A DARK AND
BROKEN HEART

A DARK AND BROKEN HEART

R.J. ELLORY

THE OVERLOOK PRESS
NEW YORK, NY

This edition first published in hardcover in the United States in 2017 by
The Overlook Press, Peter Mayer Publishers, Inc.

141 Wooster Street
New York, NY 10012
www.overlookpress.com

For bulk and special sales, please contact sales@overlookny.com,
or write us at the address above.

First published in Great Britain in 2012 by Orion, an Hachette UK company

Cataloging-in-Publication Data available from the Library of Congress

Manufactured in the United States of America
ISBN: 978-1-4683-1128-0

First Edition
1 3 5 7 9 10 8 6 4 2

"Things come apart so easily when they have been held together with lies."

—Dorothy Allison
Bastard Out of Carolina

1

BAD AMERICA

The reason Vincent Madigan didn't kill the guy was because the guy looked like Tom Waits. Okay, he was Polish and his name was Bernie Tomczak, but he still looked like Tom Waits. Like Tom Waits did some Eastern European girl and this A-hole was the result. Not only that, but Bernie didn't squeal or cry or plead for his life. None of the regular drama. And Bernie didn't try to be a hero either. He just took the beating, and somewhere after the tenth or twentieth or fiftieth time that Madigan smacked him there was a grudging respect coming in out of left field. Madigan could go with that. He could run most of the way to anyplace with that. And amid all the blood and all the grunting and the sound of teeth breaking or whatever was going on, Madigan wondered if Bernie wasn't the toughest guy he'd ever . . . Ever what?

Madigan hit Bernie again, and whatever thought might have been there just disappeared. That always happened with bad coke and Jack Daniel's. And then Madigan stepped back and felt this rush of something in his chest, and his chest was thin glass like a lightbulb, and he figured if someone hit him back he would just shatter like . . . like . . . like something that shatters, and the feeling in his chest became nausea, and then he started retching and then Bernie fell down and there was a smile on his face, and that smile accompanied the realization that Madigan didn't have the will or the strength to hit him again.

"Jesus, Vincent," Bernie said through his broken and bloody teeth.

"You shut the hell up," Madigan replied. "Pay Sandià the money you owe him or I'm gonna come back and kill you."

Bernie Tomczak tried to smile. It didn't pan out and he just looked worse. "Vincent, seriously . . . I'm gonna pay the guy when I've got the money. But however long that takes, you ain't gonna kill me. If you kill me then no one gets nothing . . ."

"Screw you," Madigan replied.

A few minutes later Madigan got himself together, walked back down the alley, and got in his car. Then he drove away, and he figured if a motorcycle cop pulled him over for weaving back and forth all over the road, he would have to shoot the cop in the head and that would be another story.

Cars went by on all sides, and then he thought about his wife. The second one. Thought about the last time he'd seen her. Standing there in the doorway with that expression on her face. She had that look in her eyes, the look that told Madigan she wasn't alone. He wondered who was in the apartment, what was his name, and most of all he wondered what the guy looked like. And she said, *Hey, Madigan . . .* Her tone was all sassy and she was half-smiling like she knew she was being a bitch and she just loved it. *Hey, Madigan, how goes it?* And he remembered when he met her and how she was just working so hard to be someone, to be *anyone*, and how that naïveté and innocence had seemed so appealing. And now she had half his money and half his balls and half his everything. And then he remembered the other one, the wife before that. She had the other half of every-damned-thing, and that was a different story as well. And Madigan? He had nothing. Like he'd started with nothing and had most of it left. And it was all because of her. Because of both of them. All of them. All the same. And Jesus Christ, he felt like crap.

A block and a half into the Bowery and Madigan couldn't see the road anymore. He pulled over and got out and tried to stand upright, but it was no good. He got in the backseat and lay down, but the roof looked like it was coming down to crush him to death. So he sat up again, and that's when he knew he was maybe going to be sick some more.

He got out and leaned against a streetlight, and then he heaved dry noise into the gutter. Some woman looked at him like he was a piece of garbage, and he told her, "Go to hell, lady," and that shut her up. She hurried away and didn't turn back. He looked up and saw the facade of the Rodeo Bar, and he remembered that place. Inside they had a bar made out of a bus. He saw some girl singer there a while back. Sexy. Had a smoky voice like Billie Holiday. Ingrid something. Italian-sounding name. Ingrid Lucia. That was it. Where the hell was he now? Murray Hill?

After a little while he felt better and he reckoned he could drive a straight line to pretty much anyplace. He got in the car and pulled away from the curb, and he went a good way up the street. Then he remembered where he was going and made the turn. Places to go. People to see. Things to do. Important things. Most things in life are bullshit. Everything good is hiding. You got to look for it a long time, and when you find it you're never certain it was exactly what you were looking for. You only know it's worth something when it's gone. Seems like life is there solely to teach you about all the ways you can hurt.

Six blocks and Madigan was there. There was a taste of coke in a twist of paper in the dash, and he hunted around and found it. Then he dabbed his finger moist, picked up most of it, and rubbed it in his gums. He waited a moment, and then he felt better—like he was coming alive again—and he opened the car door, got out, went up to the warehouse door and knocked, and they opened up and let him in.

"Hey, Groucho," Chico said.

Madigan nodded. "Everyone here?"

"Harpo is; Zeppo ain't. He called. Be here in five."

"Good 'nough," Madigan replied, and he took off his jacket and walked across to where Harpo was waiting to go over everything again in the most detailed detail imaginable. That was the way it had to be. Details were everything. The devil was in the detail.

"Groucho," he said.

"Harpo," Madigan replied.

Madigan knew their names. All three of them. They didn't know his. He knew everything about them. They knew nothing in return. This was the upper hand, the royal flush against a pair of jacks, a three of aces against a something of whatever else. They looked the way such people always looked. They spent their time in the joint just working out, putting on muscle, and once they were out they let it go. They smoked too much, drank too much, maintained a minimal level of personal hygiene. They would all go unnoticed in a crowd—regular height, dark-haired, clean-shaven, but who they really were was in their eyes.

Madigan sat in the chair, lit a cigarette, and closed his eyes for a moment. Harpo said, "You okay, man?" Madigan looked up and smiled. "I wanna do this thing," he said.

"Tomorrow is the day," Harpo said.

"I know tomorrow is the day," Madigan replied. "But I wanna do the thing now. This waiting bullshit is . . . is—"

"Bullshit?" Harpo ventured.

Madigan smiled. "Bullshit is what it is," he said. He smoked his

3

cigarette and waited for Zeppo—aka Laurence Fulton, an ugly son of a bitch who did three-to-five upstate for a GTA beef, another term sometime before that, now had another thing pending with the DA for accomplice to armed robbery; a man with more balls than sense, a raw red fist of a temper. Most important of all was the rape charge. The rape charge that never stuck. His word against that of a thirteen-year-old Hispanic girl out of East Harlem. Fulton was always late. Always apologetic. *My old lady* this, *My old lady* that. More crap from people who'd had a lifetime's experience of talking crap. Hell, what did they think? That other folks had a never-ending appetite for it?

Madigan dropped his cigarette on the floor. He put it out with his heel and then put the butt in his jacket pocket. Leave nothing behind. No prints, no beer cans, no food wrappers, nothing. We were here, and then we were gone. Gone like ghosts. And this place was so damned far from his own haunts that they could look for months and find nothing. Like looking for a handful of air in a paper bag; you knew it was in there, but you just couldn't see it.

Fulton arrived. He started up about something-or-other, everything tagged with a sad apology, but Madigan didn't listen. The four of them sat around the plain deal table in the middle of the empty warehouse, and they got out the plan of the house, the plan of the street, the plan of the park and the surrounding block. Then they went through it one more time, and then another time for good luck, and Madigan believed they'd got it enough for him to call it a day.

He looked at the three of them—Laurence Fulton, Chuck Williams, Bobby Landry. Print their sheets in one go and you could wallpaper a duplex. Fulton and Landry were two strikes down, Williams was a one-time deal. All three of them—among so many other things—were sex offenders, the kind that slid like oil off glass. Nothing ever stuck. Those cases were the hardest to prosecute, the easiest to defend. These three were somewhere out beyond the lower levels, the bottom-feeders. That's why he used them. If they wound up dead then it was no one's loss, everyone's gain. And Madigan himself? He had never been inside, intended to keep it that way. If he went inside, knowing what he knew, he was dead, no question. Fulton and Landry were both lifers if they were pinched, though Fulton was in the end zone compared to Landry. Landry was dangerous, unpredictable, even psychotic, but Fulton? Fulton was an out-and-out sociopath. Hell, they were all lifers if this thing went the wrong way. This was the kind of deal where a good number of people were going to die on the scene. They had a matter of minutes for the in and out. Soon as there was gunplay there could be soldiers running from all quarters. Silencers were out of the question, even homemade ones. Hit like this it was best to go in noisy. The shock factor played in your favor. At least there would be no police, not for this gig. Not until later. But hell, anyone who figured *any* plan was a cert was dumber than a box of sand. That was the trick: Anticipate every which it could go wrong, and you upped the odds on it going right. And if the thing didn't go down, then Madigan knew his whole sorry life would be history anyway. The heist was a straight fifty grand apiece, maybe seventy-five. The moment they got inside they had to be all over that money like stink on shit. If the money made it out the back door, they were screwed. That's why timing was of the essence. This was the deal. Mess this up and it got deeper than a hole through the bottom of hell. The better part of a quarter mill was going into a house up near First and Paladino at ten in the a.m., Tuesday the twelfth, and Vincent Madigan, Laurence Fulton, Chuck Williams, and Bobby Landry would be in for that money at 10:05. At 10:10 they had to be out of there and running. Madigan needed the money for the lawyers. He owed more than twenty in alimony alone. And then there was Sandià himself. That was the bitterest irony of all. He could give the lawyers ten and keep them in the woods for a few more weeks, but Sandià needed everything else. That was where his cut needed to go. Forty grand toward a seventy-five-grand debt. Mr. Sandià—loan shark, bookie, dealer, pimp, King of East Harlem, and all-round Man of the Year. Like the Bernie Tomczak gig that morning—chasing up Mr. Sandià's other debtors bought Madigan time, but never a discount. And if the house job came back to him, then Madigan was in deeper than he could ever comprehend. He could imagine the meeting that would take place between him and Sandià. *Vincent . . . I know it was you. I have the evidence here. You killed my people and you stole my money to pay your debt to me. You paid me back with my own money. And don't insult me by telling me you didn't. Tell me the truth and I'll kill you quickly. Lie to me and I will have someone torture you for a month.*

Madigan looked at the men around him. Three pedo grunts out of Leavenworth on a day pass for cheap whiskey and cheaper whores. That was what he had. It didn't get much worse than this.

"So we're good," Fulton said. "We're here at eight thirty

precisely, out of here at eight forty. No later than nine thirty we're on the corner of First and 124th, and then we're on hold until we see that money go in the house." He smiled. "And then, my friends, we are up."

Williams reached into his bag, brought out a fifth of rye and four plastic cups. He shared the bottle between the cups, passed them around.

"To Joe DiMaggio," Madigan said.

"Joe DiMaggio?" Landry asked.

Madigan smiled. "Anyone who can hit that many home runs and bag a babe like Marilyn Monroe deserves a toast every time I take a drink."

Landry smiled. "To Joe DiMaggio."

They drank. The cups and the bottle went back in Williams's bag. Madigan was the only one to ensure he wiped his cup before he returned it to Williams.

"We're done," Madigan said, and he got up. He wiped down the seat, the edge of the table, everything he'd touched. He made his farewells and went out to the car. He looked for any more drugs in the dash; there was nothing but half of some white pill that could have been anything from aspirin to Benzedrine. Madigan licked it. More than likely a bennie, so he dropped it dry. He would either get a buzz or lose a headache, either which way was fine.

He drove a while. He parked ahead of some $9.99 All-U-Can-Eat chop suey joint and looked in the rearview. From how many mirrors in how many restrooms in how many bars had that worn-out face looked back at him? Too many? Or too few? Once, maybe a long time back, he'd been a handsome man, a man with a crooked smile and some kind of charm in his eyes. But now all he saw was the other side of himself, the darker side, the side that he hid from the world. Maybe he'd just lock himself in a motel room and drink himself to death. Maybe that would be simpler.

Madigan smiled at himself. "A-hole," he said to the reflection, and then he started the car and pulled away from the curb.

He was hungry all of a sudden—cheap burgers and greasy fries kind of hungry.

WALKIN' WITH THE BEAST

*T*hings happen. Most of them bad. Too many things to remember. You forget the details, of course. Details are unimportant until they're important, and when they're important they're vital. Life and death kind of vital. How you came to be where you are can never be attributed to one thing only. Like the destination never comes down to one facet of the journey, and if we're talking about life then the destination you planned for and the destination you get are never the same damned thing anyway. And there is never one thing that causes you to lose control, to have your life become something other than your own. If there was one reason, then maybe you could go back and fix it. That's what you keep thinking. You keep turning it over, like a video loop or something. But it's not that simple. Nothing's that simple. When you take a good look, even the simplest things are a great deal more complicated than they at first appear.

Things color you bad. Takes more than a prayer and a promise to uncolor you. This stuff stains your soul. Deeper than that even. And for a while your mind can get all twisted around in figuring out how to go backward and fix things up. The drugs, the booze, the wives and the kids you messed up. And then—almost imperceptibly—you start to wonder if you can go forward and out the other side. It starts to make sense. You can't get off the rollercoaster midflight. You ain't never gonna jump clear of this thing. But maybe it stops somewhere. Or maybe you can do something to make it stop. And then you can get off.

Comes down to it, profiling is a lie. It is bullshit. I am neither a loser nor a loner. I do not live with my mother. I have been married twice. I have four children from three different women. I am fertile, focused, and right now—right at this very moment—I am screwed. I am surprised every morning I wake up and find out someone hasn't killed me. I can sell two different lies out of separate corners of my mouth at the same damned time. I saw a girl die three weeks ago. I knew she was ODing, and there was nothing I could do. I knew she wouldn't make it to the hospital, and I knew I could never save her, and it's things like that that *make me wonder what the hell is going on in this world. No one gave a damn about her. Not her dealer, not her pimp, not her mom or dad or brothers or sisters, and sometimes I wonder if I am going to die that way—forgotten, unknown, irrelevant. It's that kind of thing that gives me nightmares, and, like Tom Waits says, it takes a whole lot of whiskey to make the nightmares go away. And I have nightmares. A lot of nightmares. And they're getting worse. I gotta do this thing with these three whackos tomorrow. I gotta get this money and get Sandià off my back. I gotta get the lawyers sorted with the alimony, and then we're good to go. I'll get cleaned up. I'll get straight. I'll drink carrot juice and take vitamins and slow down on the booze, and I'll stop chugging bennies like they're PEZ. I'll get a girl, a nice girl, and things'll be good. I'll have some money in my pocket, and we're all gonna be fine an' dandy. That's what we'll be.*

I think all these things, and then I think: Who the hell are you kidding? You think you're gonna fool anyone with this, most of all yourself? You're a dumb son of a bitch. Hell, you couldn't pour piss out of a shoe if the instructions were written on the heel. Five minutes in your company is the best argument anyone could ever get for compulsory sterilization.

And then I take a couple of bennies, maybe a Adderall or Desoxyn— whatever I can get—and it all kicks into life. I see things in a different light, and I think: To hell with it; it's all gonna be fine. Balance it all out with some Klonopin or a Xanax or two, and I start to make sense of things. Things start to look less fractured, more straightforward. Get some drinks. Maybe the Cedar Tavern where they have that old bar that was saved from the Susquehanna Hotel. Go down there and hang out with the ghosts of Ginsberg and Kerouac and Vincent O'Hara, and then drive down to the Bridge Café for soft-shelled crabs and a hanger steak . . . World sure looks seven shades of different after that.

I'll do that tonight, but I'll keep Jack Daniel's—great friend that he is—at arm's length. For tomorrow I need my wits and my wisdom. Tomorrow is the day when it starts to turn around one eighty and go in the right damned direction.

It has to.

Just for once, it has to.

LIKE CALLING UP THUNDER

The inside of the Ford Econoline E-250 cargo van smells like a post-game locker room on a hot Sunday afternoon. Four men have sweated inside it for the better part of an hour, back and to the left across the junction, out of line of sight of the building. Vincent Madigan is up front, passenger side; Bobby Landry is behind the wheel; Laurence Fulton and Chuck Williams in back. Landry will stay in the vehicle, keep the motor running. Vincent Madigan will lead the assault, in through the back second-floor windows, coming at them like a tidal wave of shock and awe. That's the ticket here. This is the free pass for the job. They'll never expect it, and that element of surprise is the only damned thing they have. Madigan has a sawn-off three-inch Mossberg on a loop from his shoulder and under his overcoat. He has a .44 in back of his waistband. Williams has an M-16 in a canvas duffel. Fulton doesn't like long-shooters, and has gone for a .45 and a .38. It's going to be very noisy. And they plan to leave no witnesses.

By reckoning, by past experience, trusting everything that has happened before, Madigan expects four men in the house. The rear of the house is not where they keep their eyes. Eyes are always out front. Eyes look for the money, and when the money comes up, well, then—and only then—are they all eagle-eyed out back. These guys may be tough, but they're not the brightest lights in the harbor. That, and the simple fact that Sandià owns the whole neighborhood and no one in their right mind would even consider robbing him . . .

But Madigan hasn't got any room to maneuver; desperate situations call for desperate measures.

Madigan, Fulton, and Williams will be up on the roof of the outbuilding before the delivery's even made. The outbuilding adjoins the property, its roof sitting beneath the window by three feet, no more. The way it goes is this: Landry's out in the street. He sees the money going in the front. He radios Madigan, and

Madigan, Fulton, and Williams are coming through the upper floor as the money reaches the top of the stairwell. The four goons are dead in a hail of gunfire, and then the money goes out the back, along the alleyway beside the house, into the van, and away. Five minutes, tops.

Madigan closes his eyes. He feels the rush. He feels the punch of the thing in his lower gut. If this goes, then maybe there's an out for him. If this dies a death, then regardless of whether he makes it out of the house there's no chance. If he doesn't get caught by the cops, Sandià will find him. And then there will be the inevitable conversation, and Sandià will torture Madigan for a month and leave his heart in a box on the sidewalk in front of the apartment where his kids live. This is what Sandià will do. This is the kind of man that he is.

Landry grips the wheel. His knuckles are white. Madigan watches him for a moment, and then he glances over his shoulder at Fulton and Williams. Any other day and he would be kicking the crap out of people like this for the money they owed Sandià. But today? No, not today. Today is different.

"We're out of here," Madigan says quietly, and such is the tension and anticipation in the van that they would have gotten that message had he only thought it.

Fulton opens up the back door.

Williams goes first. Blue jeans, tan work boots, a black jacket with the collar up against the cold. Over his shoulder is the duffel. It's all in his eyes, his body language, his gait—the fear, but also the *need* to feel that fear.

Madigan nods at Fulton. Fulton does the two-fists-clenched, *I'm ready for this* gesture, and then he's out the door as well. He follows Williams, is no more than ten feet behind him, and Madigan waits for a good five minutes. He allows ample time for them to walk back around the block and come up to the alleyway beside the house from the far side.

"Whatever happens," Madigan tells Landry, "whatever you hear, whatever the hell you think might be going on in there, you don't take off until I'm back. I don't care if Zeppo comes back here with half his head blown off. I don't care if half of Costa-fuckin'-Rica comes out of that house with Harpo's head on a stick and his balls in a paper bag. You don't go anywhere until I'm in here with you. You get me?"

"Hey—" Landry starts, and he smiles. He's done this kind of

thing before. He knows the score. He knows what's *meant* to happen and what *really* happens are sometimes as far from each other as north and south.

"Hey nothing," Madigan says. "You just say, 'Yes, sir, Mr. Groucho.' That's all I wanna hear right now."

Landry nods. "I got it, man. I know the deal here." He bangs the steering wheel with his palms a couple of times for emphasis, and then he grips it again like a lifeline.

"So we're good?"

"We're good, man. We're good."

Madigan tucks the leather loop of the Mossberg over his shoulder and buttons his overcoat. He jerks back the lever and the door opens. He steps down into the street and looks back one more time at Bobby Landry. He's a young guy, only twenty-five. He has a thin film of sweat varnishing his forehead.

Madigan closes the van door and starts walking. At the corner, he glances back. The only giveaway is the thin cloud of fumes issuing from the van's exhaust. In this neighborhood? Someone parked up in a vehicle with the engine running? Well, that person has something going on that someone else is going to disagree with, for sure.

Madigan nods one more time at Landry, and then turns the corner.

At the rear of the house, Fulton and Williams are already down on their haunches side by side, backs against the wall of the outbuilding. The roof of the building is no more than ten feet from the ground. A simple boost, and they're up there. They sit quiet—all three of them—and Madigan can see the light in their eyes. He knows he has it too. It's a light like nothing else. It isn't fear, not exactly. Maybe it's fear and excitement and anticipation all bound up together in that moment when you know you might die. Madigan has experienced it so many times it's like one of the family. It's something that regular folk will never understand. You could give it a name—could be the best damned name in the world—and people still wouldn't understand it. Not even soldiers, because they're not fighting two enemies. Here he has Sandià's people, and he has the police. The *po-lice*. Screwed either way.

Madigan breathes deeply. It is cold. He exhales and watches his breath dissipate. His pulse is regular, his heartbeat too, and he feels the blood in his veins, thin like water. He did a couple of

Dexedrine earlier. Kicked things up a notch. He's okay. He feels a balance. He did just enough, and it's all good.

He checks the handheld. Can't miss word from Landry in the van. That delivery arrives at the front door, and in that moment they're up on the roof and over to the window. In that moment. No sooner, no later. The money coming in through the front door puts all eyes on the street. No one will be looking their way. These guys ain't that good. And if they're seen from a property that faces the rear of the building . . . well, this is the neighborhood. No one says a thing. Not a word. And sure as shit no one calls the *po-lice*. Down here it doesn't work that way. This isn't Gramercy Heights or Chelsea. This is East Harlem. Suck it up, motherfuckers; only way out of here is in a squad car or the coroner's wagon.

Fulton goes to speak, but Madigan silences him with a shake of his head. Williams has got the bag laid out flat at his feet. It's unzipped, and Madigan can see the dull sheen of the M16's barrel. Fulton is a gangbanger, and Williams isn't that far off. They want blood and mayhem. No class. No subtlety. They want to see people exploding. Fireworks in a butcher's store. And when they're done, they're gonna want to go and screw teenagers. These are the kind of folks he's now socializing with.

The handheld crackles once, but it's just a burst of static. He checks the volume, the small red light on top. Williams instinctively reaches for the M16. There is electricity everywhere. He can feel the raw copper taste in the back of his throat.

Madigan stays his hand. Williams closes his eyes and holds his breath for just a second.

A bead of sweat breaks free from Madigan's hairline and starts down his forehead. He wipes it away.

"To hell with this," Williams hisses, and it's little more than an exhalation of pent-up nerves.

"Chill, chill," Fulton says, and Madigan looks sideways at the man, and behind the light in his eyes he sees the thing that makes them do this. The *hunger*. That's the only word to use. It's a hunger, a need, a reason to live. More often than not it's a reason to die, but until then it's just who and what they are. They kowtow to no one. They grant respect to no one but their own kind, and even then it is granted begrudgingly. These are precisely the kind of people who would do something as foolish as robbing one of Sandià's drug houses. That's the second reason Madigan chose them.

*

When Bobby Landry saw the beat-to-shit Chevy Caprice pull up in front of the house, he slowed down inside. Everything went quiet. He held the radio in his hand for a moment, and then raised it to his mouth. His finger hesitated over the TALK button. He watched carefully. He had expected an inconspicuous car, something that no one would give a second thought to, but this was taking it to the extreme. This could be nothing more than a crowd of Costa Rican junkies after a score.

He breathed slowly. Timing was everything. If the crew went in the back before the money arrived, they'd be dead. If they went in too late they be dead all over again.

If they'd known faces it would have helped. Any of Sandià's people could be on the delivery run. And Sandià had no shortage of mules and carriers and grunts.

Three men came out of the Caprice. Two crossed the sidewalk and stood at the gate. The third hung back with the car. They were scanning the street, no question. If a fourth man got out, and if that fourth man was carrying a duffel, a suitcase, a backpack— anything that was big enough to contain a quarter mill in used bundles—then Landry would be on the radio to the crew at the back of the property.

Landry held his breath. It was good. This was it. This was the deal. Right here, right now.

The man at the side of the Caprice leaned down to speak to someone in the car. That someone then came out slowly, glancing back over the way, all eyes and ears, and once he was out of the vehicle and upright Landry saw the bag.

This was it.

The gig was on.

He pressed TALK.

Madigan was on his feet, his back to the wall, the side of his face against the left edge of the window frame. Williams stood to his right, Fulton over on the other side, and through the glass Madigan watched for the first sign of the door opening at the base of the internal stairwell. He'd been inside once before. He knew the layout well enough. The front door opened into the lower hallway. The stairwell started not six feet away and ran a straight line up to the second floor. The window was ahead of a turn in the stairs. From his vantage point he could see the light from the street as the front door opened, see the light disappear as the front door was closed behind the delivery crew, and then they would start up the stairs. One man ahead, the carrier behind him, the other two behind him. Madigan's Mossberg through the window would take out the lead man, maybe the carrier. In that moment of stunned confusion generated by the attack, all three of them— Madigan himself, Fulton, and Williams—had to be through the aperture and firing before these assholes even had a chance to tell the time. The narrow stairwell, the fact that the two front men would fall backward into the latter two—these things Madigan counted on. Surprise and gravity. Shock and awe. Bodies in motion and then at rest.

The light was there.

Madigan even heard voices.

He reached out his right hand and stayed Williams once again. He nodded to Fulton. Fulton looked like a man with a fire in his gut. He had the .45 in one hand, the .38 in the other. Doc-fucking-Holliday.

The delivery crew started up the stairs. The lead man was eight or ten steps up before the front door closed below him. One more step, one more second, and then Madigan was turning, the Mossberg ahead of him like an extension of his own body, his finger jerking, the slide coming back a second time, a third, the window exploding inward.

The first barrage took the guy's face away. Madigan hit him just beneath the chin, but the trajectory was angled upward by just a few degrees. The instinctive response of the lead man to pull his head back away from the source of the blast meant that his face was parallel to the angle of the shot. Most of his features were on the ceiling before he knew what the hell had happened.

The weight of the front man, the fact that he fell backward into the carrier, the narrow stairwell—all these things worked in Madigan's favor. He was through the devastated window and firing more shots down into the melee of arms and legs before any one of them had a chance to pull a gun, let alone fire it.

Fulton and Williams came in behind Madigan, and the three of them let fly with a barrage of gunfire sufficient to decimate not only the four men now heaped at the bottom of the stairway, but the risers themselves, the banister, and much of the lower hallway. Plaster and wood fragments, chunks of masonry, carpeting, blood, bone, flesh, teeth, and the smoke and noise and screaming of the men beneath them. Another day in hell. It was a turkey shoot. It was a massacre.

Madigan stopped firing only when there were no shells left.

Fulton and Williams followed suit.

The silence was eerie, far more unsettling than the war that had just taken place. The smoke hung in a thick pall above them. The smell of sweat and cordite and blood was thick enough to taste.

Madigan took the stairs at their edges for greatest support, descending tentatively, hoping that the risers didn't collapse beneath him. The idea of landing feet-first in the disaster zone that lay there not ten feet below him was . . . well, picking Costa Ricans out of the treads and welts of his boots was not something he'd scheduled for this Tuesday afternoon.

Williams, using his common sense, lay down on the landing and leaned over toward Madigan. He held out his hand, and Madigan gripped it. From halfway down the stairs he could reach the bag, but it was beneath bodies, and it took Madigan some time to work it free. One of the handles was snapped, the bag punctured in numerous places, spattered with blood, but the bodies had acted as a shield against it and it was remarkably intact considering all that had taken place.

Madigan pulled it up by the good handle, and Williams assisted him in his return to the upper landing.

At the top Madigan took a second to check the contents of the bag. Thick wads of hundreds and fifties. Looked like a great deal more than he'd anticipated. He smiled to himself, but gave no outward acknowledgment to Fulton and Williams.

"Go," he mouthed, and followed them to the window. He indicated with his hand, knowing full well that they would be hearing nothing clearly for a while. In his own ears the ringing was intense, deafening almost.

They were out, across the roof of the outbuilding, down into the alleyway and into the street within thirty seconds.

The van was already on the go as they reached it, Madigan up front with the bag, Fulton and Williams in back with the weaponry.

Landry took the first three hundred yards at speed, and then he hit First Avenue and slowed right down. He headed southwest, followed a road parallel to the FDR Drive, kept within the limit, took it easy, and when he crossed East 117th, he started to relax. No sirens. Not a sound. No one following them.

"Okay, where to now?" he asked Madigan.

"Change of vehicle near the Metropolitan Hospital. There's an alleyway off of East 109th. Get to the junction with Second and I'll direct you."

Madigan glanced over his shoulder. Fulton and Williams were grinning like crazies queuing for meds.

Went like clockwork. Went like a dream.

Half an hour's work for way more than a quarter mill.

Madigan clutched the bag on his lap. He could feel the bundles inside. This was the way out. Lawyers, Sandià, whoever the hell else wanted a piece of him, they were all history. Rock *and* roll, motherfuckers . . . Rock and fucking roll.

4

SHAME AND PAIN

*M*y heart goes like a train. The four fifteen out of Grand Central. I've got the bag on my lap. My hands are sweating. I would choke someone to death for a couple of Mandrax. A couple of shots of Jack. Anything.

Jesus Christ.

The way those people just exploded down the stairs. It was a slaughter; no other word for it. Didn't even have time to see our faces. The guy up front I'd seen before. I know his face. I've seen him with Sandià.

I daren't hold out my hands. They shake. I can feel them as they grip the bag. I can feel the money inside. Like freedom. Feels like freedom. Maybe.

Landry is driving steady—not too fast, not too slow.

Williams and Fulton are laughing like jackasses in back. I want to smack the pair of them quiet, but I'm not saying a word.

Just need to get to the storage unit, change cars, get as far away from these guys as possible, and then disappear into . . . into where?

Through the window I see familiar streets. We're out of East Harlem and heading toward Yorkville.

My scalp itches. The palms of my shaking hands are sweating. I look down at them. They feel like someone else's hands. The hands of Orloff.

Jesus, I'm losing it.

Williams is laughing like a hyena. I turn round and look at him for a moment. He has kids. Fulton does too. Landry doesn't. None of them are married. Smarter than me on that count. Some marriages work because each person thinks the other's too good for them, like what did they do to deserve this person, you know? They try all the harder to keep the show on the road, and they're both trying real hard and it kind of works out for a while. Me? Hell, after they got under the surface, when they really started to see behind the facade of charm and self-control, all the women I was ever involved with soon understood that I was way beneath them. Maybe it was exciting for a while—the unpredictability, the dangerous edges and sharp corners that lay just beneath that thin, thin veneer of

17

social respectability. But that veneer wears away real quick, and then what you got? You got Madigan, Vincent Madigan, and all the demons of the underworld he brings along for the ride.

Hell, where did it all go so wrong?

Landry says something. I look at him for a moment and wait for the words to register, and then I get it . . .

5

DEATH PARTY

"Left," Madigan says, "and then sharp right at the end."

Landry follows the instruction, and the van bears left and then takes a right at the end of the alleyway and comes to a stop.

Madigan sits quiet for a moment.

They are all waiting for him to say whatever he's going to say.

He says nothing.

Opening the passenger door, he climbs down from the van, walks to the end of the alleyway, and produces a set of keys from his pocket. It is only then that he notices how much blood is on his right shoe. He doesn't have another pair. That was dumb. That was a case of not thinking it through. He would have to stop someplace and buy some sneakers or something, get rid of his shoes as fast as possible.

He opens up the door, steps inside, flicks a switch, and waits as the garage door comes up slowly. The van is already nudging its way into the darkness before the gate is all the way up. Once inside, Madigan closes the door and switches on the lights. Back against the wall is a dark sedan, plain and inconspicuous. In the rear seat are four canvas duffels, all matching. Madigan brings them out and puts them on the floor.

"Let's see it," Landry says.

Madigan upends his bag and the bundles of money fall out.

Williams whistles through his teeth. "Jesus Mary, Mother of God," he whispers.

Madigan is down on his knees. He's fanning through the tied bundles, opening them up, counting out fifties, hundreds, twenties.

"Separate them out by denomination," he says. "Count up what you got, and then we'll divide."

It takes a good twenty minutes. There's a lot of money.

"Four eighty-five," Madigan finally concludes. "That's one-twenty-one, two-fifty each."

"Shit, man, you do that math shit in your head?" Williams asks.

Madigan smiles. He starts dividing up the money.

A hundred and twenty grand. Better than he expected. Enough to give Sandià the whole seventy, thirty to the lawyers and have twenty left over. Maybe he'd go buy Cassie a car for her eighteenth. That would knock the shit out of all of them.

"You as happy as me, man?" Fulton asks.

"I'm happy," Madigan says, and then he's got his money bundled into his duffel. He's over at the sedan, reaching in through the driver's side door and retrieving his handgun from the glove box. He tucks it in the back of his pants and straightens his leather jacket. He looks down at his right shoe again. There sure is a hell of a lot of blood. It must have just come spraying up from below as those poor motherfuckers got blasted. Hell of a thing.

"So you're dumping the van," Madigan tells Landry. "Take it a long way away. I'm serious, now. Drive it for sixty, seventy miles upstate. Find some parking garage, somewhere huge that has no security cameras. Just park it in there, wipe it all down, and walk away. Don't stop on the way, don't speed, don't get pinched by the highway patrol, okay?"

"I know, man. I know. Trust me. I've done this before, and I sure as hell mean to do it again." Landry looks at Madigan like a scolded kid.

"Good 'nough," Madigan says.

Fulton and Williams are standing by the front of the sedan.

"Guns now, all of them," Madigan says. "Over there by the wall. I'll take care of their disposal."

The three other men comply, dropping their guns in a pile against the far wall.

"Ready?" Madigan asks.

"For some wild-ass party, yeah!" Fulton says.

Madigan shakes his head. "You go easy, Zeppo," he says. "Stupidest thing you could do right now is flash that money around the place."

Fulton laughs. "Think we can do without the dumb nicknames now. Don't you?" he says, and there's something in his eyes.

Madigan says nothing.

"I mean, hell, man, we're all friends here now. Brothers in arms, partners in crime an' all that shit." He glances at Landry. "Me an' Bobby ain't strangers. We did some work together a little while back, and this guy over here," he adds, indicating Williams, "sure wasn't keeping his name a secret. Were you, Chuck?"

Williams looks pissed. He shakes his head at Fulton and looks away. He knows Madigan is staring at him, but he can't face him down. Doesn't even try.

"You are full of shit, Zeppo," Madigan says. "I said what I said, and what I said I meant. Don't fuck with me—"

Fulton sneers. "You think I don't know who you are?"

Madigan's eyes widen. This is not what he planned for, not what he expects, not what he needs. He is aware of the .44 in the back of his waistband.

"Seriously? You think I don't know about you . . . about who you are, your reputation?"

"Shut the hell up, will you?" Williams says urgently.

"Yeah, shut the hell up," Landry echoes. "We're done. The whole thing is done. Let's get out of here right now."

Fulton stands his ground. He's cock of the walk now. He stands straight, like someone jammed a stair rod up his ass.

"You know who I am?" Madigan asks.

"Sure as shit stinks, I know who you are," Fulton replies. "You're Vincent Mad—"

Madigan would later marvel at his own speed. He has the .44 in his hand before he is even aware of it himself. The bullet hits Fulton in the stomach.

Williams and Landry don't move. The sudden noise, the sight of Fulton looking at his own stomach, the way he just goes on standing there smiling his condescending smile. And then the blood starts coming and he knows he's in trouble, that it isn't his imagination. He drops the duffel full of money and clasps his hands to his gut, and he goes on standing there for a good ten seconds before he finally lets out a noise like *Neeeuuuggghhh* and drops to his knees. Fulton looks up at Madigan. Still the disbelief is there in his eyes. Madigan doesn't say a word. Fulton's eyes roll back, and then he falls sideways. His right foot is twitching.

Williams starts hyperventilating. "Oh Jesus, oh Jesus, oh Jesus. What the fuck. What the fuck . . ."

Landry steps away from the front of the car. He looks down at Fulton—there on his side, still now, not a flicker of motion—and Landry says the only thing that he can think of in that moment which is, "I don't know who the hell you are, and I sure as hell don't wanna know."

Madigan looks at Williams. Williams slows down. He calms a little. He's gripping the handles of the duffel like a lifeline to something. He's breathing heavily.

Madigan knows what to do. It comes together like a jigsaw puzzle. He walks to the wall and retrieves Fulton's .38. He points it at Williams.

"You know who I am?" Madigan asks him.

Williams is shaking his head vigorously, but Madigan knows he's lying. He knows they're both lying. Fulton found out who he was and told both Williams and Landry, and now he has to deal with it.

"You know Ben Franklin?" Madigan asks.

"I don't know anyone," Williams says. "I don't know you, and I don't know any Franklin guy."

Madigan smiles. These guys really were dumber than dog crap.

"Benjamin Franklin, the President of the United States . . . *that* Ben Franklin."

"Sure, yeah. Sure . . . Heard of him, yeah . . ." Landry says. He takes a step back. He's clutching his duffel to his chest like it's bulletproof.

"Said something that makes a great deal of sense in this situation," Madigan continues.

"Yeah, okay . . . Okay, man," Williams replies. "Ca—can we just get the hell out of here now? Fulton's dead, okay? He was an asshole and he opened his dumbass mouth and now he's dead. We'll split up his share, you and me and Bobby here . . . No, forget that. You just take Fulton's share, and that'll be the end of that—"

"You haven't heard my Ben Franklin quote yet," Madigan says. He takes a deep breath. He doesn't understand why he feels so calm. He hefts the .38 in his hand. "He said that a secret between three people is only a secret if two of them are dead."

It takes a second before either Landry or Williams understands the significance of Madigan's words.

A second is too long.

Madigan shoots Williams first, right through the heart, and he's close enough for the force of impact to spin Williams right over the bumper of the car and onto the ground.

Landry looks like he's going for the wall.

Madigan takes one step forward and shoots him in the face. Both of them are down. He checks vitals. There is nothing.

He gathers up the four duffels, opens one up, takes a good three or four handfuls of notes and scatters them across the floor. He turns the bag out and empties it beside Fulton.

Madigan wipes his prints off of the .44 and puts it in Williams's hand. He cleans off the .38 and reaches down to put it beside Fulton.

Fulton opens his eyes and looks back at Madigan.

Madigan starts suddenly.

Blood bubbles from Fulton's lips as he tries to speak. Madigan stands straight. He pockets the .38. He cannot shoot the man again. A second shot would preclude any possibility of this being read the way he intends. It needs to be clean, simple, a closed case. Three people robbed one of Sandià's drug houses, and those same three people had a go at each other in a storage unit near the subway. Three shots, three DBs, case closed.

Madigan backs up the Econoline and opens the door. He sits sideways in the seat, now no more than three or four yards from where Fulton lies on the ground in an ever-widening pool of blood. The man's leg twitches once more, a brief flurry of motion, and the side of his shoe draws an arc of blood out from the edge and across the concrete.

Fulton tries to speak again, and blood bubbles grow and burst from his mouth.

"It's over, Larry," Madigan says. "I ain't takin' you anywhere. You do understand that, right? You and me are just going to have to sit here until you die."

Fulton's eyes tighten with whatever ravages of pain are coursing through his gut. Stomach wounds are the worst—the slowest, the most painful, the most difficult to repair.

"You been a bad guy," Madigan says. "Hell, what goes around comes around, eh? Seems to me that something like this is the only way it could end for you."

Madigan pauses, wonders if this will be the way for him as well. Sometime.

Fulton is down on his right side. He tries to lift his left arm, but he has no strength. His fingers are trying to reach for something he cannot see, perhaps reaching out toward Madigan in a last, desperate attempt to provoke some slight sense of mercy.

Madigan closes his eye and exhales. The adrenaline has gone. He is exhausted. He feels as if the edges of his mind have been frayed and weathered by some terrible storm.

He feels the weight of the .38 in his pocket. He needs to get it into Fulton's hand and get the fuck out of there. He cannot leave until Fulton is dead.

Madigan stands. He surveys the scene around him—the bodies, the blood, the money, the Econoline. Devastation every which way he looks. Kind of like his life.

He takes three steps and is down on his haunches beside Fulton, careful not to get any more blood on his shoes.

"Just fucking die already, will you?" Madigan says. "Just die and go to hell where you belong, you piece of shit."

Madigan gets the next words that Fulton tries to utter. He can lip-read enough to see *Fuck you* amidst the blood.

"Fuck you too, Larry," Madigan says, and the temptation to just reach out and close his hand over Fulton's nose and mouth and let him suffocate is very strong, but he cannot touch the man.

Madigan waits.

Larry Fulton's mouth opens and closes a couple of times, and then he is gone—eyes wide, looking right back at Madigan, and the light behind them goes out.

Madigan takes the .38 from his pocket, wipes it down, and puts it in Fulton's right hand. He moves the hand slightly and lets it come to rest in half an inch of blood. The blood, still fluid, closes around the hand, and the scene is set.

Madigan spends a good ten minutes wiping down every possible surface in the Econoline, and then he's behind the wheel of the sedan. He manages to maneuver it out past the van and up to the door of the storage unit. He looks back at the scene. On his passenger seat are three duffels, over three hundred and sixty grand in cash. He doesn't know what he's feeling. He doesn't need a Mandy anymore. He could use a Brooklyn Pilsner, a shot of Jack, a smoke. That would do him right now. The adrenaline has lit a fire in him, and it ain't going out anytime soon.

Eight minutes later Vincent Madigan is heading toward the Triborough and home. That's when his cellphone goes off. That's when he checks the number of the caller and feels his balls tighten.

He hesitates, then pulls over, takes one more look at the phone, and answers it.

"Detective Madigan . . ."

6

THE LIE

"You are *not* the light of the world," Angela said. She was his first wife, back when things were straight and clean, back when things were far closer to how he'd imagined they should be. She was beautiful and smart, and Madigan was handsome and charming and humorous. They were a great couple, at least for a while. And between them they made Cassie, Madigan's first child, and anything that produced such a girl as Cassie couldn't have been wrong.

Cassie was the brightest, the best, the one that seemed to have inherited all his good and none of his bad. Cassie was everything to him. And though Madigan now saw Cassie infrequently, she seemed to be the one person in his life who recognized who he really was.

Madigan could hear Angela's voice anytime he chose. He just had to close his eyes and remember her face, and with her face came her voice, and with her voice came all the subsequent years of accusations and bullshit that seemed to have been part of both his marriages. At least at the end. After the fire had died.

Angela soured the pitch, always and forever. She seemed to have adopted it as a crusade. "Maybe it's my job to remind you what an asshole you are. Maybe it's my task on this earth to keep Vincent Madigan apprised of the fact that the universe does not revolve around him and his desires."

One time, close to the end of the marriage, she had slapped his face. He raised his hand but didn't slap her back. Then they made out like sixteen-year-olds, right there in the kitchen, right there on the cold Mexican ceramic tile floor. Aggressive, almost vindictive, like fucking for revenge.

Angela Duggan knew what kind of man Vincent Madigan was. She married him regardless. She knew what kind of man would do the kind of things he did. Bad things. Dirty things. Dealing with the scum of the earth. The dealers and pimps and killers and psychos and the filth that floated up to the surface every once in a while. She knew that to deal with that kind of thing you had to *be* that kind of thing. At least a little of you. It had to be there in your soul. Only way you could survive that kind of toxic horror was to be related to it.

And now she never missed an opportunity to remind him of who he was, of how little he meant.

"Marcus Aurelius," she said one time. "He hired a slave to follow him wherever he walked, and whenever anyone showed him respect or told him what a great guy he was, well, that slave had to lean forward and whisper, 'You are just a man' in his ear. Kept him grounded, Vincent; kept his feet on the same planet as the rest of us. You could do with some of that, you know? You could do with a little grounding."

And so she kept him grounded. *You are not the light of the world,* she said, and he tried so hard to believe her.

Moments like this—driving back toward the Sandià house, summoned to the very scene of the crime he had just committed, he wondered if this was the time they'd get him.

Madigan stopped en route to Louis Cuvillier Park. He wiped down his shoes as best he could, found a store, bought a new pair, and once back at the car he bagged the blood-stained ones and buried the bag beneath the driver's seat. The sooner he had a moment to dispose of them properly, the better. He drove on, and parked a block away from the park. He didn't want any questions as to why he wasn't driving a precinct vehicle. He put the money in the trunk, checked it was locked, walked ten yards, went back, and checked it again. He felt nauseous. Now he wanted something, anything to settle his nerves. He had nothing. Maybe it was better that way. Maybe it was better to be on edge, feet hanging over the precipice. Needed to be on his toes, sharp as a paper cut. Needed to be seeing three ways simultaneously, backward as well.

The house was lit up like the Fourth of July. Red and white flashes, yellow crime scene tape, the hum and buzz and crackle of a dozen radios from a dozen cars, a crowd of spectators already gathering along the sidewalk, that insolent screw-you attitude so evident in their eyes as a uniform tried to herd them back away from the road.

Madigan had his wallet out, flipped his badge, and tucked it into his breast pocket. He lifted the tape and went under, was met by

Charlie Harris and Ron Callow from Madigan's own unit, Robbery-Homicide, 167th Precinct.

"Got a whirlwind of mystery meat up and down the stairwell," Callow said.

Madigan smiled. "And good morning to you, my friend. Nice weather we're having."

"Jeez, Vincent, you look wiped out, man," Harris commented. "You didn't sleep so good, huh?"

"The schedule is the schedule, my friend," Madigan replied. "How many we got?"

"Four," Callow said, "and man, have they let themselves go."

"You are such a wiseass," Madigan replied.

"Looks like a hit-and-run. Figure they were bringing in some dope maybe, some cash perhaps, but someone was out back and came in through the upper window. Usual story, though," he added, glancing up and around at the crowd of onlookers across the street, the facing apartment buildings. "No one saw a damned thing. Couple of folks said it sounded like a firework display, but beyond that nothing. This is business. No one's gonna get involved."

"This is one of Sandià's places, right?" Madigan asked.

"Sure is," Harris said. "He's gonna have a hard-on to get whoever. You know?"

"He'll find 'em before we do," Callow interjected. "We'll turn up a couple of stiffs without their balls and their eyes in a Dumpster someplace before the week is out. Whaddya wanna bet?"

"Think you're right," Madigan said, and started up toward the house.

Once inside, he marveled at his own handiwork. Looked like an incendiary device in an abattoir. He tried his best not to tread the stuff around, but there was barely anywhere to stand that didn't have some part of someone all over it.

He was surprised at how little he felt. He remembered the shock, the noise, the adrenaline, the panic, the sheer maelstrom of gunfire that had erupted here such a short while before. And he— Madigan—had been right in the middle of it. Perhaps he was insensate. Perhaps he had seen this kind of thing so many times before that he had grown numb to it. Perhaps it was simply because he cared nothing for these people. What had happened here went with the territory. Occupational hazards. Play with fireworks, you're gonna get burned sometime or another.

27

Madigan stood amid the madness and took a deep breath. He believed he could smell his own sweat and adrenaline in the air.

He thought of Fulton, Landry, and Williams—dead like Elvis back in the storage unit. Someone would find them sooner or later, and then everything would fall neatly into place.

Callow was beside him then. "Had Al on the radio. He wants you to do this one."

"You are kidding me?" Madigan replied. "You guys have a helluva lot less traffic than me."

Callow smiled. "Al says what he says, Vincent. He wants you on this one. Says you know the Sandià business better than anyone."

Madigan knew there was no point arguing. Squad Sergeant Alvin Bryant, three years from retiring, had already bought the boat and the Winnebago, and he ran Robbery-Homicide like a prison yard. You ate when you ate, you slept when you slept, you worked the assigned cases, no leeway left or right. Bryant was a rock, an anchor for everyone, and he gave a damn about his people. However, he was a realist, a man of method, and he ran the 167th on the understanding that his word was law.

Madigan signed deeply.

"You love it, man; you know you do," Callow said sarcastically.

"Whatever," Madigan replied resignedly. "Look, help me out on this one, would you? At least do the prelims with me. You, me, and Harris could get this wrapped in an hour."

Callow hesitated. "We got our own messes to deal with—"

"Just the preliminaries," Madigan interjected. "Then I'll take it from there."

Callow looked at Harris. "Hey, Charlie . . . you wanna help Madigan with the prelims?"

Harris shrugged. "Sure, whatever."

"An hour," Callow said. "No more."

"I owe you," Madigan said.

Crime Scene descended en masse. Four bodies, at least what was left of them, and Madigan, Harris, and Callow had a hard time maneuvering their way up the stairwell to the second floor.

"Looks like the freakin' Green Berets came in through the window here," Harris said, and stooped to pick up pencil-sized splinters of frame that were scattered across the carpet for four or five feet either way.

"So I figure we got these four clowns coming in downstairs,"

Callow said. "They're bringing home the bacon—cash maybe, more likely the dope—and out here on the roof we got whoever is waiting for them." He took a moment to lean out through the aperture and look down toward the rear yard.

"You know this place?" he asked Madigan.

"It's Sandià's. I know that much. Beyond that—" He shook his head.

Harris was up the second short stairwell—no more than four or five steps—and he stood there for a moment.

"You hear that?" he asked.

Madigan frowned.

Harris leaned over the banister and looked down at the Crime Scene guys taking pictures of bullet holes and blood spatter.

"Hey . . . quiet down a minute!"

It was eerily quiet. Suddenly. Madigan believed he could hear his own heart, the blood in his temples, the sweat breaking free from his hairline and starting down his forehead. He knew he was imagining it.

Callow opened his mouth to speak, and then he heard something too.

Like something scratching through the wall.

"Jesus," he said through his teeth. He had his gun out.

Madigan's heart skipped a beat or two. He felt something tighten up in his chest, his lower gut.

He heard it then. A scraping sound. What the fu—

Someone in the other room. Someone or something in the room to their left.

Harris was up the well and over on the other side of the door.

Callow followed suit.

Madigan hesitated, and then he moved after them and stood right there with his back against the banister, his gun in his hand, his eye on the handle of the door.

He raised his foot.

Someone was in there. He knew it. Someone was in there and had seen what had happened, and he was going to go right through that door, Callow and Harris on his heels, and whoever was in there was going to get the surprise of their lives.

Madigan hoped like hell that they were armed. Maybe backed up in the corner, gun in their hand, anything in their hand that could pass for a gun, and he could shoot them without hesitation. Shoot them right where they crouched, and that would be that. There would be an internal, IA would be all over it, Officer-Involved Shooting would tie him up in paperwork for a week of Sundays, but it would be done. Bottom line is that there'd be no living witness, no one to tell everyone that the lead investigator had in fact been the perpetrator.

Madigan held his breath. He let fly with the sole of his shoe and the door gave way like cardboard.

He rolled sideways as he went through the doorway. Gun in his hand, elbow hitting the ground with a sickening thud, but he didn't feel a damned thing—maybe the bennies, maybe the adrenaline. It didn't matter. He felt nothing. Saw everything. Gun up ahead of him, finger on the trigger, ready to just let fly with a barrage and down whoever was in there.

But they were down already.

Down and bleeding. Clutching the stomach, scarlet-soaked T-shirt, eyes tight shut, hair in pigtails, a little yellow bow at each end, and blood on the floor, on the walls, and skid marks where she'd tried to get up and failed . . . Whatever strength she might have possessed was fading fast. Madigan could see it in the way she looked at him. Her head against the carpet, and blood there too, so much blood . . .

She opened her mouth to say something, but nothing came out. Just a breath. An exhalation.

She couldn't have been more than seven or eight, and the wound in her stomach was the size of a man's fist.

Madigan wondered whose bullet she'd taken—his or Landry's or Williams's or Fulton's. To his right were the holes. Nothing more than studs and drywall between the upper landing and the girl. How many bullets had come through? Ten, twelve, twenty, fifty?

She'd taken one. Taken one right in the gut. Worst kind of shot. Slow bleed-out, slim chance of making it, a great deal of pain while it happened.

"Jesus Mary, Mother of God," Madigan heard someone say, and then Harris was out on the landing, screaming, "Medic! Medic! Get a fucking medic up here!" at the top of his voice.

For some reason Madigan fell to his knees. His gun slipped from his hand, and with that same hand he reached out toward the little girl. He saw nothing but fear and sadness in her eyes, and it went right through him like a knife.

7

LUPITA SCREAMS

*T*hey're taking her to Harlem Hospital up on West 136th. Harris says she will die.

"She don't weigh more than seventy pounds," he says. "Half her blood is on the floor." He shakes his head. "She ain't gonna make it."

I watch as the ambulance peels away, lights flashing, siren hollering, and I try and convince myself that Landry shot her. Or Williams. Or Fulton. But not me. It couldn't have been me.

It feels like something is coming apart inside me. The seams are weak. I knew that already, but now it feels like maybe there's no seams at all.

Who was she? What the hell was some little kid doing in one of Sandià's drug houses? What the hell was she doing there? She couldn't have seen anything. Not a prayer. Not through the wall, however thin that wall might have been. And hell, even if she did see something, it doesn't matter a damn now because she's gonna die anyway. That's what Harris thinks. Harris says she doesn't have a hope in hell. I wish her dead. Right now, I wish her dead. And then I feel bad for thinking such things . . .

No, this shit is karmic. It doesn't have anything to do with me. I am not responsible for this. Shit like this happens every day in every way imaginable, and it doesn't just happen here. It happens all over the world. People die. Kids die too. Little kids. Littler than this girl. And they die in worse ways, and that's just the nature of things, and maybe there's predestination in all of this, and it was just her day to die . . . and if she hadn't been in Sandià's house then she would have been someplace else, and she would have died some other way . . .

This is the way life works. This is just the way of things.

I know it. I believe it. I have to believe it.

The siren disappears. I wonder if she'll be dead by the time she reaches West 136th. I think of the medics, the furious activity in the back of that ambulance as they put in lines and saline and glucose and call ahead for blood, and they've got an oxygen mask clamped over her face and they're telling her to breathe, breathe, breathe goddammit!

*And I wonder whose daughter she is, and if her mother is someplace
out there and knows already that something bad has happened.*
This is collateral damage.
That's all it is.
Nothing more nor less than that.
I'll feel better after a couple of Quaaludes.

8

COOL DRINK OF WATER

After the ambulance left, Harris and Callow went too. Madigan didn't see them leave. They were there, and then they were gone.

He went back in the house, up to the room where the girl had been found, and he crouched on the floor and looked out onto the landing through the holes in the drywall. He could see the Crime Scene johnnies doing their thing and he knew that he had to get some 'ludes and a drink before his heart exploded with the tension.

This thing was screwed. This was a seriously screwed thing.

Half a block away there was a stolen car with three hundred and sixty grand in the trunk. Money that had come from this very house. Money that had come from four dead guys who were still on the stairwell. And now there was a dead kid too. Mostly dead, at least.

Jesus Christ.

He had to keep it together. He *could* keep it together. This was just another job, another day, and he'd dealt with this kind of thing before. Many times before. He was no stranger to this business.

Madigan stood up. He felt light-headed. He breathed deeply, and then he turned back toward the door. As he did so he looked down at the floor, and there he saw a vague pattern in the nap of the carpet. The outline of the little girl's head and shoulder. Blood had pooled around her and soaked into the carpet, and it was unmistakable. Like she was still lying there. He started to lose his balance. He put his hand against the wall and steadied himself.

He took another deep breath, but all he could taste was that coppery ghost of blood in the back of his throat. Like he was breathing her inside him.

He retched dryly, and he knew he had to get out. He went out to the landing, but the stairwell was crowded with people. They had

33

stretchers, gurneys down below in the hallway, and they were starting the process of taking the dead guys out to the meat wagon. To Madigan's right was the window, shattered glass all across the floor, most of the wooden framework in pieces on the floor, but he could see the roof out there. He stepped across and put his hand on the wall. Carefully, doing everything he could not to lose his balance, he lifted his foot over the sill and lowered it to the roof below. Within a minute he was out there, walked right to the edge and looked down into the rear yard. It seemed like minutes since he had crouched right there with Landry, Fulton, and Williams. Seemed like minutes, and yet seemed like an eternity. Everything was the same, yet everything felt different. There was no easy way to describe how he was feeling, and thus he did not try. He jumped to the yard and walked down the alleyway. He was out in front of the house and looking up at it from the sidewalk when the first body came out.

He knew the guy. Couldn't remember his name, but knew his face. All these guys were related anyway. Cousins of cousins of cousins. And he'd chosen to spend his life among these people? What did that make him? And how many times had he thought to get out? One last job, one big job, and he'd be gone. But it was a drug. It was an addiction. He could no more get away from this than these gangbangers could stop doing their own coke. This was also the nature of things, and Madigan knew—better than anything—that you didn't fight nature.

He decided to head back over to the 167th and write up the prelims. Bryant would be all over it otherwise, insistent, matter-of-fact, demanding that Madigan apply himself to it relentlessly. Internal Affairs was in the shop, headed up by some guy called Duncan Walsh. Always made the atmosphere tense. Madigan didn't know Walsh from Adam, but these guys were all the same, trying their damnedest to short-circuit the hard work to a gold shield. Pedantic, officious in the main, inflated egos, admiring of their own importance as they went about the business of policing the police.

Hell, he had enough going on without having to investigate four murders of his own doing. Ironic. Really freaking ironic. Maybe even karmic.

Madigan didn't have time to drive back to the Bronx and dump the money. And he would have to park the car a good ways from the precinct. Last thing he needed was some eagle-eyed traffic cop running the plate and impounding it. And it wouldn't be smart to leave the cash in the car, regardless of where he parked it. The money would have to go with him, right into the precinct house, right into his locker. Safest place for it. More irony. His life seemed to be one irony after another.

Six blocks from the southeast corner of Louis Cuvillier Park, Madigan parked some ways down toward the corner of Third and 112th. He walked back past the school and took a left, went up the front steps and through reception. He barely had time to get the duffel into his locker before Bryant was behind him.

"So?" was Bryant's opening question. He started walking, took the stairs to the second floor, Madigan following him.

"Four dead, and a little girl wounded. I think she might be dead already."

Bryant shook his head. "She's alive, Vincent. She's in some deep trouble, but she's alive, thank Christ. Apparently she crunched herself up, knees to her chest kinda thing, and that slowed the blood loss. One very lucky little girl."

"We have an ID?" Madigan asked, the only question he could think of in the heat of the moment. He felt the rush. He felt the punch in his lower gut. The little girl was alive. The little girl might have seen something. More important, she might have seen some*one*.

Madigan tried to breathe deeply without making it obvious. His heart was a clenched fist. There were some downers in the bottom of his desk. He needed one. One would be enough to just smooth out the universe and get the world on an even keel.

Jesus Christ. The girl was alive.

"So who were these DBs?" Bryant asked. "Sandià's people, right?"

Madigan nodded.

"Enough of them left to see who they were?"

"Saw one. Know his face. Can't get his name. I'll look through the files and sort out who was who."

"Heard it was a turkey shoot. A massacre."

"Near as damn it. Looks like people were waiting on the back roof, and these guys came up the stairs and got it full frontal. They didn't have a prayer."

"Dope or cash?"

"Don't know. Could have been both."

35

They reached Bryant's office, went inside, took seats on either side of the desk.

"Oh, come on, Vincent. You know the routines better than anyone. That's why I want you on this thing. You knew this place. You knew it was one of Sandià's houses. You go down to the morgue and take a good look at these guys, and I bet you can tell me their names without looking at the damned files. Tuesday, second Tuesday of the month, four guys coming into that house. What are they gonna be bringing?"

"Cash, most likely."

"How much?"

"Two hundred, maybe a quarter mill."

"And everyone is gonna know about it, right? Anyone who works that zone, anyone who lives within two blocks, anyone who deals out of the park . . . They're gonna know about this delivery schedule, aren't they?"

"Sure."

"But they ain't gonna risk anything 'cause it's Sandià's money, right?"

"Right." Madigan felt the muscles tighten in his face. He was trying to look relaxed, nonchalant, like this was just a regular day, a regular meeting with Bryant, a regular investigation. The very money of which Bryant spoke was right there in his locker on the ground floor.

"So the question is this, Vincent . . . Who is either dumb enough or ballsy enough to rip off Sandià on his own turf? Who's got the cojones to do that?"

"That is the question," Madigan said.

"Sure as hell is. And that's the question you need to get me an answer to, Vincent. I need a real answer to that question, and I need it fast. I can't have four dead guys and nothing for the show 'n' tell. I need you to get on this as a priority, okay?"

"Okay." Madigan started to get up.

"Oh, and we got this guy Walsh from IA all over the place. Duncan Walsh. Career cop. Doing his IA shift to get a gold shield before he's forty. You know the routine, right? Stay out of his way, but if he catches you, act polite and helpful but say nothing. Usual beat."

"He asked for me?"

Bryant smiled. "Why? You worried he's going to ask for you?"

Madigan tried smiling back. It felt awkward, out of place, and he dropped it. "You show me one cop in Robbery-Homicide who's got time to talk to IA. Everyone can hang for something, Sarge. You know that."

"Go do your worst, Vincent. I need the crew who pulled this stunt, and I need them faster than yesterday."

Madigan reached the door.

"Oh, and Vincent?"

Madigan turned back.

"Get the kid ID'd as a priority. She's up at Harlem. Be good to know what the hell she was doing in that house this morning."

Madigan made it ten yards down the hallway, and then cut left into the restroom. He barely made it to the sink before he retched dryly. Had he eaten anything, perhaps he would have been sick.

He sluiced his face, scooped some cold water, and drank thirstily. Went down like ice, burning right through his chest and into the pit of his gut.

When he looked back at his own reflection in the mirror he wondered if anyone else could read the guilt and fear painted large in his eyes.

9

STRANGER IN MY HEART

I search out a Quaalude. I chew it dry. It tastes like shit. I sit there for a
minute or two and wait for something to happen.

I think of the money.

*I think of the guy's face as we came through that window and let rip
with a tornado of gunfire.*

I think of the little girl.

I wish she were dead.

*If she was dead I would feel bad that she was dead, but I would feel
better that she was dead.*

I am confused.

I think I should take another 'lude, but I don't.

*And then I think about my own kids. Cassie's birthday is coming up.
She'll be eighteen on February 11. Christ, where do the years go? And her
mom? Angie Duggan . . . Hell, she was the love of my sorry life. At least
I thought so then. Six years and three months we lasted, and then it all
went to shit. Met Ivonne in the middle of that, back in . . . When the hell
was that? Ninety-four? Yeah, it was July of ninety-four, just after
Independence Day. That affair went on right through the divorce from
Angie, and Angie never knew a damned thing about it. Suspected sure,
but never got me on that one. But she accused me of playing around long
before I ever did. She was always accusing me of things I hadn't done.
We used to joke that she'd make a great cop. And so there was Ivonne
and me, and then there was Adam, the child I had with her. My boy
Adam. Light of my second life, star of my heavens. And he's just turned
thirteen, for God's sake. He's a little man. The Little Man of the House.
Haven't seen him since Christmas. Ivonne won't let me in the damned
door. And then there was Catherine, and we stayed married for over
seven years, even longer than with Angie. And we had two kids—Lucy,
all of six years old, seven years old a week before Cassie turns eighteen.
And Tom. Three years old. Smarter than all of them put together. Two
wives, one mistress, four kids. And all of those kids are being told I am
a waste of space. They're young, though. I can win them back, despite*

everything. Maybe I can win them back. Cassie, she would help me. Cassie knows who I am. She sees the truth. She sees that underneath all this madness is a father she could love, perhaps even respect.

I try to think how I would feel if I heard Lucy was shot. She ain't a helluva lot younger than the Hispanic girl we found. So how would I feel if she was shot in the gut and up in Harlem Hospital? And then I wonder how I would feel if a cop was assigned to investigate her shooting, and that cop was just like me.

Then I try not to think. It does no good to think.

There's a stranger in my heart. He has arrived uninvited. I wish he would leave, but I know he will not.

I am in deep.

But there's a way out.

There's always a way out.

I need my wits. I need all my smarts. I need everything I've got and more besides.

I should eat something now and drink some strong black coffee, but the 'lude is creeping up on me and I'm starting to settle a little. I'm starting to think that maybe I can hang it all together in such a way as it stays together . . . and it's all going to be fine . . .

I also know that when the 'lude wears off I'll still be full of shit.

I stand up. I go downstairs. I retrieve the duffel from my locker. I feel for my center of balance. I find it. I start walking. I'm going to get rid of the car. Wipe it all down and get rid of it. I'm going to secure the money. I'm going to take care of everything.

It's gonna be fine.

Seriously.

It's karmic. I am invincible. I do too much good to be waylaid by this shit.

Off I go.

10

PORT OF SOULS

There was something about hospitals. Something unique and specific and troubling.

Harlem Hospital up at Lenox was a Level 1 Trauma Center. Madigan had been there a thousand times. Triage, most days, was an indoor car wreck. Too many people, too few beds, same as any other public hospital. Noise was unbelievable—those who weren't screaming were shouting; those who weren't shouting were trying to be heard over the screamers and shouters; and in the middle of it all came the doctors and nurses, every one of them doing their damnedest to hold it all together despite the fact that it was all falling apart.

Hospitals made Madigan nervous.

Souls were everywhere. Souls departing, souls arriving, all of them looking for new bodies. That's what it felt like. It scared the crap out of him.

There was also a lot of drugs. Made him feel like a quit smoker in a cigar store.

One time he'd come to question a gunshot victim and the duty doctor took him aside and asked if he was okay.

"You don't look so hot," the doctor had said.

Madigan was taken aback, left without words for a moment. He wondered how many others could read what was really going on with him. "I always look like this," Madigan said, and he tried to smile. He could hear the false bravado in his own voice.

"Then you're probably in worse shape than you think. You anemic?"

"Nope."

"Diabetic?"

"Nope."

"You on medication?"

Madigan had glanced away, back again, turned his mouth down

at the corners. "Take a painkiller every once in a while. That's all . . ."

The doctor had smiled knowingly. "You think I don't see you?" he'd said. "You think I can't tell?"

"Tell what?"

"You are off somewhere, my friend. You are somewhere in the clouds. Look at your pupils; look at your skin tone. You think I don't know? What the hell have you taken?"

Madigan hesitated for a moment. He felt transparent, hollow, like nothing. "Taken enough of your bullshit, for a start," he replied, and walked away.

Only when he reached the door did he appreciate how much his hands were shaking.

This time one of the duty nurses was helpful, businesslike, no personal questions. He flashed his ID, asked after the gunshot girl, was directed to the Trauma Unit in back of Triage.

Madigan found a couple of uniforms. He recognized one of them.

"She doing?" Madigan asked.

"Nearly bled out. Slim at best. They say she's fifty–fifty. Next few hours will tell."

"She say anything?"

"Asked if she could get a BLT and a root beer, side order of fries."

"The sarcasm we can do without," Madigan said.

"Far as I know she hasn't said a word. You want to go in and see her?"

"Sure."

The uniform stepped aside and let Madigan pass.

In the bed she looked half the size she had at the house.

Tubes everywhere. Nose, mouth, stuff stuck in her arms, her legs.

Madigan stood there for a week. That's what it felt like.

It crept up on him. The guilt. The conscience. It crept up on him with every passing second, every second that made him see how small she was, how pretty she was, how fragile and delicate and broken and impossibly damaged.

He saw her like she was his own, could have been, might have been.

He remembered Cassie at eight, nine years old. He saw Lucy, not so much younger than this one. He remembered holding her when she was newborn, and feeling that sense of power and duty and responsibility and fear. Fear that he would get it wrong, that he would do or say something that would irreparably damage her. He saw his own children, every one of them, and they were all in that bed, and they were surrounded by wires and tubes and humming machines, and it was all because of him . . .

There was a sound behind him and he turned.

"Was a through-and-through," the nurse said. The nurse was black and pretty and she had cornrow hair, and when she smiled there was something deeply sympathetic in her expression, like she had enough patience to care for the whole fucked-up world.

"Missed most of her vitals, but punctured a lung and put a hole in her gut on the ricochet. Went out her back."

"Odds?" Madigan asked.

"Odds are never great with the little ones. Big bullets and small bodies don't play well together."

"You her attending?"

"Yes, I am."

"What's your name?"

"Nancy. Nancy Lewis."

Madigan gave her his card. "Keep me posted, huh? She wakes up, I need to talk to her."

"We're keeping her sedated," Nancy said. "Think it's gonna be that way for a while. Only way to stop her moving. She's been stabilized. They fixed the hole in her lung, but she's back in surgery in . . ." She glanced at her watch. "An hour, maybe an hour and a half, depending on her vital signs and whether there's any adverse to the transfusion."

"Just let me know if there's any significant changes, okay?"

"I might have to call you and tell you she died."

"Had plenty of those calls before," Madigan replied.

Nancy left the room.

Madigan took another step toward the bed. If the shot was a through-and-through then the bullet was still in that room some-where. It would have pancaked for sure, but there'd be enough of it remaining to determine the caliber. He tried to recall the weaponry. He'd carried a Mossberg, had the .44 as backup but he could not remember if he'd fired it in the house. Even if he did, it wouldn't matter. The storage unit would tell them what Madigan wanted them to believe. Williams shot Fulton with a .44; Fulton shot Landry and Williams with a .38. So Williams must have been carrying the .44, and if a .44 went through the girl and into the wall then Williams must have done it. Neat as paint. That .44 was a lift from a crime scene. Trace that back and it'd wind up somewhere in Harlem, some dealer's house, the scene of some other killing at some other time. It would never come back to Madigan. Madigan was a ghost.

He began to settle.

He took his cellphone from his pocket and held it up above her face. He snapped the picture, checked it, snapped again. It would have to do. He'd have to have something for people to look at if he was going to trawl around East Harlem and the park asking questions.

Collateral damage. That was the truth of it. That was what he told himself, what he tried to make himself believe.

Sometimes it was just your day to die.

Outside the room Madigan spoke to the uniform again.

"Fingerprints?" Madigan asked.

"They're being run."

Madigan shook his head. "They won't find her that way. She has a mother somewhere, a father too, and someone's gonna miss her before too long. I'm gonna head back there and start checking up on neighbors and whatever." He started away, turned back. "You know if her picture was sent over for Missing Persons to chase up?"

"Not a clue."

"Okay, I can do that too," Madigan said.

"You want I should call you if anything happens?"

Madigan smiled dryly. "No, I'll tell you what . . . Why don't you write me a letter and post it a week from Tuesday?"

The uniform shook his head resignedly. Sometimes the only way they got on was to talk crap to one another.

Madigan handed over his card and walked away.

He didn't look back.

11

NOBODY'S CITY

It took the best part of an hour to drive home. He went Triborough, then 278 and 87, all the way up to the stadium before heading east on 161st.

Madigan took the bag of cash from the trunk, the shoes from beneath the driver's seat, and walked it into the house. He upended the bag onto the kitchen table and looked at the money. He could smell it. It smelled used and dirty, like all money did.

He bundled it back into the bag, and then hurried upstairs. He pulled back the carpet at the end of the upper landing, lifted a floorboard, and pushed the bag down inside the cavity. He reached left, lifted out a small wooden box, and from inside he took a ziplock evidence bag. He tipped a half dozen pills into his palm, put one in his mouth, the rest in his jacket pocket, returned the bag to the box, the box under the floor, the floorboard to its rightful place, and tucked the carpet back against the wall.

He got to his feet and stood silently for a moment. He took a deep breath, exhaled slowly, and then went left to his bedroom to get a clean shirt and jacket.

Back downstairs in his makeshift study he switched on the computer and plugged his phone in. He accessed the picture he'd taken at the hospital, tried his best to sharpen the image, soften the contrast a little, and then he printed off a dozen copies. While the printer did its thing, he made coffee in the kitchen, smoked a cigarette, waited for the lithium to stabilize him.

He collected his pictures and his shoes, went back to the stolen car. He had his own vehicle parked on Teller near the corner of 169th. He pulled up on Morris at the southwest edge of the park, wiped down the wheel, the dash, the glove box, the seats, everything. He covered the outer handles, the lid of the trunk, everywhere he'd touched. He knew what he was doing, had done it a dozen times before. He left the car unlocked, walked a half block, dropped the keys down a storm drain, and hurried across the street. A day, maybe two, and the car would be gone for good—joyriders, out-and-out thieves who would strip it down to anonymity within an hour; whichever way, the car would be history before anyone from the PD realized there was another car to even look for.

It would be faster back to East Harlem. The traffic would be better. An hour, maybe an hour and a half and it would be dark. He wanted to find out who the girl was before she died. If she was still alive people would be more helpful. Once she was dead she became part of the history. It didn't matter so much anymore. Even if they did answer up, what good was it going to do? It wasn't going to bring her back, was it?

Madigan made two detours, the first at the precinct to give a copy of the girl's picture to the duty uniform in Missing Persons.

"Start looking soon as you can," he said.

"Without a name?"

Madigan shrugged. "Way it goes, my friend," he said, and smiled.

"You know how many pictures we got back here?"

"Oh, I reckon maybe ten or fifteen, twenty at most," Madigan replied.

"Jesus, you guys are unreal," the uniform countered. He turned his back and disappeared.

The second detour was to an auto-salvage place he knew. Here they crushed cars, recycled windscreens and tires, other such things. They also possessed a small incinerator unit where they burned what couldn't be sold. It was into this unit that his blood-stained shoes went, and he slipped a fifty to the owner, an old acquaintance. Madigan had turned a blind eye to a few stolen vehicles over the years, and they had an understanding.

Madigan headed back up First. As far north as 128th, west to Third, east to the FDR, and south to 110th. That was the deal. That was the zone, the territory. They called it the Yard. That was all. Just *the Yard*. Eighteen blocks up and down, eight from left to right. Little more than a mile one way, three quarters of a mile the other. Never ceased to amaze Madigan how much garbage could be packed into someplace so small. Gentrification was overdue here. Hell, maybe they could do it as well. They'd worked some on the Bronx, the Village, the Fulton Fish Market, Tribeca. It was all going upmarket. East Harlem was the latecomer. Maybe the Yard wouldn't make the qualifiers, would never make it to the Big

Show. Did it matter? Hell, no. Not to Madigan. He was going to take what he could and run. Staying here was not an option. He'd been good for too many years, smart for too few. Right back to July of '89 when he'd taken the academy exam, he was looking for the angle. No one *wants* to be a cop. That never happened. There were some who *had* to be a cop, some who *needed* it, but none who wanted it. That was not the way it worked. This wasn't a job. It was a vocation. And if it wasn't a vocation, well, it was an angle. You heard the stories, and for sure they were true. Little kid sees the tapes go up someplace, the black and yellow crime scene tapes. He sees the big guys in the blues, the even bigger guys that the blues saluted, and those guys didn't come in uniforms; they came in slacks and sports jackets and they had shirts and ties and there was a holster on the hip and a badge folded outside the breast pocket, and they went right on inside wherever and saw whatever shit had been done. And most often it was some bad shit, and how bad it was no one knew except the guys with the hip holsters and the sports coats. The kid makes a decision. *I wanna be that guy. I wanna see what that guy sees. I wanna know it all.* But the *knowing* wasn't the end-all. Knowing had a reason. Always had a reason. You wanted to know something because . . . Because what? Because it would get you rich or laid or powerful or free or safe or protected, or something. What it did, well, it didn't matter. Different for different people. And maybe the kid on the sidewalk watching those guys go in the house where the family had been shotgun slaughtered for forty bucks and a wireless had no inkling of what he wanted to know, even why he wanted to know it, but he knew enough to recognize the truth. The more you knew, the stronger you were. Dead people were dumb. That was the simple fact. The dumber you were, the deader you got. Not old people. That's a different thing. We're talking people dying ahead of nature, ahead of the natural order of things. Those were the dumb ones. And usually it came down to one thing. They say "wrong place, wrong time." Well, that didn't make sense. It could only be one or the other, never both. More often than not people got killed because there was one thing about which they were ignorant. Had they known that one thing, well, they'd still be alive.

Life wasn't complicated. At least Madigan didn't believe so. Life was simple. Take or be taken. Eat or be eaten. Kill or be killed.

Six months academy, four years patrol officer at the Twelfth, thirteen months as suppression officer in the Manhattan Gangs

Division, three years in Investigative, two years in Vice, six years in Robbery-Homicide to secure Detective First Class, a year in Organized Crime Control Bureau, and then a requested transfer back to Robbery-Homicide. Six one-eighty-ones for excessive force, eleven officer-involved shootings, thirteen commendations from the mayor's office via the police chief, a fifty-one-percent average arrest-to-charge rate, thirty-one lifers, countless ten-to-fifteens and six-to-tens, a taxable salary of ninety thousand, additional sources of income bringing in another hundred or so. He'd do a year or two more of this, and then cut out for greener pastures. Pick up another twenty a year in Nassau, Suffolk, maybe Westchester or Rockland, someplace where people didn't crap in their own backyards and expect the stink to vanish by itself. Someplace where the bureaucrats possessed some organizational skills, a basic understanding of manpower assignment and resource utilization. Down here they couldn't organize a blowjob in a whorehouse.

Madigan had been back in Robbery-Homicide since September 2008. Forty-two years old, two marriages, one mistress, all gone by the wayside. Four kids, youngest three, oldest seventeen. He had his issues. He smoked too much, drank too much; he slept around some. He had his medicinal predilections and proclivities, but nothing he couldn't control. It was all a question of balance. Too much coke, take a Xanax. Too much Adderall or Dexedrine, well, just smooth off all the rough edges with some lithium, a couple of 'ludes, maybe a Percocet or two. The road of excess did not lead to the palace of wisdom. Blake might have been smart on everything else, but he was dumb on that one. Look at that poor, dumb fool Jim Morrison. Where the hell did a philosophy like that get him? Less than thirty years old and he was in a hole in the ground in Paris, that's where.

It was true. New York was nobody's city. And because it was nobody's, then—in a way—it was everybody's. And Madigan was as good an *everybody* as anyone else.

He pulled over to the sidewalk on 117th. He picked up the pictures of the little girl from the passenger seat and looked at her.

He felt what he felt, but he convinced himself he did not. He could not afford to feel anything.

Maybe she would die, maybe she wouldn't. Ballistics wouldn't get him, and he did not believe the girl had seen any faces. Landry, Williams, and Fulton would be found in the storage unit. Two and two would make four. It was a home run, and he wasn't even out of breath, hadn't even skidded to base.

It was all collateral damage.

Madigan tried to smile, gave it up as a bad idea, opened the door, and started walking.

12

GREAT DIVIDE

*T*his is the thing. People are not the same. It's that old adage: All victims are not created equal. Sure, that's the case wherever you go. Like the fire chief said, "I ain't never put out a fire in a rich white guy's house." You live up in Chelsea or someplace, then you're gonna get the best of the best. Some upmarket Detective First Class Gold Shield shiny-shoed son of a bitch, and he's gonna be all over your case until someone's in the hole for whatever they did to you. Down here, here in the Yard, you're gonna be one of twenty-nine homicides I'm investigating, and three weeks after the coroner signed you off I'm still gonna be chasing a requisition form for Crime Scene snaps.

I do this for an hour and I've already had enough.

First guy I talked to was some dirty-faced, semi-incoherent white guy with filthy hair woven into ratty dreadlocks. He smelled like a penitentiary toilet in high summer.

The only thing I'm thinking while I'm talking to these people is, "Why are these motherfuckers lying to me?" Not about the girl. Not that. About everything else. Their lives are lies. Lies upon lies upon lies. Layers of lies. They lie to their husbands, wives, their kids, their neighbors, and they lie to themselves. And those are the biggest lies of all, the ones they tell themselves every goddamned day: I am different from everyone else. I am different from all these people around me, and things are gonna get better. Maybe not today, maybe not tomorrow, but soon. Soon they will get better, and I will be out of here. This is not my life. This is a way station, a bus stop, nothing more than that.

Bullshit. You're born here, you live here, you die here. It ain't never gonna change. You ain't gonna win the lottery. You ain't gonna sing one time and find some Warner Brothers A&R guy was just happening by, and lo and behold, all of a sudden you're Beyoncé or Alicia Keys. Not a prayer. That shit happens in other peoples' lives.

I see the lies in the eyes of the guy who serves me at Chicken Shack. He knows I'm a cop. He can see it in my attitude, in the way I walk and talk, in the bulge of my hip holster.

He thinks I'm a piece of shit. He thinks I'm no one. Less than no one.

I'm thinking right back at him, "Hey, buddy. You're what? Thirty-five years old, and you're still wearing a name tag to work. You tell me who made the wrong career decision."

But I say nothing. This guy'll spit in my chicken if I piss him off.

I tell him, "Thanks," and I take my chicken back to the car and eat it.

I sit there chaining smokes, like I don't want to breathe the air down here. Whatever six thousand toxic chemicals they put in my Luckies is one helluva lot cleaner than the shit they get to breathe in the Yard.

I have spoken to fifty people, maybe more. They don't want to know. They say they don't know the girl before I even show them the snap.

I say, "Look at the picture before you tell me you don't know her," and they get that defensive light in their eyes, all superior and condescending. And then they look at the picture without really looking at it, and they say they don't know her again, and it's little more than an echo of the first denial.

Makes me wanna smack them. Smack them hard. Hard enough to go down and stay down.

"Don't screw with me," I want to say. "You have no idea the whirlwind of shit I can bring down around your life if you screw with me. Today I killed three people. Three white people. Three pedophile loser scumbags sure, but I killed them for pissing me off less than you are pissing me off right now."

But once again, I say nothing. I was raised up polite, see?

And it is then—just then—as I am thinking these thoughts, as I hold the lighter to the tip of the last cigarette I will smoke before I get out of the car and start down the other side of the street, that my cellphone goes off.

I think, "What the hell now?" and I take it from my pocket and turn it over, and I see the name flashing on the screen.

And my heart stops for a moment. My heart stops and my stomach sort of swallows itself, and I feel the hairs on the nape of my neck stand to attention, and I feel my scalp tighten . . .

The phone won't stop.

I hesitate, my finger hovering over the little green telephone, and then I push it.

"Yes," I say, and already I can hear it in my voice. The edge. The nerves.

"You gotta come see him," the voice says. And it doesn't matter whose voice it is. It could be the president of freaking Cuba, for all that it

matters. It's just that the message will have come from him, and him directly.

"Get me Madigan," Mr. Sandià will have said, and there won't have been the slightest doubt in his mind as to whether or not I would comply.

"Now?" I ask, like six feet of stiff shit.

"No, dickhead," the voice says. "Why don't you come next Christmas?"

The line goes dead.

Oh fuck, I am thinking. Oh fuck, oh fuck, oh fuck.

13

PROMISE ME

His name wasn't always Sandià. His name used to be something else, and something before that, but none of these names was the one with which he was born.

Now he was just Mr. Sandià, and this was the name by which he was known and the name that everyone used.

Anything that went before didn't matter.

Madigan sat for a while in the smoke-filled car.

He felt nauseous, light-headed. He wished he hadn't taken the lithium back at home, and then he thought that the smartest thing to do would be to take another one. And so he did.

He chewed it dry, and it tasted bitter in the back of his throat, and he took the empty cup from Chicken Shack and pulled off the lid. There was a half inch of melted ice water in the bottom. He drank it, sucked the last ice cube into his mouth and chewed it. He lit another cigarette, opened the window, tried to breathe deeply and couldn't. His chest was too tight. Everything was too tight. He loosened his tie, his top button, even his belt. He opened the door and let the cool air in, and then he slammed it shut and started the car. He tried to clear his throat. It was tourniquet-tight. His fingers drummed nervously on the wheel.

Come on, he thought. *Lithium, lithium, do your worst.*

He was at the junction of a 119th and Pleasant before he could even get his thoughts straight.

Mr. Sandià wanted to see him.

That morning he—Vincent Madigan—ably assisted by three dead scumbags, had busted one of Sandià's houses. Sandià's courier and accompanying entourage had been massacred in a hail of gunfire, and all the money had gone. Four hundred grand, give or take some change, more than three hundred and sixty of which was in a bag under the floorboards on the upper landing of Madigan's own house. Next to that bag were several boxes of pills—everything from Demerol and Quaaludes to Dexedrine and

Bennies. Besides that there were three unlicensed handguns, a Tec-9, about ten grams of coke, and a half dozen wraps of smack. What a field day Walsh would have. And what a fun time Madigan would have explaining it all away. Walsh had nothing. IA never had anything. They relied on informants and snitches within the division, and they never got them. They said they did, but they lied, just like most everyone else. Walsh was not only chasing Madigan, he was after Charlie Harris and Ron Callow and a dozen others. Some rumor that three or four of them had lifted a crate of Zegna suits from Evidence, sold them on to whoever was interested. Those suits had gone missing for sure, but it wasn't the suits that were the item of interest. The suits went into a furnace, and the six kilos of grass that has been vacuum-packed in coffee cartons and buried at the bottom of that crate had been trafficked into the network within twelve hours of leaving Evidence. That hadn't been Madigan's gig. Weed was bullshit. Six kilos? Jesus, you could make that much money off of three ounces of coke if it was cut right.

No, Duncan Walsh had nothing, and hell, the guy was out of there within three months if the grapevine was anything to go by. He'd move on up, gold shield clutched in his greedy, sweaty paws, and end up behind a desk in the chief of police's administrative division, bullshitting war stories from the good old days when he busted cops for smoking reefer in the precinct garage.

Madigan was off-track. Thinking about Walsh and IA and Zegna suits was avoiding the issue. Sandià had called.

You gotta come see him.

That meant nothing. It inferred and implied and gave away nothing. The message was always the same, the same tone of voice, the same kind of call. Didn't matter what you were doing or where the hell you were. Your kid's first birthday party, and if you don't stay your wife is going to divorce you. Your daughter's marriage, and you're right there in the damned church about to give her away to some slick-haired dentist out of Yonkers with a brand-new Lexus and a weekend chalet on the edge of Blue Mountain Lake. It didn't matter. You were summoned by Sandià, you went. End of story.

Despite the lithium, Madigan's nerves were all over the place. He thought about taking another, but he didn't want to be drooling and tongue-tied like some hopeful kid on prom night.

This was it.

Showtime.

He turned left at the lower end of Paladino Avenue and started on up toward Sandià's tenement. Sandià was up top, right there at the peak of the mountain, six floors beneath him filled with Hispanic junkies and hookers and dealers and loan sharks, the topmost level a fortress of solitude and safety. You wanted to get to Sandià you had to walk a gauntlet of security like no other. The mayor, the chief of police, the state senator? Not a prayer. The security around such people was a tissue-fine web of nothing compared to that provided for Sandià.

Madigan parked fifty yards away. In and of itself, there was no concern that his car would be seen and identified, either by his colleagues or the assholes that prowled this neighborhood and kept Sandià informed of who was around and what they were after. Madigan was supposed to be in the area. He was looking for the girl. That was the official line. The unofficial line? Well, anyone who was *anyone* in the Yard knew that he and Sandià had a working relationship. In reality, it would take six divisions of cops and most of the National Guard to bust open Sandià's tenement. It was a castle. Perhaps it was the last bastion of real opposition to the mayor's progress machine. There would be no gentrification here. Perhaps Sandià was paying the world to take no notice. Madigan knew some things, but not others. He knew more than most, but when it came to whatever *working relationship* that might have existed between Sandià and the real powers that be, well, Madigan was in the dark. There was an uneasy alliance, a tenuous rapport, and for as long as Madigan could remember it had held in this part of the city. Raids happened, of course, but it was always the little guys who bit the bullet. It was in the dealers' houses, in the crack dens, the cluster of dilapidated condos where Sandià's hookers plied their trade that the busts were made. Never here. Never up close and personal.

Madigan started walking back the way he'd come. He'd left both his guns in the car. Take them with him and they'd keep them until he came out again. Unless he was up for a suicide mission, there was no hope of killing Sandià on his home ground. And before today there had been no reason to kill him. Before today he hadn't hit Sandià personally and directly.

And if Sandià already knew that Madigan had taken the house that morning, well, Madigan would be dead within the hour. His head, hands, and feet would be a dozen pounds of hamburger by nine, most of it in the New Jersey swamps, a little in the East River, maybe some in the Hudson. By midnight the fire department would be traipsing through the wet, smoldering wreck of his house, and the office of the chief of police would be making a statement to the *New York Times* about how sorely Madigan would be missed by his colleagues and his family.

And Sandià would make sure that his connection to Madigan never saw the light of day.

It was that simple. It was always that simple with Sandià.

At the lower entrance to the tenement Madigan was waved through into the foyer. Here he went through the customary pat-down—collar, shoulders, underarms, waist, thighs, calves, ankles. His hip holster was empty, as was the one at his ankle. He was escorted to the elevator, and one of the apes rode up with him. Nine floors, all of it in silence, the aged elevator clunking and creaking every foot of the way. The ape didn't smell so good. He needed a good hosedown. Maybe six three, two ten, two twenty perhaps, his face like a wet sack of sneakers. He had a buzz cut all over, but at the sides there were lightning streaks cut down to the scalp. He had a vicious scar dissecting his left ear, and right down to the edge of his jaw. The ear had been severed, but had knitted.

"Machete," the ape said, aware that Madigan was staring.

"That so?"

"Sure is."

"Gotta smart, huh?"

"Just a little."

"Wouldn't want to see the guy that did that to you," Madigan ventured.

"You ain't gonna," the ape replied.

The elevator shuddered to a halt.

Madigan waited for the door to slide back. The lithium had slowed his heart, but he could feel the pressure of his own blood in his veins, in his brain, in the arteries in his neck. His hands were moist with sweat. His scalp itched something fierce. He needed to be the way he always was with Sandià—respectful, yet nonchalant and unhurried. They had history together, all of fifteen years, all the way back to the Gangs Division. Back then Madigan had been twenty-seven, Sandià something around forty. He owned a piece of a half dozen things. Nothing was big by itself, but everything together made him matter. He had some cars, some girls, a couple of chop shops, a few runs in and out of the cargo bays at JFK for cigarettes, liquor, videos and electronic gear. He had a crew of three or four dozen. They weren't a gang. They didn't wear colors or fly flags. Sandià was too smart for that. No, Sandià knew where to invest his time and resources. Start with the cops already on the take. Get them on your side. Those that weren't, well, there was always a way. Put a couple of girls in a hotel room, make a call, have a cop arrive for a possession bust, maybe a solicitation or something. The girls take care of the cop so as not to get the ticket, and everything is on film. The cop gets a couple of stills in the mail, he faces a costly divorce, a screwed career, or he gives word to Sandià every time there's a planned raid on a traffic route.

Madigan's own introduction to Sandià's little world had been a mutual thing, a river that ran both ways. Back then, the mid-90s, there were things going on that made today's business pale in comparison. Madigan was still married to Angela, his first wife. He went up to Manhattan Gangs in July of '94. Cassie had been two years old and a handful. Neither he nor Angela were sleeping so good. They were fighting, but still at the stage where they didn't fight around Cassie. There was some vague semblance of their former relationship, perhaps even the belief that they could work through their problems and survive. A year later it would be a different story. A year later they were sleeping in different rooms, Cassie in with Angela, Madigan in the den with a bottle of Jack. It was a bad time, and would stay bad until the final split in early '97. Madigan already had something going with Ivonne Moreda, a girl he met in July of '94, the same month he came out of the 12th Patrol and went into Gangs. He'd been twenty-seven, she was all of nineteen, and he had her up for possession with intent to distribute, resisting arrest, unlawful possession of an unlicensed firearm. He hadn't gotten laid for a year. She was a drop-dead perfect ten. It didn't take long for her to convince him that there was a better way to iron out the situation than throwing her in the jail with a crew of crack whores and gangbangers. They stayed together until September of '99, and Adam—their son—had been born in November of '96. He was a beautiful kid. He was quiet and calm and he looked like all the best of Madigan, all the best of Ivonne. He was the kind of kid who'd solicit admiration from people no matter where he went. Now Adam Moreda was thirteen, Ivonne was thirty-four, and Madigan hadn't seen either of them for as long as he could recall. But Ivonne had been Madigan's introduction to Sandià, if not directly, then certainly indirectly.

The Hispanic gangs were a world apart from the blacks and the Orientals. The Hispanic gangs—Los Carniceros, El Equipo Séptimo, and Los Fantasmas among others—were vying for bit-and-piece territories all around Louis Cuvillier Park, west to the FDR, north to the junction of MLK Jr. and First by the Triborough. There were incidents. People got stabbed and shot and gutted and burned. Then it all went quiet. Nothing for days. Madigan spoke to Ivonne, and she just smiled. She said, "It's him. The Watermelon Man. Mr. Sandià. He has it all worked out. He gets them all working together instead of fighting between themselves. He is the mayor of East Harlem now. He has some people killed and now he is the big boss."

So Madigan asked questions, got word back, met this Mr. Sandià in January of 1995. Madigan could remember the day as if it were yesterday. Bright, cold, the air fresh and clean. The meeting had been in a small house on East 124th. Lunchtime. Madigan went on up there. The door was opened even as he approached it. A narrow-shouldered man in a good suit waved him in, smiling. One gold tooth on the right side, the rest artificially white. When he turned and led the way down to the kitchen in back Madigan saw the bulge of a handgun in the small of the man's back. A second man rose as Madigan entered the kitchen. The smell of fried meat and cheese filled his nostrils. It was a good smell.

Sandià got up from the table. He was smiling too. He was no more than five eight or nine, but solidly built. His hair was thick and crimp-curled. His complexion was fair, almost Caucasian, but the warm depth of his eyes and the pitch black of his hair made him nothing but Hispanic.

"You are Madigan," he said, and there was but the faintest hint of accent.

"And you are Mr. Sandià."

Sandià smiled again and extended his hand. "We are eating," he said. "Simple, but good."

And they ate, and they spoke little—merely of the cold weather, the upcoming political changes, the deterioration of educational standards for children in the area—and all the while Madigan knew that here was a man who possessed no small aspirations. And when lunch was finished and they sat smoking, drinking coffee, Madigan merely said, "There is work for both of us here, Mr. Sandià," and Sandià, nodding slowly, said, "And what line of work would be of the greatest interest to you?"

It started small. Madigan gave Sandià heads-up on traffic lines for the black gangs. Consignments coming in were detoured, redistributed. In exchange Sandià gave Madigan the inside line on the Orientals, even supply lines for the dealers who provided for the white college kids and student nurses who drove up from Yorkville and the East Side. Sandià got rich. Madigan got a bust sheet the length of the Mississippi, and all was well. August of 1995 Madigan was promoted to investigation detective in the Gangs Division, and there he stayed until October of '98. From there it was 3rd Class at Vice until January of 2001, and then six years in Robbery-Homicide. But the roots had been planted here, all those many years before, and he and Sandià, differences aside, had worked hand in glove for the better part of fifteen years.

It was this history that was always there, always present. Though tacit, unspoken, there was still a contract between them. A promise. One hand washes the other. One good deed deserves its recompense.

What Madigan had done that morning was a violation of everything that had ever taken place between them—every word and every action through every year of that decade and a half.

And it was this—this painful awareness—that he was doing his utmost to hide as he stepped out of the elevator and walked down the hallway to Sandià's room.

14

GHOST ON THE HIGHWAY

W alsh should not have been called out, but he was one-time Homicide and was the only detective in the precinct when the call came in. Callow, Harris, the others—they were all out on other jobs. There was a dead twelve-year-old in a Dumpster near St. Paul's Place; a domestic on 125th near the subway station that had gone so terribly, terribly wrong; something that looked like an erotic-asphyxia case in a shitty apartment overlooking Thomas Jefferson Park that looked more like a setup with every question asked of the deceased's boyfriend. A regular evening's work. So Walsh it was. Duncan Walsh, thirty-nine years old, New Jersey born and bred but sounded like someplace else. Unmarried, living with a woman three years his senior, no kids. Walsh went into the PD in New Jersey. Took his exam late, already twenty-six years old, but he sailed it. Out of the academy into patrol, he did three years feet-and-seat, half the time in a black-and-white, the rest on the sidewalk. Eighteen months in Homicide, and then an about-face that took him into the SWAT Program. SWAT didn't suit him or vice versa, because four months into that he cut and ran, transferred to NYPD in the early part of 2003 and spent the next four years jockeying a desk in PD Veteran Admin. The mayor's office PD public relations department came looking in the fall of 2007, and he went; spent a year smoothing out the creases and tucking in the corners, and then he decided it was time for a gold shield. That's why he wound up in Internal Affairs, the guaranteed fast-track to detective without doing the real grunt work.

Walsh may have been New Jersey, but he wasn't real New Jersey. His father was Scots lineage out of Pennsylvania, his mother from the South. Duncan had been an only child, neither spoiled nor ignored, but hovering somewhere in the middle ground. Later, after both of them were dead, Walsh looked back on his parents and wondered if they'd had a child not because they wanted to, but because they were supposed to. That's what people did. They got married and had kids. His folks tried it once and figured it was someone else's game.

Work was his thing. That was what Walsh did. He latched on to the police career for lack of some other vocation. He forced himself to identify and relate. It was neither a case of personal reconciliation, nor conditioned response, but the simple fact of having to do something that possessed meaning. Walsh's problem had always been the expectations afforded tomorrow. It would be better *tomorrow*. What was up ahead was infinitely better than what had gone, or what was now. A trait he took from his father. Not pessimism, more a belief that everything was a way station en route to something better. It was a double-edged sword. You didn't rest on your laurels, and yet neither did you acknowledge your immediate successes. Always in limbo, Walsh worked and watched and waited for his chance to prove something. What he was trying to prove he was as unaware of as anyone else, but that didn't change the fact that this was what he felt. Such an attitude, such a *philosophy*, gave him a degree of perfectionism and attention to detail that was almost obsessive. He had been that way in PD Veteran Admin, in the mayor's office, and before that in Homicide. SWAT had been a different ball game. SWAT had tested everything that he was, and he had been found wanting. Walsh knew himself better than most. He recognized a hiding to nowhere, and he got out before he arrived. Acceptance of limitations was not defeatist as far as he was concerned; it was simply realistic and pragmatic.

That Tuesday evening, when the call came through from the desk to say that a triple homicide had been reported in a storage unit off of East 109th, Walsh's first response was, "Who told you to give it to me?"

"Squad sergeant," the desk told him.

Walsh called Bryant, and Bryant said, "We have no one else. I'm not asking you to take the case. I'll pass it on to whoever comes back first. I just need someone with half a brain to go down there and secure the scene. That's all."

"This is *so* not my job—"

"You think I don't know that? Jesus, Walsh, stop acting like six feet of bullshit. Right now you're all I have . . . oh, aside from three dead fellers and a crapload of cash all over the floor of some storage unit garage. Gimme half an hour of your precious time, will ya?"

"Crime Scene been called?"

"Yep, but they say another twenty minutes or so."

"Give me the address," Walsh said, and he was already reaching for the jacket on the back of his chair.

Uniforms had put a black-and-white on either side of the storage unit. Already there were people haunting the edges of the thing. Walsh pulled over, flipped his badge, and tucked it into his breast pocket. He glanced at his watch. Five fifteen.

Bryant had been good to his word. Inside there were three DBs, a bunch of cash scattered this way and that, a lot of blood. Only vehicle was a Ford Econoline E-250. Looked like the party had all gone to shit. Crime Scene would have a field day.

There were three dead, two of whom still held handguns—a .38 and a .44. The guy holding the .44 had a chest wound, looked like he'd taken a slug right through the heart. The guy with the .38 had been shot in the stomach, and from the wide pool of blood around him Walsh figured it had been a bleed out. The third man had gone down with a head shot, looked like a .38 as well; he was without a weapon, and there didn't seem to be a weapon anywhere on the floor of the storage unit. Walsh's first question was who shot who first? The only way it could have worked was for .38 to shoot the one with no weapon. No weapon is down and finished, no argument. We're good so far. Then .38 and .44 have a face-off. Did they fire simultaneously? One gets it in the head, the other gets it in the stomach, and then .38, he bleeds out? Seemed to work in theory, but Ballistics and Forensics would confirm.

Walsh backed up to the storage unit's entranceway, then headed back to his car for his digital camera. He took shots of the Econoline treads, the tread marks on the floor near the wall. He snapped the three DBs, the entry and exit wounds, the handguns, the bodies themselves from each corner of the storage unit, the van, and then the blood-spattered tens, twenties and fifties across the floor.

This was the aftermath of a robbery, a robbery executed successfully, and then someone got greedy. Maybe someone had been greedy all along, and this had been inevitable.

Walsh returned to the door as he heard a vehicle draw to a stop outside. Crime Scene, three of them, booted and suited, business-like as always.

Unit First acknowledged Walsh, listened to Walsh's résumé of the prelim.

"We can tell you who shot who, no problem," Walsh was told. "Don't know how long it'll take, however. We've had a busy weekend and I got traffic backed up from late Saturday."

"I'm just on secure detail," Walsh said. "I'm staying until someone gets here from Robbery-Homicide; then it's their problem . . ." Then he hesitated and added, "But sure, yes, if it's no trouble. Send me a copy when you get through with it." He gave the Unit First his card.

"IA?" he asked. "You're a little far from home, aren't you?"

"This is the breaks," Walsh said, and smiled. "Like I said, I'm just on secure detail until the cavalry arrives."

Walsh left them to get on with it, headed back to the car, and sat patiently. It was another fifty minutes before someone showed. Ron Callow, some new guy in tow.

Callow and Walsh shook hands, always polite yet never friendly.

"Appreciated," Callow said.

"No problem."

"You get a take on this?"

"Nothing much. Looks like a robbery went down, someone got greedy, they had a falling out, and it all went to hell."

"We'll go see," Callow said. He turned back after a moment. "You done?"

"Not until eight," Walsh replied.

Callow and his partner headed for the storage unit. Walsh got back in his car and started the engine. As he pulled away he glanced back at the strange glow of the arc lamps that emanated from the doorway of the storage unit. Was there something that he missed about this? It had been there, hadn't it? He'd felt it. Standing over those dead bodies, the blood spatter, the money sent in six different directions . . . the rush that came, that feeling in the base of the gut. Eighteen months in Homicide had taught him a great deal, but also it had embittered him, given him an edge of cynicism. That was something he'd never wanted to keep, and thus he had moved on, just as he had at SWAT, the same thing that had prompted the transfer from New Jersey to New York. It was the edge that was so visible in people like Callow, in Bryant and Harris and Madigan. And yet Madigan was something beyond even that. Madigan possessed something that was uniquely Madigan. Madigan, Walsh believed, was the best of them. He had a hell of an arrest record, a lot of people put away for a long time. But Madigan was also the hardest to deal with, the toughest to nail down, the quickest to vanish. Madigan was also the man Walsh believed he himself would have become if he had failed to see the signs. They were there, just like the signs on the freeway. Speed limits, stop signs, detours and diversions. There was a reason for those signs, and if you ignored them . . . well, if you ignored them then your career ceased to be a career and became simply a means by which the days and weeks could be made to disappear. Madigan had become such a man; so long a cop there was now no other life he could lead. Two divorces, two different sets of kids, more than likely living in some shitty little apartment, boxes in the hallway containing everything he owned, still there from the day he moved in. That was not a life, certainly not the kind of life Walsh wanted. And yet Madigan inspired a degree of respect, simply because he had not compromised that sense of purpose.

Walsh saw it in most of them—fifteen years in and they were worn out, half-beaten to death, suspicious of all offers of help, cynical not only about the law, but any real possibility of justice, forever angling for any kind of letup that would ease the pressure. And yet they kept on going, kept on doing the job, and they did it as best they could.

Walsh had been in twelve years already, and by the time he reached a decade and a half he wanted the gold shield, the rank, the office, the salary. He had convinced himself that he would not become another Callow, another Harris or Bryant, and certainly not another Madigan. And yet, even in convincing himself of this, he knew that he would never have what they had: a sense of pride in the simple fact that they hadn't quit.

Walsh took a left after Thomas Jefferson Park and headed down the incline into the parking garage beneath the precinct. There was no reason to feel anything as he walked from his car to the elevator, and yet he did. An uncharacteristic anxiety had settled somewhere in his lower gut, and as he rode up the two levels to his floor he could see little but the scene that had confronted him in the storage unit.

Something hadn't made sense. He wondered who had been robbed, and how much had been taken. He wondered about the identity of the three dead men, the way in which that final scene had played out. He tried to imagine how they must have felt—believing that whatever they'd done had been a resounding

63

success, that here was the money they needed, a way out, an escape route, and yet swiftly understanding that this was the point at which it would all end.

The elevator doors opened. Walsh hesitated outside his office door. He had the digital camera in his hand. Why had he taken those pictures? It was not his case, not his crime scene, and why had he asked the Unit First to info him on the treads and ballistics?

This was not the way to go. He was not about to turn back. Robbery-Homicide was not where he wanted to be. IA was swimming against the current for sure, but IA was a means to an end. The destination was the thing, not the journey.

Walsh sat down and switched on the camera. One by one he deleted the images from the memory, and then put the camera in the desk drawer.

That was the end of the matter, and there was nothing more to be considered.

15

ETERNITY IS HERE

*C*ourage is not what you believe it to be. Courage is misconceived. Everyone wants to survive. No one wants to die. I think courage— more often than not—comes out of a certainty that you are screwed anyway. Sort of dead if you do, dead if you don't. Like a nothing-to-lose proposition.

I don't believe anyone is really courageous. At least not naturally. People are scared. They don't want to die. Even the crazies, the out-and-out psychos. They get scared too when they know it's coming.

Seen two executions. Both lethal injections. Didn't sleep for days afterward. Didn't dare. Those men sobbed. I mean really sobbed. They were all attitude until the moment they knew it wasn't a game, it wasn't a dream, and they weren't going any other way than a deep hole in the bottom of hell. Because that's where they belonged, both of them, and no doubt about it. And still they sobbed like little girls.

I've had guns in my face. I've been shot at. I've had big people come at me with baseball bats and knives and sticks and broken bottles and one time a chainsaw that had already cut someone's arm off at the shoulder.

I was scared. Damned straight.

But not scared like now.

This moment.

Crossing the threshold, passing out of the hallway and into the room where Sandià waits patiently for me.

"Get me Madigan," he told someone, and the someone made a call, and Sandià never thought for a second that I would do anything but come a-running.

Does he want me because he knows? Or does he want me because he doesn't know?

If he knows, well, I am dead. No question about it. "You killed four of my people," he will say. He will shake his head. He will look away for a moment, and then he will turn back to me and smile philosophically. I will see that expression, the one I have seen so many times before. A sense of regretful reconciliation, as if he has appreciated now that there is nothing more that can be done. Like Pontius Pilate. Even if he felt something different, there would be nothing he could do. The decision has been made. It has now been washed out of his hands.

I am sad. Not for me. Not for the hopelessness of my situation. I am sad simply because it has come to an end. I am forty-two years old. It has all been and gone in the blink of an eye. What did I expect? What kind of life did I believe I would have? Only thing I know for sure is that it was something other than this. Of that I am certain.

I have a feeling in my chest. Someone has gripped my heart and they are squeezing it hollow. The constriction spreads to my lungs, my throat, even my nose. I am finding it hard to breathe. The walls seem tissue thin. If I touch them they will move.

I think of the girl who OD'd three weeks before. I think of how my life has become as meaningless as hers.

I think of Landry and Williams and Fulton. I wonder if anyone has discovered their bodies yet. I wonder if Crime Scene are—even now— taking pictures, putting two and two together, and I try to imagine what I would do if I were assigned to the investigation. I should have gone farther. I should have chosen a storage unit out of jurisdiction. I should have gone back and checked and double-checked that there was nothing to tie me to the scene in that building.

I should have done a lot of things.

This is it now.

This is the moment.

Like that child killer on the table when they stuck those IVs in his arms and he knew the sodium thiopental and the pancuronium bromide was on its merry way.

"So this is it?" he asked, and he looked through the glass right at me. "Eternity is here."

16

DAY TURN TO NIGHT

"Such things as this are neither forgiven nor forgotten," Sandià said. "It is never an issue of how or why, but simply a matter of who. That's all I need to know, Vincent. Who did this thing?"

Sandià stood near the window, his left hand in his jacket pocket, his right holding back the curtain. He was looking down into the street below, had been doing so when Madigan had entered the room, had not even glanced in his direction.

The escort had left. Madigan stayed as close to the door as he could, believing that if he narrowed the distance between himself and Sandià then Sandià would hear Madigan's heart beating.

"Who did this thing?" Sandià repeated. He shook his head slowly.

Was Sandià playing games? Did he know it was him? Was he giving Madigan a chance to come clean, to admit his own guilt and thus lessen the penalty?

I gave you a chance, Vincent. I gave you as good a chance as I could. I was hoping you'd speak, that you'd say something, that you'd tell me what happened and why and how you were sorry. But no, you didn't say a thing. You have disappointed me, Vincent. Seriously disappointed me. I believed we were friends, that all the years behind us counted for something. Evidently not. Hell, Vincent, I don't want to do this to you, but now I have no choice . . .

"My sister's boy," Sandià said. "They killed my sister's boy." He stepped away from the window. "Four of them . . ." He shook his head, waved his hand in a dismissive fashion. "The other three . . . The other three were bad enough, but my sister's boy?"

Madigan swallowed the knot in his throat. It was the size of a baseball.

That was the one he'd recognized as the stretcher had been taken out. That was the one whose face seemed so familiar. Sandià's nephew. Hell, could it get any worse?

"Come," Sandià said, and he waved his hand toward Madigan. "Come sit with me, Vincent."

Madigan took a step away from the door. He was trying so hard to read Sandià, to see what was in his eyes, in his thoughts, but Sandià had never been an easy man to predict. That's what made him good. That's what made him successful. No one ever knew what Sandià would do next, and that edge of unpredictability gave him leverage.

From the dresser against the wall Sandià took a bottle of scotch and two glasses. He two-inched each glass, held one out to Madigan. Madigan could delay no further. He walked forward, accepted it, took a seat facing Sandià. Sandià sat down, held the glass against his cheek for a moment, and then sipped. He closed his eyes as he swallowed.

Madigan drank too. For a moment he believed he would cough as the heat of the spirit invaded his throat, but he quelled the sensation. He willed his heart to slow down. He willed himself to look directly at Sandià and show nothing of what was occurring in his thoughts.

"I am disappointed," Sandià started, and Madigan knew this was it.

I gave you a chance, Vincent.

He could feel the cool glass in his hand, felt the tension in the muscles of each finger.

"I am disappointed in people—"

I was hoping you'd speak, that you'd say something . . .

And as his grip increased he wondered if the glass would shatter right there.

"Disappointed that they take me for such a fool—"

Hell, Vincent, I don't want to do this to you, but now I have no choice . . .

"That there are people who honestly believe they can do such a thing as this and . . ." Sandià shook his head resignedly once again. "That they think I won't find out. That they think I won't discover the truth of what happened, who they are . . . that I will just let it go."

Sandià closed his eyes. He held the glass to his lips but did not drink.

Madigan started to wonder if he'd been wrong, if he had misjudged the situation.

Sandià looked at him closely. "Are you all right, Vincent?"

Madigan nodded, almost involuntarily.

"You seem pale. Are you not well?"

"I—I'm okay, sure."

"This has upset you too, I imagine?"

Madigan frowned.

"You knew him, didn't you? My nephew."

Madigan tried to show nothing on his face. He cast his mind back, the moment he and Fulton and Landry and Williams came through that upper window, the guy at the top of the stairs, the guy with the money. What was his name? What was his—

And then it came to him.

"Alex."

Sandià nodded slowly. "You saw him? At the house today?"

Madigan's heart missed a beat. The bottom dropped out of his stomach. "Saw him?"

Sandià smiled knowingly. "You think I was unaware of your involvement, Vincent?"

Madigan's eyes widened. It was as if the glass in his hand literally bent with the pressure of his grip.

"That you had been assigned to investigate this? You think I didn't know?" Sandià rose from his chair and walked once again to the window. "You forget how many friends I have, eh?"

Madigan wanted to scream. He wanted to run from the room, his heart bursting from his chest, his mouth wide, his eyes bright with terror and desperation. He had never felt anything like this before. He never wanted to feel anything like this again.

Madigan opened his mouth to speak. His tongue was stuck to the roof of his mouth. Even as the whiskey crossed his lips he knew that he had missed the inevitability of his own death by nothing less than seconds.

"Yes," he said. "Sometimes I forget."

"Well, if there was ever a choice, Vincent, then you know I would choose you."

Sandià returned to his desk and sat down. "Tell me what you saw, Vincent . . . Tell me exactly what you saw."

Madigan shifted uneasily. "It was a massacre," he said. "They had no chance. Whoever did this came in through the upper window. They waited until the escort had arrived at the head of the stairwell, and then they came through. There were three, perhaps more. We are still trying to work out exactly how it occurred."

Sandià then dismissed the comment with a wave of his hand, as if, in hearing it, he realized that he did not want to hear it after all. "*How* is of no concern to me, Vincent. Neither *how* nor *why*, but *who*. This is all I need to know. Who did this thing? I do not care for the money. It is of no significance. Regardless, the money is no use to whoever took it. Start spending that money and they'll get no farther than the next 7-Eleven—"

"No use?" Madigan asked.

Sandià smiled dryly. The expression in his eyes was one of superiority. "Marked," he said.

"I'm sorry . . ."

"The money. It was marked. All of it."

Madigan's heart stopped. He heard it stop. It was like the sound of a car hitting a wall.

"So, understanding that whoever took it will probably wait a while before they start throwing it around, I need you to help me."

"Of course," Madigan said. The words, just two of them, were like mouthfuls of dry dust. He felt disoriented, elsewhere. Had this all now been for nothing? Marked money? How the hell could it be marked? This did not make sense.

"There is also the matter of the girl."

"Yes," Madigan replied. "The girl."

"I was given a responsibility, Vincent, a responsibility to care for this child. I was taking care of this child for a very good reason, and now she is in the hospital, and from what I understand there is a good possibility that she may not survive." Sandià took a deep breath, exhaled slowly. "If the child dies . . . Well, Vincent, if the child dies I will be very unhappy, not only because it is never good to see the death of a child, but because I will have failed in my duty in this matter. You understand?"

"Yes, of course."

"So I need your help here as well."

"What do you need me to do?"

"I need you to work on this case diligently and with all speed, Vincent. I need you to find out who did this thing, and before you make any arrest I need you to tell me who these people are, and where they are hiding."

Madigan said nothing.

"Second, I need you to keep this girl safe. I need her to live, Vincent. I don't know how much more I can stress this. I need the girl to live. I need her to make it through this."

"Can you tell me her name?" Madigan asked. "We still have been unable to identify her."

Once again Sandià waved his hand in a dismissive fashion. "Her name is unimportant. Who she is and where she came from are unimportant matters. I just need you to ensure that no further harm comes to her—"

Madigan sipped his whiskey. The tension in his chest had become an intense nausea. His eyes felt too large for the sockets. His tongue was like a rough stone in the dry pit of his mouth.

"And my gratitude will not go unrewarded, Vincent," Sandià added. "You have a far better memory than me," he went on. "How much do you owe to these gambling people of mine?"

"Seventy-five," Madigan said. "Seventy-five thousand."

"You do these things for me, Vincent, you tell me who these people are and where they have run to, and you do all you can to make sure the girl comes out alive, and we are even. The debt is wiped from the slate."

Madigan sighed. He tried to smile. "That is very generous—"

Sandià rose from the chair and walked toward the dresser. He lifted the bottle of scotch from the tray. "You know me as well as anyone, Vincent. My generosity is matched only by my anger. The people that did this thing . . . Well, let us say no more, eh? Have another drink with me, and then you must go and take care of these matters."

"Yes," Madigan said, and he held out his glass for Sandià to refill it.

17

JACK ON FIRE

I *am sick for nearly an hour.*
I retch and heave and gag until everything in my body is gone, and then I retch and heave and gag until the blood vessels in my eyes are ready to burst.

I am in the washroom in some bar. I have locked myself in a cubicle, and three times someone has called out, "You okay in there, buddy?" "Hey . . . you all right?"

"Okay," I have replied through a mouthful of saliva, my nose blocked, my eyes stinging, my breath coming short and fast and shallow.

I got in the car and drove away from Sandià's place. I kept on driving, ended up somewhere near the park, somewhere between the museum and Mount Sinai. I pulled over. I remember crying, crying like those guys in the chamber when the needles went in. Crying like a bitch. Jesus. Jesus Christ Almighty. I don't know what the hell I am doing. Sometimes I wonder if I am even awake. Is this a dream? Is this just some sick, deranged nightmare, and I am going to wake up and find myself in bed next to Angela or Ivonne or Catherine? Or maybe I'm still a kid, and this is some kind of surreal premonition about what will happen to me if I take this path . . .

But it is none of these things. I know this.

Sandià needs my help. He wants to know the identity of the people who robbed his money and killed Alex, his nephew. I remember when I last saw Alex. He seemed like a good guy. He worked for his uncle, as all Sandià's nephews did, but he didn't have that arrogant bullshit attitude that so many of them assumed. They assumed it because they were related to Sandià, and because they were related they could get away with it. But Alex didn't have that thing going on. He seemed out of place, a fish out of water, and yet that had been all of six months before, and Alex was still working for his uncle. He'd been there today. The courier. And now he was dead. So were the three others, and so were Fulton, Landry and Williams. And there was only one person left alive, and only one person who really knew the truth of what had taken place, and that was me. Madigan. Vincent Madigan. Jesus Christ.

And what had Sandià meant about the money being marked? What did that mean? Marked by who? Surely not Sandià. Was it already stolen? Had that money come from a bank robbery? Was it all recorded, every serial number noted somewhere, ready to flash up on some government screen somewhere as soon as it passed hands at a till someplace? Or was it an offhand comment? Did it mean nothing at all? Was he speaking figuratively?

Christ, it didn't even matter now. He had stolen Sandià's money to pay his own gambling debts to Sandià. And now? Hell, Sandià himself was going to wipe the very same debt! Was that the greatest freaking irony, or what? Find out who did it, let him know before an official report or arrest was made, and the debt would disappear! Jesus Christ! I'll call him now. "Hey, I got a name for you. I'm right here, my friend. Right here! Come get me and we're all quits. I'll even tell you where the money is, okay? It's in a bag under the goddamned floorboards on my landing!"

I retch again.

"Hey! Who's in there? You gonna be okay, buddy? You need me to get some help?"

"I'm okay," I shout back. "Just a few too many. I'm gonna be fine."

"Okay, buddy, if you say so. But you sure don't sound so fine."

And he's right. I don't sound good outside, and I sound even worse inside.

If I thought I was screwed beforehand, well, I was playing kindergarten.

Now I'm up for the big show. Now I'm in the big leagues.

Vincent Madigan is swinging for the fences, and the whole world is there to see him strike out.

What have I done?

And the girl. What is the deal with this little girl? Laid up in the hospital, bullet wounds, bleeding out. Maybe she'll make it, maybe she won't. And he wants me to take care of her, make sure she makes it through, and yet he won't even tell me her name.

Who the hell is the little girl, and what was she doing in that house?

I try to stand. I have puke down my shirt, on the waistband of my pants, on my hands, my shoes, on the floor.

I back up out of the doorway and lean over the sink. I look at my reflection in the mirror. I can see how I appear to myself, yet I wonder how I would appear to someone else.

Like a dead man, I think.

That's what I must look like to the world: a dead man.

18

A HOUSE IS NOT A HOME

It was past midnight, closer to one. Madigan knew he would not sleep.

Upon arriving home, he went directly upstairs and pulled back the carpet. He took out the bag of money, upended it onto the floor, and stared at the bundles of twenties and fifties and hundreds. He figured he might as well burn it. He could not spend it, neither to pay the outstanding alimony to the lawyers, nor his debt to Sandià. He could not pay a bar tab, nor buy his groceries, nor get a pack of smokes from the liquor store on the corner. It was dead money. He—Vincent Madigan—was a dead man, and he had three hundred odd grand of dead money.

The simple question now was where to go from here?

Officially he was lead detective on the Sandià drug house robbery, the four homicides that had taken place. Unofficially he was Sandià's inside line on who had carried out the same robbery and killings. Officially it would be a case that would stay open indefinitely. That had always been the intention. No names, no identities, he and the three others remaining strangers from that point forward. But what had he expected? Had he honestly believed that neither Fulton nor Landry nor Williams would figure out who he was? And what choice had he been given? As soon as Fulton had opened his mouth—*You think I don't know who you are?*—the outcome had been inevitable. Fulton had to go down, and if he went down, the other two had to go with him. Ben Franklin was right: A secret between three people was only a secret if two of them were dead. And now there was the other side of the same coin: Madigan was supposed to come back to Sandià with the names and location of those who had killed Alex, and beyond that the responsibility of ensuring the safety of a potentially fatally wounded child, a child without an identity.

Madigan put the money back in the bag. He put that bag under the floorboards once more. He looked at the ziplock baggies of pills. He looked at the handguns, the Tec-9, at the boxes of ammo. He sat with his back against the wall, his knees drawn up to his chest, his hands around them. He needed to think clearly. He needed to sleep. *Then* he would think clearly. A couple of Ambiens would do the trick, and he had some in the bathroom cabinet. But he didn't get up. He didn't make his way down the hallway to the bathroom. He just sat there, his eyes closed, his fingers interlaced, his feet going numb as his circulation slowed down. After twenty, twenty-five minutes he stood up. He leaned against the wall until feeling had returned to his calves and ankles, and then he withdrew the pictures of the little girl from his pocket. He looked at her, the tubes in her nose, her closed eyes, the frailty of her features. She was about the same age as Lucy, the eldest child of his second marriage. Lucy was six, would be seven come February 10th. Lucy was the image of her mother, and if she grew up like her mother then she would break more hearts than a girl should ever have the right to break. Catherine Benedict, longest relationship Madigan had ever had. Seven years and two months. Two kids—Lucy and Tom. Before that Ivonne, before that Angela. Other lives. Lives he had left behind. Kids he had forgotten about. Bad actions did not make you a bad person. He could hear his own thoughts, and for a moment he was disgusted at himself. He looked at the baggie of pills again. There was enough there to kill a horse. He could, couldn't he? He could just end it. Be done with all the bullshit and lies, all the running and hiding and lying and cheating and . . .

Hell.

He leaned down, picked up the floorboard and replaced it, pulled the carpet over, and stamped it flat to the baseboard.

Even as he entered the bathroom he felt the picture of the nameless girl fall from his hand. And then he was sitting on the edge of the tub with his head in his hands, and had he been asked he was unsure he could have repeated his own name.

Twenty minutes later he was in the kitchen, his throat sore, his eyes gritty, in his hand a glass of Jack Daniel's. There was no right or wrong. Not anymore. The things that had happened, the things he had done—these things exempted him from consideration in such a light. Ethics, morals, the law? It was all so much horseshit. There was no law. Not really. Ask any man in the street if there was such a thing as justice—real justice—and he would laugh at you.

The law served the lawyers. The courts served those who leveled judgments, but never those who sought restitution for wrongs. The society was corrupt. Everyone had a price. There was no one who could not be bought. Madigan knew that, knew it with certainty. The dividing line between himself and Sandià was not a line. It was a shadow. If you considered the truth of such a statement, then the lawyers and the police were the worst. At least people like Sandià were not pretending to be something else.

And who was he? Who was Vincent Madigan? Who the hell was he fooling but himself? Evidence planted, evidence removed, drug raids where the money and the drugs went *unrecovered*. People like Walsh at IA spent every waking hour looking for this kind of thing—the internal corruption, the shadows around people where the law ceased to inhibit and started to be an advantage. Not everyone. No, not everyone. There were some who held it all together, kept their lives on track, stayed lawful and honest and coped with the ever-increasing sense of frustration of one failed investigation, one failed testimony, one prosecution after another.

You will never win, Sandià had once said. *The police, the courts, the legal system will never win. And I'll tell you why, Vincent. I'll tell you why. Because they no longer have the people on their side. The people know you are as corrupt as anyone else. They know where your true interests lie. They see the ulterior motives, they see the bargains and trade-offs, they see the way the law is compromised, the way it turns and twists until it fits whoever possesses the greatest influence or the most money. That is why you will never win . . . Because you people stopped taking care of the man in the street long before we did.*

That had given Madigan pause for thought. It was a truth. Perhaps not a complete truth, but a truth nevertheless.

The law did not serve the common man. And thus the common man had no desire to serve the law.

Madigan drained the glass. He set it down and lit a cigarette. It was a few minutes after one, morning of Wednesday the 13th.

He needed to find out who the little Hispanic girl was. He needed to know her name. He needed to know why she had been in that house near Louis Cuvillier Park. He needed to know how she was connected to Sandià, and why Sandià needed her to survive.

Perhaps he needed to know these things for himself. To give himself something to hold on to. His world had slipped off of whatever axis it might have been balanced upon, and it was spinning wildly out of control. He was caught—he knew that—caught between two things far worse than the devil and the sea, however deep or blue that sea might have been. Follow this investigation through—whether officially or unofficially—and he was dead. As was the case when he'd taken something bad, or taken too much of something, the only thing he could do was hold on to a single thing—whether physical or mental, it didn't matter. Just hold on to a single thing, a point of reference, an anchor, and stay connected to that thing until everything else stopped moving.

He was going to find out who the girl was. He could do that. That was information that Sandià had been unwilling to give him, information that was unknown to the department. Information was power. Information was valuable.

He would try and sleep, at least for an hour or two, and then he would go looking once more. Someone had to recognize her. Someone had to know her name.

Madigan got up from the kitchen table. He looked around at the bare walls, the empty cupboards, the microwave oven—still in its box from more than six months ago.

What had happened here? Where had his life gone? His marriage to Catherine had been over for more than a year and a half. In that time he had seen her—what?—perhaps twice, three times? The last time he'd stayed no more than an hour. Their words had been bitter, acrimonious, a rerun of the previous meeting, the one before that. And his daughter? Well, she hadn't recognized him. More important, he had barely recognized her.

And if Sandià took him out of the game, then who would care? Ex-wives, an ex-mistress, children who didn't remember him? And if he avoided Sandià—somehow—but ran afoul of the department? If they closed down his career, if they sent him to prison for what he had done—what then? The people he worked with—people like Callow and Harris and Bryant—would perhaps think of him for a week, maybe two, and then he would disappear in the track of time and be forgotten.

Madigan stood in the hallway. For a moment he felt the pressure of it, the crushing sense of impending defeat and overwhelm. It had come down to this now. He had created his own Sword of Damocles, and it hung heavy and ominous above him. Was there a way out? Perhaps, perhaps not. But he could resign himself to the inevitable end, that end dictated by someone other than himself, or he could do his utmost to evade the personal and professional crucifixion that would follow close on the heels of discovery. He was not a stupid man, but he had been stupid. Taking Sandià's money, killing the nephew—that had been ill advised. Using Landry and Williams and Fulton had not been smart. He had arrested Fulton twice, Williams also, and hadn't Fulton said that he and Bobby Landry were friends? Hadn't that been one of the very things to leave his lips before Madigan shot him in the throat? Had they spoken to anyone before they did the job? Had Fulton mentioned to anyone that he was doing something with this cop from the 167th? *Hey, man, gotta tell you, I got me a sweet gig. Can't do better than this one, right? Three hundred grand, and the whole thing's being run by a cop! Yeah, you better believe it, man. A fucking cop!*

Madigan sat on the stairs. He put his head in his hands. His breath was coming short and fast. He hadn't even noticed. He was winding himself up. He was thinking too much. Sandià didn't know. Sandià wanted him to get the inside line on the killings. Sandià wanted him to take care of the little girl. That was all he wanted. Hell, if he did those things he would be off the hook. Sandià would wipe the seventy-five grand, and that would be finished. Williams, Landry, and Fulton were dead. Madigan had the money. As it stood now, there was very little chance that they would see the work of a fourth man in this thing. But if they did, if there had been some detail overlooked, if the money was marked and they counted up what was on the floor of the storage unit and started to ask questions about the remainder . . .

Madigan stopped in his tracks.

The fourth man.

Of course, there *had* to be a fourth man. Not himself, but someone else. Any remaining clue regarding his own presence would then be attributed to whoever he chose.

And how would that fourth man be identified? By the money, that's how. Put that money someplace, and no matter what happened, no matter what was said, whoever was in possession of that money would be the fourth man. It was that easy.

Madigan got up. He felt his head clear. He felt his heart settle, his pulse slow down. It was simple. Find a patsy. Find somewhere to put that money, and he would have someone to take the fall. Give word to Sandià, Sandià takes care of things, retrieves his money, and Madigan winds up with a closed case, Sandià off his back, no debt, and a clear conscience.

Yes. No question. The most complex situations were always resolved with the simplest solutions.

And then he remembered the girl. There was still the girl, the agreement he'd made with Sandià that he would ensure no further harm came to her. Why was she important? That was something he needed to know. And if she survived, would she be able to identify Madigan from the assault on the house? Surely not. She had been in another room. She had seen nothing. Couldn't have seen anything, could she?

Madigan was buzzing. He was electrified. He would never sleep, not now, not now that he had a solution worked out for this. All that remained was the girl—her name, her identity, the part she played in this game.

Madigan left the house. He walked to the car, got in, pulled away from the sidewalk, and headed for Harlem Hospital.

19

A DEVIL IN THE WOODS

"What is it?" she said.

She stood in the doorway. She had on a robe, her hair was tousled, her eyes sleepy.

"I didn't mean to wake you," Walsh said.

"You okay?"

He smiled. "Sure."

She came forward, sat facing him, reached out and took his hand.

She said nothing. Walsh liked that best about her. Carole Douglas. A woman who had the ability to say nothing and yet communicate everything that needed to be said.

"Something bothering you?"

He shrugged. "Work stuff."

"Tell."

"Went out to a crime scene. Three dead guys. Bryant asked me to go, didn't have anyone else to secure the scene. I went to be helpful, that was all."

"And?"

Walsh smiled wryly. "The bug's still there," he said.

Carole nodded. "As if that's a surprise."

He gripped her hand. She read him better than anyone.

"You say what you say, Duncan, but what you say and what you feel are rarely the same thing. Whether that's a man thing, or that's just your thing—" She smiled briefly. "No, it's a man thing. Anyway, regardless, you are a policeman because you want to be a policeman. It's not a job you choose; it's a job that chooses you. I get why you didn't follow through with SWAT, but I never did get why you left Homicide—"

"Because it's a circus, Carole. Because it's a joke. Because it's bullshit."

"And—what?—Internal Affairs is any less bullshit?"

"We're not having this conversation."

"Sure we are. You don't hear yourself talking already?"

Walsh sighed.

"You sighing about me, or you sighing about yourself?"

"Myself."

"So tell me what happened today."

"There isn't much to tell. I went out there. Three dead guys, a whole pile of money all over the floor of this storage unit. I wanted to see beyond what was there. I wanted to see something that no one else would see. I wanted to understand what had happened there, what had really happened, and I haven't felt that for so long."

"You think no one can do the job as well as you?"

Walsh shook his head. "No, of course not. I just know how important it is to close cases. I know that it's often easier to accept what appears to be, rather than dig any deeper . . ."

"So say something."

"Say what? That I have a hunch? That I have some intuitive feeling that something isn't right, but I don't know what it is?"

"Duncan, you were born for this stuff. I've always said that. I knew that when I met you, and I've hung in there for the last seven years because . . ." She shook her head. "You want to know what I think?"

"I guess I'm gonna find out whether I want to or not, right?"

"I think you're running away from commitment—"

"Carole—"

"Shut up a minute, okay? Hear me out. I know you won't marry me. I've accepted that we'll not have kids together. That was a big deal, okay? We've been over this before, and I'm not going to get into it again. Loving someone is sometimes about sacrifices, right? But the sacrifices I've made, well, you know how I feel because I've said it before. The sacrifices I've made have been a great deal bigger than the ones you've made. I've done the marriage thing before. I've got two kids. That makes it easier for me. And we've stuck it out, we're still together, and it's working fine. But one thing I will not do, and I'll tell you this right now, is sit and watch you fold your career up nice and neat and put it in a box in the basement—"

"What the hell is that—"

"What you're doing means something, okay? I don't give a damn whether you do Homicide or SWAT or IA or the mayor's office, but if you're not going to be a husband or a father, then the very least you can be is a man with a career that means something to him."

"Carole, I—"

She shook her head. "Carole nothing," she interjected. "It isn't a rehearsal, Duncan. It isn't a quick go at something to see if you like it. You're either in or you're out. You're thirty-nine. Past forty, you're getting into the zone where it's a little tough to start from scratch in an entirely new direction. You were a cop before I met you, and you're still a cop now, but you act like it's something you're doing weekends."

"Carole, I want to go back to Homicide."

"I don't think you should have left Homicide in the first place."

"Well, you could have said something—"

She raised her hand playfully. "Asshole," she snapped. "The number of times I—"

"I know. I know," Walsh replied. "I was just teasing you. I know what you said, Carole, and I listened. But I figured I knew better."

"Isn't that always the way?"

Walsh didn't rise to the bait.

"Come on," she said. She glanced at the small LED clock in the hood of the stove. "It's nearly four in the morning. Get a couple hours' sleep. We'll talk about it more later."

Walsh got up from the table. At the kitchen door he grabbed the cord of her robe and pulled her back. He just held her for a while, and neither of them spoke, and he knew she was right, and she knew she was right, and that was the main reason they worked so well together. Walsh possessed a sense of humility, an ability to be wrong without feeling challenged or emasculated, and that lack of self-importance had made it impossible for her to give up on him even when he was at his most infuriating. She was a senior nurse. She was good at her job. She had never questioned her purpose to do what she did, but she knew she was in the minority. Some people spent their entire lives trying to figure out who they were and what they should be doing. She'd been one of the lucky ones and got it right straightaway.

"A devil in the woods," she said.

"You what?"

"You know something's there, but you try and convince yourself it's not. That's the way most people live their lives. They think if they can't see it, it isn't real."

Walsh said nothing. He felt what he felt. Something had

happened in that storage unit, something real and tangible and unavoidable. First time he'd seen a real crime scene in nearly eighteen months. Pictures, sure; there were always pictures. There was the story the duty guys told you, the ones you followed up on when there were officer-involved shooting reports to corroborate, the endless paperwork, the words you heard from so many people about the same damned thing, but none of that was *real*. Not like that storage unit. Not like three dead guys and a whole heap of cash, blood and tread marks and abandoned cars and the unmistakable tension he'd felt when he stood there with the camera and took his pictures.

Something didn't make sense. Something didn't add up. And he was damned if he knew what it was.

Devil in the woods.

Maybe it was time to walk home in the dark and face him.

20

HUMANESQUE

*W*here did I go?

　　Where did who I was and who I have become take different routes?

How did this happen?

I stand there. I am silent. I can hear the sound of the machine that helps her breathe, the machine that monitors her heart, her pulse, her blood pressure, the drips of saline and glucose and sedative as they make their way into her frail system and keep her distant from the pain.

I wonder about her name, her home, the identity of her parents. Does she have brothers, sisters? Are there people—even now—out of their minds with worry, frustrated by the seeming inability of the police department to do anything to help?

I see my own children—every one of them. I see their faces as best as I can recall them. Cassie, Adam, Lucy, Tom.

I know that they don't look the same way as I remember them.

It all moves so fast—so exhaustingly, terrifyingly fast.

The decay is observable, but slow. Like the wearing down of rocks by rain. Ideals, a philosophy, an uncompromising viewpoint, and then you arrive at the place.

It even has a name.

We call it the Trade-Off.

You've got someone. Some A-hole. He's done something. He raped or assaulted or butchered or stabbed or shot someone. Usually a kid. Pretty much one-for-one it's a kid. You have him in the tank. It's a done deal. Now it's just a matter of paperwork.

And then something happens.

You're sitting there on the other side of that plain deal table, five or six hours in the interrogation room, and someone knocks on the door. You go to the door and you think it's such and such a person for this or that reason, and you get the look.

You open the door and you see the look.

There is an almost imperceptible shake of the head, and then they look down.

The search warrant wasn't signed; the warrant didn't extend to his garbage pail, and the garbage pail was where you found some nine-year-old kid's underwear covered in her blood and his DNA; the confession has been kicked back by the ADA; there's a rumor about coercion, unnecessary force, something . . .

He's going to walk.

And it's not like you couldn't let it go. Hell, shit happens. Maybe you could let it go. Maybe you could convince yourself of the existence of karma, some grand order of things, some master plan within which we all fit like jigsaw pieces . . .

Yes, maybe you could let it go.

But when you see that look on his face; when you see the deadlight in his eyes, the shadows that sit behind them, and the way that arrogant, condescending smile creeps around his lips, you know that even as he rises from the chair and makes his way to the interrogation room door, there's someone else in his mind, some other little kid, the next one he's taking . . .

That's the Trade-Off.

And you do it for the right reason. You so do it for the right reason.

Three hours later the perp is pulled over on a suspected DUI. Some bullshit. The cycle cop searches the car while the perp stands aside and smirks. What d'you know? There's another article of the dead kid's clothing right there under the backseat. The perp pleads ignorance. Now he isn't smirking anymore. He's handcuffed. Another unit comes out on backup. They bring the boy in and he's fucked. He's arrested, charged, arraigned, bail is denied, and someone gives the word to someone who gives the word to someone, and some other perp puts a shiv in the boy's ribs in the shower room. Honor amongst thieves. Even the worst of the others can't abide a child killer.

The sense of satisfaction when you see that wide-eyed disbelief, the sense of vindication you feel when that guy comes back in on a different charge and he knows he can do nothing about it . . . Well, that sense of satisfaction is like a drug. You need it, but you hate it. You have to have it, but it costs so damned much.

You tell yourself it's necessary. The system will screw you before it screws those who buck that same system. You have to do your own dirty work. The law can go only so far. Lawyers are worse than the assholes they defend. What would you have me do? Let these bastards just walk the streets and do whatever the hell they want?

No, justice has to be seen to be done, even if it's distasteful.

So I did those things. I did all those things for the right reasons. There were a few that slipped through the wires, that made a run for it and we never got them, but that was rare. And when Sandià entered the picture, when the information we needed had to come from a source other than our own CIs and intel operatives, well, that's when it got crazy.

There are things I have done I can never talk about.

Not to anyone.

People are dead. People are in jail. People have been executed.

I'm not saying they didn't deserve it. I'm not going to say that. It is always safer to say nothing.

But this? This little girl? This is different now. What did she do? Why was she there? Why was Sandià hiding her in that house?

If she had not been there, then she would not have been hit. But she was there, and the reason for her presence seems irrelevant in the face of a far more brutal and necessary truth.

If I had not done this thing, then she would not be dying.

Because I look at her and I believe she will die. Sometimes you can tell. It's touch and go, and it all comes down to how much fight the person possesses. Not how old, or how big, or how strong, or anything else. Just how much fight there is left in them.

I don't think she can fight.

I think she started out with two strikes against her, and I delivered the third.

I think about Sandià, about what he said when I asked him her name.

"Her name is unimportant. Who she is and where she came from are unimportant matters."

And I hate him for saying that.

Her name is important. Who she is and where she came from seem to be the most important matters in the world right now.

I look at her once more, and then I turn away.

I am tired. I am emotionally shattered. I know I will feel different tomorrow. Tomorrow I will think of her as I first thought of her: collateral damage.

Shit happens.

Sometimes I just get too emotional, too involved.

It's a dangerous route. You cannot afford to be emotional. You cannot afford to get involved. If they see your weakness they will eat you alive. You want to play with the tough guys, then you have to be tough. This is the nature of the beast.

I hesitate at the door. The girl is so small she is barely visible there beneath the covers.

Hell, she isn't my daughter, and from the turnout it looks like she's no one else's either.

If the rest of the world doesn't care, then why should I?

21

GIVE UP THE SUN

"Tell me what you have," Walsh said. He leaned back in his chair. The call had come through from the coroner's office, and he'd taken it. He'd asked Crime Scene from the storage unit to keep him apprised. Unit First had agreed, and was now being good to his word. Unit First's name was Luke Fraschetti.

"You've got three guys, all with sheets. We picked them up on AFIS. Robert Landry, Laurence Fulton, Charles Williams. Fulton got it in the stomach with a .44 from Williams, more than likely bled out within half an hour. Landry was hit in the head with a .38, and then Williams got it in the heart with the same .38."

"You can tell the sequence?" Walsh asked.

"This is Crime Scene, not the Ouija Board Squad, but I'd say that Fulton shot Landry first, then Williams—figuring he was next— shot Fulton with the .44, but it wasn't a kill shot, so Fulton had time to get Williams before he went down. Whichever way, you got three dead and no one to argue about how it played out."

Walsh was silent for a moment. He closed his eyes. He pictured the scene in the storage unit. He put himself right back there.

Apart from the DBs, it was just the money and the Econoline . . . and then he had it. He could see it clearly, as if it was right there before his eyes. The tread mark at the edge of the blood pool. A car went out of there after the shooting had happened.

Walsh's nostrils cleared like ammonia. He felt a cool, electric sensation up his spine and across the back of his neck.

The devil in the woods.

"Well, there we have it," Fraschetti said. "That's just the prelim stuff. You want more, I can send it over when we're done. You're not the lead on this, though, are you? It's Callow, right?"

"Yes," Walsh said. "Ron Callow."

"Okay, well, you said to call you and I did."

"And it's really appreciated. Thank you."

"No big deal. Anyway, got to go. Places to be, people to see."

The line went dead.

Walsh replaced the receiver in its cradle. He sat for a moment in silence.

There was a fourth man. A ghost on the highway. Maybe there had been a great deal more money, and whoever now had it had killed the three guys in the storage unit and just driven away.

Walsh left his office. He found Charlie Harris in the squad room.

"Ron Callow around?"

"Callow? No, he's off."

"Off?"

"Two weeks. Gone like a bird." Harris shook his head. "Lucky son of a bitch has a vacation."

"And his cases?"

Harris shrugged. "We do what we can with the people we got." He glanced up at the actives board. Each detective's name, the case numbers of his ongoings, the date opened.

They were there already—the triple from the storage unit, Callow's name beside them.

"So who takes that triple from last night?" Walsh asked.

"Well, if I can somehow just get this paperwork through to the NYPD Cloning Division—"

Walsh smiled at the sarcasm. "It'll stay right there until Callow gets back," he said.

"I don't know. It might, it might not. We're stretched six ways to Sunday as it is. You know the beat, Walsh; you did Homicide. If I get a break on some other stuff I might be able to take a look at it. But, hell, it's three scumbags. They probably got what was coming. I don't think the chief of police is gonna be down here anytime soon wondering why there's no progress on that one."

"Understood," Walsh said.

Back in the hallway he hesitated, and then he went left and up the stairs.

Bryant was in his office.

"Sarge, I want the triple from the storage unit."

"You what?"

"Last night, the triple homicide in the storage unit. You sent me out there on secure. Callow took it, but he's on leave for two weeks, and I want to pick it up."

Bryant frowned, shook his head. "You on drugs, or what? What do you mean, you want to pick it up? You're IA."

"I'm IA, but I did eighteen months in Homicide, and you'd sure as hell rather have me working one of those cases off the board than snooping around Evidence to see who's stealing what."

"This isn't a joke, right? You actually want to take an active case and run it?"

"Sure I do. I'm still a detective, irrespective of being IA."

"And your superiors?"

"I can handle them. I can log it as a supervisory investigation."

"Why the change all of a sudden, and why this one?"

Walsh stepped forward. He sat down facing Bryant.

"I went out there, Sarge. There's money and guts all over the place. Three dead guys, all with sheets. Way I see it, there was a fourth man. The money came from somewhere. It all went to shit. Number four kills one, two, and three, and off he goes. I figure there was a great deal more money going out of there with number four than he left on the floor. I think he wanted it to look like three men did a job, three men disagreed, and three men died. End of story—"

"And how do you figure this? How do you know there's a fourth man?"

"There was a tread mark through the blood, and if that tread mark is different from the tires on the van they left behind, then it means someone drove out of there after Fulton was down."

Alvin Bryant took a deep breath. "Hell, I don't know, Walsh. You don't exactly got a good reputation around here . . ."

"What the hell is that supposed to mean?"

"Ah, come on, man. Don't be so naive. You think they like having you here? You're IA, for Christ's sake. IA are the enemy inside the castle walls. They see you running something like that, they're gonna think you're investigating Callow."

"Well, tell them the truth. Tell them we're overloaded and I've volunteered to pick up a nonstarter. Callow didn't even get the ME's prelims. He's off on vacation, right?"

"Sure, sure."

"So let me do it. You tell whoever you have to tell. I'll say whatever to my superiors. And the fact that they're not the same thing is beside the point. If I bust it, I'll credit Callow. And if it's still running by the time he gets home from wherever—"

"Saratoga Springs."

"Huh?"

"Where Callow has gone . . . Saratoga Springs."

"What the hell is in Saratoga Springs?"

"Exactly what I asked him. Fishing, apparently. Anyway, back to the matter at hand." Bryant rose from the desk and walked to the window. He looked out and down into the street, buried his hands in his pockets. "Okay," he said eventually. "I give you this. You do it as a supervisory. I tell everyone here that you're just helping to ease the load. You bust it, you credit Callow; you don't, then Callow gets it when he's back from the fishing trip."

"Right."

Bryant turned and faced Walsh. "And this is not some line, okay? This is not some bullshit internal secret inquiry into something or other?"

Walsh raised his hands, his expression one of disbelief.

"What? You don't think I know how IA works sometimes? Come on, Walsh. You've been too long around these corridors—"

"Straight up, Sarge. It is what it is. I want to do the thing, okay? I just want to do this thing."

"Good enough," Bryant said. "Report to me, no one else."

"I can live with that."

"Okay, so go do your worst, G-Man."

22

UP ABOVE THE WORLD

When Madigan woke he felt differently about a great many things. He'd known he would, but it was good to find the familiar sense of certainty that had been absent the previous night.

Leaving the hospital at some unknown hour, he'd made it home again and crashed on the bed fully clothed. A handful of hours of sleep, he then woke and showered and shaved. He drank coffee, took a couple of bennies, even ate half a bagel, and then stood in the kitchen and chained smokes until he felt ready to leave.

Today he had to find out who the girl was.

That was priority number one.

The drive from the Bronx to East Harlem cleared his head. The traffic was light for the time of day, and when he passed under the expressway on Third and crossed the river he tried to imagine the worst-case scenario. Always best to imagine the worst, and then anything better than the worst was a small success. He was forty-two, a veteran of the PD, and his life had not been a straight highway to health and happiness. He was also on the take, had an armful of files that IA could open wide and blow apart; he was drinking too much and taking too many pills. That was a fact. But such things were relative. Everything was relative. He was worse than some, better than others. Honestly—and he had to be honest about this, if nothing else—he was worse than most. But, once again, such a thing was relative. Ultimately Madigan believed he did more good than not. This was the rationale, the small saving grace that preserved his sanity. Life was not only what you made it; it was also what you took from it. And who did he take from? The scumbags, the lowlifes, the worst of the worst. Sandià was in a category all his own. Sandià did not possess a soul, nor a heart, nor a conscience. Sandià—sometime back—had ceased to be a human being in the accepted sense of the term. His dealers sold to kids. He knew it, and on it went. Some of his girls carried the kind of diseases that killed you. Still they worked on his payroll, and on his terms, and they met the demands of the job for fear of far greater retribution than some pissed-off homicidal john could ever have delivered. And then there was his name. Sandià. The Watermelon Man. He reveled in it. People who knew him when he was no one had even forgotten his real name. Such was his reputation. Such was the effect created by what he had done and why he had done it. Once such a thing had entered the realm of urban myth, there were few who would cross him, few who would even have considered it.

But Madigan had.

Madigan had not only considered it, he had planned it, executed it, had murdered seven people—four in the house, three in the storage unit—and was now sitting on Sandià's money.

There was a way out of it. It was simple enough. Put the money in someone's possession. Alert Sandià. Sandià's people make a visit. They interrogate the guy. He denies any involvement. He keeps on denying any involvement until the money is found, and then it's all over. Madigan's debt is wiped clean, the case is closed, Sandià is happy. Madigan walks away a hero on both sides, and then . . . Then he would still have to handle the lawyers, pay the alimony, and get himself the hell out of this situation. It was not tenable. It was not a good way to live. Too much stress. Too much thinking.

Arriving at the 167th, there was a message at the desk for Madigan. Bryant needed him, and needed him now.

Bryant was an anchor in a storm of madness. Bryant was a decent man, a good squad sergeant, and he had always expected great things of Madigan. Madigan delivered, for the most part. And if Bryant possessed any suspicion that Madigan was not on the up-and-up, he didn't raise it. Bryant knew how hard it was to find a good homicide detective. Had he known how deep Madigan had gone, how out in left field Madigan really was, Bryant would act, and act swiftly. They had a tight relationship, but they were not social friends. Ultimately, it was always business with Bryant. He kept his private life and his work very clearly delineated, and he expected his crew to respect that decision.

Madigan went on up, stood in the corridor for a moment. He straightened his jacket, cleaned off the toes of his shoes on the backs of his pants, took a couple of deep breaths, and knocked on the door.

"Come!" Bryant hollered.

Madigan opened the door, stepped into the office, and not until he was closing the door behind him did he see Duncan Walsh seated across from Bryant.

What the hell was this?

"Vincent . . . Good, come in," Bryant said, and he rose from his chair and came around the desk.

Walsh acknowledged Madigan with a dry smile. Walsh was always matter-of-fact, always businesslike. The man lacked humor. The man was IA.

"Vincent," Bryant said. "Very simply put, we have a situation—"

Madigan didn't move. He felt the color draining from his face. The mess of nerves in the base of his guts was tightening furiously. He felt his muscles cramping. His mouth was dry, his tongue stuck to the roof of his mouth.

"Vincent?" Bryant asked.

Walsh turned to look at him, frowned.

"You okay, Vincent?"

Madigan nodded. "I think I have a bit of food poisoning . . ." he said, and held his right hand to his stomach.

"You okay to be in today?" Bryant asked. "You need to go get something for it?"

Madigan shook his head. "Just some water . . . I'll go get some from the machine . . ."

Walsh got up. "Hey, sit here, Vincent," he said. "Take it easy. I'll get the water."

Madigan watched him leave the room, took the man's chair, waited in silence until Walsh appeared with a bottle of Evian.

Madigan drank thirstily, most of the bottle, and then he sat back and closed his eyes. He breathed deeply, tried to let it go, tried to think nothing, to feel nothing, to let it all slide away. *If this is it, then so be it.*

"We can do this another time, if you want," Walsh said.

Madigan opened his eyes, looked at the man—perhaps for the very first time—and the expression on his face seemed to be one of genuine concern.

Madigan raised his hand. "It's okay. Let's get it over with."

Walsh frowned again, shook his head, and then turned back to Bryant.

"You sure you're okay, Vincent?" Bryant asked.

"Yeah, sure. I'll be fine . . ."

Bryant sat down. Walsh took a chair from behind the door and sat beside Madigan.

Madigan tightened his grip on the bottle. He was waiting for the opening salvo. He was waiting for them to ask for his gun and his badge.

"We have a situation here, Vincent," Bryant said. "Not only to do with the thing that happened in the house that you're working on, but also a triple homicide in a storage unit out near East 109th . . ."

Madigan felt a drop of cool sweat running from the nape of his neck down to the middle of his spine. He believed he would start hyperventilating. Any moment now. That, or maybe he would just puke. They would drug test him. Ordinarily he got a tipoff on the drug test and he stayed off of anything for a week or two. But this? This was different. This was something for Vincent and Vincent alone.

Fuck. Oh fuck oh fuck oh fuck . . .

He started to think about Cassie, about the car he'd planned to buy her for her eighteenth. He thought about Sandià's nephew, the one face he remembered from the turkey shoot at the house.

And then he thought about the kid at the hospital, who she was and how she was connected to Sandià, where her parents were and what the hell she'd been doing in that place . . .

"Last night," Bryant said, "we got the three DBs in this storage unit. I asked Walsh to go out there on secure until Ron Callow could make it over there, and we figured it for nothing but a heist gone wrong, maybe some inter-crew rip off. Who the hell knows, eh?" Bryant got up and walked to the window. "But then Walsh picked up on something." He paused, as if for effect. He looked at Madigan. Madigan's heart was a runaway horse.

This is it this is it this is it . . . What have I done? Jesus Christ . . . What the hell have I done . . . ?

Madigan could see an interrogation room, a team of suits from IA, a courtroom, a jail cell . . .

"There was a tread mark through the blood, and that tread mark could only have come after the shooting."

Madigan's thoughts stopped dead.

"I expedited the report, and Forensics have confirmed that the tread mark through the blood in the storage unit does not match the tread on the van that was left behind. Additionally—and this caught both of us unawares—there were blood smears in the back of that van that match the vics at the house you're working on."

Madigan felt his eyes had widened to twice their size.

"So it seems the robbery at the Sandià house from yesterday morning is the same case as the three DBs in the storage unit."

Madigan tried to look surprised. He drank some more water. Without it he didn't think he'd be able to speak. "So the three dead guys in the storage unit were the ones that hit the house?"

Bryant nodded. "Seems that way, except we don't think it was three guys."

"It was four," Walsh interjected. "That's the premise we're working on, due to the simple fact that someone drove out of that storage unit after the shooting was over."

Oh, you dumb dumb dumb son of a bitch . . . What the hell were you thinking? Why the hell didn't you trust your instinct? Why didn't you go back and check over everything again?

Bryant sat down again, leaned forward with his fingers steepled together. "You get anywhere on this little girl?"

"On it again today," Madigan said. The words came with difficulty. He drank the last of the water. "Nothing as yet, but I don't think it'll be too long before we track her down."

"We need that ID," Bryant went on. "Maybe that's not related to the robbery, but I sure as hell would like to know what she was doing in that house."

"So where to now?" Madigan asked.

"Walsh here is gonna work on the storage unit DBs—"

"What?" Madigan asked. "You're IA. What the hell are you doing on a homicide?"

Bryant raised his hand to silence Madigan. "Walsh here did eighteen months in Homicide. He knows the ropes. He's got some breathing space, okay?" Bryant smiled wryly. "And we sure as hell would prefer Detective Walsh here to be sticking his nose into a triple homicide than anything else. Right, Vincent?"

Madigan hesitated, and then he smiled suddenly. "Sure, sure," he said. "Sure thing."

"So this is what we're doing," Bryant went. "You run the case as it is. You work on the house, the ID of the little girl, all that that entails. Walsh here is going to work on the three DBs and finding that second vehicle. You are working the same case, essentially, but I don't want you partnered. Partnered is not going to work. You coordinate with each other, but you do that through me. I ain't getting shot from guns for letting Walsh here run a Homicide case. But with Callow away, I sure as hell can use the extra pair of hands. You get the girl and Walsh goes after the fourth man. That's the way I want it."

"If it's the same case why don't I just run it as one?" Madigan asked, doing everything he could to disguise the utter disbelief and horror that he felt.

"No, you have enough on your plate," Bryant said. "I've gone over this with Walsh, and this is the best way to work it. This is seven homicides, a little girl up in Harlem Hospital who might just be the eighth, and I need this off the books as fast as possible. I figure that, despite the inevitable differences of opinion, you pair might be able to work together, don'tcha think?"

Madigan said nothing.

"Not a problem for me," Walsh said. "You okay with this, Vincent?"

Madigan nodded. "Yeah, sure," he said. "Won't be any problem at all."

23

IDIOT WALTZ

*L*aurence Fulton is dead. He lies on a mortician's slab somewhere. His skin is cold and blue and his limbs are stiff, and his heart is like a clenched fist of dead muscle and I left tire tracks in that storage unit and someone is peering at them and trying to figure it all out . . .

And I am a dumb, dumb, dumb son of a bitch.

And I have Sandià's money and a bunch of unlicensed and unregistered weapons, and a crapload of ammo and drugs right there under my floorboards.

Most often I am staggered by the stupidity of others.

Right now I am stunned breathless by my own.

I stand at my desk, and then I sit down. Harris is somewhere. I can hear him talking to someone about something. Outside Bryant's office Walsh said it was good to be back on a real case. He walked with me to the stairwell, and then he said he'd forgotten to tell Bryant something and he turned around and went back.

I tried to be nonchalant. I tried to act like a man who had nothing to hide. I tried to act like a normal person, but for the life of me I don't even remember what a normal person is.

It was a good fifteen minutes before I could even feel my heart and my pulse, and they were still going ten to the dozen. I was ready to piss myself. I was ready to just piss myself and cry like a brokenhearted schoolgirl.

If I ever had nine lives, I just lost eight of them.

In too deep to get out now. In so deep the only way out is through the other side.

I feel like a crazy man. Maybe I am a crazy man. Maybe all the crazies think they're not, and they think that everything they're doing possesses the greatest reason and rationale. Isn't that the case with psychos and sociopaths and serial killers? They got it all figured out. They know what they're doing. They're the only ones who really understand the truth.

Am I any different?

Yes, I must be. I must be because I doubt myself, because I question myself, because I take time out to try and calculate the odds.

And right now? Right now the odds are stacked against me. Seriously stacked.

Jesus Christ Almighty.

I head outside for a smoke. I stand in the parking lot behind the precinct. My hands are shaking. I need a drink. I need a couple of lithium. I need something.

What I don't need is Duncan Walsh looking for the fourth man. A man that is not supposed to even exist. But he does, and that man is me. That's the truth. But truth is relative. And they won't find the second car, and they won't find my bloodstained shoes, so what have they really got? They've got the house and the storage unit linked. They think there's a fourth man, but they can't prove it. They have a partial tread from a stolen car, and that car could never be traced back to me. They have ballistics reports on all the weapons that were used, both at the house and at the storage unit and none of those weapons carry my prints. Aside from what I scattered on the floor of the storage unit, I have all the money, and none of it has gone into circulation. Put that money in someone's house and they're screwed.

It's the only way. The only, only, only way.

I have to ID the girl, and I have to find myself a fall guy.

And then we're done.

I smoke another cigarette. The tension in my chest eases fractionally.

I can do this. I am Vincent Madigan. I can sell two different lies out of separate corners of my mouth at the same damned time.

If anyone can pull this off, it's me.

And then it's finished. I'm up at the big show. I'm right there on the plate. Strike out and it's all over, but one home run and we're done. Change the job, change the city, take whatever money I can find and go.

But first the girl . . .

24

CRY TO ME

Late morning. The streets and houses and faces and words are all the same. We saw nothing. We know nothing. We don't *want* to know anything. This is not our problem. Leave us alone.

Madigan knew this routine all too well. You don't spend any time at all in inner-city Homicide without knowing the enervating frustration of canvassing for eyewitnesses.

He tried to forget about Walsh. He tried to tell himself that he had covered all bases, that there was nothing in the storage unit, nothing in the personal residences of Fulton, Landry, or Williams that would place him and them together. Even if they found the warehousing unit, he had been careful with every bottle, every cigarette butt, every piece of paper. The only thing he could not predict were the words that might have been shared with friends, associates, bar buddies. And whether any of them had written anything down. Something on a scrap of paper. Madigan's name, even his first name, a phone kiosk number he had given to call him at a particular time. There was no way in the world to predict what may or may not be among their personal effects, and to try and guess would drive him crazy. Better to think of nothing at all. Better to empty his mind of all considerations, and just take each day, each hour as it came. To do anything but strenuously pursue the identification of the girl would be foolish. He had to appear professional, focused, in the game. Walsh would work on the DBs, the storage unit, the Econoline. Madigan would give Sandià the irreducible minimum of information, and coordinate everything regarding Walsh through Bryant. It was a small circle, a tight circle, and he centered it. He needed three-hundred-and-sixty-degree vision, and he needed it all the time. He was going to have to keep off the pills, keep the booze at a manageable level, try and get some sleep. Eat properly. All that shit.

Madigan was back in the car just before eleven. A minute or two to smoke a cigarette, just get himself settled before he started down some other street, listening to the same kind of losers bullshit the same kinds of stories.

It was then that he looked in the rearview. Tilted it to see himself dead square.

He looked older than his age. His hair was edging into gray at the temples. The shadows beneath his eyes were now becoming permanent. He carried that worn-out look, ragged and frayed and wearing thin at the edges. Lost was the man that his wives had married, the man that had attracted the mistresses. He was an advertisement for how to do most everything the wrong way. But he would never apologize. Not to himself. What the hell use was that? And he didn't need redemption or salvation or absolution or forgiveness. What had he read one time? *If I forgive you, that's me saying you can just go ahead and hurt me again and I'll do nothing.* No, he didn't need forgiveness from anyone. He wasn't here to argue for his own defense. He was here just to make the bullshit go away. That's all he needed to do right now. Just make the bullshit go away.

He rooted around in the glove box. He found a baggie with a couple of Xanax. They chilled him right down when he'd done too much coke. He broke one in half and raised it to his lips. He remembered the taste of them. Hell, these pharmaceutical guys were so damned smart, how come they couldn't make these things taste like Reese's or M&M's or something? He closed his eyes for just a second, and then he lowered the window and dropped the tablet into the gutter. If he was going to try and keep it together, then he should start right now.

Madigan left the car, the pictures of the girl in his hand, and he started up another street.

Three doors in he got a rise.

It was a hesitation, would've gone right by him had he not been looking directly at the girl when she saw the picture.

The girl was twenty-five, maybe thirty. She had that spiritual beat-to-shit look that they all had down here, the ever-present certainty that however hard they fought there was never really such a thing as escape. They were all defined by the past, and they tried so hard to forget it. The Russians had a saying: Keep an eye on the past and you'll see the future half-blind; forget the past and you'll be blind altogether. They went at it blind, and they went at it angrily, and blind anger had a way of undoing pretty much everything in a bad way.

"Happened to her?" the girl asked.

"Someone shot her. Left her in a hell of a mess . . ."

"Well, I can see that. I mean, who the hell would do something like that to a . . ." Her voice trailed away. There were plenty of people, and Madigan figured she could probably name a half dozen without trying.

"You know her, right?" he asked, his tone assured. It was more a statement than a question.

"No."

"Who'd you think of when I showed you the picture?"

The girl shrugged. "Who I thought of and who it is ain't the same damned thing." There was the defensive tone. Madigan heard it. Now the girl was walking on eggshells. She knew if she said a single thing more she was involved. Involved meant statements. It meant more questions; it meant the possibility of face time with more police, other people in the neighborhood getting word that she was talking, and all of a sudden she doesn't have any friends and she's looking over her shoulder when she comes home in the dark.

"What's your name?" Madigan asked.

"Hell business is it of yours?"

Madigan smiled. "None of my business."

"Then what you askin' for?"

"'Cause we can do this nice or we can do it shit. We have a real short conversation now. You tell me who you think it might be. You tell me as much as you know. I walk away and you never see me again. Other way we can go is I take off and get a warrant. I come back here with a black-and-white and a couple of uniforms, and they stand outside your place while I come in and listen to whatever bullshit might be going on and then I leave with the same information. Oh, and tell me what you know now and I'll give you fifty bucks for your trouble."

"I tell you who I think it is, you give me fifty bucks, and then I never see you again?"

"Right."

I think it's Isabella's girl."

"Who's Isabella?"

"Used to live up on Pleasant. That was a while back."

"You know the child's name?"

"Nope."

"You know Isabella's surname?"

103

"Nope."

"Anything else you can tell me . . . *anything* at all?"

"Think she went to the school over by St. Paul's . . . Yeah, pretty sure she did."

"Good," Madigan said. "That's good." He took out his wallet, gave the girl two twenties and a ten.

"So we're done?" the girl asked as she took the notes. "I ain't never gonna see you again?"

"Sweetheart, I never even seen you this time."

Madigan turned and walked back down the street to his car.

St. Paul's was three blocks west, right by the 116th street subway station. He knew the school as well. He hoped to hell they knew her.

By the time he arrived most of the kids were taking lunch. He got in through reception and waited for the deputy principal to come on down and see him. When she came, Madigan was surprised she was white. She was good-looking, maybe mid-thirties, a little heavy perhaps, but a great smile.

"Detective Madigan? I'm Catherine Carvahlo, deputy principal. How can we help you?"

Catherine. Same name as his last wife.

Madigan rose, asked if there was somewhere they could speak away from the main corridor.

"One of the classrooms," she said. "Down here. The children are all at lunch for another twenty minutes or so."

Once inside, the conversation was brief. Yes, Catherine Carvahlo recognized the girl. She was a pupil there, but had stopped coming about two weeks earlier. This was not unusual. Happened all the time. The school reported the absentees to the board. The board reported them to the local education department. The education department put them on a list, and when their turn came around, the parents got a visit to find out what had happened.

"Her name is Melissa," Catherine told Madigan. "Melissa Arias."

"And you have the home address?"

"Of course, yes," Catherine replied. "In the office. If you come with me now, I'll get it for you."

They walked side by side. Madigan waited for the questions. *What happened to her? Do you know who did it? How is she? Is she going to make it?* But Catherine Carvahlo asked nothing, and in a strange kind of way it didn't surprise him. There were those who wanted to know everything, and those who wanted to know nothing. The *nothings* tried to go on believing that the world was a good place. They lived in some disconnected la-la land where people were nice to each other all the time. They wound up dead in a home invasion, or shot by a crackhead in a 7-Eleven robbery. The *everythings* carried their suspicions and cynicisms like a burden. They got depressed and frustrated, but they were smart enough to get their groceries in daylight and stay indoors after dark.

As Madigan left, in his hand a small piece of paper upon which was printed the name *Isabella Arias* and an address no more than five blocks away, Catherine Carvahlo did pause for a moment. She was going to ask something, and then she evidently decided against it.

Madigan looked at the piece of paper, at the woman's too-neat schoolma'am handwriting, and he said, "It's okay, Miss Carvahlo. Sometimes it's better not to know."

She knew then that he saw right through her. She looked embarrassed, as if she'd been caught in a lie. *I do care*, she wanted to say. *I do care. About all of them. But I have to try and care for the ones I've got. The ones I lose . . . I would've lost them anyway . . . Oh hell, I don't know what I'm saying . . . Forgive me . . . It doesn't make sense . . . I am a good person really. I promise I am . . .*

"I'll let you know what happens," Madigan said, and he knew he wouldn't. Catherine Carvahlo knew it too, but the fact that he'd said it made the end of their meeting all the less tense.

He walked away, didn't look back, reached his car and headed for East 117th between First and Second.

25

LONG LONG GONE

Walsh pulled their sheets—Landry, Fulton and Williams. There was a wealth of information, a good roster of contacts, all ex-cons, all with sheets themselves. It would take a month to trawl through what he had in front of him. Who the hell knew who'd said what, and when they had said it? The vast majority of these guys couldn't keep their mouths shut about anything. They talked about past jobs, present jobs, future jobs. They talked about ideas—smalltime, much of it, and then the wildcat shit that was going to make them a million and get them out of New York. And then there were the lies. These guys were born lying. They started out lying and they just kept on going. They lied to one another, to their friends, their wives, their girlfriends and mistresses and mothers. They lied to the police, the lawyers, the judges, the prison crews, and their cellmates. Most of all they lied to themselves. They had to, or they'd go mad. It was hard work, that kind of life. Always trying to remember what you'd said, who you'd said it to. Five, six, seven cellphones, all with names written on the back of who had this number, who had the other. If you're going to call such and such a person, do it from this phone, not from some other number. Exhausting. Just utterly exhausting.

Bobby Landry was a two-timer, once on a GTA, second time on a B&E. Had he not been shot in the face with a .38 he would have wound up somewhere three strikes down, career criminal, out for life and never coming home. Landry was thirty-one, hailed out of New Jersey. His father—Charles Francis Landry—had done a five-to-seven for robbery, but there was a catalog of other charges, cautions, notices, fines, suspended sentences, and God only knew what. He was questioned about a reported instance of sexual abuse against the daughter of a woman he was sleeping with. Daughter was nine years old. Her word against his. Never went anyplace. Even Landry's mother had done six months for solicitation. Hell of a family.

Charles "Chuck" Williams was out of the same petri dish. One term only, a three-to-five for assault with a deadly weapon. Did it without any trouble, came out on parole after forty-one months, ran his probation clean and didn't go back. Probation report painted him as a misguided individual, a temper-driven reactive who went off the rails at an ex-girlfriend's new lover. His outburst was a one-time thing. Bullshit. Read his sheet and he was in and out of precinct houses all over the city. He never got charged. There were no arraignments. But he was implicated in eleven robberies, two GTAs, assault on a minor, pandering, a gang-rape, possession and intent to distribute. Mom and Dad must have been proud. Williams walked all of them, maybe because he was just so charming. Walsh looked at his picture. His was a hard face. Dark eyes, bitterness in every facet of him, the sort of awkward bastard who believed that everybody and the world owed him whatever he wanted. He was a New Yorker, came up out of the Lower East Side as far as Walsh could work out. And when he got up close and personal with the concrete floor of that storage unit—one slug in his chest, a second in his head—he was thirty-four years old.

Laurence Fulton made Landry and Williams look like kindergarten cons. Fulton was also a two-timer, a three-to-five upstate for a multiple GTA, something a couple of years earlier in and around Atlantic City, and he'd had an armed robbery charge pending trial. He was out on bail—a seventy-five grander, said bail posted by his mother. Seemed she'd put her house on the line for her delightful child. Well, she wouldn't have to worry about that anymore, her delightful child now lying in one of the ME's chill drawers with most of his throat and the back of his head someplace else.

Fulton looked like the roughest of the three. He'd done juvy as a pre-teen, in and out of an assortment of facilities between fourteen and seventeen, forever skipping around the edges of something or other. His sheet was twice the length of Landry's and Williams's combined. He was boosting cars at eleven, pulling 7-Elevens when he was fifteen. They got him a few times, but he bullshitted his way around the system somehow or another. As a teenager he robbed grocery stores wearing a leather jacket with olive oil smeared all over the sleeves and back. Someone grabbed him they could never hang on. They even got him for such a stunt one time, had the coat, had the store guy with oil all over his hands, but there was no way to prove that the oil on the guy's hands was the *very same oil* that covered Fulton's coat. He walked again. Or slithered maybe. Got himself criminal defense lawyers who were as slippery as the jacket. Fulton was a violent man. Was up for a rape charge one time, but that went away too. Lack of evidence. There were reports of domestic abuse, visits to his house on numerous occasions due to reports of screaming, an endless history of ER visits made by the various girls he was sleeping with, and yet no one ever pressed charges. Not once. He was cautioned, interrogated, kept overnight a dozen or more times, but without a charge there was nothing that could be done. He didn't only beat his girlfriends senseless, he beat them scared. He instilled such a terror of retribution that they wouldn't say a word.

Walsh felt sure that Fulton was the heavy hitter of the three, so much so that he decided to focus his energies on Fulton's contacts, Fulton's known associates, maybe some of the girls that he'd kicked six ways to Sunday, and in among all of that he might find someone who remembered Fulton saying something about taking down one of Sandià's houses. Such a venture was not undertaken lightly. Walsh knew of Sandià; there were very few people in the PD who didn't know of Sandià, especially in the Yard and surrounding territory. No, whoever decided to go up against Sandià was either crazy, extraordinarily clever, or just plain suicidal. Fulton was crazy, no doubt about it, and maybe Landry and Williams were crazy too. But what they were and why they got involved was not important now. All that was important was the fourth man, and Walsh believed that Fulton's world—the one that still existed, the one that still contained his memories—was where he would find the ghost on the highway. He believed, however, that the fourth man might not be crazy, that he might be the clever one of the pack. Why? Because he'd been the one to walk away with the money. Walsh was certain that the few thousand dollars on the floor of the storage unit was nowhere near the sum total of the robbery. And the fact that he'd left three men behind—all of them dead, thereby creating the appearance that some internal conflict had resulted in the three perps wiping themselves out—had been a smart idea.

Perhaps the fourth man believed he had pulled it off, this master plan. But there had been a mistake. Just that one tread mark, that one small thing, and it had taken on a whole new slant.

Now Walsh had to contend with his own self-appointed return to the world of Homicide, the fact that he was investigating one half of a case while Vincent Madigan investigated the other, and there was yet a third matter to take into consideration—the simple reality that Sandià would be even more driven than the police to identify who had committed this crime against him. He would want his money. He would want revenge. He would want his own pound of flesh. He would get word out that no one should speak of this matter to the police. His own people would be taking care of things. And he would not want it made known that he had been ripped off. It would not serve his reputation well. Both Walsh and Madigan would be up against a wall of silence.

No, this was not a simple case of three dead guys in a storage unit. This was something else altogether, and Walsh realized how much he had missed it. He had two weeks before Callow returned, two weeks to prove to himself, to prove to everyone, that he could do this thing, that he belonged here, that he had learned how to make a mark that counted for something in this territory.

Somewhere there was a fourth man with a great deal of money and a car with tires that matched those treads, and this was going to be legwork and late hours, the usual routine for such cases. Homicides fell into four main categories—premeditated and intentional, everything from domestic murders for the insurance money to contractors employed to make someone disappear; those occasioned in the execution of another crime—bank robberies, kidnappings and suchlike; crimes of passion—the drunken ex-husband stabs the wife's new lover; finally, the gang-related and territorial homicides. Pretty much everything fell into one of those boxes, and what had happened with the Sandià robbery was the latter. Until the fourth man was found there was no way to determine whether or not it had always been his intention to kill the other three, but this didn't change the nature of the crime. It was an internal thing, something that fell within the bounds of the criminal fraternity, and there was little going on in that fraternity that someone somewhere didn't know. It was a matter of finding that person, or getting something on someone that could then be used as leverage to find that person. That's all it would take. Walsh would begin with Fulton's closest people, the ones whose names appeared most frequently as accomplices, those with whom he had shared a cell and then maintained a connection post-sentence. That was how the vast majority of these partnerships were founded. There was little to talk about in a twenty-three lockdown aside from what they were going to do once released.

Walsh set everything else aside and combed through Fulton's file. Three names figured prominently, two of them from prison terms. One of them was back inside, and thus was out of the loop. That left two, the first being Fulton's cousin on his mother's side, the second a cellmate from the upstate three-to-five. His name was Richard Moran. Fulton played booster, Moran was the driver. So, if they'd worked a few things together, why wasn't Moran brought in as a driver on the Sandià hit? Because Fulton was a hired hand, that's why. The fourth man was the contractor, not Fulton. The loyalty lay with the money, so Fulton may have suggested Moran, or Number Four might already have secured his driver before Fulton joined the crew. Walsh pulled Moran up on the system. He had a sheet like Fulton's—B&Es, GTAs, assault and battery, possession with intent—and though he'd done eighteen months a while back, he seemed to have slid through everyone's fingers for the rest of it. Seemed that the PD spent the vast majority of their time and resources chasing the big guys, the guys like Sandià, and Sandià would never see the inside of a jail cell. Otherwise, they were chasing the small-timers, the kids with the dime bags, the speeding offenders, the traffic violations. In between was a whole world of violent, single-minded thieves and dealers and sex offenders, every one of them protected by the lumbering inefficiency of the system. This was the nature of the beast, and if you didn't care for it, then this was not the line of work to pursue.

The second connection—the cousin—was named Edward "Eddie" Fauser. Fulton's maternal aunt had married one Jerry Fauser, and Jerry Fauser was a star. He was inside even then, serving an eighteen-to-twenty-five for armed robbery. He'd gone down in May of 1994, had done sixteen, looked like he'd be doing at least another three or four. Two parole applications had been denied, next one wasn't due until after the following Christmas. Eddie was definitely his father's son—looked like him, behaved like him. Followed in the family business, started young, worked hard at it, and by the time he was nineteen he'd already done a year for aggravated assault. On his sheet were charges of attempted robbery, malicious wounding, physical abuse of a minor, an assorted collection of robbery-related things, but—once again—he appeared to have maneuvered his way through all of it with a certain deftness and aplomb. He was out and about too, didn't have anything pending, but the last time his name had been linked to that of Laurence Fulton had been four years before.

Fulton and Moran, however, had been marked up as prime suspects for questioning in a recent robbery. Nothing had come of it, and they were not pursued. But it had been recent, and that's why Walsh felt his time would be better spent following up on Moran. If that went nowhere, then he could go running after Eddie Fauser.

Moran's last-known address was on the outskirts of the Yard, up around West 132nd, just near the point Park Avenue crossed the Harlem River. Walsh called down to the pool for a vehicle, took his jacket from the back of his chair, and made his way out.

Bryant saw him leaving, called him back.

"Got word from Madigan . . . Looks like he has a lead on this girl, the one from the Sandià house," he said. "And where you off to?"

"After a buddy of Fulton's, see if Fulton was a talker."

"Good 'nough." Bryant smiled, added, "And, hey, let's be careful out there."

"That is such a crap impression. Did you ever *actually* watch *Hill Street Blues*?"

"Yes, I did, wiseass."

"Well, you take it easy as well, Sarge."

"Fuck you very much," Bryant replied, and turned to head back to his office.

Walsh watched him go. Bryant was a good man, a good sergeant, but it was the first time Bryant had ever cracked wise with him in all the months he'd been there. IA was a hell of a way to make no friends.

26

BAD LUCK AND TROUBLE

Three blocks south and he would be outside the 167th—that's how close he was—and for a while Madigan stood ahead of the beat-to-shit tenement building and wondered whether there was anyone inside who would talk to him. And if he found someone who was willing to talk, would they know anything of consequence? The Arias apartment was up on the third. Madigan took the stairs. He didn't trust elevators at the best of times, and in buildings such as these it was best to trust them not at all. Even as he entered the hallway on the third floor, as he checked door numbers for the right apartment, he had an uneasy feeling. For Madigan, it was never a question of whether or not to trust his intuition. Intuition was vital. Intuition was a faculty to be cultivated—not necessarily depended upon, but certainly cultivated. Criminology and profiling were not sciences. Not in the strictest sense of the word. There were variables in all aspects of these subjects, and the guys that had worked on them initially, the ones who had built the foundations, well, they had originally gone with their intuition. In that moment it was intuition that told him the apartment was empty. Number thirty-seven, supposedly the residence of Isabella Arias and her daughter, Melissa, missing from school for two weeks, now laid up in Harlem Hospital with a gunshot wound. The terrible irony was not missed on Madigan. Had he not hit the Sandià house, the girl would not have been shot. Had he not been carrying seventy-five grand's worth of gambling debts, he would not have hit the Sandià house in the first place. Had he spent a little more time concerning himself with his own relationships, his own duties as a father, then he would not have been gambling. Now he was out here concerning himself with the well-being of someone else's child, a degree of concern far greater than he had shown his own children. All the while he was aware of the fact that if too much of what he learned

112

became common knowledge then he was dead, if not physically then certainly professionally.

He raised his hand and knocked on the apartment door.

"Ain't there," a voice said behind him.

Madigan turned, came face-to-face with a middle-aged white woman. "Sorry?"

"She ain't there . . . She's gone. Left us with three hundred bucks of unpaid rent."

"Us?" Madigan asked.

"My brother and me. He's the super. I do all the money stuff, collect the rent and what have you. She just took off a couple of weeks back and that was that. Haven't seen hide nor hair of her or the brat kid since."

Madigan was beginning to get irritated by the woman's tone. He flipped his badge. She looked at it nonchalantly and shook her head.

"So what? She's dead or something?"

Madigan closed his eyes for a moment and took a breath. "I'm looking for her," he said. "What's your name?"

"Elizabeth."

"Elizabeth what?"

"Elizabeth Young."

"And your brother's name?"

"Harold. Harry."

"And you own the building or just supervise it?"

The woman cracked a bitter smile. "You think I'd live in this rathole if I owned it? No, the place is owned by some real estate people in the city, far as I know. I don't deal with them. I deal with the property agent. I collect the rent, bank it, do the paperwork an' all that."

"And these people, the woman and her daughter—"

"Isabella Arias. That's her name. And the kid's name is Melissa."

"And when did you last see them?"

"Two weeks maybe. Something like that. Three hundred bucks behind and they just took off. I've been in there. There ain't nothin' worth nothin' for us to sell and make it back. Hell, I don't know who these people think they damn well are."

"Do you remember the exact day you last saw them, Ms. Young?"

Elizabeth Young looked at Madigan for a moment. She seemed

to stand a little straighter. She was being addressed politely, a little respectfully perhaps.

"Well, yes, as a matter of fact I do," she said. "It was the last day of December, middle of the day."

"New Year's Eve."

"Right. New Year's Eve."

"And were they coming in or going out?"

"Coming in, just her and the girl. Had some bags, groceries, I reckon. Didn't pay much attention, to tell you the truth. I'd let the rent slide for a while, it being Christmas an' all, but I reckoned I could only let it go so far. People I answer to don't know the meaning of compassion, if you know what I mean. Besides, I hadn't seen them for a good few days. Figured they might have gone visiting with family or something, considering all that had happened. So I waited a couple of hours and then I knocked on the door. No answer. Not a sound. I imagined they'd just gone out again without me hearing them. I went over the day after New Year's, knocked again. Same thing. Left it a couple more days and still there was no answer. I kinda got worried then, because like I said, I was rememberin' what happened to her sister an' all—"

"Her sister?"

"Sure, her sister, Maribel. Pretty girl. Really pretty. Ever such a sweet girl, couldn't have been more than twenty-five or thereabouts. Anyway, considering what had happened to the sister I got a little worried—"

"I'm sorry, Ms. Young, I need you to back up here. What was it that happened to her sister?"

Elizabeth Young frowned. She looked at Madigan like the comings and goings of Maribel Arias were common knowledge. "She was murdered. Murdered just the day after Christmas."

The hairs rose on the nape of Madigan's neck. "Murdered?"

"Sure. Yeah. It was all over the building. They found her head in a Dumpster someplace, the rest of her a block or two away. You didn't know about that?"

"No," Madigan said. "I didn't even know she had a sister."

"Yes, she definitely had a sister, and that sister definitely got herself murdered. Anyway, as I was saying, I kinda got worried seein' as how this thing had happened to Maribel, so I opened up the apartment and took a look inside. Nothing to see. Everything looked like it had before. I got to thinking that maybe she just got scared or whatever, and she just decided she was going to take off someplace. That was the only thing I could think."

"And did you report this?"

"What's to report? People bail out on their rent all the time. There was nothing to tell anyone. She was there, and then she was gone."

Madigan was quiet for a moment. He was trying to think, trying to put something together. "I want to see inside," he said eventually. "You have the keys?"

"Sure do," Elizabeth replied, and then she hesitated. "You need a warrant or something?"

"Unpaid rent, tenant gone, and your brother's the super? I don't need a warrant. I just need you to say it's okay."

Elizabeth shrugged. "Okay with me." She went back into her apartment to get the keys.

She opened up, left him alone in there, went back to her own place. Inside it was as the woman had described. Madigan stood for a while in the silence of the room. The air inside was musty, a little dry. No air-conditioning, no open windows for two weeks, that was all. He walked through the living room into the kitchen, opened drawers and cupboards, opened the fridge, the microwave. He went back through and looked in both bedrooms, the small bathroom, an adjacent closet. Someone could be home any moment now. That was how it felt. On the floor of the girl's room were a couple of dolls, a coloring set, a scattering of cheap toys, the kind that came with fast food kids' meals. Didn't appear to be any missing clothes. The mother's room was the same—a cheap dresser, cosmetics on top of it, a bed that had been slept in and left unmade, the cupboards and drawers full of clothes. Where is it that people go where they need to take nothing with them?

Madigan went back to the living room and stood in the middle of the rug. He closed his eyes. The mother and daughter were seen two weeks ago. They vanish within a couple hours of being seen. They leave all their clothes and possessions behind. A week or so before that the mother's sister was murdered—decapitated, her head found in a Dumpster, the rest of her elsewhere. There had to be a connection, and that connection—Madigan suspected—possessed a great deal to do with the little girl's presence in the Sandià house. It was this thought that chilled him.

He went through the rooms again, looked more carefully, looked beneath the rugs, behind the fridge, behind the TV.

In the bathroom he stopped. Behind the door, low and near the ground, there were a series of dark scuff marks on the paintwork. Madigan closed the door, put his shoulder against it, and then pressed the edge of his shoe against the lower part of the door. The scuff marks were in precisely the position they would be had he tried to prevent someone getting in. Had someone come here for the girl and the mother? If so who, and why? Sandià? What would Sandià want with a woman like Isabella Arias? More to the point, what would he want with her daughter? And did their disappearance relate to the death of the sister, Maribel?

That would be the first port of call—to find out about the sister. When had she died, when and where had she been found, and who had found her? It may have been handled at the 167th, and if so it made his life a great deal easier. The last thing he needed was to officially involve another precinct in this mess.

He left the apartment, knocked on Elizabeth Young's door.

"I'm done in there for now," he said. "Before I go, I just want to clarify these dates. The sister was murdered on the twenty-sixth, right?"

"Well, I don't know when she was murdered, but that was when they found her."

"Okay, and then you saw Isabella and Melissa on the thirty-first, New Year's Eve?"

"Yeah, New Year's Eve."

"And you hadn't seen them at all between the twenty-sixth and the thirty-first?"

"No, not a sign of them. Like I said, I figured they'd gone away visiting family or something, the sister having died an' all."

"Okay," Madigan said. "And between the time they arrived and when you knocked on the apartment door a couple of hours later you heard nothing suspicious?"

The woman smiled and shook her head. "My brother is deaf like a plank. He has the TV on so damned loud I have to go shut myself in the kitchen. World War Three could break out in the lobby and I wouldn't hear a damned thing." She hesitated, and then she frowned. "Why? You think something happened here? She gone and got herself killed as well?"

"I don't know, Ms. Young. I really don't know. I'm just trying to find her right now, that's all."

"Well, if you do find her tell her to get her ass back here pronto.

Another two weeks they're gonna come empty the place out, paint it maybe, and then it'll be someone else's apartment."

"If I see her, I'll tell her. And is there anything else that you think might be useful for me to know . . . people who came over, recent visitors, anything out of the ordinary?"

"Not that I can think of," she replied. "I've told you everything I know."

"That's really appreciated, Ms. Young."

Madigan gave her his card, asked her to call him if there was any news of Isabella Arias or her daughter. He did not tell the woman that Melissa Arias was lying in a bed in Harlem Hospital. Such a piece of information would be everywhere in the building, everywhere in the neighborhood, before nightfall. And the last thing he needed was for word to get back to Sandià that he was looking into the murder of Maribel. He did not see how they could be anything but connected. The sister is murdered, the woman and her daughter disappear, and the daughter is found in Sandià's house. Two plus two makes four.

He left the building, and as he walked back to his car he began to appreciate that whatever concern Sandià possessed about Melissa Arias, it was a great deal more important than three hundred grand and the death of his nephew.

Madigan was scared. There was another facet to everything now, another factor to take into consideration. Something was going on, and that something was important enough to have justified the killing of Maribel Arias and the kidnap of the child. Maybe Isabella was dead too. Maybe she'd been cut up and scattered around some other part of the city, and it was merely a matter of time before someone found her.

Madigan, however, did not think so. He believed that Isabella Arias was out there. Hiding, terrified, perhaps unaware of what had happened to her daughter. Above all else, she needed to be found, and found fast. Madigan needed to get to her before Sandià.

He started the engine and headed back to the 167th. There were case files on the sister's murder that he needed to locate, and if those files were outside the Yard then he was screwed.

More than he already was? For sure, no question about it. If there was one thing he knew from hard-won experience, it was however deep the hole there was always a way to dig it deeper.

27

CLEOPATRA DREAMS ON

There is usually one way to get things right, but there are countless ways to get it wrong.

Among the things you don't want to get wrong are your family, your marriage, your kids, your career, your finances. All the important shit.

The little things don't matter. They get fixed or they fix themselves.

With me, it's always been the other way around, and in hindsight I have recognized the problem. I am short-sighted. I see today, tomorrow, maybe next week. Guys who get things right—the important things— look a little farther. They have five-year plans. I can't comprehend five years. What does that even mean? Sometimes twenty-four hours is a struggle. A day. A single day. And I'm expected to be planning the next two thousand? Some kind of joke that is.

No, I have been short-sighted. I have listened to the epithets and clichés. People who aim for nothing are sure to hit it. Some people dream of success while others get up and work hard at it. To hell with that. You need a hit. Just one good hit, and it's all done and dusted. Sandià's money was going to dig me out of a hole. Hell, the guy can afford it. He makes that much money between every heartbeat. But me? No, not me. I get it organized, I get it straight, I get it all figured out—all the details. But I miss the important shit. I miss the vitally important life-or-death significant keystone that holds the whole thing together. You don't ever crap in your own backyard. I should've known that. What was I thinking? Chewing pills like M&M's, drinking a fifth before dinner, another fifth before bed. Jesus, could I have been dumber? Sure I could. Have been dumber than that before. Dumb enough to get involved with Sandià. Kind of bullshit stupid thing was that? Well, it wasn't at the time. Smartest thing I could've done. That's what I thought. I can play both sides. I can make a little here, a little there, keep the PD happy, make some busts, all the while the left hand is right behind me taking a fat bonus from Sandià for keeping the noise down around his place.

And now? Now I have only one advantage. It's simple really, too simple to ignore. Sandià trusts me. Why else would he ask me to take care of this thing? He needs the girl alive; he needs to know who took his money and killed his nephew. So who does he call? He calls Vincent. Good old Vincent. Vincent will take care of it. Vincent can play both sides. Vincent can see around corners. This is what Vincent does. This is Vincent's specialty.

And it all comes down to the money. Only thing you need to get anyplace at all.

Am I dreaming?

Is this all a figment of my imagination?

Have I just taken too many pills and emptied too many bottles to even remember where reality and imagination divide?

Jesus, what the hell have I done here?

What the hell am I doing now?

And if I get this wrong? If I screw this up? Hell, I don't even want to think about it.

I think a thought, and it's a strange thought, an uncharacteristic thought—at least for me. For a second—just a second—I wonder what it will do to the children. Cassie, Adam, Lucy, and Tom. What would it do to them if they found out the truth about their father?

Angela, Ivonne, Catherine . . . what they think doesn't matter now. They're all grown up. They can handle it. They knew what they were taking on, and if they didn't when they started they sure as hell did by the time they were finished.

It was a game. That was all. Just a game.

And then it became something else. What, I don't know, but it became something else. It got serious. It started to mean something.

I have to get back to how I was. I have to be the old Vincent Madigan, the one who didn't give a damn for anything but today, right now, the next five minutes.

Right now anything else would be suicide. It's all right to give a damn, but you have to give a damn about the right things. That money has to wind up somewhere, and that will be the clincher. Someone has to take the fall for this and then it will all settle down. I got to think fast, think both ways at the same time, and then we'll get through and out the other side.

Things always look better looking backward. Slow down, take a sidestep and you'll never get there. Hindsight may well be the cruelest and most astute adviser, but until something is past there ain't no such thing.

This is not going to be the end for me. This is not the thing I will be remembered for.

This is not going to be the thing that kills me.

28

GOOD TIMES

F inding Moran was the easy part. Everything else was a different story. Moran was heavy-set, taller than Walsh, and when he opened the door to the walk-up he looked down at Walsh with an expression of certainty. Walsh was a cop. There was no doubt in Moran's mind.

"Richard Moran?" Walsh asked.

"Who's asking?"

Walsh had his ID out. "Detective Walsh, 167th Precinct."

"And if I am?"

Walsh took a step back. He didn't want to appear too aggressive. "A friend of yours was killed and I wanted to see if you could help me—"

"And why would I want to do that?"

Walsh hesitated. He looked back and to the left, across the hallway toward a woman coming out of her apartment with a squalling baby. "No reason," he said, turning back to Moran. "Except maybe self-preservation."

"How so?"

"What goes around comes around," Walsh said. "He was into a thing, the thing went bad, and anyone who was connected might run into some difficulty."

"Who's to say I even know what you're talking about? Who's to say I was connected?"

"You were his friend?"

Moran shrugged his shoulders. "I got a lot of friends."

"Sure you have, but I don't think Fulton did."

Moran frowned. "Larry Fulton?"

"Yeah, Larry Fulton."

"Shee-it."

"You didn't know he was dead?"

"Nope, didn't know a thing."

"Well, he is," Walsh said. He took another step backward.

"Someone shot him in the stomach with a .44. There ain't a great deal of his cheery smile left."

Moran looked genuinely concerned for a moment, and then he seemed to realize that giving anything away was a mistake. His expression was deadpan once again.

"But, hell, you know how it is," Walsh said. "Shit like this happens every which way each and every day. If you didn't know he was dead, and you don't know anything about what he was working on, then I'll leave you to your business." Walsh turned, his hands in his pockets, and took a step down to the sidewalk.

"Hey, wait up," Moran said.

Walsh turned.

Moran came out of the doorway. He had on a sleeveless T-shirt, jailhouse tats scattered up and down his arms, around his shoulders, the base of his neck. His jeans were scuzzy, his boots worn-out, the laces hanging loose. He looked three days short of dereliction, and yet there was something about the way he was dressed that seemed contrived. Maybe he looked this way because he was supposed to look this way, to fit in, to belong.

"When'd he get it?"

"Yesterday."

"He alone?"

"Can't say."

"Can't or won't?"

Walsh didn't reply.

"Hey, man, it's a give-and-take scenario here." Moran smiled, held out his hands in a conciliatory fashion.

"He was not alone," Walsh said. He didn't move, still standing there in the hallway, hands in his pockets, everything about his body language saying he was really not that interested, that he really had other more important places to be.

"And what would you say if I said that he told me he was doing a thing?"

Walsh nodded slowly. "I'd say that I was interested in what he might have said to you."

Moran held Walsh's gaze. Everything that was going on behind his eyes was right there, as clear as day.

"Whatever it is, I can help you," Walsh said.

"You don't know what it is," Moran replied.

"Do I want to know?"

"That depends on whether you want to know anything else."

"And this is a conversation you want to have in the hallway?"

"You ain't gonna wanna sit in my kitchen, man. I don't have no old lady cleanin' up after me."

"You think I give a crap about your housework?"

Moran smiled. "Well, maybe I'm not so concerned about the dirty dishes as something else."

"Then I'll just see the dirty dishes, my friend, and I won't see the something else."

"You don't have no warrant; you don't have no probable cause. I'm inviting you in here and that's all."

"That's all, Richard."

Moran laughed. "Hell, man, no one calls me Richard."

"What do they call you?"

"They call me Cutter."

"Is that what you do?"

"I do a lot of things, man, but we ain't talkin' about me today. We're talkin' 'bout Larry Fulton and what he might have told me."

"So lead the way," Walsh said, and when Moran turned and went back in the apartment Walsh followed him.

Moran had been right. The place was a sty. The kitchen sink was stacked high with dishes, the smell of rotting food from the trash can almost overpowering, but it was the presence of mason jars, coffee filters, surgical tubing, and bottles of hydrogen peroxide that gave up the show. Moran was cooking tina—smalltime sure, but big-time had to start somewhere.

"A sideline," Moran explained, aware of the fact that here was traction on him if Walsh needed to press him for information.

"I don't see anything," Walsh replied.

"We all got selective blindness when we need to, right?"

"Right." Walsh took a seat at the table. He didn't look at the up-ended coffee cup, mold growing on the spill of liquid that must have gone unattended for weeks. He didn't concern himself what whatever filth he might find on his jacket and pants when he left. He just sat there and waited for Moran to talk.

Moran was silent for some time. He lit a cigarette and smoked most of it before he spoke. He surveyed his stained fingers, the backs of his hands, even the sole of one sneaker, and then he shook his head slowly and said, "We had some good times."

"You and Larry."

"Sure, me and Larry, 'cept no one called him Larry. I was Cutter, he was Bone, like in that movie, right?"

"Right."

"We did a bunch of stuff together. Little things, nothing big. We did a while together in the box, and then when we came out we sort of hung around a while."

"He was doing a three-to-five. What were you doing?"

"I was doin' a seven-to-ten, but I busted it in five and a half. We spent the last three years in the same room."

"He was a good guy?"

"You tellin' or askin'?"

"Asking."

"Sure, he was a good guy. Had his moments, like everyone, you know?" Moran nodded toward the stove. "He did a little too much crank, man, and that can get to you. Wears off the varnish, right? Makes everything sharp and awkward. He didn't sleep good. He was burning himself up a good deal."

"Was he trying to get out?"

Moran laughed. "Hell, man, who isn't? Shit, I bet you're even trying to get out of something. 'S what it's all about, isn't it? Life is getting stuff you want, getting rid of stuff you don't."

"Yeah, s'pose it is."

Moran was quiet again. He lit another cigarette, reached over and picked up the spilled coffee cup to use as an ashtray. He smiled. "If I'd known we were having guests, I woulda cleaned up some."

"Don't worry about it," Walsh replied.

"Oh, I won't. You can be sure of that."

Walsh smiled. "So what do you need me to fix?" he said, affecting as nonchalant a tone as he could. He needed to sound anything other than desperate. He needed to sound like whatever Moran had to tell him he could find in a dozen other places. In reality, the tension was almost unbearable. Within hours of taking this on he had located someone who could give him something of real use.

Moran cleared his throat. "I got a thing going on. It ain't a big thing, but it's number two for me. And if I got number two, then number three ain't gonna be far away and then I'm a lifer."

"What is it?"

"A possession beef."

"What?"

"Some coke, a bit of weed, nothing heavy."

"How much?"

"Gram of powder, maybe a half ounce of the weed."

"Not enough for intent, but enough for a term."

"Hell, I don't know. It blows hot and cold, man. Seems like one week they want to get you inside as fast as possible, another week they want to keep you on the street."

"Places get overcrowded," Walsh said. "Has more to do with numbers than anything else. Numbers and politics determine whether you get a term."

"Well, I don't wanna risk it, you know what I mean? I ain't goin' up on a beef and just wishin' on a star, right?"

"Right."

"So you can sort it out?"

"Maybe."

"Maybe ain't worth shit."

"You ain't told me anything worth shit, Richard."

"Oh, but I got something, baby. I got something hot and heavy."

"And if what you got is so hot and heavy why haven't you angled for a let-up on the possession bust?"

"'Cause I didn't know the motherfucker had gotten himself shot, did I? Jesus, the thing only went down yesterday."

"The *thing*?"

"The gig that Bone had goin' on."

"You knew he had a gig yesterday?"

"Maybe."

Walsh paused. It was like teaching a blind guy to play checkers.

"So—"

Moran shook his head. "I'm gonna need assurances."

Walsh frowned. "Assurances? What the hell are you talking about?"

"I know some shit, and—like I said—it's good shit, hot and heavy shit, and it's worth a good deal to whoever has an ear for it."

"I have an ear for it."

"So I need an assurance from you, and if you don't have the stripes to give me an assurance, then I need someone up the ladder to give the go-ahead."

"Who's the arresting officer?"

"Some asshole called Levin."

"You know which precinct?"

"One I went to was the 158th."

Walsh didn't hesitate. "I can straighten out things at the 158th."

Moran leaned forward. He looked directly at Walsh, and there it was. There was the psycho, the killer, the tin man, the crank cooker, the unpredictable whacko who'd stab someone in the eye with a pencil for a wrap of coke.

Walsh didn't flinch.

"What does that mean?"

"Means I have a couple of friends at the 158th. I make a call, your paperwork goes walkabout, and lo and behold we don't hear a thing about it for six months. And then the ADA and whoever the hell else doesn't give a crap about it because we're not looking for possessions anymore—we're looking for suppliers—and even if we were still looking for possessions it wouldn't matter because there's no paperwork on you anyway."

"You're tellin' me straight?"

Walsh leaned forward. He met Moran's unflinching gaze. "Straight as a highway."

"How do I know to trust you?"

"You don't."

"We're doin' this on a handshake."

Walsh shook his head. "We're not doing anything, Richard. I don't know who you are. You don't know who I am. This conversation never took place. All that happens is you tell me what you have. I make a call. We both walk away happy—depending, of course, on whether or not what you got to tell me is worth shit." Walsh heard himself talking, and all of a sudden he was ten years younger, smart and fast and on the ball. It felt good. He was lying backward and sideways at the same time, but it felt good because he was doing it for the right reasons. This was how the game worked, and this was a game he could play.

"Oh, it's worth shit all right."

"How do I know we're even talking about the same gig?"

"Fulton, Bobby Landry, Chuck Williams, right?"

Walsh—once again—felt that narrow twist of electricity along the length of his spine. He said nothing.

"So we're talking about the same gig, right?"

Walsh nodded.

"I tell you what I know, you make the possession beef go away. This is the deal?"

"That's the deal."

"Give me your word."

"I give you my word."

Moran leaned back. "I don't know why the fuck I'm even trusting you—"

"Because you aren't dumb, and neither am I," Walsh said. "You don't think I know what you're capable of? I turn this over and it goes bad for you, what you gonna do? You're gonna come after me, right? You're going to get loaded up on some of that home-made shit and come find me. That stuff inside of you, hell, you won't even think twice about putting me down."

Moran smiled. He nodded slowly. "I am the Cutter."

"So talk."

"Was a bullshit thing from the get-go," he said. "I don't know much, but what I do know counts for a good deal. Some guy set it up. He was the leader of this crew. He was recruiting. He was the one who got Larry into it, and then Larry comes back and says there's two others as well. Four in all. The head honcho, then Larry, this guy Williams, lastly this other one, Landry. Takes a while to get a handle on the main guy, but Larry got something. Didn't tell me his name, but he told me something else."

"And this was the robbery of the house?"

"House? I don't know, man. I don't know what they were robbing, but I know *what* they were robbing, if you get my drift."

Walsh raised his eyebrows.

"Bank money."

"You what?"

"They were taking bank money off of someone. Some other crew turned over a bank, the money was traveling, and this main guy—whoever he was—had a gig going on to lift this money." Moran laughed coarsely. "It was like something out of some god-damned Hollywood movie. Some crew turns over a bank, and before they can get it into their system to clean it up, some other crew comes along and takes it right off of them."

"You know which bank?"

Moran shook his head. "Not a clue. But I'll tell you this . . . The main guy, the one that recruited Bone, he didn't know it was bank money. He thought it was drug money."

"So how did Larry find this out?"

"Larry knows people. He knows enough people. He can get info on anything."

Walsh was already working this through. The money was traceable. That money was going to start showing up somewhere pretty soon.

"You say that they robbed a house?" Moran asked.

"Yeah, someplace up in Harlem."

"There you go, then. It all makes sense. This main guy brings Larry into the crew. Larry does his own homework, finds out that the cash they're going to lift is bank money, all of it typed and traceable and serial numbers in some system somewhere. But the main guy doesn't have a clue. Larry had his own guy ready to take his percentage and clean it up for him after the fact. He was going to get maybe seventy, seventy-five on the dollar and get the hell out of here. He didn't want to be around when those other schmucks started spending their bank money."

"But if he knew it was marked money, why did he get involved? Soon as the others started spending that money they'd bring them in. One of them was sure to give up Larry on a plea bargain with the DA's Office."

"Mexico," Moran said. "Hell, man, there wasn't nothing for him here. He reckoned he'd get the money cleaned within twenty-four hours, be in Mexico in forty-eight, and that would be the end of that."

"But surely if he was going to Mexico he wouldn't need to get the money cleaned?"

"I don't know. Jesus, man, I'm just tellin' you what he told me. I don't know what was going' on with him—"

"Okay," Walsh said. "But still one hell of a risk."

"You gotta speculate to accumulate. That's what he said. Higher the risk, the greater the danger, but the bigger the return."

"So that's all you've got for me?"

Moran shook his head. "I've got something else. This is the shit man, the real shit . . . And hell, if he wasn't dead I wouldn't tell you, but he's dead 'cause someone shot him. And if what he told me is true, then it ain't only Larry Fulton that had a problem with this guy. I'd say that you have one too."

Walsh shook his head. "I don't understand what you mean."

"That's 'cause I ain't told you yet."

"So tell me."

"We got a deal, right? I tell you this, you make the call, I'm in the free and clear on that possession beef."

"That's the deal."

"Hold on to your freakin' hat, man—"

"Just tell me . . . Tell me, for Christ's sake . . ."

"The main guy, the one who brought Larry and the other two in . . . He was a cop, man. He was a fucking cop."

29

LOVE AND DESPERATION

Maribel Arias's body had been found in the Yard. That made her the 167th's problem. Her head had been discovered in a Dumpster behind an empty store near the 125th Street subway station. The rest of her was in garbage bags, the heavy-duty ones used by builders for masonry and pipe work—her legs in one, her arms in another, her torso sectioned in two more. Those bags had been found by a homeless guy rooting around behind the North General Hospital. Used needles, that's what he was after. Said he sold them on to junkies who used them once again. What remained of Maribel Arias was still on ice with the ME. Eighteen days had elapsed since the discovery, but the case—assigned initially to Charlie Harris, then transferred to a relative newcomer to Homicide, John Faber—had stalled within seventy-two hours and moved nowhere since.

Faber had come up from Vice at the 27th, had a clean track, a solid record, but he was one of the methodical, pragmatic types. Faber did not have intuitive strikes, or so he told Madigan.

"It's all legwork," he said. "It's a numbers game, right? Talk to enough people and you're gonna find someone who knows something."

Madigan didn't disagree, didn't argue. All he needed was a look at the files. Faber was all too eager to cooperate. Give him another year in Homicide and he'd be as suspicious and awkward as the rest of them.

Madigan took the files to his own office. He read through the initial scene of crime reports, the ME's findings—decapitation, clean severance, the body parts separated with a narrow-toothed mechanical saw, the lack of tearing on the bone indicative of a high-quality blade, possibly carbon steel, and the extensive notes that Faber had himself made as he tried to talk to enough people *to find someone who knew something*. As yet Faber had not located that mysterious and singular individual who could shed light on what befell Maribel Arias. As was always the case, irrespective of the nature of death or the victim, the more time that elapsed the less likely any new information would be forthcoming. More often than not it was a crapshoot. Chance eyewitnesses, unknown to perp, unknown to police until the police knocked on enough doors and found them. Faber was right, at least to a degree, but the thing he was missing was the certainty that there was *always* someone who knew something, and often it was nothing but the intuitive *shift* that led you in their direction. The *shift* was a change of perspective, an alteration of viewpoint. It wasn't science, rocket or otherwise. It wasn't even a sixth sense, per se. It was an appreciation for tone of voice, body language, eye movement, for all the other myriad details that passed by you until you started to read them for what they were.

It was as he read the file that Madigan remembered something. An event, a circumstance, the thing that had prompted his enrollment in the New York Police Academy back in July of '89. A woman was raped. She was an acquaintance of Angela's, his first wife. He had only just met Angela, and it would be another two years before they were married. They'd had a date booked, but Angela had called him to say that she didn't want to go.

Why, he'd asked.

Because of this thing that happened to a girl down the street.

What happened?

She got attacked by some guy. He raped her.

Did he kill her?

No, Vincent, he didn't kill her. But you wonder if something like that happened to you whether you'd be better off dead. I mean, how the hell do you go on living after something like that happens to you?

Anyway, she hadn't wanted to leave the house where she lived with her folks. Vincent drove over and fetched her. They went on the date, and after an hour or so she stopped talking about this thing and they'd had a good time.

A couple of months later they got the guy. Arrested, charged, arraigned, the whole show. But there was a problem. Vincent heard about the problem from Angela. There was a hitch with the warrant, some administrative thing, and all of a sudden the guy's arrest was invalid, and the guy was out on the street again. And the girl he raped? She committed suicide. Angela didn't know the girl any better then than she had when the attack had taken place, but it cut her up bad. She was inconsolable for a while. She went on about how she could have spoken to the girl, befriended her, been there for her. I mean, hell, she lived down the goddamned street. All it would have taken was a three-minute walk and a knock on the door. Maybe, just maybe, if she'd done that, the girl would still be alive.

Vincent told her no, that's not the way things work. But then he started thinking. He started wondering about the people on the street. He started wondering about their thoughts, their intentions, their motivations. He started to get it into his head that maybe things were not *just that way*. How that resulted in him becoming a cop he was never sure, but it was a watershed, a point of change. He spoke to Angela about it and she was all for it.

You'd make a good cop, she said. *You get decent money, a good pension. It's a career, Vincent, something that you can raise a family behind.*

It seemed to make sense. He went for it. The academy loved him, and he got a kick out of the fact that he was actually good at something for the first time in his life.

A natural. That's what the instructors said. *Vincent Madigan is a natural.*

And it started out fine, but then it went bad—and it went bad in proportion to the number of times he found his hands tied. Just like those guys must have felt when their rapist walked and the vic killed herself.

You can do only so much good, people said. *We ain't here to save the world. The world is too messed up for anyone to save it. This is damage control, that's all. This is the best it's gonna get, and if you're hoping for any more then you're in the wrong line of work.*

That's when things had changed. The slow, insidious undermining of faith in the system. The loss of faith becomes a sense of resentment, bitterness, a deep-seated frustration that founds a sense of disillusionment. You doubt the system, then you doubt yourself, and that begins an unforgiving deterioration in self-belief. *If I could have been so wrong about my career, what else could I have been wrong about? My marriage? My ability as a father?* And swift on its heels comes the effort to replace all that exists with something else. A mistress instead of a wife. Another child that your wife knows nothing about. And then the desire for more money creeps in. *If only I had more money I could . . .*

And then comes the day.

The day.

Vincent Madigan, seated there at his desk, remembered it now as if it were yesterday. Monday, January 16, 1995. The day it all turned inside out. The day he made the decision. The day he met Sandià for the first time. Of course he had known of the man beforehand. Madigan had been in the Manhattan Gangs Division, and anyone in Gangs knew of Sandià, if not personally then professionally.

That had been the day everything changed.

The drinking started a month later, maybe less. The pills soon after. A little more than a year and things were irreconcilable between him and Angela. A year later they were divorced. He'd already been seeing Ivonne for three years, Adam was eleven months old, and in that moment it seemed that everything was right again. He had never loved Angela. Not really. Not the way he loved Ivonne. And Cassie, his first child, the daughter he had with Angela? She was a girl. A beautiful, wonderful girl, and that was the worst thing of all. That was like wrenching out the very center of his soul. He bonded with Adam, but not the way he had with Cassie. That made him feel guilty and cheap. Made him feel like a liar. But he knew it was all of his own making, and he knew he couldn't fight for custody of Cassie. Nevertheless, he tried. He drank less, he cut down on the uppers that kept him going, the downers that let him sleep. But the world got to him again, and other things happened, and the guilt kicked in, and all of a sudden Adam was two years old, getting on for three, and he and Ivonne were seeing each other less and less frequently, and even when they did speak they didn't really speak. They shouted, they screamed, and that started Adam screaming. And the kid was supposed to be out of diapers, but he was such a freaking wreck he would wake every night, his bed soaking, his eyes swollen red with crying, and Ivonne was telling Vincent to *get the hell out of here you drunken son of a bitch, you asshole, you useless druggie piece of shit . . .*

And so he went.

Madigan closed his eyes and took a deep breath. He tried so hard not to think of these things, but this was it. This was the deal now. This is where he was, and he had carried himself here without anyone's help.

Except Sandià.

Sandià wanted him messed up and drunk and out of control.

Sandià wanted him in the palm of his hand. Sandià wanted to play him for advantage any which way he could.

Sandià. That was where the problem had started, and that's where it had to end. He had to get out of Sandià's business dealings. He had to get away from the man. The money would serve a purpose, but only to get Sandià out of the picture.

Madigan looked back at the pictures of Maribel Arias in the file before him. She was a pretty girl. Twenty-nine years old, her head in a Dumpster, her body cut up and left in trash bags behind North General Hospital. What had she done? Had she done anything? Why had she been murdered? Why cut her up? Why separate out her head and her torso and leave them in two entirely different locations? Too many questions, and—as always—too few answers.

Madigan took a photocopy of every document in the file and returned it to Faber.

"How's it seem to you?" Faber asked.

Madigan shook his head. "Could be anything. Psycho, contract, ritualistic, sacrificial, religious, ex-lover on the rampage. Like Paul Simon said, there's fifty ways to leave your lover."

"Well, I sure as hell hope I never have a girlfriend pissed enough with me to do that."

Madigan thanked Faber and headed back to the office. Before he left again he typed a quick e-mail to Bryant. *Good ID on girl and mother. Melissa and Isabella Arias respectively. Am following up potential connection to murder of girl's aunt, Maribel Arias. Questions around area of residence, also back to Harlem Hospital to see if the girl has had any visitors.*

He hit SEND and stood up to get his jacket. Even as he did so the phone rang.

"Vincent, it's Bryant. Got your e-mail. Walsh has come back with something as well."

Madigan felt something cramp in his lower gut. Was he afraid? "Shoot."

"He managed to track down one of Fulton's associates. The guy was probably off his head on crank, but he did say a couple of things that Walsh is going to follow up. First, from what Fulton told his buddy, the money that was taken from the Sandià house was the proceeds of a bank job. Anyone spending that stuff . . . well, we're gonna know about it within a couple of hours."

Madigan took an audible breath. He knew now precisely what

Sandià had meant. *The money is no use to whoever took it. Start spending that money and they'll get no farther than the next 7-Eleven.*

"You okay, Vincent?" Bryant asked.

"Sure, sure . . . Got a little indigestion . . ."

"Anyway, here's the other ballbuster. This guy . . . hang fire a moment . . ." The sound of rustling paper. "Richard Moran, that's his name. Anyway, he said that Fulton was hired for this job by some guy, went to check it out and there were two others on the payroll, presumably Chuck Williams and Bobby Landry. That ties in with the ballistics and crime scene info on the storage unit shootings, the fact that there must have been a fourth man, and from what this guy is saying he was the one who put the job together—"

"What about the fourth man?"

"Well, this Moran character says that the fourth man was a cop."

Madigan stopped breathing. There was an awkward, tangible silence between him and Bryant.

Suddenly he spoke. He had to. "You are bullshitting me."

"Hell, Vincent, it's some crank cooker. And he got it from some guy who was no better. These guys talk crap to each other most of the time, and the rest of the time they're talking worse crap. The bank money thing interests me, but as you can imagine, Walsh has got a big hard-on for the cop connection."

"He's taking it seriously?"

"He has to, Vincent, he's IA. This is what he does. I agreed to have him help out on this thing. Better to have him inside pissing out than outside pissing in an' all that, but now he's got a legit reason for sticking his nose anyplace he wants to on this."

"What, because some junkie says some other junkie said that a cop was involved?"

"Hey, hey, don't take it personally. We all feel the same way about these scumbag dealers and whatever. You can't lose sight of the game here, my friend. You can't lose sight of why you're doing this in the first place. Jesus, you've been around long enough to know that these assholes will say anything to impress one another, and most of it is BS. Anyhow, do what you gotta do on your end, and leave Walsh doing whatever he's doing. You guys shouldn't cross paths much anyway. Let me know if you find anything on this other murder, the kid's aunt, okay? You think there's a connection here?"

"I don't know, Al. I don't know. Give me some space and I'll come back to you."

"For sure, Vincent. For sure."

The line went dead.

Madigan hung up the phone.

He leaned back in his chair and closed his eyes. He breathed deeply—three, four times—and all he could hear was Bryant's voice . . .

Well, this Moran character says that the fourth man was a cop . . . says that the fourth man was a cop . . . fourth man was a cop . . .

All of a sudden the world seemed terrifyingly small, and there was pressure from every direction.

It was a good ten minutes before he moved. And when he did he knew he had to get a drink, a drink and a couple of Librium, a couple of anything just to get rid of that feeling, that terrible, terrible feeling that it was all going to end like this.

And he thought of the kids again—Cassie, Adam, Lucy, Tom. But Cassie figured large, larger than all of them, and he realized that of all of them—of all the people he knew, all those who knew him—the one that he hoped would never discover the truth was his daughter.

And then he thought of Melissa Arias—eight years old, lying in Harlem Hospital with a fist-sized hole through her little body.

Maybe I deserve it, was the thought he had as he left the precinct house and started toward his car.

Maybe everything that happens now is my own inevitable justice for all the shit I have caused.

And then a final thought.

Okay. So be it. But if I go, then Sandià is going with me.

30

WILDWEED

*T*his is who I am.
  I am the fourth man.
  I am the one they are looking for.
  I stand in a restroom stall. I am sweating profusely. I don't even know what time it is. I have forgotten which bar I am in. I think it might be dark outside, or getting dark. Dusk maybe. Something like that.
  I am supposed to be over at Harlem Hospital. I am supposed to be in Maribel Arias's apartment on East 118th between Lexington and Third.
  But I am not.
  I am here.
  Taking a ride on the Black Train.
  Jesus fuck Jesus fuck Jesus fuck Jesus fuck . . .
  Fuck.
  What the hell am I doing now?
  I gotta go home and change. I gotta clean myself up and get back out there. I gotta find out if whoever killed Maribel put Melissa in the Sandià house, and if they made Isabella disappear . . .
  And the Sandià money came from a bank?
  And Fulton knew this?
  How the hell did I not know this? How the hell did that one get by me, when some asshole druggie crackhead like Larry goddamned Fulton knew about it?
  I am losing the edge. I am losing the game by inches.
  And who told Fulton about the money? Who did he speak to? How many people other than this guy, Richard Moran, knew that Fulton was doing a job with a cop? And did he tell anyone the cop's name? Is there someone out there who knows that Larry Fulton, Bobby Landry, and Chuck Williams were doing the Sandià house with a cop called Vincent Madigan?

137

And which of those people are gonna hear about the three dead guys in a storage unit off of East 97th and put two and two together?

Up to my neck and sinking fast.

I need another drink.

31

SENSITIVITY

Walsh left with two other names. A second *compadre* of Laurence Fulton, a man by the name of Bernie Tomczak, and Karl Benedict, the 158th Precinct arresting officer on Moran's possession beef. Walsh had bullshitted Moran. He didn't know whether he could make the bust go away. He needed to do whatever it took; he might need Moran again, and—with Fulton dead—Moran would have to play his part in confirming that a cop was the fourth man on the Sandià heist.

With this information it had become an entirely different case. A case that Walsh could legitimately pursue within his official brief. A crooked cop. A cop that set up a robbery of a drug dealer's house, the proceeds of that robbery seemingly the earlier proceeds of a bank heist. Which bank, well, Moran hadn't been privy to that info. Walsh didn't want to make a big noise about the bank robbery connection. *It'll bring the feds in*, he told Bryant. And Bryant had backed his call. *Play that down*, he told Walsh. *I don't want the feds here any more than you do. Hell, dealing with you gives me enough of a headache.*

Play that down was the phrase Bryant had used, and Walsh had read it both ways. Bryant was working with him, making things as straight as he could. IA dealt with the department's dirty laundry. That was bad enough. To have that laundry hung out to dry in public was another issue entirely. Irrespective of the precinct, a bad cop was a bad cop. It reflected on the department, not the divisions or the units or the precincts. It made the whole NYPD look bad. And this was robbery and multiple homicide. This wasn't some rookie taking a twenty to lose a traffic violation ticket. This was murder.

First of all, Walsh went out to the 158th. He asked after Karl Benedict. Fortunately Benedict was on duty and in the building. Walsh waited in the foyer, wondered which way the conversation would go. He was soon to find out.

Benedict, suspicious at first, curious why IA from the 167th would want to talk.

"I need you to drop a charge," Walsh told him.

"Drop a charge? What charge? Who is it?"

"Guy called Richard Moran. You were the arresting officer on a possession beef, and it needs to go away."

Benedict—early thirties, five years in the department, smarter than he looked—smiled and shook his head. "I don't just make possession busts go away, Detective Walsh."

"I can get him later for something bigger and hand it to you."

"I can do my own work."

"I know you can, but I got this guy here and he's cooperating with me on something big . . . something very big . . ."

"You're IA, right?"

"Yes, I told you."

"So something big for you is gonna be something on a cop, right?"

"I can't say."

Benedict nodded. He looked down at his shoes, looked back up at Walsh. "Think we're done here, Detective." He started to turn.

"Yes, it's a cop," Walsh said. "But bad. Multiple homicide . . . maybe."

"That so?"

"Looks like it."

"And Moran is your CI?"

"Unofficially."

"And you made him a deal already?"

Walsh didn't say anything. He maintained Benedict's gaze, direct and unerring.

Benedict looked at his shoes again. "Tell you something, Detective Walsh . . . Way it works, as far as I can see, is that you already owe me for this."

"I can see that."

"You already got one of my busts thinking that his charge is gonna vanish, and when he comes on back in here he's gonna shout for his lawyer. He's gonna tell his lawyer that he made a deal with you. And that lawyer's gonna be all over me like a bad case of something."

"This works the way it works. We're playing the same game here."

Benedict stepped closer. He lowered his voice. "I'll tell you how I think it works. How I think it works is this . . . You come here and tell me you need me to do something. I listen to you. I understand your predicament, of course. And believe me, I am sensitive to your situation, Detective Walsh, and I am also the only person who can fix this." Benedict paused. He seemed to be taking pleasure in this. "Taking everything you have told me into consideration, I guess you know what am I thinking?"

"You're thinking you want something in return."

Benedict smiled.

Walsh had predicted the way this conversation would go. He was self-assured. He was in control. "What you got?"

"I got an officer-involved shooting review a week on Monday," Benedict said.

"And what do you need?"

"I need it postponed for a month . . . No, better make it two."

"And is this your first review on this case?"

"Third and final."

"Postponed already?"

"Twice."

"And you want me to get it postponed again?"

"That's the deal. You get the OIS review postponed for two months and I'll drop the bust on Moran. Then you got your informant and I got what I need. Everyone walks away happy."

Walsh looked at the man. He was IA. He could get an OIS review postponed with a phone call. He had no intention of letting Benedict know how easy it would be. He had his trade-off.

"Okay," Walsh said.

"You're gonna fix it?"

"I am."

Benedict extended his hand. Walsh took it.

"I get word that the review is postponed and Moran's paperwork takes a vacation."

"Deal."

"Deal." Benedict let go of Walsh's hand. "Good doing business with you."

Benedict turned and walked away.

Walsh watched him go, and then he left the precinct house and headed back to his car.

He sat for a while. He turned the radio on, anything to drown his thoughts, but it merely served to irritate him. He thought about what he'd just done, how smoothly he had done it. It had been necessary. This was the way the game went, this was the field, and these were the moves. He was good at this. This was his territory. There were lines. There were spaces between the lines. You recognized where those spaces were, and you used them to your advantage.

From his pocket he took the slip of paper upon which he'd written Bernie Tomczak's name and address. That's where he was headed now. Some other buddy of Laurence Fulton, someone who'd known something about this house that Fulton and the rest of the crew had robbed. He would speak to Tomczak, find out if he knew anything beyond what Moran had already told him.

Walsh started the engine and turned the car around. Tomczak's place was up on East 128th near the Harlem River Drive. It was a good half hour through the early-evening traffic, more if there was gridlock. That gave him time to consider his situation, to consider his next move, the move beyond that, and to see the different possibilities that could arise from the play he was making. Maybe he was a natural. Maybe, after all was said and done, this was what he was really meant to be doing.

32

CITY IN PAIN

The woman had made an effort. There was no question about
that. Her apartment was in the same kind of rundown tenement building as that of so many others in this neighborhood, but
once inside, Madigan could see that Maribel Arias had done her
best to leave the world outside the walls. Nevertheless, the world
had found her, and that world had cut her head off and left it in a
Dumpster behind an empty store eight blocks northeast of where
he now stood.

The super had let him in. The remnants of crime scene tape were
still adhered to the frame of the outer door, but Faber and whoever
else was interested had been and gone.

Evidently there was nothing of further consequence here.

Madigan found pictures of the daughter, Melissa. There was no
question in his mind as to her identity. With her was a woman
who looked very similar to the pictures of Maribel in Faber's case
file. This was undoubtedly Isabella, the missing mother. He took a
seat in the small kitchen. He held the picture there in front of him
and looked at the three faces. One dead, one hospitalized with a
gunshot wound, one missing. This was the Arias family as he knew
it. The girl's father? No idea. Isabella Arias was more than likely
unmarried, and if not then at least estranged, or she wouldn't be
using her own family name. There was no record of his name save
in Isabella's memories.

Madigan left the picture on the kitchen table and went through
the remainder of the apartment. Cheap ornaments, cheap furnish-
ings, cheap artificial flowers in a plastic vase on the windowsill in
the bedroom. She was fighting against a tide. The tide had pulled
her under and she'd drowned.

Madigan felt sober, as sober as possible under the circumstances.
Seeing the woman's apartment had cleared his head somewhat.
Seeing her apartment made her real, and that reality occasioned
another reality, and yet again one more. It resulted in a slow

acceptance and appreciation for his situation. He was in a corner, but he was still on his feet, could still punch well for his weight. He could drop now, or come out fighting. It was going to be smart-fighting, using his mind more than his fists. Come out like a dockyard slugger and he was screwed. This had now been elevated from checkers to backgammon.

So where now? How did he find out what had happened to Isabella Arias? The hospital. See if the daughter had received any visitors, if anyone had requested permission to visit. Didn't matter what situation you were in, if your kid was sick, you were going to want to see them, to be there, to do anything and everything you could. Unless you were Vincent Madigan, of course. If you were Vincent Madigan, it was a long-shot that you were even going to know about it until well after the fact.

Madigan took the photo from the kitchen and left the building. He let the super know he was done on the way out, thanked him for his help.

"They find out who killed her?" the super asked.

Madigan shook his head. "Still going."

"Hell of a shame. Real nice girl. Her sister too."

"You knew the sister?"

"Sure, knew her as good as Maribel. She was over here with Melissa all the time. Real nice people."

"Have you seen Isabella since Maribel was murdered?"

"Sure. She's been here a couple times. Think she wanted some bits and pieces, stuff that the kid left here, maybe something to remember her sister by."

"How'd she seem?"

"A mess. Helluva mess. Usually so cheerful, both of them, and then this happens." The super was dismayed. "Jesus, what the hell is this world coming to, eh?"

"When was the last time you saw Isabella?"

"What are we now? Wednesday, right? Saw her Monday evening, maybe eight, eight thirty. She was here for twenty minutes, no more, and then she was gone."

"Her daughter wasn't with her?"

"Nope, no daughter." He paused. "Come to think of it, I haven't seen Melissa since we heard of Maribel's death."

"How did Isabella seem then . . . on Monday night."

"The same. Looked a wreck. Looked like she'd slept in her clothes, and that is just not her, you know?"

Madigan gave the super his card. "You see her again you call me. She may be in danger, and I need to get her under some sort of protective watch."

"You think someone was after the pair of them?"

"We don't know," Madigan said. "We really don't know. But I have to make sure that if someone was after the two of them then they don't get to Isabella."

"She's a tough lady. She has her own mind. I'll tell her what you said, but there's no guarantee she'll call you."

"I appreciate that, but you just tell her I'm on her side, interested in her welfare . . . and her daughter's too."

"Sure thing."

Madigan left then, headed to the car and turned back up toward 135th Street and the fastest route to Harlem Hospital. If Isabella Arias had heard of her daughter's condition—from a friend, a contact, even read it in the city papers—then there was little doubt in Madigan's mind that she would make an effort to see the girl. What mother could possibly leave her child in a hospital bed and not attempt to see her?

The roads were clear and Madigan made good time. He parked behind the hospital, put a police notice behind the windshield so as not to get towed, and headed inside. He knew where he was going, but the receptionist called him back, asked for ID, said that Melissa Arias had been moved to another unit.

Madigan didn't want to ask why.

The receptionist sensed his alarm. "She must be doing better," she told Madigan. "She was in ICU; now she's in the Rehabilitation Ward. They wouldn't have transferred her if they didn't reckon she was going to pull through."

Madigan's first emotion was one of relief, but his second was one of alarm.

His thoughts went back to the Sandià house, the possibility that the girl might have seen something.

Madigan followed the signs to the Rehab Ward, found it down the corridor and to the right of ICU. Melissa was still being drip-fed a half dozen ways, but there was no tube in her nose or mouth, and she seemed to be breathing unaided.

Madigan stood there and listened to her. Her eyes closed, her body motionless. She was so utterly, utterly frail.

He felt uncertain then, of what he didn't know. He needed to sit down. He fetched a chair from an adjoining room. Seeing the girl again had unsettled him. He had felt sure of what he needed to do, and now doubt had once again crept in.

The sound of her breathing, the almost unreadable flickering of her closed eyelids, the *drip-drip-drip* of glucose and saline and painkillers. The same age as Lucy, sure, but Madigan could see nothing but Cassie at eight years old, how fragile and delicate and perfect she had seemed to him . . .

Madigan looked up as something moved in the corner of his eye. Out there in the corridor. He frowned, got up. He felt unnerved, scared even?

She was walking away. A nurse. Looked like a nurse—same pale blue tunic dress. Madigan called after her.

"Excuse me? Nurse?"

The nurse glanced back, and Madigan caught her profile.

He started to walk faster.

She heard his footsteps quickening. She started to walk faster herself, and all of a sudden Madigan was sure. Absolutely sure.

"Isabella," he said. "Isabella Arias?"

She glanced back once more, and he saw the wide eyes, the fear present in them, and it was then that she started to run.

"Shit," he said. "Oh shit." And then he was running too, down along the corridor, down past the other Rehab Ward suites, and Madigan knew where she was headed, the *Fire Exit* signs flashing by on the edge of his field of vision. He heard the alarm go, and he knew she was around the corner and had wrenched open the door to the stairwell.

Another nurse appeared at the doorway of a room.

"False alarm!" Madigan shouted. "Get the thing switched off!" His hand was on his badge and he flashed it as he went by.

"Do it!" he shouted over his shoulder.

He was through the fire escape door then, and he could hear her down below, hear her footsteps on the concrete stairs, and he was shouting, "Isabella! Isabella! Stop! I can help you! I am here to help you!"

But she kept on going, and already Madigan was beginning to feel the tension in his chest, the light-headedness, the intense cramp in his gut as he barreled down another flight of stairs and almost lost his balance.

He grabbed the handrail and took another narrow corner of the well, and down he went—another flight, and yet another—and from the sound of her footsteps he believed he was gaining on her, and it spurred him on. And then he could see her hand as she took another corner two flights below. Madigan sped up, barely kept his footing as he went down another three, five, nine steps. His heart was pounding. His breath came short and fast. He felt sick. He believed his heart would burst in his chest before he ever managed to catch her, and then he had his gun in his hand and he was shouting, "Goddammit! Stop running, for Christ's sake! Stop running or I'm gonna fucking shoot you!"

It was another two flights before he caught her.

He was breathing heavily, almost unable to stand, and Isabella Arias was backed up into a corner of the well, her face varnished with sweat, her eyes wide, her mascara streaked across her upper cheeks, her hands clenched in tight fists. She looked like a cornered animal, ready to unsheathe claws and strike back any way she could before she died.

"Isabella Arias," he gasped, and he held his gun in such a way as she could see it without aiming it at her directly. "You run again I'm gonna shoot you in the goddamned head, okay?"

She said nothing. She glared at him.

"You understand me?"

An almost imperceptible nod of the head.

"Okay, okay . . . so calm the hell down. I am not here to arrest you, all right? I am not here to take you in. I came here to see your daughter—" Madigan tugged the last two prints of Melissa out of his pocket. "See?" he said. "I am trying to find out who shot her, okay? This is what I am doing here. Nothing else. I need to talk to you. You can help me find out what happened."

Isabella looked at him with disdain and contempt. "Screw you," she hissed through her teeth.

"I know you lost your sister . . . and now this has happened . . ."

"You are police," Isabella snapped. "You are police. You people don't care what happens to us . . . You are just pigs . . ."

Madigan lowered the gun further. He was still breathing heavily, still feeling the tight fist of tension and nausea in his chest. He looked at the woman, and he saw fear and hatred and anger and pain and grief and a thousand other things.

And he felt it.

He felt it good.

He stepped back and closed his eyes for just a second, but that look in her eyes went right through him, and for a second he didn't even know his own name . . . he just felt the piercing nature of her stare, and he was no longer anonymous, no longer in-conspicuous, no longer a ghost . . .

Madigan looked back at her and he could see himself. He could see what he had become, and it terrified him.

"I am here to help you," he repeated, and the words came out slow and staggered. *I. Am. Here. To. Help. You.*

Isabella Arias sneered contemptuously. "People like you," she said, "are only ever interested in helping themselves."

Madigan could not reply.

"My sister is dead . . . murdered by that bastard. And now my daughter is shot and lying in a hospital, and there is nothing I can do to protect her . . . And you think I don't know about the police . . . You think I don't know he is paying you to always look the other way . . ."

"Who are you talking about? Who murdered your sister?"

Isabella Arias—fierce and scared, her eyes wide, her hands clenched in fists, her whole body shaking with rage and hate—just looked back at Madigan with utter contempt.

"Fuck. You," she said, emphasizing each word so precisely. "You cannot help me. No one can help me. He will find me and he will kill me, and then he will kill my daughter . . . And there is nothing anyone can do to stop him . . ."

33

SECRET FIRES

It did not take a great deal of time, nor a great deal of work, for Walsh to find Bernie Tomczak. He was in a bar no more than three or four blocks west of the 167th, and when he saw Walsh come in the door his eyes went this way and that. Bernie could not have known that Walsh was looking for him, but Bernie knew cops.

"Jesus," Walsh said when he sat down across from the man. "Who the hell did you have an argument with?"

Bernie said nothing. He shook his head.

"Hey, I have nothing on you," Walsh reassured him. "I spoke to a couple of people who spoke to a couple more, and I was told I might find you here." Walsh looked around the small, dimly lit watering hole. It was suitably *atmospheric* to obscure all manner of transactions, suitably crowded and noisy to minimize the chance of being overheard, but it was a dump. No question about it. Aside from nursing what appeared to be a fractured jaw, both eyes blackened, a map of tiny hemorrhages across the upper half of both cheeks, Bernie was also holding on to a glass of something or other.

"Can I get you another one of those?" Walsh asked.

Bernie nodded. "Sure, why the hell not? JD straight, no rocks, no water . . . And make it a big one."

Walsh got up and walked to the bar. He glanced back over his shoulder, and Bernie was already halfway to the door. Walsh took three or four strides and grabbed his arm.

"Bernie . . . seriously . . . I just need a word or two, that's all. I buy you a drink, we sit down, share a few words, I go away. That's it, no bullshit."

Bernie seemed to hesitate then. He appeared to be considering the odds. Wrench himself free and run. Lull Walsh into a false sense of security, catch him off guard again, and then run. Or just let the guy ask the questions and then leave him to his drink.

Bernie nodded. He chose the latter. He just didn't have the will or the strength to go haring down the street with a cop on his tail.

Bernie went back to the table, waited for Walsh to bring his glass of JD.

Bernie poured his drinks into one glass, leaned back and looked at Walsh.

"So who did the handiwork on your face?" Walsh asked.

"Is that what you came to ask me?"

"Nope."

"Then ask me what you came to ask me and fuck off."

Walsh nodded. "Larry Fulton," he said.

"What about him?"

"He's dead."

"Now, there's a surprise."

"You knew?"

"I know a lot of things."

"But you already knew that Larry Fulton was dead?" Walsh repeated.

"I knew Larry Fulton well enough to know that he was never going to be long for this world."

"So his death doesn't surprise you?"

Bernie smiled sardonically. "Nothing surprises me."

"Did you know anything about the job he was doing?"

Bernie reached forward for his glass. He took a sip. He kept his eyes on Walsh but Walsh saw nothing, not even a flicker to suggest that he might possess any information that was relevant. That meant nothing. Bernie, according to his sheet, was a gambler, and gamblers practiced implacability.

"Bernie?"

Bernie put his glass back on the table. "What's your name?"

"Walsh."

"You a detective?"

"Yes, I am."

"Which precinct?"

"167th."

"Hey, that's over here just a coupla blocks."

"That's right."

"So how come we've never crossed paths?"

"Should we have?"

Bernie laughed. "Hell, man, if it has a uniform, or ever had a uniform, I have crossed paths with it."

"Because I'm not in Vice or Robbery-Homicide," Walsh said.

"So what the hell are you?"

"Internal Affairs."

"No shit," Bernie said, and not only was there surprise in his voice, there was also a sense of curiosity.

"No shit," Walsh echoed.

"So what are you doing out here asking after me?"

"Working on a case."

Bernie smiled sarcastically. "No shit."

"So did you know anything about the job Larry Fulton was doing?"

Bernie sipped his drink again. "Do you know anything about me, Detective Walsh, Internal Affairs, 167th Precinct?"

"No, Bernie, I don't."

"Well, I'm gonna tell you something now, and this is for free. If I was the only person in the world who knew the answer to that question, and in telling you that answer we could bring peace to all nations, end all wars, solve world hunger, and bring about the second coming of Christ, I would put a pencil in each nostril and bang my head on this table before I uttered a single freaking word."

"You feel quite strongly about it, then?"

"I do."

"That's a shame."

"It is."

"You know why that's a shame, Bernie?"

"No, I don't, Detective Walsh. And though I know you're going to tell me, I feel a certain duty to inform you that I don't give a rat's ass why it's a shame."

"Just so we're on the same page, right?"

"Sure, Detective . . . just so's we're on the same page."

"Well, bear with me, Bernie, because this here is the deal. Larry Fulton is dead. So are two other characters, one by the name of Bobby Landry, another by the name of Chuck Williams. They got killed by a fourth man, and that man may or may not be a cop—"

Bernie's eyes widened fractionally.

"I got your interest now?" Walsh asked.

"Go on," Bernie said.

"Well, I was talking with a friend of mine called Richard Moran—"

Bernie laughed. "Shit, man, if you and Moran are buddies then I am the second coming of Jesus Christ."

"We're friends now, Bernie. Get me? Not yesterday, not this morning, but *now*."

Bernie squinted at Walsh, his eyes like a lizard. "What'd he get from you?"

Walsh waved the question aside. "I am interested in anything Larry might have said, Bernie . . . *anything* that Larry might have said that could help me. You understand what I'm saying?"

Bernie didn't move for a moment, and then he nodded slowly.

Walsh felt the air grow light and cool in his chest. This thing was moving even faster than he'd anticipated. Two guys from Fulton's file, and both of them had songs to sing.

"So you have a think for a moment, Bernie," Walsh said. "You have a think for a moment and see whether or not there's anything you might know about this fourth man. His name, perhaps, might be a good place to start . . ."

"And if I do?"

"Well, if you do, then maybe we could see whether there's some kind of arrangement we could come to."

"Like maybe the kind of arrangement you made with Moran?"

Walsh said nothing. His heart was going at some rate. He was listening to himself, and he could barely believe what he was hearing. He had walked himself into a conversation that would give him the identity of the fourth man.

"Then, Detective Walsh, I believe there might be a strong possibility of a mutually beneficial arrangement . . ." Bernie left the statement hanging in the air between them.

Walsh—once again—said nothing. He didn't know what else needed saying. All of a sudden he was in the perfect bargaining position.

"So we each have something to work with here," Bernie Tomczak said.

"Seems we do, Bernie. So start talking."

Bernie shook his head. "Not the way it works, my friend," he said. He winced for a second, held the flat of his hand gingerly to the right side of his jaw, and then he seemed to relax. "You tell me what you want to know. I see whether I know it, or if I can find out for you, and then I tell you what I want in exchange."

"You already know what I want, Bernie. I want to know who Larry was working with."

"Whether it was a cop, and if it was a cop then what is his name, right?"

"Right."

Bernie took a deep breath and exhaled slowly. "Well, I'm gonna give you something for nothing, Detective Walsh. I can tell you right now that there wasn't no cop involved in whatever Larry was into. Larry Fulton working with a cop? Not a prayer, my friend, not a freakin' prayer. If you think Larry did business with a cop, then you didn't know Larry."

Walsh felt his heart miss a beat. He couldn't understand what he was hearing. Fulton was *not* involved with a cop? If that was the case then what the hell was Moran talking about? And what had he himself now reported to Bryant?

Walsh shook his head. "Hey, wait a minute. Moran said—"

"Moran is a liar," Bernie interjected, and then he smiled. "Okay, so I'm a liar too, but Moran is a worse liar."

"Why should I—"

"Believe me before him? I'll tell you why. Because I'm not trying to make a deal with you, see? Whatever the hell Moran asked for, well, you shouldn't give it to him because he sold you a truckful of bullshit man, a truckful of bullshit. Larry Fulton would no more work with a cop than I would."

Walsh leaned back. He didn't know who to believe, and he didn't know what to think.

"However," Bernie added, "if the thing we were talking about earlier is still a goer, then maybe I can give you something that will point you in the right direction."

"A name?"

"That's right, Detective, a name."

"Whose name?"

"The name of the man who put that job together."

"The dealer's house robbery—"

Bernie shrugged. "I don't know where they robbed, or whose house it was, but I know it was the job Larry was doing."

"How do you know it was the same one?"

"Because he told me where the money was coming from, and he told me who had it."

Walsh raised his eyebrows.

Bernie smiled. "Let's just say that by the time Larry Fulton and his crew got to that money, all the hard work had already been done. Make sense?"

It did. It made perfect sense. The hard work was the original bank robbery. "Yes," Walsh said, certain that he and Bernie Tomczak were now talking about the same job.

"So I give you the name of the man you should talk to—and whether he was the one who whacked Larry and the others is another thing entirely—but I give you the name of the man who put that shit together then you and I got a deal, right?"

Walsh hesitated. "What do you want?"

"I want you to make something disappear for me."

Walsh closed his eyes. He inhaled, exhaled slowly. They all wanted something to go away.

"What did you do?" Walsh asked. "What happened?"

"Not for me," he said, "for my brother. And it ain't no big deal."

"You brother?"

"Right, my brother, Peter. It was all a mistake. He was holding something for someone, just a .22. It was a popgun, a peashooter. No big deal. Anyway, he gets himself pinched, and I need it to go away. That .22 is in your evidence lockup, and if that was to vanish then there wouldn't be no case."

"You expect me to make evidence vanish," Walsh said.

"You can do anything you want to, Detective. Or you can not. If you don't, then you ain't getting nothing from me. You know this shit. This shit goes down all the time. You can't play ignorant with me. You either want this guy's name or you don't."

Walsh was suddenly agitated. An edge of panic had entered into his emotions, but he was nevertheless still driven. It was as if Bernie Tomczak had drawn him into a web and there was no way out but to carry on through.

"And if I agreed," Walsh said, "then what's to say I wouldn't just renege on the agreement? You tell me what you know, and then I don't carry through on the deal. I just go on like I never even spoke to you. What's to stop me doing that?"

"Nothing," Bernie said matter-of-factly.

Walsh leaned back. "You're gonna have to trust me?"

"I am. Just like you're gonna have to trust me to give you the right information."

"But I'm gonna follow up on whatever you tell me and if it turns out to be bogus then we don't have a deal."

"Right."

"So we're still back to you trusting me to hold up my end of the deal."

"We are."

Walsh looked down, noticed his hand was shaking.

"Looks like you need a little time to think this over," Bernie said.

Walsh put his hand in his jacket pocket and then withdrew it. For a moment it looked like the back wall was ever so slowly sliding to the left.

"No," he said. "You need to tell me what you know."

"You're sure, Detective?"

Walsh didn't answer.

"You're agreeing with me that if I tell you what I know, then you and I have a deal. I give you a name and my brother's .22 goes walkabout never to be seen again . . . That's the deal we're agreeing right here and right now?"

"Yes," Walsh replied, the word like a bullet from his lips.

"Then I'm gonna go find out what I need to find out," Bernie said. "Give me your card."

"You're going to tell me now, right?"

Bernie shook his head. "No sirree, not now."

"What the fu—" Walsh started to get up out of the chair.

"Sit down, Detective," Bernie said. "We're gonna do this, then we're gonna do it my way. I go away, I check something out, I call you, you tell me that .22 has disappeared, and then you find out what you need to know."

"This is bullshit," Walsh said. "This is fucking bullshit. No fucking way. This is not what we agreed. You tell me what you know now, or the deal is off—"

Bernie reached for his glass and drained it. He pushed back his chair and stood up. "We have an agreement," he said quietly. "And the agreement stands. I find out what you want to know, you take care of my problem."

"Screw you," Walsh said.

"Oh, I don't think you got a choice Detective Walsh," Bernie said, and from his jacket pocket he withdrew a phone. "This," he said, "is one hell of a phone. It takes pictures, it keeps me reminded of my appointments—and I have *so* many important appointments. Know what I mean? And it also has a recorder on it." He smiled. "The whole conversation, my friend, the whole fucking conversation, and that—whichever way you look at it—gives me a straight flush. You are on tape, my friend, agreeing to make that evidence disappear, and that—as we say in the trade—is a home run—"

Walsh lunged forward and tried to snatch the phone from Bernie's hand. Bernie took two steps back, turned and started walking.

Walsh was up and past the table. He closed on Bernie rapidly, faster than Bernie expected, had Bernie by the arm, was wrenching him back.

And then he was aware of people moving, people who knew Bernie but did not know him, people who looked a great deal more threatening and dangerous than Bernie ever could.

"You need some help there, my friend?" someone said, and in their tone was such an undercurrent of aggression that Walsh just let go of Bernie's arm and stood there.

"I think we're good here, thanks," Bernie said. He looked at Walsh. He smiled. When he spoke his voice was hushed but emphatic. "I have everything I need, Detective Walsh. You are in the deepest shit imaginable. You agreed to removing evidence. You made the trade-off. You said what you said. This winds up in the press, you are screwed. Only way out is to hold up your end of the deal. You make the .22 vanish, you get the name you want, you bust that case wide open, and you're the hero. You let me down, my friend, and this is the end of your career. If you're lucky, you can look forward to security duty at J.C. Penney."

There was nothing Walsh could do. People were looking. People were waiting for him to back down, to let Bernie go whichever way he was going.

Bernie Tomczak took a step. Walsh didn't move. Bernie took another, yet another, and then he had made it to the door. He glanced back. Walsh caught the fleeting sly smile on his face, and then he was gone.

Walsh stood there for a minute, and then he sat down heavily.

The sense of overwhelm he felt just sucked all the air right out of him. He could barely breathe, couldn't think straight at all. He had no choice. He had to make the .22 disappear. Dead if he did, dead if he didn't. Moran, Benedict . . . and now Bernie Tomczak? What the hell was he playing at? What kind of game did he think he was playing?

He could not believe the situation he had created for himself, could not believe the words that had come from his own lips.

34

SORROW KNOWS

She had finally looked at him in the stairwell, and there must have been something in his eyes that gave her sufficient pause, because she just said, "Get me out of here," and Madigan did. She didn't say a word as Madigan drove, and he drove her somewhere where no one connected to Sandià would know her. Madigan had asked her nothing—not where she'd been living, not where she got the nurses' uniform, not who she thought had shot her daughter or killed her sister.

He asked her nothing.

Every once in a while he just said a few reassuring words. *It's okay. I can help you. You can tell me what happened. Take your time. Take your time.*

Marion's Continental at 354 Bowery was a place that easily forgot you after you'd left. It was a place with history, and Madigan had forgotten how many times he'd fallen drunk in the restroom and been carried out. The sink in there had been replaced four times, broken beneath the weight of couples screwing. Despite it being a haunt of celebrities and aesthetes, their no paparazzi policy kept away a great deal of people—the kind that wanted to see celebrities, the kind that wanted to be seen. Madigan found it sufficiently discreet and off the usual beaten tracks to suit his needs. It was a good place to remain anonymous. In all the years he had frequented Marion's he had never seen another cop there, and that was reason enough to patronize the place.

It was here that he got Isabella Arias into the men's restroom and helped her clean up her face, got her to straighten up the skirt and T-shirt that she'd been wearing beneath the nurses' tunic. No one interrupted them for the few minutes it took, and Madigan was grateful for this. Once done, he sat with her at a corner table, watched her drink brandy, and waited and waited for her to wind down and settle out. Her eyes were red-swollen. Looked like she'd cried for a week without a break.

At one point Madigan glanced at his watch. It was late, past eleven, and he had no idea how long they had been sitting there.

Eventually she spoke. "I am hungry," she said. "Can we go somewhere to eat?"

"We can eat here," he said.

"No," she replied. "I do not want to stay here. I want to go somewhere else."

Madigan didn't resist. He helped her up, walked her out, opened the car door for her, and walked around to get in. He drove toward home, back to the Bronx, and he kept on driving until he found a regular haunt up on Grand past the park and the museum. He came around again and opened the door. She looked at him but said nothing. She was exhausted. He could see it in every step she took, every motion of her body. Tired and weak and scared and confused. He tried to imagine how he would feel if it had been Cassie there in the hospital, a bullet wound . . .

He tried to remember if the bullet had ever been recovered from the room where the girl had been found.

Had Crime Scene ever come back to him on that?

He should know that. He should know such a thing with certainty, and yet he could not remember.

He opened the restaurant door for her. The place was dark and empty. Here they would go unnoticed.

"Thank you," she said, and she stepped ahead of him and walked to a booth in the far right-hand corner.

As Madigan passed the bar he caught the attention of waiter. "Menu?" he asked.

The waiter nodded, brought menus to where they were sitting and asked for drink orders.

"Just water," Isabella said. "No more alcohol."

"Jack Daniel's," Madigan said. "Double, straight."

She ordered chicken-fried steak, a bowl of fries, a salad. Madigan had the same because he couldn't be bothered to read the menu. The food came. It was acceptable. She cleaned the plate and Madigan ate more than he wanted, but he felt he needed it. He could not recall the last time he'd eaten a meal of real substance.

She wanted coffee. The waiter brought it. Madigan ordered another double, and she raised an eyebrow.

"I am bulletproof," he said.

"You are driving," she replied.

"I am, yes, but I am a cop, and if I get stopped they won't bust me."

She shook her head disparagingly.

There was silence for a moment, and Madigan broke it with, "Your sister is dead."

Isabella looked at him. Had she not cried for a week, she perhaps would have cried some more.

"And your daughter is in the hospital. She's going to be okay, you know?"

Isabella said nothing. Her expression didn't change. Madigan believed she would look like this for a long time to come, as if a twelve-wheel hauler had driven through her life and left nothing but wreckage.

"They told you this?" Madigan asked.

"No," she replied. "I have been there three times. I went back yesterday and she was gone. I didn't know where they had taken her. I was panicking. Then I asked someone and they told me she had gone to the Rehab Ward. Apparently if you go to Rehab you're unlikely to die." She spoke matter-of-factly. She was holding everything inside as best she could. She was trying to convince herself that she could cope with this, that she was strong enough to deal with everything that was happening to her, with what had happened to her daughter, her sister.

Madigan watched Isabella's hands. Her fingers fought with one another, her fists clenching, unclenching, her knuckles white with the tension of what she was feeling.

"Where have you been since your sister was killed?"

She shook her head.

"It's okay. You don't need to tell me," Madigan said. "I went to your apartment. I spoke to the super. He said you had been there to collect a few things."

Again there was not a word.

"I am not the person who is investigating your sister's death," Madigan went on. "I am investigating the robbery of a house where your daughter was staying—"

Isabella looked up suddenly. Her eyes flashed angrily. "She wasn't *staying* anywhere!"

"She was being held there, right?" Madigan asked.

No response.

"Someone kidnapped her . . . Someone came to your apartment

and they took her, right? You or she tried to hide in the bathroom. You had your foot against the bottom of the door, but you couldn't stop what was happening, and they took her. Is that what happened?"

"They took her," Isabella said. "They took us both. We escaped in the street, but they came after us and they caught her . . ."

She bowed her head. Her hands went to her face. Her whole body rose and fell sharply as she stifled her sobbing.

"They caught her and took her to this house?" Madigan asked, and then he reached forward and touched her arm.

She moved her arm suddenly, rejecting his effort to console her, his attempt at reassurance. And she leaned back against the wall of the booth and simply glared at him.

"Who the fuck are you?" she said. "What do you want from me?"

"I want to help you find out what happened to your sister, and I want to see you get your daughter back."

"Why? What does it matter to you? You're a cop. You people are just as corrupt as . . ."

She didn't finish the sentence.

"As corrupt as who?" Madigan prompted. "As corrupt as the people who took your daughter?"

"I don't want to talk about it."

Madigan didn't press the issue. She would talk in her own time, or perhaps she would not.

"Do you have somewhere to stay?" he asked.

"I have an apartment I cannot go to. I have people looking for me . . ."

"You can't go on staying where you've been staying already?"

"I have been in a motel. I have very little money. I can stay somewhere one more night, maybe two if it's cheap—"

"I have a place," Madigan said.

She smiled sarcastically. "That's nice for you."

"I have a room you could use."

She looked at him. Her expression was suspicious, untrusting, even vindictive. To her, Madigan merely symbolized much of what was wrong with the world.

Madigan raised his hands. *Look*, he was saying. *No tricks.*

"What?"

"A room. I have a house. I live alone. You can stay there for a while. It isn't great. In fact, it's really crappy. But no one will look for you there and you will be safe."

"No way . . . What the hell are you—"

"It's real simple, Miss Arias. I know who robbed the house where your daughter was. I think I know who shot her. I certainly know who owns the place . . ."

"You know who shot my daughter?"

"I *think* I know," Madigan repeated. "I'm not sure. But I am sure about whose house it is, and I just want you to tell me why your daughter was kidnapped and why she was being held there."

"I can't trust you," Isabella said. "What makes you think I can trust you more than anyone else? . . . In fact, in my experience cops are the very last people you should trust—"

"You should trust me because I think we want the same thing," Madigan said.

"And what would that be?"

"We want our lives back the way they were."

"What the hell is that supposed to mean?"

"It means that you want your daughter back, and you want to go on with your life without people looking for you. And I want to get back some things that I have lost."

"Such as?"

"It doesn't matter. What matters is that you can go stay in a motel, and when you run out of money you can walk the streets and take your chances, or you can trust me enough to let me give you a room. For one night, two maybe—however long you want —and you tell me what you know and I will go and take care of all this bullshit."

She paused, and once again she looked at him just as she had in the hospital stairwell. She looked *through* him. That was the way it felt.

"You're serious," she said.

"I am."

"So who *are* you?"

Madigan smiled sardonically. "I was somebody, and then I was nobody, and now I'm trying to be somebody again."

"Are you for real? Who talks like that? This isn't a game, mister. These are real people, and my daughter is in a real hospital, and someone took my sister and they really cut her head off. You think you're in a movie or something?"

"Sometimes, yes . . . Actually, yes, sometimes it does feel like a movie." He slowly shook his head. He looked down at his empty glass and wanted another drink so badly. Then he looked up at her and smiled. "But the movie's gotta end sooner or later, right? People gotta go home. People have lives to get on with . . ." His voice trailed away. For the first time he wasn't thinking about every word he was saying. He'd lied so much and to so many people, about so many things, and every word he uttered had to be weighed and considered just in case he said something that he really shouldn't. What kind of a life was that?

"You're some crazy son of a bitch," she said, "and you want me to come stay in your house?"

"No, not really," Madigan replied. "I don't know what the hell I want most of the time, but I think you and I can help each other, and I think that if we do this together then maybe we have a chance. I think if you try and handle this alone then you're going to wind up like your sister—"

"Enough!" Isabella snapped. "You have no business—"

"I do," Madigan interjected. "I have a great deal of business talking about this. Your sister is dead and your daughter is shot, and I think I can help you get through the other side of this alive. You? Out there on your own? If this is who I think it is . . . If what I think is going on here *is* actually going on, then I'd give you a day, maybe two, and then I'll be pulling bits of you out of Dumpsters all over the city."

Isabella Arias just looked at Vincent Madigan and there was nothing she could say.

"Tell me who killed your sister," Madigan said.

"I don't know."

"You know the people who came to your apartment, the people who took Melissa?"

"Their names? No, I don't know their names."

"But you know who they work for?"

No response, and that was response enough.

"Sandià, right?" Madigan asked. "Melissa was in his house, and if Melissa was taken by Sandià's people, then Sandià must also have ordered your sister's murder. Am I getting close here?"

Again, there was nothing in the woman's expression to even suggest she was hearing Madigan.

"And if they wanted you as well, and you're on the run, then they must have been holding on to Melissa as a hostage until you turned yourself in to them. Is that right?"

Silence. Her expression was implacable.

"And if they want you that badly . . . bad enough to kill Maribel, bad enough to kidnap your daughter, then you must know something that makes them awful scared . . ."

"Sandià," Isabella said. "That's what he calls himself. That's what people call him. To me he will only ever be Barrantes . . . Dario Barrantes . . ."

Madigan's reaction was immediate. He had not heard anyone speak that name for years.

Isabella nodded. "You know Barrantes, eh?"

"Yes," Madigan replied. "I know Barrantes."

"And you know why they call him Sandià, the Watermelon Man?"

"Yes, I do."

"And you associate with him? You are one of his people?"

"No," Madigan said. "I am not one of his people. But I am a cop in the Yard. Everything that happens here has something to do with Sandià, and so we cross paths."

Isabella closed her eyes and leaned back.

Madigan was aware of his own heartbeat. He was aware of his pulse. He was frightened, tense, agitated. He didn't know this woman. He didn't understand how these things had happened, but he believed he had been drawn irreversibly into some dense and complex web. Always on the outskirts, the edges, and now?

"Okay," she said, interrupting his train of thought.

"Okay?"

"I will come with you," she said. "That's what you want, right?"

"Yes," Madigan said, almost involuntarily. "That's what I want."

"So let's go."

"Why the sudden—"

"Why? Because you are right. I have enough money for a day, maybe two, and then I am dead anyway. If you work for Barrantes, then so be it. I am dead if I go with you, dead if I don't. And if I don't do something, *anything*, then he will kill Melissa . . ." She hesitated, breathed deeply, seemed to gather herself from the edge of another abyss of grief, and then she was sliding along the seat of the booth and gathering up her jacket.

Madigan rose to his feet. And now? That had been his earlier thought. Now what? Now there was no turning back. He had come this far, and—just as he had considered earlier—the only way off the rollercoaster was to reach the end. You pay your money, you take your choice.

She walked to the door. He followed her as quickly as he could, pausing only to drop enough money on the bar to cover their check. She remembered where he had parked the car and she went on ahead. He caught up with her, grabbed her arm and slowed her down. She did not resist, did not protest. He released her and she walked beside him.

He drove slowly, five miles below the speed limit. They were at his house within ten minutes, and even as he drew to a stop against the curb he knew that something was wrong.

"Wait here," he said, and he switched off the internal light before opening the driver's side door. He had his gun in his hand, and he walked past three houses to the left of his own and cut through an alleyway into the rear of the block. He came up behind his own place, saw a silhouette against the rear door, and crouched down. The silhouette was still, and then it moved, and then the silhouette put a cigarette in its mouth and flicked a lighter.

Bernie Tomczak.

Madigan—wondering what the hell Bernie Tomczak was doing in his yard—came up out of nowhere and stuck his gun in the small of Bernie's back.

"Jesus freakin' Christ, Vincent!" Bernie exclaimed. The lit cigarette dropped from his lips and bounced in a shower of small sparks on the stoop.

"What are you doing here, Bernie? Come to stick me?"

"Jesus, no, Vincent. What the hell? Christ Almighty, you damn near gave me a freakin' coronary."

"Answer the question, Bernie . . . What are you doing here?"

"I came to speak to you. Someone came and visited me. A cop. He came and told me some shit, and I think you should know about it."

"If you're bullshitting me, Bernie . . . If this is some kind of—"

"Vincent, just shut the fuck up and listen to me, okay? I got something that's gonna help you."

Madigan frowned. He remembered the kicking he gave Bernie just two days earlier, the kicking that had left him looking like a car crash victim. And then he put two and two together.

"You want me to make your debt to Sandià disappear, right?"

"Right."

"Well, Bernie, you better have something really valuable . . ."

"Vincent, just let me in the goddamned house already. What the hell, eh?"

"Okay, Bernie, but I got someone with me."

"You on a hot date, Vincent?" Bernie smiled like a fool.

"No, I am not on a hot date, you asshole. I got a witness out in the car, and I need you to go easy, okay?"

"Whatever you say, Vincent. Whatever you say."

"Jesus, I don't know why the hell I have anything to do with you."

Bernie raised his hand and gently tapped Madigan's cheek. "Because you love me, Vincent, and you'd miss me if I was gone."

Madigan took out his keys and opened the back door. "Get in there," he said. "Make some coffee. I'm gonna go get the girl, and no bullshit, okay?"

Bernie Tomczak went on in the house and Madigan closed the door behind him.

Back around the front he told Isabella that there was someone else inside.

"Who?" she asked.

"His name is Bernie Tomczak. He's an old friend. He's okay."

She seemed unperturbed by the fact. She got out of the car and followed Madigan.

It was then, as Isabella Arias and Bernie Tomczak came face-to-face, that Madigan saw something in Bernie's expression. He did well to hide it, because Isabella seemed to see nothing, but Madigan caught it. A fleeting shift, like the shadow of a cloud across a field, and then it was gone.

Madigan told Isabella to take a seat in the front. He went out back to the kitchen after Bernie.

"What?" Madigan asked him.

Bernie frowned.

"I said no bullshit, Bernie. What the hell is it with the girl?"

Bernie shook his head. His face dropped. "She's the dead girl's sister, right? The one Sandià's looking for?"

"How the hell do you know about that?" Madigan asked.

"Oh man, you have no idea how much I know about . . . no freakin' idea at all."

35

ANGER BLUES

"**I** don't know why," Walsh said. "I don't know what the hell happened . . ."

"Oh come on, Duncan, you expect me to believe that? You, of all people? Mister Organized, Mister Predictable, Mister Routine . . . Are you even listening to yourself?"

"Carole, I am tired. I am really fucking tired, okay? I can't use this right now—"

"Well, use it, Duncan, damn well use it. Because what you've just told me . . ." Carole Douglas threw her hands up in dismay. "Christ, I can't even get my head around this." She got up from the edge of the bed and walked to the door. She started to open it, and then she turned back. "No," she said emphatically. "We talk about this, and we talk about it now."

"Carole—"

"You are Internal Affairs, Duncan. You are *Internal* Affairs. You are supposed to be the cleanest of the clean. You are supposed to be beyond reproach. You are supposed to be setting the example that everyone else follows but you make a deal with some guy to get a possession bust lifted. And then you make a deal with the arresting officer to get a review postponed. And then you make another deal with some lowlife scumbag to make some evidence disappear, and he records it on his cellphone! Jesus Christ Al-fucking-mighty, Duncan, what the hell were you thinking?"

Walsh got up. "Enough!" he yelled. "Enough already, Carole! I told you because I need to work it out. I told you because I trust you. I told you because after six years together I figured you'd be understanding enough of this situation to maybe just listen to what I have to tell you and then try and help me figure something out with being a judgmental bitch—"

"Screw you, Duncan!"

"And screw you too, Carole!"

They stood there then, seemingly for an hour, a day, one on each side of the bed just glaring at each other.

Walsh was the first to look away, but it was merely to move from the edge of the mattress and walk around to the other side.

"I am sorry—" he started.

Carole stood there for a moment, and then she shook her head. "Jesus, Duncan, what the hell are we going to do?"

He shook his head.

"I mean, who is this guy? The one with the cellphone?"

"His name is Bernie Tomczak. He's a crook, a lowlife, a gambler . . . Whatever, it doesn't matter."

"And what did you say exactly?"

"I told him I needed some information . . . important information regarding the possibility that a cop might have been involved in a robbery and a multiple homicide, and he said he had a name for me, and then he asked me to get a weapon out of evidence and get rid of it. Some bust his brother was up for, and if the weapon disappears then there's no case."

"And you agreed to this?"

Walsh nodded. "Yes, I agreed."

"And he has you recorded on his phone."

"Yes."

Carole closed her eyes and shook her head.

Walsh heard her exhale resignedly.

"So you didn't even get the information you wanted?"

"No," Walsh replied.

"How the hell—"

"You weren't there, Carole. You weren't part of the conversation. If you'd been there—"

"Duncan, if I'd been there you wouldn't have even been in a conversation with this guy. Jesus, what in Christ's name was going through your mind?"

"The purpose, that's what. The reason I do this. The reason I went to IA. It's the job I do, Carole. That's why I was there."

"But speaking to some scumbag in a bar someplace . . . How the hell is that IA business?"

"It's a long story."

Carole sat down on the edge of the bed. She grabbed her purse, took out her cigarettes and lit one. "Well, I've got time, Duncan. I've got time, and I think you better tell me what the hell is happening here."

Walsh sat down. He'd not smoked for two years, three perhaps, but he took one of her cigarettes and lit it. His hands were shaking. He felt a cold sheen of sweat across the entirety of his body. He'd not felt this way since his second month in Homicide when an OIS review had gone bad for him. For a while he was up for an accidental shooting of a civilian, but then Ballistics came back and it was not his gun. That had been the roughest three days of his life. Until now.

He told her then. He told her about the robbery of the Sandià house, the deaths of the couriers, the three DBs in the storage unit, the shooting of the little girl, the missing mother, the murdered aunt, the reason he was involved in the first place. He told her about Madigan and Bryant and his meeting with Richard Moran, how that had led to Officer Karl Benedict and the OIS Review, and lastly his meeting with Bernie Tomczak. And when he was done she was silent for some time, and then she looked at him and said, "This Madigan guy? He's okay?"

"Okay? What do you mean, okay?"

"He's a good cop?"

Walsh smiled. "Is there such a thing?"

"Hey, listen to yourself. We don't have time for anything but trying to figure this out. Now, tell me, who is Madigan and what's he like?"

"He's in Robbery-Homicide. He's a good cop. Has a good arrest rate."

"Is he straight, or does he take money?"

Walsh frowned.

"What?" Carole asked. "You think I don't know about you guys? You think I don't know how much money changes hands? For Christ's sake, Duncan, I'm not naive. Why the hell do you think there's an Internal Affairs Division in the first place?"

Walsh raised his hands in a conciliatory fashion. "Okay," he said. "Madigan? I think he does what he needs to do. I'm sure he's not the best, but I don't think he's the worst either."

"So you could talk to him in confidence? You could tell him what happened and he wouldn't go running to the police chief or something?"

"You what? You're suggesting I tell Madigan about this?"

"Duncan . . . you *have* to tell someone. You think I know what to do about this? Well, I don't. And you certainly don't have some magic solution up your sleeve. You have to get some help on this. You have to get this sorted out. If you don't . . ."

"Okay, okay, I got it," Walsh interjected. "But Madigan?"

"Well, is there someone else? Someone better? I don't care who you talk to, but it can't be the squad sergeant, and it sure as hell can't be the precinct captain. And you tell your superior in IA and it's all over. Your career is finished, and then where the hell will you be, huh? They'll kick you out on your ass with nothing."

"I suppose Madigan's the best bet," Walsh said. "He's as good as anyone else."

"So we're agreed. You talk to this Madigan guy, and see what he says, okay?"

Walsh didn't speak.

"Okay, Duncan?"

"Okay, okay, yes . . . I'll speak to Madigan."

Walsh had let the cigarette burn down in his fingers. He stubbed it out in the ashtray, and then he turned to Carole and he shook his head.

"I'm sorry for putting you through this . . ." He reached out his hand toward her.

"Duncan, I am so pissed with you. Jesus Christ . . ."

He touched the sleeve of her robe.

"Don't touch me," she said matter-of-factly. "Don't touch me right now, Duncan."

Walsh withdrew his hand. He sat there on the edge of the bed, and he felt sick—from the cigarette, from the arguing, from the situation he had created, from the thought that Bernie Tomczak was out there somewhere with a recording of their conversation on his cellphone.

He got up. "I'm going to take a shower," he said.

Carole didn't reply.

Walsh left the bedroom and made his way down the hall. He closed and locked the bathroom door behind him, and then he sat on the edge of the tub and put his head in his heads.

"Dumb, dumb motherfucker," he whispered, and he hoped like hell that Vincent Madigan could be trusted, and that he would have something useful to say about this nightmare situation.

He knew little about Madigan, save that he'd been a cop for twenty years and had seen pretty much everything there was to see.

If Madigan was the wrong choice then he—Duncan Walsh—was screwed.

36

KEYS TO THE KINGDOM

Bernie stayed in the kitchen.

Madigan went upstairs and ran a bath for Isabella. He tried to fix up the spare bedroom. He moved boxes out of there into his own room, found some clean sheets, made up the bed. He hadn't had anyone stay since . . . Hell, he couldn't even remember the last time someone had stayed.

When he was done he went down and got her. He showed her the bathroom, where the towels were kept, the soap, a spare robe, and he showed her where she could sleep once she was done.

"I have to deal with something with this guy downstairs," he said. He stood there on the landing, aware of the fact that six inches beneath his feet was three hundred grand of Sandià's money.

Isabella stood in the doorway of her room. She had a strange expression on her face.

"What?" he said.

She shook her head. "Nothing."

"Okay, so take your bath and get some sleep."

Madigan turned to the stairwell.

"Hey," she said.

"What?"

"I'm not going to say thank you."

"I don't expect you to."

"Good, because I don't trust you. I don't know who you are and I don't know why you're doing this, and I might wake up in the morning and find out . . ." She paused, shook her head. "I might not even wake up, right?"

Madigan took a deep breath. "Take a bath. Get some sleep. We'll talk in the morning."

He didn't wait for her to reply. He went on downstairs to deal with Bernie Tomczak.

*

"You know Larry Fulton, right?"

Madigan frowned. "Know the name, yes. Who is he?"

Bernie smiled wryly. "You ain't such a good liar, Vincent."

"Say what you have to say, Bernie, and then get the hell out of my house."

"You are a mean-mouthed son of a bitch at the best of times," Bernie replied. "Jesus Christ, you act like someone's pissing down your back and tellin' you it's raining."

Madigan got up from his chair at the kitchen table. He fetched down a bottle of Jack Daniel's and two glasses from a cupboard, poured drinks, took his seat again.

"I had a conversation this evening," Bernie said.

"Good for you."

"A very, *very* interesting conversation."

Madigan took a deep breath. He didn't know whether to hit Bernie Tomczak right then and there or wait a moment before he hit him.

"With a man called Walsh."

Madigan's thoughts stopped dead. He made such an effort to display no change in his expression, but the surprise was evident in his eyes.

"You want me to tell you about my conversation with Detective Walsh, Internal Affairs Division, 167th Precinct?"

"Sure, go ahead and tell me about your conversation."

"You gotta be nice, Vincent. You gotta be nice, okay?"

Madigan smiled as best he could. "I'll be nice, Bernie."

"Well, Detective Walsh went to see a guy called Cutter Moran. You know him?"

"Nope."

"Calls himself Cutter. His name is Richard, but he and Larry were close like family. He was Cutter, Fulton was Bone, like after that movie, you know?"

"Yes, I know the movie."

"Well, anyway, whatever, the thing was that this Walsh went to see Moran, and Moran told him about me, so Walsh comes looking for me and he finds me. And he tells me a real interesting story about a job that was pulled on one of the Sandià houses, and how a bunch of people got messed up real bad and then Larry Fulton and a couple of his *compadres* get themselves all shot to pieces in some storage unit someplace, and this Walsh is looking for the fourth man. Seems this fourth man was not only in on the Sandià heist, but he killed Fulton and the other two and took off with all the money . . ."

Bernie Tomczak paused.

Madigan's heart was like an angry fist trying to break out through his rib cage. His entire body was freezing cold, and yet covered in a slick layer of sweat. He felt the glass sliding through his fingers and he set it down on the table before he dropped it. He couldn't look Bernie in the eye, but he had to, he *had* to show nothing, to give nothing away . . .

"You okay, Vincent?" Bernie asked.

Madigan nodded. "Tired, Bernie. Long, long day. You got much more of this story to tell me?"

"Do I need to tell you any more of it?"

"What does that mean?"

Bernie shook his head. "Nothing, Vincent . . . It means nothing."

"So, like I said, go on and tell me whatever you have to tell me and then get out of here."

"You said you'd be nice."

"This is nice. Piss me off any more and I'll get mad."

"Jesus Christ, you really do spend your whole sorry life in a bad mood—"

"Bernie . . ."

"Okay, okay . . . Take it easy. Anyways, so this Walsh is telling me all of this, and then he tells me that Cutter Moran has told him that guy number four is a cop. Can you freaking believe it? A cop robs one of Sandià's places, wastes the three guys in a storage unit, and then takes off with the money. Jesus, the balls on this guy! So I'm listening and I'm listening, and I'm thinking all the while what I gotta do, and then it comes to me. It comes like a blinding flash of freaking lightning. Something like this comes once in a lifetime, Vincent, once in a lifetime. So here we are . . . you and me . . . and we got some shit to sort out, right?"

Madigan takes a drink. He empties the glass. He pours another. He waits.

"Right, Vincente?"

"Don't call me Vincente."

"What? You think I'm scared? You think I don't have some insurance, Vincent? I have insurance, my friend . . . I have plenty of insurance. We're gonna make a deal, you and me. We're gonna make a deal and it's gonna be really straightforward, and when you hold up your end of the deal then I am gonna just disappear out of your life, out of New York, and you will never see me or hear from me again."

Madigan knew he was cornered. This was a turn he had not predicted. Christ, which turns had he predicted? Any of them?

"So what is it?" Madigan asked.

"I got a debt to pay," Bernie said. "As you know all too well."

"How much is it?"

"One eighty."

Madigan's eyes widened. "A hundred and eighty grand. You are out of your fucking mind!"

"What? You don't think what I know is worth that much?"

"No, Bernie, I don't know how you got into that much of a hole with Sandià."

"Oh, screw you, Vincent. You know the score. You get on a winner and it's never gonna end, and then you get on a loser and you have to keep on because it has to end sometime. It's the freakin' game, man. It's the life. You know the beat here."

Madigan raised his hand.

Bernie fell silent.

"Have another drink, Bernie."

Bernie took the bottle and refilled his own glass.

"I could take you out the back here and shoot you in the head and no one would be any the wiser."

Bernie smiled. "You could, but you ain't going to."

"Why, Bernie? Tell me why I'm not going to do that."

"Because my insurance is your insurance."

"Enlighten me."

"This cocksucker, this Walsh guy . . . man, he'll be onto you in no time. He's around and about the Yard, he's talking to people, and it isn't gonna be long before he runs into someone who gives you up. He'll find someone like me, but it'll be someone who's already paid off the vig to Sandià and doesn't give a crap about you, and then where are you? He'll tell Walsh that you're working muscle for Sandià, and all of a sudden Walsh is putting two and two together and coming up fours. You've pissed off enough people, Vincent, and you know it—"

"So what you got?"

"I got a soundtrack of my interesting conversation with Detective Walsh."

"You got what?"

"What I said. I got a recording of my conversation with Walsh. Had my phone with me, and there we go . . . The wonders of modern freakin' technology, right?"

"And what did he say?"

"Well, first things first, just to show that I'm on your side, I told Walsh that Cutter was full of shit, and that the fourth man was no more a cop than I am. That threw a spanner in his works, I'll tell you. Second thing is I give him the impression I know who set up the robbery. I tell him that I know who he's really looking for. He gets all excited. He's got a freakin' hard-on for this, you see? I tell him I know who it is, and I tell him I want something in return."

"And he agreed?"

"He did."

"What did he give you?"

"Told me he'd lift a .22 out of evidence and get rid of it." Bernie smiled as best he could with his mess of a face. "He promised me a doozy, Vincent, a freakin' doozy."

Once again, Madigan could not hide the change of expression on his face. He looked away for a moment, turned back, and said, "A doozy? Who the hell talks like that, Bernie? Jesus, you sound like a schmuck."

"Whatever, Vincente—"

"I thought I told you not to call me that."

"Hey, will you just shut the hell up? This is important. I got this recording, okay? I got a recording of your IA dickhead making a deal with me, and I got it good and safe. So even if whatever the hell you're doing goes belly-up, you got some insurance against getting the bust. And what I want in return is for you to sort out my business with Sandià."

"A hundred and eighty grand."

"Yes, indeed. A hundred and eighty grand."

"And this recording is where?"

"On my phone in a safe place."

"You're asking me to trust you, Bernie."

"Yes, I am."

Madigan leaned back. He had not had time to think. Now that he had time, he didn't know what to think. He was in a box. But there was a good side. If what Bernie Tomczak was telling him was true—and there was no reason to doubt it—then he did indeed have some insurance against Walsh. It just left the matter of a hundred and eighty grand . . .

"I'd want to hear that conversation, Bernie."

"Well, I figured you might say that, and though I don't trust you enough to bring you the phone and play it for you, I did take a moment to just write it out for you." Bernie reached into his inside jacket pocket and took out a sheet of paper. He straightened it out on the surface of the table and slid it across to Madigan.

Madigan read through it quickly. Bernie possessed neither the skill nor the intelligence to fabricate such a thing.

Looks like you need a little time to think this over.
No. You need to tell me what you know.
You're sure, Detective? You're agreeing with me that if I tell you what I know, then you and I have a deal. I give you a name and my brother's .22 goes walkabout never to be seen again . . . That's the deal we're agreeing right here and right now?
Yes.

"So?" Bernie said.

"So what?"

"So do *we* have a deal?"

Madigan smiled. "You recording me now, Bernie?"

"Hey, Vincent, just because you beat the living crap out of me on Monday morning doesn't mean we're not friends anymore."

"You are such a wiseass."

"Yeah, Vincent, I know, but this time I think I maybe did it right, wouldn't you say?"

"You did good, Bernie. I have to give you that. You did good."

"So we got a deal?"

Madigan nodded. "Yes, Bernie, we have a deal."

Bernie raised his glass. "To absent friends," he said. "God bless Larry Fulton and his crackhead buddies, dumber than fence posts but good in a fistfight."

Madigan raised his glass too. By the time he'd set it down he'd already worked out what to do.

37

SLEEPING IN BLOOD CITY

*I*sabella Arias.

She sleeps upstairs.

I imagine that if I hold my breath, I could perhaps hear her breathing.

The thing I could not say, the thing I could not fathom, was how much she reminded me of Ivonne.

That moment on the hospital stairwell, again as she looked at me out on the landing . . . the way she saw right through *me . . .*

I loved Ivonne.

I worshipped her.

She worshipped me in return.

And then I killed it all, like I killed everything before, like I will just keep on killing and keep on killing . . .

Everything you touch turns to shit, Vincent.

Everything you say is a worthless lie.

You think I don't see who you are, Vincent Madigan? You think I don't see right through your heart to the small black shadow that you once called a soul?

And now here I am. Dead if I do and dead if I don't. It's a web—thinly constructed, delicate, fragile—and yet supposed to support the burden I am carrying.

Who am I kidding?

Myself, that's who.

I think back to the moment in the bar. I could smell the shampoo from her hair, the soap from her skin. I can remember the way her eyes were red and swollen with grief, and how I felt when I looked down at this woman's daughter in the hospital bed.

There is no way for me to understand how she feels, and yet I am trying. I am trying so hard.

Bernie is gone. Bernie has left me with the transcription of his conversation with Walsh. I am going to try and defend my life with this.

And if I do? Then what? What will I have? A job I can no longer do, two ex-wives, an ex-mistress, and four children who would struggle to recognize me in a lineup . . .

That's what I'll have.

Is this what my life has amounted to?

Jesus Christ.

And if I don't? If it all goes wrong . . . more wrong than it is even now? Then what? Will I be dead, or in jail, or just wandering the wilderness with an ex-career to throw into the mix?

Shame there isn't a book you can read on how this stuff works.

Shame I didn't do it right from the start.

Hindsight: the cruelest and most astute adviser.

38

MOTHER OF EARTH

"You're sure that guy won't tell anyone that he saw me here?" Isabella asked.

She sat across from Madigan in the kitchen, the same table where Madigan and Bernie Tomczak had drunk and talked the previous night. It was early, a little after seven, and Isabella had made eggs for them both. She ate quickly, and ate everything in front of her. Madigan ate slowly, struggled after the third mouthful.

"He won't say anything," Madigan assured her.

She shook her head. In her eyes was confusion, despair, most everything that Madigan himself had felt the night before. He had slept for an hour, perhaps two, and had risen awkwardly, everything aching.

"You're going to have to decide to trust me," he said.

Isabella was silent for a while. She ate some more. She sipped her coffee. "This morning I woke up," she said, "and I was here alone with you."

Madigan frowned. "What did you expect?"

"I don't know . . . more trouble? That you lied to me? That you were working for Barrantes? In a way I was surprised to even wake up in the first place."

Madigan remembered that thought: *Surprised when I wake up every morning and find out someone hasn't killed me.*

"So you're alive, and there's no one else here. Like I said, you get to the point where you think that you can trust me, then I'll be ready to hear what you have to say."

"I'll need to go out," she replied, her tone dismissive of his statement. "I'll need clean clothes."

"I can get whatever you need. Tell me what you want, the sizes, and I will get them for you."

"And you have almost no food here. Do you actually live here at all?"

"I live here, yes."

"How long have you been here?"

Madigan shrugged. He tried to remember. He had moved in a month or two after his divorce from Catherine finalized.

"Two years maybe, something like that."

"Looks like you've been here two weeks."

"I'll get groceries as well."

"And what am I supposed to do all day?"

"Watch TV. Sleep. Get some rest, for Christ's sake. Do whatever you want, but you can't leave the house."

She didn't reply.

"I have to go to work," Madigan said. "And when I get back you're going to need to start talking. I need to know why your sister was killed, why Sandià had your daughter in that house—" He was cut midsentence by the change in her expression. "What?"

"Barrantes had my sister killed. She saw something, and he found out and he had her killed."

"Saw what?"

"She saw him kill a man."

Madigan's eyes widened. Sandià never did his own work. This was hard to believe, but Madigan believed it. It must have been very personal, indeed.

"Maribel had a lover. He was a good man. At least in his heart he was a good man. But he did some things, and he made some mistakes, and he crossed Barrantes, and Barrantes killed him."

"You know his name . . . Maribel's lover?"

"Yes."

"And Maribel told you that she saw Barrantes kill him?"

"She didn't need to tell me."

Madigan frowned. "I don't understand—"

"I was there too. I was there when he killed this man. We were both in the house, but Barrantes didn't know it. And then he found out later that we were there, and when he found Maribel he killed her and now he is looking for me . . ."

"What the hell? You *saw* Barrantes kill a man? You actually saw him kill someone with his own hands?"

"I saw Dario Barrantes put a screwdriver through a man's eye and kill him."

"When? And where did this happen?"

"It was a few days before Maribel was killed. We were both at her lover's house up on East 115th. Barrantes came there with two other men, and they held him while Barrantes killed him."

"And his name? Who was this man Barrantes killed?"

"His name was David . . . David Valderas."

"And Melissa—"

"Melissa was at school, and then after these men left I went to the school and took her, and we stayed with Maribel, and she was sure that Barrantes would never find out that we saw this thing happen."

"So how did he know?"

"I do not know how he found out, but then Maribel was killed and we couldn't stay in her apartment, and so we had to get out. We went back to my apartment for some things, but they came for us. Barrantes's people were hiding inside, and then when we went in they held us both . . ."

She stopped talking. Color rose in her face, her eyes welled with tears. She inhaled deeply, held her breath, and then she exhaled. Madigan opened his mouth to speak, but she raised her hand and he fell silent.

"And if you are working for Barrantes, then you know all that you need to know and you can kill me now. I am terrified. I am more terrified than I have ever been, but I will willingly give you my life if you do not harm my daughter further . . ."

Madigan reached out and took her hand. She withdrew it swiftly.

"If I worked for Barrantes, then I would already have known why he wanted you. I would already know why your sister was murdered. I would already know why he had your daughter. And you would already be dead. I do not work for Barrantes. I know him, but I do not work for him. Go on. Tell me what happened."

Isabella looked away. Tears filled her eyes and rolled down her cheeks. Every muscle, every nerve, every sinew was wrenched to its limit. She looked as if she would just burst at the seams.

"Melissa struggled free and locked herself in the bathroom. I could hear her screaming. They went after her, two of them, and I got away from the third one, the one who was holding me, and I went to help her. They managed to get her out, and then they took both of us down into the street, and that's when I ran . . ."

Tears dropped from her jaw line onto her T-shirt. She gripped the edge of the table as if to prevent herself from losing balance.

"I ran," she said. "I r-ran away . . . I left her be-behind . . ."

Madigan reached out and touched her shoulder. She rose from the chair, Madigan followed suit, and he held her for a moment.

She was rigid, unyielding, and then she seemed to fold and bend, and it took everything he possessed to keep her from falling to her knees.

"Okay, okay," he said. "You had no choice . . . I don't see what else you could have done . . ."

"I could have saved my daughter," he heard her say. "I could have stopped them taking my daughter . . ."

"But it was you they wanted. If you had stayed they would have killed you, and then they would have killed Melissa. I know Sandià. I know he would have done this, and then you would have both been dead. Right now you're alive. He doesn't know where you are, and he has to make sure Melissa stays alive, as she is his insurance against you saying anything to the police . . ."

Isabella pulled away from Madigan and looked up at him. She looked just as she had the previous night, as if her entire body was filled with grief, and it was simply finding any way it could to release the pressure of this burden.

"So by running away you have kept her alive . . . And now we can do something. Now we can get her back and we can finish Sandià . . ."

"Finish Sandià? You cannot finish a man like Sandià. Sandià will go on forever, and when he is finished there will be someone else to take his place."

Madigan was shaking his head. "He can be brought down, Isabella. Even a man like Sandià can be brought down."

"You really don't work for him, do you?"

"No," Madigan said. "I don't work for him. I work for myself now, and I am also going to work for you."

"He has hurt you as well?" she asked. "Barrantes has done something against you?"

Madigan didn't speak for a moment, and then he stepped back and held her by the shoulders. "I have to go now," he said. "I am going to be gone all day. If you need me you call my cellphone from the landline, okay? But do not leave the house, and if anyone comes here you do not open the door. You understand me?"

"Yes," she said.

"And you want me to get you some clothes?"

"Yes, if you can. Just a few things."

"Write them down for me," he said. "I'll get them, and I'll get some more food as well."

Madigan gave her a pen and paper. She wrote down what she needed. Underwear, some jeans, T-shirts, another pair of shoes.

"Anything will do," she said.

"Okay."

Madigan put on his jacket. "Under the bath is a .22-caliber revolver. It's in a cardboard box. If Barrantes's people come here . . . if they have somehow figured out where you are, do everything you can to get away. Go out the back and down the alley to the street. Take the gun with you. If they get in here or they come after you and you know they are going to kill you, then just kill as many of them as you can before they do."

Isabella said nothing. There was nothing she could say.

She followed him to the front door, and as he opened it to step out she looked at him with a different light in her eyes.

"I told you I was not going to say thank you . . ." Her voice faded. "I cannot trust you. You understand that?"

"Be safe," Madigan replied, and then he stepped out and closed the door firmly behind him.

39

BLACK HOLE

M adigan did not think as he drove. He did not want to think. This was a mess. An unholy nightmare of a mess. He'd believed it complicated—the situation he was in—but this? This was beyond complicated.

Arriving at the precinct he went on up to his office. He took an evidence bag from his desk drawer, wiped down his coffee cup, put it in the bag, and closed it up. He went back down to Evidence, nodded at the attending, went in back, looked up the Tomczak .22, and stuck it in the back waistband of his pants. He replaced the Tomczak bag with his own, and then left.

Now, irrespective of what Walsh might say or do, the fact remained that he had agreed to remove something from Evidence, that agreement was on record with Bernie Tomczak, and that precise something was now missing.

In his office, Madigan stripped down the .22, dropped the pieces into a Subway bag, folded it up tight, and put it in his inside jacket pocket. He would find a street-side trash can, and within a couple of hours that .22 would be lost somewhere amid the collected mass of garbage en route to the municipal dump.

Next item on the agenda was to find out all he could about this Valderas murder. East 115th. At least it was in the Yard. The case should have run out of here, the 167th, and that meant the files wouldn't be too hard to find.

Madigan had been seated for no more than five minutes before Walsh appeared in the doorway.

"Vincent," he said. "I wondered if you had a few minutes."

Madigan looked up at Walsh, frowned, leaned back in his chair. "What's up?"

Walsh seemed hesitant. He had his hand on the edge of the door. "Can I close this?" he asked.

Madigan knew what was coming. "Sure," he said, "go ahead."

Walsh closed the door slowly and quietly, almost as if he wanted no one to know he was doing it. He paused once more, and then he approached Madigan's desk and sat down. He closed his eyes for a second, took a deep breath, and said, "I have a situation, Vincent, and it is not a situation I have . . ." He shook his head, looked away toward the window.

"The case you're working, right?" Madigan asked.

Walsh nodded.

"The three dead guys in the storage unit," Walsh said. "The one . . . Larry Fulton . . . he had a friend, someone he knew, a guy called Richard Moran. You know him?"

Madigan thought for a moment. "Can't say I do." He could feel the tension between them. Madigan did not know exactly how much Walsh knew, and Walsh did not know that Bernie Tomczak had already spoken with Madigan.

"No mind," Walsh said. "Anyway, this guy Moran was a friend of Fulton's, and I went to see Moran. Moran told me something. He told me that the fourth man was a cop—"

"Bryant told me," Madigan interjected. "You really believe that?"

"Hell, Vincent, I don't know what to believe . . ."

Madigan didn't know where this was going. Walsh looked really distressed.

"I told this guy Moran that I would help him out with something if he gave me the information. Now I don't know whether the information he gave me was correct . . ."

"About the fourth man being a cop?"

"Right."

"So what makes you think it's not true?" Madigan asked.

Walsh shook his head. "That comes later. Something else happened. I made this agreement with Moran that I would help him out on a possession bust if he told me what he knew. He told me, and so I have to hold up my end of the deal otherwise any case I might build comes apart because Moran won't confirm it. Anyway, I go and see Moran's arresting officer on this possession thing. His name is Benedict. He's a uniform at the 158th. He tells me that he can fix this thing about Moran if I help him with something else. He has an OIS review. He's moved it twice, wants it moved again. So now I'm having to agree to that to get Moran's bust lifted . . ."

"But you said that this information from Moran was not good, right? If the info he gave you was bullshit then you don't have to get the bust lifted."

"Sure, sure . . . But I don't know if it's good or not, and that's not the worst of it."

"There's more?" Madigan asked, feigning surprise.

"There is," Walsh replied.

There was silence between them.

"So?" Madigan asked.

"What we say here stays here, right?" Walsh asked.

Madigan frowned. "What? You have to ask me that?"

"Okay, okay . . . Christ, Vincent, this is one hell of a mess. I've never been in a situation like this before . . ."

"So tell me what happened."

"You know a guy called Bernie Tomczak?"

"Yes," Madigan replied, knowing that his name was all over Bernie's yellow sheet. If he denied knowing Bernie he could so easily be caught out.

"I went to see him," Walsh said. "Moran gave me his name. Bernie Tomczak was a buddy of Fulton's too, and I tracked him down in some bar. I told him the whole story, and then he told me he wanted to make a deal."

"He wanted a bust lifted as well?" Madigan asked.

"Not specifically, no," Walsh replied. "He wanted me to get a weapon out of evidence, a .22 that his brother was busted for."

Madigan tried to look confused. "But you haven't done this, right? You haven't taken the .22 out of evidence. What's the problem?"

"He recorded the conversation."

Madigan paused. He looked at Walsh. The expression on the man's face was priceless. "He did what?"

"He recorded the conversation, Vincent . . . recorded everything I said. Everything about Fulton, about Moran, me making an agreement with him . . . And he denied that the fourth man was a cop. He categorically denied it, said that Fulton would never work with a cop."

God bless you, Bernie, Madigan thought. *God bless you, you dumb drunk gambling Pollock motherfucker.*

"Oh," Madigan replied. "Oh Christ . . ."

Madigan paused to think of the Subway bag in his jacket pocket, the pieces of the .22 inside it.

"I don't know what the hell to do, Vincent . . . I just wanted to—"

Madigan raised his hand. "Hold up there," he said. He got up from the desk and walked to the window. He buried his hands in his pockets, stood there in silence for a minute or so, his expression pensive.

"Okay, okay, okay," he said. "So Fulton does this job. He tells his buddy Moran that the fourth guy was a cop, but there's no evidence to indicate this. Bernie Tomczak denies there was a cop. But you made an agreement with Moran about the possession bust, and then you have this situation with the uniform at the 158th."

"Right."

"But the worst thing is the conversation you had with Tomczak has been recorded."

"Right."

"Recorded on what?" Madigan asked.

"His cellphone."

Madigan returned to the desk and sat down.

"So what do I do?" Walsh asked.

"You do nothing."

"Huh?"

"You do nothing. Absolutely nothing. You go on dealing with your regular caseload. You drop this storage unit thing. Drop it like a stone. I'll tell Bryant that I'm going to run it alongside the thing with the girl who was shot. The one in the hospital. They're one and the same case, for Christ's sake. It makes sense. I'll speak to Moran. I'll speak to Bernie Tomczak as well. I'll twist his arm somehow and get the phone off of him. You have to step away from this now. You're compromised. Anything you do has the potential to make the situation worse . . ."

"Vincent . . . Christ, I don't even know how this happened. If you can help me on this, it would be—"

"It's gonna be fine," Madigan said. "We look after each other, okay? We take care of things. We're on the same side here."

"I'll owe you, Vincent . . . Seriously, if there's something I can do for you—"

"I'm sure there will be, Duncan. I'm sure there will be. But don't worry about it for now. You go do whatever you have to do on your other cases. I'll take care of this thing, and if there's something I need from you to help out on it then I'll let you know. Otherwise, this conversation never happened."

"Vincent . . . I don't know what to say."

"Say nothing. You understand me? Don't say a word to anyone. Like you said before, what we say in here stays in here."

Walsh got up. He shook Madigan's hand.

Madigan walked him to the door.

"I won't forget this, Vincent," Walsh said.

"Neither will I," Madigan replied, and he opened the door for Walsh and watched him walk down the corridor to the stairs.

Even as Madigan closed the door, a faint smile on his lips, even before he had a moment to congratulate himself on the way this was playing out, his cellphone rang. He knew who it was before he looked at the screen. He pressed the green button.

"Yes," he said.

"You gotta come see him."

40

DESIRE

I *have all the pieces.*

Walsh is backed off. He has tied himself in knots around this thing, and he cannot move. He will do nothing on the storage unit murders. Not until I say so. Isabella Arias is an eyewitness to a Sandià murder, and no one knows where she is but me. Sandià will want to find her more than anything, but as yet he has not even spoken her name to me. He should have had someone at the hospital. How easy would it have been to find a nurse, pay her off, get her to report back to him regarding any visitors? Too easy. And David Valderas, whoever the hell he was, will be an out for me in the deal with Sandià. Bernie is on my side, God bless him. Jesus, who the hell would have expected that? Beat the guy half to death on Monday, and he comes back two days later as my savior. But then he wants out too. He wants his one-eighty debt to vanish, and then he can start over. Is that what we're all fighting for here? A chance to start over? Even Sandià . . . Not from his life, not to escape from who he is, but to be free of the Valderas killing. That was a mistake. A big mistake. People like Sandià should never get their own hands dirty. That's why they have people, people like me, people to break bones and dent heads for them. And then there's Moran, but Moran is unimportant, a sidebar to the main story. And if I make all these pieces fit together, and they tell the story I want, then I will be home free. No debt to Sandià, no connection to the robbery, and thus no implication in the murders of Fulton, Williams, and Landry.

Home free.

What could go wrong?

Everything, that's what.

Everything could go wrong, and if there is one thing I have learned by experience it's that everything that could go wrong will go wrong.

Never expected a smooth ride, but I didn't expect anything as rough as this.

You want something? You just have to desire it enough.
It's a tightrope.
Have to step careful now.
The drop is long and sudden and I would never survive it.

41

BAD INDIAN

Madigan couldn't help it. He had to take something before he went out to see Sandià again. Just a little something—three inches of Jack Daniel's to wash down a couple of Librium—and the edges wore off a little smoother and he felt grounded.

By the time he got out to Paladino he was less anxious. He felt settled in what he had to do. The game had changed, and changed fast, but it had swerved in his favor. Having Isabella in his house was a three of aces, but Walsh's confession and request for help was a royal flush.

Madigan believed that Sandià wanted nothing more than a progress report on what had been learned about the robbery, but when Madigan entered the room, there was something about Sandià's manner that told Madigan that he was there for a different reason.

"It's not possible," Sandià said.

Madigan walked forward, took a seat.

"It is not possible for someone to simply vanish into thin air."

"Who are you talking about?" Madigan asked.

"I am talking about a woman called Isabella Arias." Sandià smiled. "There, I've said it. My new policy. Tell the truth. Speak of things as they are. I need this Isabella Arias woman found, and I need her dead."

"Can I ask who she is?"

"She is the mother of the child who is in the hospital."

Madigan's nostrils cleared. The line around him, the parameter within which he could operate, had all of a sudden narrowed a thousandfold. The distance between himself and the sheer number of things that could go wrong had decreased dramatically.

"You need her dead," Madigan repeated.

"Yes, Vincent, I need her dead," Sandià said, and he came away from the window and sat on the other side of the desk. "And, yet again, I am speaking the truth. No hesitation, just the truth as it is." He smiled. "It is somewhat liberating."

"Can I ask why you need her dead?"

Sandià smiled. "You can ask, Vincent, but I will not answer you. Business is business."

Madigan nodded. "So I didn't ask."

"So tell me, my friend, what news of these people who took my money and killed my nephew?"

"I am working on it. I have spoken to a lot of people. I am getting closer—"

"But you have nothing specific."

"No, nothing specific."

Sandià shook his head. His expression was cold, distant. "Then you are of less use to me than I thought."

"Sorry?"

"Well, you say you have nothing specific, and at the same time I have discovered something very specific. That means that my intelligence network from outside the police department is better than the intelligence network you have inside the police department, and if that is the case then it means that you are redundant."

Madigan smiled. "Someone spun you a line."

"What? What do you mean?"

"You're telling me that you have some information that I don't have?"

"Yes, I am."

"About the fourth man, right?"

Sandià hesitated, and Madigan knew what he was dealing with immediately.

"The fourth man was a cop. Someone told you this, right?"

Sandià didn't reply.

"You have been told that the fourth man was a cop. Is that so?"

"You believed yourself the only bad Indian in the camp, Vincent? You think you're the only person who tells me what I need to know?"

"I'm the only person who tells you the truth, it seems," Madigan replied. He could feel his palms sweating. Had it not been for the Librium his heart would have been racing.

"What? You're telling me that it wasn't a cop?"

"Who told you this? Someone inside the department?"

"Who told me is my business, Vincent, you know that. You

would appreciate it if I gave out your name every time someone asked me how I learned of something?"

"Well, if this information came from inside the department, then it's already been contradicted. There are people involved here, people who want other people to believe certain things, and they have their own vested interests and motives, and they want certain people implicated who have nothing to do with it. The story you've been told is yesterday's story, and today's story is a different thing altogether."

"Vincent, I'm getting angry now . . . What the hell is this you are telling me?"

"I'm telling you that whatever you heard is old news. Leave this thing with me. I will find your man. It may be a cop; it may not be. Right now it looks like it isn't, but tomorrow everything could change again."

"Jesus Christ!" Sandià snapped, and he slammed the flat of his hand on the desk.

Madigan jumped, startled, but gathered himself quickly.

Sandià got up. He paced back and forth behind his desk, and then he slowed and stopped. He turned and looked at Madigan. Again Sandià held that distant expression, the absence of emotion, the absence of any real humanity. Suddenly the distance closed and his eyes flashed with anger.

"I need to know what happened, Vincent. I *need* to know what happened. You have any idea how this makes me look? I can't even keep hold of my own money. I can't even protect my own family. This makes me look weak, Vincent. It makes me look like a man who is losing control of his territory."

"I am handling it, okay?" Madigan said. "You asked me to deal with this thing and I am dealing with it. I need you to tell whoever else you are working with on this, especially if this is someone inside the department, to just back the hell off and let me handle it. I really don't need someone else muddying up the field here . . ."

"You have to promise me, Vincent. You have to promise me that you are going to take care of this, and fast—"

"I've had a day," Madigan interjected. "One day. There was word that a cop might have been involved. You know where the information came from? A crackhead. Some dumb druggie loser. So I take a look. If it's a cop then I am very interested. I speak to some other people, more reliable, straight-up people, and now everything points to it *not* being a cop. Then you tell me I am pretty much useless because you got word from somewhere else that it *is* a cop. This is old, okay? This is half a day old, and I need you to give me free rein to sort this out, and I will."

"Vincent, I understand—"

"What are you saying here? . . . You're saying that you don't trust me anymore?"

Sandià smiled.

Librium and Jack Daniel's, Madigan was thinking. *Librium and Jack Daniel's. Shit, this stuff just puts me in a bad mood. Best place to be right now. Offense is the best form of defense.*

"Vincent, seriously, when have we ever really trusted each other? People like you and me do not found a relationship on trust. You tell me what I need to know, and I take care of things for you. It is simply a mutually beneficial arrangement."

"So let me do what you asked me do, okay? Just let me do what you asked me to do, and get whoever else might be involved out of my fucking way."

Sandià leaned back in his chair. It creaked slowly, so audible in the tense silence that hung there between them.

"How long have we known each other, Vincent?" Sandià asked.

"What the hell is this? . . . You gonna be the Godfather now?"

Sandià smiled. "You go fuck yourself, Vincent Madigan."

Madigan laughed. "You spend too much time worrying, you know that?"

"Hey, if I don't worry, who will? My nephew is dead. He was a young man, pride of my sister, and whoever did this thing must pay. The money—" Sandià waved the comment aside. "The money itself is unimportant. Pocket change, you know? But it is the principle of the thing, the message it sends out. Sandià cannot take care of business. Sandià is losing his grip. Sandià can be taken over by some punk-ass kid out of the barrios . . ."

"Believe me," Madigan said, "I don't think anyone has such an idea."

"I need to make sure no one has such an idea. I can believe all I want, but belief and faith and hope are redundant and worthless commodities in this business. I need to know who did this thing, and I need them dead."

"And you need the girl's mother."

"Yes, Vincent, I need the girl's mother. More than anything, I need that woman."

"And the daughter?"

"The daughter is a bargaining chip, nothing more. When she is well enough to move, I will take her again. If I take her now she will die, and she is worthless to me dead. But if the woman is found then I do not need the girl."

"So if you want me to find her you need to tell me everything you know about her."

"What I know? What I know is her name. I don't know anything else about her, and I don't need to know anything else except where she is. If she is dead then fine, bring me her head in a bag to prove it. If she is not, then I need her however she comes —willingly, unwillingly, it doesn't matter. She can believe she is coming to see me in order to save the life of her daughter, or she can come because she believes she can make a deal with me—"

"Why would she want to make a deal with you?"

Sandià rested his elbows on the arms of the chair. He pressed his fingertips together. He closed his eyes for a moment. "I ask questions, Vincent. I don't answer them. I agree to back everyone else away and you will do your work. This is the agreement here. You find out who took my money, you find out who killed my nephew, and you owe me nothing. Your debt is gone."

"And if I bring you the Arias woman . . . What then?"

"You bring me the Arias woman, dead or alive, and I will not only clear your debt, I will give you another fifty thousand dollars."

Madigan nodded. "Okay, you have a deal. But I work this alone, at least the robbery and the murders. You can have whoever you like looking for this woman, but if I find her I get the fifty grand."

"Working with you is never complicated is it, Vincent? It was always the money, right?"

Madigan smiled wryly. "Hey, what the hell else is there? You got enough money then all the shit just goes away."

"You believe that?"

"I never had enough money to find out one way or the other."

"But you're working on it."

"Aren't we all?"

Sandià rose from the chair and came around the desk. Madigan stood also. Sandià gripped Madigan's shoulders. He looked directly at him. "I continue our relationship because you are a thief and a liar and a murderer, Vincent Madigan. I continue it because you and I are almost the same person. You do this thing for me and your life will be a great deal simpler, I assure you."

Sandià released him. Madigan turned and walked to the door.

"You find out anything important—I mean really important—and you let me know, okay?" Madigan asked. "Half the game here is knowing what everyone else knows."

"Well, there's the difference between you and me, Vincent," Sandià replied. "I couldn't give a damn what anyone else knows. Only thing that concerns me is that I know more."

Madigan smiled. He opened the door, stepped out into the hallway, and closed it silently behind him.

42

THUNDERHEAD

These were new curves. Not only had Sandià spoken of Isabella Arias, but he had admitted the presence of someone else inside the department. To say that this came as a shock to Madigan would not have been correct. Had Madigan thought about it, well, it would have made perfect sense. It was just that he had never really thought about it. Which division, which unit, which precinct—there was no way to know. He could have people anywhere, and—knowing Sandià—he more than likely did. But the closeness of it disturbed Madigan—the fact that Sandià had another incoming line on the robbery and storage unit homicides. And Sandià's concern for Isabella Arias had been single-minded and definite. Sandià wanted her gone. He *needed* her gone. It confirmed what Isabella had told him. Fifty grand was nothing to keep Sandià away from a homicide rap, but Sandià would not have wanted to alert Madigan to the seriousness of the task by offering some huge amount. Sandià would have paid five million to avoid the homicide beef, but he was not about to telegraph that to the world. Madigan was still a cop—good, bad, indifferent, he was still a cop—and Sandià could not afford to let his guard down or display all his cards. As Sandià had said, he stayed powerful because he knew more than others. He stayed powerful because of others' ignorance.

Madigan returned to the precinct. He needed to find out about David Valderas, the murder that the Arias sisters had witnessed. He wanted to know who was on that case, and whether or not they were on Sandià's payroll.

There was a message at the desk. Bryant wanted to see him. Madigan went on up, knocked and entered.

"The little girl," Bryant said, getting up from behind his desk. "She's gonna make it for sure. She's a tough cookie, this one, and I need you to liaise with whoever's looking after her and get the heads-up when she's able to talk."

"Should think it will be a while," Madigan replied.

"Whatever, Vincent, I just need you there the moment she is given the go-ahead for some questions."

"Will do."

Madigan hesitated.

"Something else, Vincent?"

"Yes," Madigan replied. He sat down. "I have to be honest with you, Sarge. I have to tell you that I think it's a mistake to have Walsh all over these homicides."

"How so?"

"Because he's been a desk jockey too long, and even a month in IA gets you looking the wrong way."

Bryant didn't reply for a moment, and then he seemed to nod in affirmation of Madigan's concern. "Okay," he said. "So I'm thinking I should put Charlie Harris on it."

"You don't need to. I've got it covered. They're the same case, no question. You've got a fourth man somewhere, and we just need to find him."

"Any more on this rumor it was a cop?"

Madigan shook his head. "That came from the crackhead, like you said. I don't think there's any truth in that. I mean, for Christ's sake—"

"Vincent, you've been around the block. Something like that would really surprise you that much? It could have been a cop. Jesus, it could have been the freakin' ADA."

Madigan laughed.

Bryant laughed too.

The tension dispersed.

"So what do you want to do?" Bryant asked.

"Just let me run both cases as one."

"You want Charlie to work it with you?"

"Nah, just give me a uniform for the legwork as and when."

"You can handle it?"

"No, Sarge, I'm gonna just make one royal fuck-up of a disaster—"

"Okay, okay, okay," Bryant interjected. "Go do your worst."

Madigan got up.

"And, Vincent?"

Madigan looked back at Bryant.

"If this *is* a cop then I need to know before anyone else. I am not naive. I know how dirty this business is. I know what these guys go through day in and day out. I know how easy it is to fall by the wayside, to lose sight of the bigger picture. I know that one mistake can destroy a career, and a wrecked career more often than not means a wrecked family." He shook his head slowly. "I really do give a damn about the guys that work here. All of them. Their wives, their kids, whatever the hell their personal circumstances are, well, they put it all on hold to do something that is frustrating and thankless at the best of times. The more heads-up I have, well, the more damage control I can do. You understand what I'm saying?"

"Yes, Sarge, I understand exactly what you're saying."

"So keep me in the loop. Whatever you know, I need to know it next, right?"

"Right."

Madigan walked to the door, stepped out into the corridor, and it was only as he reached the stairs that he realized his heart was going ten to the dozen.

Back in his own office, the small sanctuary within the madness, Madigan went back over the Maribel Arias file. The head in the Dumpster, the rest in garbage bags behind North General. Christ, Sandià was a freaking animal. If he had done this thing . . .

Madigan thought of his name—the Watermelon Man. Yes, Sandià could so easily have done this to Maribel Arias. He would not have blinked an eye.

And then he went on the trail of David Valderas. On the system he was listed as an active homicide, case registered on Wednesday, December 23, 2009. ME's report said that Valderas had died approximately eighteen hours before on the Tuesday, his body having lain undiscovered in his house on East 115th. Again, Madigan took note that the address was the same one that Isabel had given him.

Cause of death had been a fatal puncture through the right eye into the frontal lobe of the brain. The murder weapon—a flat-head screwdriver, just a regular $1.99 cheap screwdriver available from a thousand places in any fifteen-block radius—had been left protruding from the socket. The driver's shaft was all of five and three quarter inches, and it had been buried to the hilt. Paralysis of the entire nervous system would have been instantaneous, consciousness lasting no more than a handful of seconds, but in that handful of seconds David Valderas would have been aware of his own imminent death. A hell of way to go, and so much like Sandià. When there was no way that someone could say anything further, then Sandià would want them to know everything.

Valderas's case had been picked up by the second duty detective, and that evening it had been Charlie Harris. Charlie had canvassed the street, spoken to a half dozen neighbors, had come away empty-handed. Had anyone known it was Sandià, they would have said nothing. People in the Yard knew enough to know nothing. Always the way. Charlie was a good cop—thorough, methodical—and had the case been originally assigned to Madigan he doubted he would have found out any more. But then he doubted that Charlie Harris would have spoken to the same people as he would have. The irony was immediately evident. Had this been some other case, some other homicide, the first person Madigan would have contacted would have been Sandià himself. A murder such as that would've had to be sanctioned, or at least bought off. From the jacket, it seemed that Valderas had in fact been busy. Three pickups on possession, one of possession with intent, two grievous-with-intents, a GTA, a B&E, a spell in the pound for illegal firearms, a couple of community service orders with no indication that he satisfied them, finally a pending warrant for the robbery of a 7-Eleven. His house, right there on 115th was a stone's throw from Paladino Avenue. With Valderas's sheet, well, there was no way he was working for anyone but Sandià. So if someone other than Sandià had wanted Valderas to disappear, Sandià would've had to have given his blessing. If it had been advantageous to Sandià to lose Valderas, then the blessing would have been cheap. If the beef had been legitimate but personal— perhaps Valderas had raped some other big shot's kid daughter or some such—then the big shot could have paid for the privilege of dispatching Valderas to the hereafter. Going rate was two years' profit. Whatever Sandià made from Valderas, double it, and that would have been the fee. So Sandià would have known about the killing, and maybe he would have given some information about it to Madigan, but there would have been a cost to Madigan for that. Let some other wife-beating, vest-wearing Hispanic hothead off of a possession-with-intent rap, and Sandià would have given the nod on the perp. Madigan gets a line on the killer, picks up the homicide bust, Sandià gets the killer's territory for safekeeping while he's up at the Big House, and everyone is sweet. It was the way it worked, the way it had always worked, the way it would work from here on out. In one hand and out the other, and everyone looked lily white and perfect. Organized crime had always been there. The Mafia wasn't 1940s Sicily. The Mafia went back hundreds of years. The Asians weren't the Triads; they were the Yakuza, the Ronin, and way back a thousand years to the first time one guy wanted another guy's rice paddy and was prepared to kick his ass to get it.

But this? This was Sandià himself. This time it wasn't Sandià giving Madigan a nod on a killer in his midst. It was Madigan getting the word on Sandià for a homicide. So Maribel Arias got diced and sliced because she was in the house when Sandià stuck Valderas with a screwdriver, but why did Valderas get stuck? What had he done? How had he upset Mr. Sandià that fateful Tuesday in December?

That was a question with no answer as of yet, and a question to which Madigan would have appreciated an answer.

Madigan decided to say nothing to Charlie Harris. From all appearances, Charlie had not moved the case at all. Madigan decided to work it as a sideline; he wanted nothing official to say he had taken it on.

And then there was Walsh. Walsh was backed into a corner. Bryant would inform him he was off the homicides. Walsh wouldn't argue. Madigan would take them on as part of the same case. Madigan picked up the phone, dialed internally and got Walsh after the second ring.

"Walsh, it's Madigan."

"Hey. Yes. How's it going? Is everything okay?"

Madigan could hear the anxiety in the guy's voice. He was on eggshells.

"Everything's okay," Madigan replied. "Now, listen . . . I had a word with Bryant and he's given me the three storage unit DBs. I'm gonna run the whole thing. I might need you to do a couple of things, but if I do they'll be off the clock. Know what I mean?"

"I understand. Yes, of course," Walsh replied. "But I can't do anything that would jeopardize—"

"That would jeopardize what? Are you serious? Christ, man, you have any kind of idea how deep a hole you're already in? You want me to help you out of this, then you're gonna have to play ball, okay?"

There was silence at the end of the line.

"Okay?" Madigan repeated.

"Okay, okay . . . but—"

"But nothing," Madigan interjected. "I might not need anything from you, but if I do, then I'm gonna need you to handle it. That's all there is to it."

He paused for just a second, and then he hung up.

The game was in play, and—as was always the case—if you made the rules, then you shortened the odds.

43

PREACHIN' THE BLUES

There were people Madigan could talk to, but he decided to go home. En route he stopped at a clothing store, bought the things that Isabella had listed. The store assistant asked Madigan what size he needed.

"What size *I* need?" Madigan asked.

The girl smiled. She had a pretty smile.

"No, sir, I mean the size of the lady you are buying these things for."

"Christ knows . . . Your size maybe, a little smaller in the . . . you know, up there . . ."

"The bust?"

"Yeah, sure, whatever."

"And do you know what style she likes? What color T-shirts she wants? Her underwear?"

"I haven't a clue," he said. "Just get a bunch of stuff that you like and I'll take that."

The girl smiled again. "What every girl loves to hear, right?"

Madigan frowned. Was she hitting on him? Jesus, she couldn't have been more than twenty-five.

"Yes, right," he said, and he felt his cheeks color up. What the hell was this all of a sudden?

The girl went away. She came back ten minutes later. She had two pairs of jeans, some T-shirts, a blouse, a couple pairs of shoes, some underwear. "These okay?" she asked.

"Look good to me. How much?"

"Hundred and twenty-five fifty."

Madigan counted out a hundred and fifty bucks, told the girl to keep the change.

"Thank you, sir," she said.

Madigan bundled the things into two bags and left the store.

He stopped at a supermarket coming out of Morrisania. He

bought coffee, tea, milk, sugar, eggs, bread, ham, salami, mayonnaise, mustard. He bought canned goods, a bunch of vegetables, a few pounds of hamburger, a jar of dill pickles, a six-pack of Schlitz, two bottles of red, two of white, a bottle of rosé, a liter of Jack Daniel's. He got a kid to help him haul the lot to the car and gave the kid a ten. The kid seemed overjoyed.

Back toward home he wondered when he'd last done grocery shopping. He could not remember. It didn't matter, save to highlight the fact that everything had been lonely since May of 2008. Better part of two years alone. Better that way. It had to be. He didn't have to contend with what color underwear, which kind of wine.

Isabella seemed happy to see him, as if she'd imagined he would desert her. He showed her the clothes he'd bought.

"You did good for a guy," she said. She smiled. It was the first real smile he'd seen since he'd found her. The smile did not last long, however, as if she had caught herself relaxing and knew that to relax her guard was to invite even greater trouble. There was no mistaking the fact that she had been crying, and thus he relayed the message he'd gotten from Bryant.

"She's doing real well," Madigan said. "There is no question that she's gonna be fine . . . And considering what I have worked out, I don't think it's going to be too long before you get her back. Right now she's not able to answer any questions. The doctors don't want her stressed. But I've been put in charge of the whole case, so no one will speak to her before I give the okay. That way, whatever I find out from her you'll find out right away."

"And can I see her? Am I going to be able to see her?"

He shook his head. "No, you can't see her. That's tough, I know. But say it had been another cop there when you showed up at the hospital, huh? Say it hadn't been me. Then you'd be having an entirely different conversation. You'd either be in a jail cell for your own protection, or you'd have been delivered up to Sandià."

"By the cops?"

Madigan looked at her. He did not believe that she could be so naive as to consider such a thing impossible. "You don't have to try and make me feel better," he said. "I know that some of those inside the PD are far worse than those on the outside."

"But not you?" she said. "You are helping me, right?" The tone in her voice was definitely that of a question. She was afraid, alone, suspicious, defensive. There was no way in the world that Isabella

Arias would be won over with one night's sleep and a bunch of cheap clothes.

"Yes," Madigan said. He hesitated. "Yes, I am helping you. But I'm also helping myself."

They were silent for a moment, and then she said, "I'll make some food. You are staying now?"

"No," Madigan replied. "I have to go and see someone, but I'll be back in a couple of hours."

"I'll make food," she said. "I'll make dinner, and then we can eat when you get back."

"Sure, that'd be good."

Madigan walked to the front door. She followed him, but he turned and told her to hang back. "I don't want anyone in the street to see you here," he said.

"You're thinking of everything," she replied. She reached out her hand to touch his sleeve, but Madigan read the gesture as more of an effort to convince herself that here was someone she might possibly trust. She was not trying to express any degree of affection for him.

Madigan flinched.

"What?" she said. "You afraid of me?"

He tried to smile.

"Everything about you is lonely," she said. "Your house, your cupboards, the rooms . . . lonely. Everything you say sounds like something a lonely man would say." She paused for a moment, looking at him intently.

Madigan found it disconcerting. He just wanted to leave.

"You and I are not so different," she said. "I do not trust you. You do not trust me. Right now this is the way it is, and this is the way it has to be. I appreciate what you have done so far, Vincent Madigan, but I know that people are never who they appear to be . . ."

"I don't expect you to trust me, but I do need you to believe what I am telling you," Madigan replied. "For the moment, all I need you to do is stay here. This thing is going to go one of two ways, and we will either come out of this alive, both of us, or we won't. It's that simple. But you do anything other than precisely what I ask of you, then we shorten the odds significantly."

"I will stay here," she said. "And I will do what you say."

"Good enough," Madigan replied, and with that he opened the door, closed it quietly behind him, and didn't look back.

*

Four blocks southwest, heading back toward the Third Avenue Bridge, Madigan pulled over at the side of the road and wondered what the hell was going on.

This was a circus, the whole thing, and he either kept his head together or he could wish goodbye to everything. The girl was merely a tradeoff for Sandià. Someone was going to win and someone was going to lose. Hell, maybe both of them would. Those were the breaks.

Enough already. Get busy living, or get busy dying. Just like the man said in *Shawshank*.

On MLK Jr. Avenue and Second, Madigan pulled up and came to a stop against the curb. He sat for a moment, smoked a cigarette, decided to drop a Percocet, and then decided not to. He got out, flicked the cigarette butt across the sidewalk, and started left toward the corner. A third-floor apartment, the building that overlooked the junction, and even as he approached he saw the curtain flicker.

Vincent Madigan and Freddy Virago went back a thousand years. Once upon a time they had been tight, but life happened, things happened, and there had been a rift. The rift was as healed as it ever would be, but the friendship they'd once possessed was a thing of the distant past. Now their tolerance of each other was born out of a mutual respect.

A good fifteen years older than Madigan, Freddy Virago had run a hundred different names. He had ex-wives and mistresses scattered throughout the Yard and beyond. Twenty years before, it was a running joke that if some girl hadn't carried one of Freddy's kids then she wasn't a real Yard girl. Approaching sixty, Virago had done enough years inside to know he didn't want to die there, and so he stayed outside of everything. He knew what was going on, but he was never involved. Madigan believed he didn't even smoke reefer these days. He had a drink or two, as Madigan himself did, but the line had been drawn. Go down that route and you wound up doing something crazy.

Madigan buzzed; the door opened. Virago had seen him coming a hundred yards away.

Madigan took the stairs, and Virago's door was open by the time he reached the landing on the third floor. A young woman was there waiting for him—eighteen, nineteen perhaps, her hair a tight mess of jet-black curls, her skin olive and swarthy. She was pretty in that wild, unkempt way of so many Hispanics, a look that had broken Madigan's heart on too many occasions.

"Mr. Vincent," she said, and smiled.

"Hey, sweetheart."

She frowned. "You don't remember me?"

"Sure, I remember you," he replied, and even he could hear the uncertainty in his own voice.

Now she would want him to say her name. Madigan racked his brain. But she merely smiled a little wider and said, "Uncle's inside . . . He's watching a game."

Okay, so she was one of the nieces. Good enough. Virago had five sisters, all of them with a billion kids.

"How's your mom doing?" he asked the girl.

"Moaning, as ever. She wants me to stay on and do more school. I want to get a job. You can understand that, right?"

"Sure, I can."

"I want to do hairstyling. I want my own shop. Maybe more than one. I could have a chain and call them Caterina's. That sounds good, no?"

Right, it was Caterina. Madigan still couldn't remember her from Eve, but at least he had her name.

"That would sound great, sweetheart, but you know, sometimes moms have a point. The better your education, the better your chance of making the business work. You know how to fill out the tax forms, right?"

Caterina frowned.

"See, right there you got a problem. You don't know how to fill out your tax forms then the IRS'll be all over you like a bad rash, and they can just snatch your business right out from under you. They're a bunch of mean bastards, Caterina, and you gotta have some smarts to deal with all that shit."

"Caterina!" Virago hollered from the back of the apartment. "Caterina . . . tell that lazy bastard to get his ass in here and shut the damned door!"

Madigan smiled. He stepped on inside the hall and closed the door behind him. He followed Caterina into the kitchen, where Virago was seated at the table, a plate of something in front of him, the small TV on the top of the refrigerator playing some rerun of a baseball game.

"Hey, Madigan, what the hell? You want some mystery meat?"

Caterina playfully smacked the back of her uncle's head.

Virago laughed. "This girl is the best damned cook in the whole city, let me tell you." He turned around and grabbed her, hugged her around the waist. "I'm just teasin' you, honey. You know that."

"I'm good," Madigan said. "I got dinner waiting for me when I get back."

"That's bullshit," Virago said. "Last time you had dinner waiting for you is when someone left what they didn't want in a diner."

"Seriously, I got some dinner . . ." And then he stopped. If he had dinner, who was making it? That would be the next question. Virago—loyal though he might once have been—was a man with a past. If Sandià got word that Madigan had visited, well, he just might come over and visit Freddy himself. Half an hour and Freddy would give Madigan up, tell Sandià every word that Madigan had uttered.

"Okay," Madigan said, "but just a little. I don't have much of an appetite these days."

"You look a little better than last time I seen you. You know that?" Virago said as Caterina fetched a plate for Madigan. "You staying off the sauce?"

"Yes, sure I am," Madigan said. "This is the new and improved me."

Virago smiled. He pushed his plate away and reached for his cigarettes. "You don't need no one to tell you anything, Vincent. That's the way it always has been. That's the way it always will be, right? You're a smart guy, you know? You know the inside and the outside, and all of it from three fucking miles away—"

"Uncle . . ." Caterina said. She put a plate of chili in front of Madigan, a tortilla on the side. There were some slices of avocado, a quarter of lemon.

"I'm sorry, sweetheart," Virago told the girl. "She says I curse too much."

"You do," Madigan replied. He picked up the spoon and started eating. The meat was good—rich and fresh. He squeezed lemon over the avocados. He had been utterly unaware of his own hunger. He would eat this, and then eat again when he got home.

"You have some reason for being here aside from my Caterina's cooking?" Virago asked.

"I do."

"You want a barley pop or something?"

"Sure."

Virago turned to Caterina. "Sweetheart, get us a coupla beers, would you, and then maybe go watch a bit of TV for a while. Me and Vincent here got something to discuss."

Caterina brought the beers. She seemed to appreciate that some things were not for her to hear or understand. Madigan figured her smart enough to appreciate the kind of conversations her Uncle Freddy had in the kitchen; smart enough not to get involved.

She shut the door behind her and Virago leaned forward. "So, what you doing here?"

"Valderas," Madigan said. "David Valderas."

"What about him?"

"He's dead."

"You don't say?"

"Freddy, don't be a wiseass . . . What was the deal with him?"

"You really wanna know?"

"No, I guess I don't. Thanks for dinner an' everything and I'll be on my way."

Virago leaned back, lit a second cigarette in as many minutes.

Madigan looked down. He'd cleaned off the plate. He could've eaten the same again.

"Valderas went bad," Virago said. "He did a thing with one of Sandià's nephews. A bank thing. They came away with three, maybe four hundred grand."

Madigan—thankfully—had already swallowed the mouthful of beer. Otherwise it would have sprayed all over Virago's lap. The bank job. This was it. This was the real deal. Where the money came from originally.

"Anyways, they did this thing, all fine and dandy . . . Came away with however much. But it seemed that Valderas approached the nephew with an idea to scam Sandià, like they should run away with the money. Dumb, dumb motherfuckin' son of a bitch thought that Sandià's own freakin' nephew was gonna go turncoat on Sandià. What an asshole that boy was."

"The nephew tells Sandià, and Sandià deals with Valderas, right?"

"Sure he does, as anyone would. But the irony, the real irony of this, is that some other crew muscles in on the proceeds, and they take this bank money off of this nephew in one of Sandià's houses. The nephew is dead . . . Hell, man, everyone who showed up is dead. Even three of the perps that did this are found like mystery meat in a storage unit someplace, and it seems there's a fourth guy and he got away clean with everything. Now Sandià is ready to bite his own freakin' arm off to get this guy. He doesn't give a crap about the money . . . Hell, to him it's only spare change. But someone has come down to his yard and screwed him good, made him look like an asshole, and he isn't gonna sleep well until he knows who the guy is and he has his head in a bag."

"Well, whoever the guy is, he better get a long way away pretty fast."

"Ah hell, Sandià ain't that smart and you know it. Problem with these guys is that they run these operations with fear. Everyone's terrified, everyone's scared outta their minds and they do whatever they're asked. The problem is that sometimes the little guys wind up more scared of what happens if they rather do than what happens if they don't. Then the big boss comes tumbling down and the whole thing has to start all over again. I've seen too many Sandiàs come and go to be worried about people like him anymore. A year, five, maybe ten, and there'll be someone else in that tenement on Paladino. It's the nature of things, Vincent." He smiled sardonically. "This too shall come to pass an' all that, right?"

"You know the nephew's name . . . the one that got killed in the house robbery?"

"Calvo, Alex Calvo."

Madigan was silent for a time. He took one of Virago's cigarettes from the packet and lit it.

"How are you involved in this?" Virago asked him.

"I'm on it, officially," Madigan replied. "Not the Valderas killing, but the robbery of Sandià's house, the three dead guys in the storage unit . . . the little girl in the hospital. You know about that, right?"

"That Arias girl? Sure, I know about it. I also know that Sandià is after the girl's mother, and that the aunt was Valderas's lover."

"Jesus, Freddy, is there anything you don't know?"

"Not really," Virago replied. "Oh, yeah, maybe there is one thing I don't know. I don't know why the hell you're here asking me about it. That one is still a mystery to me."

"I'm here for the reason I said . . . To find out about Valderas."

"Sure you are. But nothing is ever simple with you, Vincent. You say one thing, you mean another. You do one thing, well, it's always to facilitate something else. If I were you, I'd be surprised every morning I woke up and found out someone hadn't put a bullet in my head."

"I am, Freddy. Believe me I am."

"So whatever else might be going on, I think you need to slow down some."

Madigan frowned.

"You have always drank too much. And you were always chuggin' pills like there'd be none left for tomorrow. If I know you, then you don't got a woman. You're all a-freakin'-lone as usual, and the world still owes you a living. Your age . . . Christ, man, I'd start getting wise."

"A lesson in survival skills I do not need, Freddy, especially from the likes of you."

"Well, fuck you very much, asshole," Freddy replied. "I'm doing okay here. I got nothing going on that would interest the PD. I got enough money. I got Caterina and a whole bunch of other daughters and nieces coming over to get me dinner and fetch me some beers, and I take care of all of them. I don't have a family, Vincent. I have a real honest-to-God dynasty. I sleep good, and I don't spend all my time wondering who the hell is behind me. I guess you don't even know what that feels like."

Madigan shook his head. "Haven't a clue, Freddy. Haven't a clue."

"That's what I'm saying, Vincent. It doesn't do you any good to be living like this. I've done it both ways, my friend, and this is one helluva lot better."

Madigan finished his cigarette. He ground the butt into the ashtray and pushed his plate aside.

"So you got anything else for me on any of this?" he asked.

Freddy shook his head. "What else is there? David Valderas was a dumb, greedy son of a bitch. Alex Calvo was loyal to his family. Both of them are dead. There's a bunch of other guys that got wasted in the house robbery, another three guys dead in a storage unit. There's a fourth man for sure, and he got away clean, and I doubt he's within a five-hundred-mile radius right now. If he is . . . well, if he is, then he's either really freakin' dumb, or he has stainless-steel cojones the size of City Hall. Valderas's girlfriend got chopped up and stuck in a Dumpster, the little girl wound up in hospital, and now Sandià has the whole world looking for two people—the dead girl's sister, and the guy who offed his delivery boys in that house and ran away with the cash. Real simple."

Madigan nodded. Freddy Virago had the thing nailed to a tee. What he didn't know was that one of those people was sitting right there ahead of him, and the other was in Madigan's house making dinner.

"This is the war we fight," Virago said.

"We go to the mattresses, right?" Madigan said, and he smiled ruefully.

"You're going now?" Virago asked as Madigan started to get up.

"I am, yes."

"Good to see you. Like I said, it always surprises me how you're still alive."

"Surprises me too, Freddy."

Virago walked Madigan to the door. Caterina appeared. Madigan wished her farewell. "Do good," he told her. "Try not to give your mom too much heartache . . . You gotta save all of that for the men in your life."

"Bye, Mr. Vincent," she said coyly, and she smiled like the little girl she once was.

Madigan shook hands with Virago. Virago gripped his shoulder.

"You take care of yourself," he told Madigan, "because sure as shit no one else is going to. You know that, right?"

"I know that, Freddy."

Freddy Virago closed the door and went back to the kitchen.

Madigan walked the block to his car and got in. His conversation with Freddy had done exactly what he'd hoped: confirmed that there was no part of this that he didn't already know. Before he pulled away and headed home he thought about the hole he'd dug for himself.

This really was it. This really had to be the end of everything. This was not a life he could go on living forever.

44

MY DREAMS

Isabella was waiting for him. That's how it felt. It felt like she was waiting for him, and it felt like he was coming home to Ivonne. He remembered that feeling, and it was good.

She had gone through all the clothes he'd bought her, and she smiled and said, "You had someone get these for you, right?"

"I did, yes."

"I can tell."

Madigan smiled. He shrugged off his jacket. His shoulders ached. He took off his holster and set it atop the refrigerator. "You can tell, how?"

"Because you don't seem like a man who's used to dealing with anyone but yourself."

He didn't respond, didn't know how to respond, so he reached for a glass, the bottle of Jack, got some ice cubes from the freezer drawer. "You want one?"

She shook her head. "Some of this will be fine," she said, holding up the bottle of rosé. She opened it, poured a glass, set the bottle aside.

"Whatever you made smells good," Madigan told her. He sat down with his drink, lit a cigarette.

"You shouldn't smoke."

"So the world keeps telling me," he replied.

She sat facing him. Her hands cupped the glass, as if she wanted to feel the coolness radiate through her. "Today has been a little better. When you told me Melissa had been moved, that she was going to be fine, I started to feel a little less scared."

"Don't do that yet."

"What?"

"Get less scared. Sandià is looking for you. He will keep on looking until he finds you, or until someone stops him looking."

Isabella closed her eyes and took a deep breath.

Madigan saw her cheeks color up.

"Your sister," he said.

She nodded.

"Sandià is a truly, truly dangerous man. You know why he has this name, right? Sandià? The Watermelon Man?"

"I know the story."

"Well, then you know that exactly what they say he did, well, he did it."

"He killed my sister . . . He just murdered David, and then he killed my sister . . ."

"David tried to cross him. David was stupid. You get involved with someone like Sandià, then you are already in trouble . . ." Madigan hesitated; he was speaking of himself. *He* was in trouble, had been in trouble the entire time he'd known the man. He also knew that he was speaking to Melissa Arias's mother. This terrible irony did not escape his attention. Her daughter, the daughter she now felt so much better about, would never have been in the hospital had it not been for Madigan. He imagined Isabella's reaction if she were to ever discover the truth. She was seeking refuge in the house of a man responsible for the near-fatal wounding of her only child, a man so closely associated with Maribel's murderer that Sandià himself may just as well have shared dinner with them. Was he—Madigan—not just as evil as any of them?

"Doesn't matter how stupid he was . . ." she started, and then she caught herself. "People like Sandià take as much as they can and they hurt people as much as they can. Maybe they think this will proof them against the hurt and pain caused by others, or maybe it is all they can do, and they do it because if they don't have this then they have a life of nothing."

"People like Sandià are just plain evil," he said, aware of the fact that he could so easily replace *Sandià* with *us*.

"You believe that?" she asked.

"It is necessary for me to believe it."

"I don't."

Madigan frowned. "What? Even after what happened to David and Maribel . . . after what happened to Melissa?"

"I think people start out good," she said, "and then every time they do a bad thing a little of their inherent goodness is taken away. Eventually there is nothing left but the bad. Like when you hurt someone, you give them the power to steal your dreams, and eventually all that remains are the nightmares."

"That's a very beautiful concept," Madigan said, "but somehow it seems a little innocent and naive."

"So what do you think?"

Madigan swallowed most of his drink. He reached for the bottle and refilled his glass a good two inches. On his own it would have been three inches, maybe four, but for some reason he was concerned with her impression of him. He had nearly killed her daughter, but he was worried she might think him an alcoholic? Madigan was losing it—he knew it—but there was nothing he could do about the way he felt. Later, he would go upstairs and drop a couple of Xanax.

"What do I think?" he echoed. "I think some people are just born bad, and once they start out that way, there's very little you can do for them. People around them spend their whole lives in chaos. Everything is damage control. Everything is geared toward minimizing the destruction. You speak to some of these people out here, the junkies, the dealers, guys who were in juvy before they were out of diapers, guys who are gonna spend more years of their lives inside than out, people who are going to die in prison . . . Hell, speak to some of these people and tell me that people are basically good."

"You need to be reminded of the basic goodness of humanity."

"I need to be reminded that there's a reason to get up and go to work each day. Things have gotten worse, no question. It's not that people do more bad. It's just that more people are doing bad than ever."

Madigan swallowed the contents of his glass, went for the bottle again.

Isabella moved the bottle beyond his reach. "Enough . . . for now," she said. "Eat first, okay?"

He looked at her. For a moment he felt challenged. For a moment he felt an intense rage boiling inside him. How dare she? How dare she come into his house, come right on into his house, take advantage of whatever miniscule sense of goodness that he still possessed, and tell him what he could and could not do . . .

Madigan stopped.

It was as if he could hear his own voice, and the voice sounded like another man entirely. He realized what she was doing. If she had to trust Madigan now, if Madigan was the man who would stand between her and Sandià, then she wanted him sober.

Self-preservation. It was that simple. She did not care about him; she cared for herself and her daughter.

She let go of the bottle.

"Okay," he said. "That would be nice."

They ate. It was good, like restaurant food, but a good place where someone gave a damn about the customers. He drank wine, just one glass, and for a little while it felt like he didn't want to drink anything else. She made coffee, he smoked a couple of cigarettes, and then they sat at the table and there was a strange and comfortable silence that was broken only by Isabella. Madigan felt no need to fill that silence with anything but the sound of her voice. He wanted to listen to her. He wanted to hear what she had to say.

"You know what it's like when someone dies—your mom, your father, a child maybe?"

"A sister?" Madigan ventured.

"Yes," she replied. "A sister too."

"Tell me."

"You stop. Your life stops. Everything stops. You cannot understand how things will ever start again. You cannot understand how it will be possible for life to go on after this. You are yourself, but you are also your family. There are parts of you in them. One of them dies and the parts of them that are within you . . . I believe they die as well."

Madigan smiled. "You are quite the thinker, quite the philosopher."

"My daughter doesn't know her father," Isabella said, going on as if Madigan wasn't even there. "I don't know . . . I don't know what to do for the best. She's growing up without a father, and there's going to be parts of herself that she doesn't understand. We all pass on facets of ourselves to our children, don't we?"

She looked up at Madigan. She looked like she was ready to start crying again. He wondered if he should give her a couple of lithium.

"Our children?" he said, and he thought of Cassie and Adam and Lucy and Tom, and he wondered if that was really true; if there were inherent and native parts of himself that would automatically be transferred to each of them. He wondered which parts. He wondered if Tom would be a thief, if Adam would be an adulterer, if Cassie would be an inveterate and compulsive liar, and if Lucy would be the drunk, the junkie, the violent one . . .

He closed his eyes.

"You can talk too," she said.

"No, I can't," Madigan replied. "I want to listen to you."

"There are things that have gone wrong for you . . . your family, your children?"

He laughed suddenly, a retort, a reaction more than anything else. "I have screwed up so many things," he said. "That's how come I know so much about how things can get screwed up."

She smiled.

He didn't. "I'm serious," he said. "You do things, you know? We're like kids all of our lives. Like when a kid does something that they shouldn't do, and you sit them down and you ask 'em what the hell they did that for. What the hell did they do that for, right? Always comes back to the same answer. Because it seemed like a good idea at the time. That's always the reason. And we're no different. We do things because it seemed like a good idea at the time. If we're a bit smarter, you know . . . If we want to justify it, well, we call it instinct, survival instinct, but it isn't anything but greed and hatred and prejudice. That's the truth. Most things that people do, they do out of greed and hatred and prejudice—"

"That's a very warped and cynical view of people."

"People are very warped and cynical."

"You believe that?"

"I know it."

"You know, I have a dream," she said.

"About what?"

"About the future."

"And what's that? What's this dream?"

"That my daughter will keep the happiness I have seen and lose everything else."

"Pretty unrealistic dream."

"Why d'you say that?"

"Because she's already out there with one strike against her," Madigan said. "She's Hispanic. She's not white. You're white, then, okay, you got a chance. You're black or Hispanic or whatever, well, you're walking against the tide before you even get to the beach. You know that. And the fact that we got a black man in the White House means shit. Government is more corrupt than any of us. That old saying: It doesn't matter who you vote for, the government always wins. The country is screwed, the planet is screwed, and we're all screwed too. Only business we should pay attention to is dealing with whatever it takes to make sure we're covered."

"That doesn't make sense. Your logic doesn't work."

"Why?"

"Because I'm here. Because you're helping me . . ."

"You think that's out of the goodness of my heart? You think that this is some act of humanitarian selflessness?" Madigan shook his head. "Sandià has haunted the edges of my life for years . . . ever since I've been a cop really. I'm going to bring him down, and you're going to help me."

Isabella Arias looked directly at Vincent Madigan. Her gaze was unflinching, unerring, and Madigan looked back at her and felt invisible. He did not look away. He wanted to say something, but he did not know what to say.

"You do have a heart, Vincent Madigan," she eventually said. "Dark and broken it may be, but you still have a heart."

"Whatever you say," he replied, and then he reached for the bottle of Jack.

They spoke little after that. She washed dishes. Madigan sat on the couch and surfed the TV for an hour, and then she came and said she was going to bed.

"Okay," he replied. "I won't be long. I'll keep the volume down."

"It's your house," she said. "Do as you wish."

I will, he thought after she'd gone. *And it's my life, and finally I will do with that as I wish . . .*

45

THE MIDNIGHT PROMISE

*W*hat did McCarthy say about politics? People went into politics because they were smart enough to understand it, but dumb enough to think it was important? Something like that.

Hell, that could apply to pretty much everything in life.

Do I want to fuck her? No, I don't. She is good-looking, this Isabella Arias. I've had a little less to drink than usual. I am able to string a sentence together. But there's something about her that just makes me mad. Self-righteous? No, that isn't it. I think it's her naïveté. Hell, her daughter just got shot. Her daughter could have died. The girl's father is nowhere to be seen. She has no money, lives in some two-bit piece-of-shit apartment in Crapsville, and she talks about hopes for the future, dreams for her daughter. Get real, sweetheart. Your daughter's gonna be a whore or a crack addict or both by the time she's seventeen. This is the life you've got to look forward to. These are the dreams that await you, sweetheart.

That's why I didn't try something. That's why I didn't want to fuck her. Because she looked at me with an expression that said, "I know this. I know that . . . You are too negative, Vincent Madigan."

To hell with you.

Life is negative. People are negative.

Wake up and smell the despair.

I took the bottle to bed. I didn't bother getting undressed. I lay there on the mattress and I could hear her in the bathroom, and I thought about the clothes I bought for her, the food she made, the feeling I'd experienced as I'd driven back from talking with Freddie Virago, and how I figured it would be nice to have someone to come home to again . . .

I have to get out of this life.

I promise I will get out of this life, one way or the other.

If I gotta die to do it, then so be it. Whichever way the shit flies, well, you got to deal with it.

*

Someone is talking to Sandià. Someone other than me. What does that tell me? Tells me I am naive too. Tells me I am a dumb schmuck for thinking that I was the only one who had my hand in the guy's pocket. The whole thing tastes sour now. The whole thing seems bitter and small-minded and petty. We did this for money. Always for the money. Sold out on every front. And what do I have to show for it? Nothing, that's what. Three hundred grand of worthless money under the floor, a drink problem, and loneliness. That's what I got.

Gonna take a bunch of Ambiens and Quaaludes and get some sleep.

Tomorrow I have to figure this shit out. Someone has a line to Sandià. Charlie Harris? He was the investigating officer on the Valderas murder. Somewhere in that house they figured out that there was a witness to the Valderas murder, and whoever the hell is on Sandià's payroll got that information to him. Maribel is dead. Now he wants Isabella dead. Could it really be that Charlie Harris has got a line in with Sandià? Seems unlikely. Not Charlie Harris. But then, wouldn't he say the same thing about me?

I have to know who it is.

There has to be a way to find out.

I'll give something to Charlie, something that would interest Sandià, and then we'll see if I get a call from Sandià.

I cannot sleep.

Not with all this noise in my head.

For a while I sit by the window and look out into the street.

Then I stand in the corridor outside the room where she sleeps.

Isabella Arias.

I press my ear against the door. Can I hear her breathing, or is that my imagination?

Am I crazy now?

Have I just slipped away from all the moorings and drifted?

Christ, I don't know what's happening anymore, and the fact that I don't know scares me more than anything else . . .

46

THE LIGHT OF THE WORLD

She was up and awake and showered, and she was making breakfast by the time Madigan came downstairs.

"Pancakes," she said. "Bacon, too. There's a 7-Eleven on the corner—"

"You can't go out, Isabella," he said. "I told you that already—"

"I put a coat on, one of yours, and I tied a scarf around—"

"Not again," Madigan interjected. His voice was stern, direct. "Don't go out again. Seriously."

"But—"

"No buts. No reasons. Nothing. You stay inside. You don't go out again. They find out you're here, then both of us are dead. This is not a good time for me to die, okay? I have some things I need to do."

She looked at him, started to smile. His expression was intense. Her smile disappeared.

"Okay," she said. "I won't go out again."

"Good," Madigan replied. "I appreciate that you wanted to make breakfast. I appreciate that you needed to get outside. But this is something you cannot screw around with, Isabella."

"I got it, Vincent. I really do. Now sit down. Eat. Shut up with the talking."

He sat down. She poured him a glass of orange juice.

Madigan ate as best he could. He had not drunk as much as usual the night before, and he felt a little sharper for it. He needed to speak to Charlie Harris. He needed to give Charlie something, and then see what happened. He felt wired, attuned to what was going on around him, and when Isabella asked what he wanted to eat that evening, he said, "It doesn't matter. Whatever you can make with what we have."

"You didn't bring a great deal for me to work with."

"Then I will bring take-out," he said. "I am not doing any more grocery shopping, and nothing is going to be delivered here."

Isabella said nothing in response. She'd picked up on Madigan's tone. What they planned to eat that evening was utterly insignificant in the face of what was really happening here.

"I have to go," he said brusquely. "I have a lot to do."

Isabella looked at him, and Madigan knew she was going to speak.

"I don't want to die . . . like my sister," she said. "And I don't want them to kill Melissa . . ."

Madigan put on his jacket. "You're not going to die," he said, "and they're not going to kill your daughter."

"You promise?"

"Jesus, no, I can't promise something like that . . . But what I can promise is that I will do everything I can to make sure that all of us come out the other side of this. I am also going to do everything I can to take Sandià out of the picture."

"I am starting to believe that you are a good man, Vincent."

Madigan shook his head. He smiled sardonically. "You have no idea, Isabella . . . absolutely no idea."

Madigan left without another word passing between them. It was staying impersonal, and he needed it to remain that way until the end.

The call came four hours later.

Madigan had arrived at the precinct house before nine. He shuffled papers in his office for twenty minutes, drank a cup of coffee, and then he wandered down the hall. He found Charlie Harris at his desk.

"Hey, Charlie."

"Vincent. How goes it?"

"It goes, you know . . . slowly."

"Always the way."

"Had something on my radar yesterday . . . a case you looked at a while back. Guy got stabbed in the head with a screwdriver."

Charlie Harris stopped typing. He frowned, seemed uncertain, and then he said, "Yeah, of course. Some Hispanic guy. Got dug right through the eye."

"That's the one."

"What about it?"

"Wondered if anything ever came of it."

Charlie shook his head. "Can't say it did. Some drug gang shit more than likely. These assholes are digging each other all the freakin' time with whatever comes to hand. Why you looking at it?"

"I'm not," Madigan said. "Not directly." He walked forward and took a seat facing Charlie. "I got a little girl who was shot in one of Sandià's houses up near Paladino. Little girl's mother has vanished, her aunt got murdered, and the aunt was your guy's girlfriend. Looks like they might be connected."

"No shit."

"Yes shit."

"Helluva thing."

"It always is," Madigan replied. "So your man, name of Valderas, gets himself dug in the head with a screwdriver, his girlfriend is this Maribel Arias DB they found all in pieces in a Dumpster and wherever, and now it looks like word is out on the sister, name of Isabella. And the little girl up in Harlem Hospital just happens to be Isabella's daughter. Is that a bunch of too-coincidental coincidences or what?"

"Sounds like all one thing. So who you after?"

"Seems it all started with whoever put a hole in your guy's head."

"Would seem that way."

"And you never got a lead on this . . . no names, no faces, nothing coming up on it?"

"Not a word. No eyewitnesses, no tip-offs, no CIs coming out the woodwork. No-man's-land on this one, Vincent, just no-man's-land."

"Okay," Madigan said, and started to get up. "You heard this thing about the robbery on the Sandià house . . . this thing about how there might have been a fourth man on the scene?"

"Sure did."

"Any ideas?"

"Nothing," Charlie said. "Pulling a stunt like that. What kind of crazy son of a bitch would do something like that?"

"You figure it might have been the same one who did your guy? Stabbed him in the head?"

"Jesus, Vincent, I don't know what you're smoking, but it's doing wonders for your imagination."

"Yeah, crazy idea," Madigan said. "Anyway, I'm gonna snoop around on it, and if anything comes from it I'll give you the heads-up before we take it to Bryant. It's still your case, the screwdriver thing."

"Appreciated, Vincent. But don't bust your balls on it. Hell, he was only some smalltime dealer. Neighborhood'll do better without him."

The conversation ended. Madigan walked away. He made some calls, chased files, went out for lunch. When he got back, four hours had elapsed since his meeting with Charlie Harris and that was when his cellphone rang.

"You have to come see him," the voice said, just the same as always.

It was the second time in as many days—the drive to Sandià's place, the elevator ride, the goons on either side of the doorway. Madigan wondered what it would feel like never to have to do this again. En route he had taken a moment to pull over and drop the Subway bag with the disassembled .22 inside it into a municipal trash can.

"We have a good relationship, Vincent," Sandià said, once Madigan was again seated on the other side of his desk. "Would you agree that we have a good relationship?"

"Yes, we do. No question."

"I thought you would feel that way, Vincent. And good relationships—doesn't matter whether they are personal, a marriage even, and especially business—these relationships are based on mutual respect, sometimes a little faith, but always respect. Wouldn't you agree, Vincent?"

Madigan nodded. He was thinking about Charlie Harris. He was thinking about all the years he'd known Charlie, the cases they'd worked together, the drinks they'd shared after successes, the drinks they'd shared when the bad guy got away, and whether or not it was Charlie Harris who was in Sandià's pocket.

Christ. Jesus Christ Almighty.

"So we have had our differences over the years, Vincent. I know that. But they have never been differences that we didn't ultimately resolve . . ."

"What do you want me to do?" Madigan asked, knowing full well the answer before he'd asked the question.

"I want you to leave the death of David Valderas alone."

Madigan didn't respond. Not a flinch, not a raised eyebrow, nothing. He smiled inside. "Okay," he said after a moment's pause. "I can do that."

Sandià smiled. "You are a good man, Vincent Madigan."

Madigan smiled again, internally. Sandià was the second person to say that today. If only they knew what he knew.

"I am not a good man," Madigan replied. "Neither of us is. If we start to believe that, then we really are in trouble."

Sandià smiled. It was a cold expression. Madigan drank to forget his conscience. Sandià did not drink—Madigan knew that—and thus to live with his conscience, he must have worked ceaselessly to convince himself of his own rightness.

"So perhaps we are not good, but we are realistic and we are efficient. This is business, Vincent, nothing but business. And as any businessman will tell you, it is kill or be killed out there."

The tone irritated Madigan. The sense of self-importance, the certainty with which Sandià uttered his edicts and bullshit aphorisms. Madigan was unarmed—protocol dictated he leave his gun outside, but there were many things in the room—letter openers, a glass paperweight, a lamp stand on a nearby table—and he could have taken any one of them and killed Sandià right there and then. He would never have escaped the building. That was a given. But he would have perhaps gone some way toward redressing the wrongs that had been perpetrated by both of them.

Maybe that was the way this would end. Both himself and Sandià dead.

He thought again of Charlie Harris. Maybe Charlie Harris needed to die as well.

"So, otherwise . . . how does this thing progress?" Sandià asked.

"I am turning over every stone," Madigan said. "That was how I found the connection to Valderas. But if you tell me that I need to look no further in that direction, then I will look no further."

"It will give you nothing," Sandià said. "This man had nothing to do with what happened at my house . . . It had nothing to do with whoever stole my money and killed my nephew."

"Good enough for me," Madigan said, and started to get up.

Sandià raised his hand. "Stay a moment," he said. He shifted in the chair, leaned back, seemed to relax. "We never talk, Vincent. We used to talk. Years have passed, we are older, and we should have found more time, but it seems we always have less."

"Always the way," Madigan replied. He wondered what bullshit was on the way now.

"I worry about you, Vincent."

Madigan frowned, and then he smiled. "Don't," he said. "I'm a lost cause."

"Well, perhaps I have chosen to be the Patron Saint of Lost Causes."

"No, my friend, we are the Patron Saints of Liars and Thieves and Killers. That's who we are. That's what we do—"

"You have not spoken with your children recently, have you?"

"Sorry?"

"A man loses touch with his children, he loses touch with the most important things in his life. When was the last time you saw any of them?"

"I don't remember."

"See? I told you. You need to see your children, Vincent. You need to be reminded of the importance of the future, what you leave behind."

"I'm afraid the best I'm going to leave behind is a lot of damaged people . . . and some dead ones as well."

"As we all are, Vincent, as we all are. But still the fact remains that you have children, and they may or may not become what you wish, but they are yours. And I see you are lonely, and there is no one to look after you. A man needs someone to look after him . . ."

"And he reciprocates by looking after that person too, right? Well, it was that part I was never very good at." Madigan got up. "I appreciate your concern, I really do, but I have a lot to do, and—"

Sandià threw something—something pale and oblong—and it caught Madigan off guard. He snatched it out of the air before it hit the ground.

An envelope. Manila, thick—about an inch and a half.

"Expenses," Sandià said. "And maybe to buy a little something for your children. Okay?"

"I can't—"

"You can, and you will. If you deny me this, then I will be offended. I expect you to accept that courteously—a little bonus for helping me deal with these matters—and we shall say no more about it."

"Thank you," Madigan said.

"Say my name, Vincent . . . You never say my name. Time was that we would talk like friends and you would always say my name."

"Thank you, Dario . . . I appreciate it. I really do."

Sandià got up from behind the desk. He walked around the front and stood for a moment. He stepped forward, extended his arms, and then he embraced Madigan.

"Don't forget to care for your children," he whispered in Madigan's ear. "Don't forget to love them. If children grow up without a father, there will be things about themselves that they will never understand."

Madigan felt every muscle in his body go tense. That was the second thing that Isabella had said that Sandià had now repeated.

I am starting to believe that you are a good man, Vincent.

If children grow up without a father, there will be things about themselves that they will never understand.

Sandià let go of Madigan.

"Thank you, Dario," he said. He could hear tension and uncertainty in his voice.

"I have upset you, Vincent?" Sandià asked.

"No, you have just made me think about things that I didn't want to think about."

"Maybe that is a good thing," Sandià replied. "Maybe that is part of my job as the Patron Saint of Lost Causes."

"Maybe it is," Madigan said, and he turned to the door.

"Keep me informed of your progress," Sandià said as Madigan stepped out into the corridor.

"I will, Dario. I will."

Madigan closed the door quietly behind him and walked down the hallway with the thick manila envelope in his hand.

He knew that Sandià had threatened him. Indirectly, simply by mentioning his children, Sandià had threatened him. And then given him money. That was the game here. Give with one hand, take with the other.

It was about time Sandià was the subject of his own methods.

It was time for the imbalance to be redressed.

GO TELL THE MOUNTAIN

Walsh was waiting for him in the corridor. He seemed agitated. "Vincent," he said. "I need to talk to you."

"Now?" Madigan didn't need Walsh right now; he needed some space to think this thing through. Was Charlie Harris the one who had called Sandià? Was it also Charlie who had informed Sandià of Maribel's presence in the Valderas house? And if so, how did he know that Maribel had been there?

"Yes, now," Walsh replied. "Can we go into your office?"

Madigan opened the door. Walsh hurried after him, glanced back into the corridor as if alert for someone following him. He closed the door, stood with his back against it, and looked directly at Madigan. Madigan noticed then how pale and exhausted the man looked.

"I have been in Evidence. The gun is missing. The .22 that Tomczak spoke of . . . It's gone. Christ, Vincent, I don't know what to think. I'm really in a fucking mess here."

Madigan laughed. "You're worried because an item of evidence is missing from storage? Jesus, Duncan, will you just calm the fuck down? If I had an inventory done right now, I guarantee that at least twenty-five percent of the stuff that is supposed to be there is no longer there."

Walsh sat down. Then he stood up again. He paced back and forth between the door and the desk.

"Hey, seriously . . . calm down, will you?" Madigan said. "I don't think this is anywhere near as serious as you think. To tell you the truth, the fact that it's missing might be a good thing."

"A good thing? How so?"

Madigan could just feel how tense and anxious Walsh was. Walsh was precisely where Madigan needed him to be, and yet he had to calm him down a little. Too anxious, too desperate, and Walsh could do something stupid. More often than not, desperate situations did not call for desperate measures, but for something quite the opposite.

"Well, if it ain't there then you don't have an excuse for not removing it, right?" Madigan said. "And whatever the hell kind of investigation might ensue as a result of its disappearance isn't going to implicate you. You can't lie about something you didn't do."

"That won't matter a damn, Vincent. Tomczak has a recording of me making an agreement with him—"

"You could cover this so many ways," Madigan said. "You're doing a setup. You're working on a project to identify a suspected leak inside the PD. Bernie was a test case. You wanted to find out if something you said to Bernie got back to the department . . ."

"It doesn't work that way, Vincent . . . I get even the slightest suspicion—"

"Walsh, I got it covered," Madigan said. "I'm taking care of it, okay? Just leave it to me and I will make this thing go away for you."

"What do you mean, make it go away?"

"Like I say, make it go away. I got it covered. Stop fucking panicking, okay? You really don't have anything to worry about."

"How can you say that? How the hell can you say that?"

"Because I'm taking care of it, right? That's how I can say that."

"And what happens if something goes wrong?"

"Walsh, just sit down, for Christ's sake."

Walsh looked at Madigan, and still that expression—drawn, overwhelmed—told Madigan that Walsh just did not get it.

"Sit down."

Walsh complied.

"Look, it's real simple. Someone has something on you, you have something on them . . . Well, in this case I have something on them. You have to stop worrying about this thing. It's gone, okay? It's just gone."

"This guy . . . Bernie Tomczak . . . you have something on him?"

"Jesus Christ, Walsh, could you be any more clueless? Hell, man, I have things on everyone."

"Including me, right?"

"I don't have anything on you. Bernie Tomczak, now, he *does* have something on you. But we're taking care of it."

"We? What d'you mean *we*?"

"Jesus, it's just an expression. We—you and me, okay? *We're* taking care of it."

"And what do you want from me?" Walsh asked, all of a sudden his tone both anxious *and* suspicious.

"From you? I don't want anything from you. What the hell would I need from you?"

"I'm IA. I can make internals go away. I can make OIS reviews change date . . ."

"I don't want anything, all right? And as far as all that bullshit with whoever about moving OIS reviews and this and that, just forget about it. This bullshit information you got from Moran about the fourth man being a cop, well, that wouldn't hold up under any kind of scrutiny. So if the information that Moran gave you was shit, then you don't have to get his possession bust lifted, and if you don't have to get the bust lifted—"

"Then I don't have to get the OIS review postponed for Benedict."

"Right."

"And you're sure that the fourth man was *not* a cop?"

Madigan laughed, and he was amazed at how spontaneous and natural that laugh sounded. "You really honestly believe that a cop would go into one of Sandià's houses, kill a bunch of guys, Sandià's nephew included, and make off with a bunch of cash . . . And then, just to get the party going full swing, he decides to whack his three *compadres* in a storage unit? Jesus Christ, that is some wild bullshit out of an airport paperback."

Walsh smiled. He tried to smile. It came out looking strained and awkward.

"Get some sleep, okay?" Madigan said. "You don't look like you've slept for a week. Take some time off sick or something . . ."

"Two days," Walsh interjected. "Two days, no sleep, barely eaten. Worried sick about this . . ."

"Hell, man, you should've come and seen me earlier. This is just nothing, you understand? This is just nothing to get all wound up about. It's gone. It's history. Okay?"

"I really appreciate your help, Vincent . . . And if there's some-thing I can do for you—"

Madigan looked pensive for a moment. "Well, now that you mention it, my friend, there was a robbery I did, and I killed a bunch of guys, and I wondered whether you might just help me sweep it under the rug, so to speak."

Walsh smiled. He started to laugh. "Vincent . . . you're a good man, and I really appreciate your help."

There it was again. *Vincent, you're a good man.* What did they say? Once was happenstance, twice coincidence, third time was a conspiracy? Maybe the world was trying to make him a better person.

"Forget it," Madigan said. "Go take a sick leave for the day. Get some rest. You look like crap."

Walsh paused as Madigan held the door open for him. He extended his hand. Madigan took it and they shook.

"I won't forget this, Vincent," Walsh said.

"That's exactly what you need to do."

"I don't mean the thing with Bernie . . . I mean—"

"I know what you mean," Madigan interjected. "Go," he said. "Eat. Sleep. Get some freakin' space, will you?"

Walsh nodded. He left the office, walked down the corridor, glanced back at Madigan as he reached the end.

Madigan stepped back and closed the door. He returned to his desk, sat down, and felt the shakes coming long before they arrived. He managed to get the manila envelope out of his jacket pocket and put it in the desk drawer, but by the time the cellphone rang his hand was shaking so much he could barely hold it steady.

"Vincent?"

"Isabella . . . what's up?"

"I'm scared, Vincent. Someone came to the house. Someone knocked at the door. I think it was that man who was here the other evening . . ."

"Which man? Bernie?"

"I don't know . . . He had a hat on when he came the other time . . ."

"Yes, that's Bernie. Don't worry about Bernie. He's fine."

"He didn't look fine, Vincent. He looked real bad. He looked like someone had given him a real good beating."

"Okay. Do nothing. Go nowhere. I'll find Bernie and find out what's going on, okay?"

"Okay, Vincent . . . but . . ."

"But nothing, Isabella. Leave it to me."

"All right, Vincent, if you're sure. I'm just scared, real scared."

"I know you are. There's no need to be. No one but me knows where you are. Just leave Bernie to me. Now, hang up and go watch TV or something, and I'll see you later. Okay?"

"Okay," she said. "Thank you, Vincent, and I'm sorry for calling."

"It was the right thing to do. Hang up now. I'll sort out what's going on."

She did so. Vincent put his cellphone on the desk. What the hell was this now? What was Bernie doing going to the house?

Rock and a hard place. If he called Bernie to ask him why he was at the house, Bernie would know someone had been inside. Bernie Tomczak wasn't the kind of person to let such a thing lie. If he didn't get hold of Bernie, then he wouldn't know whether he looked beaten up because of the beating Madigan himself had given him four days earlier, or if someone else had caught up with him. If it was the latter, well, if it was the latter, then Madigan needed to know if it was connected to this thing. Hell, Bernie was going to be in only one of three or four places. Madigan was going to have to trawl them for sight or sound. When he found him, it was going to have to be a coincidence.

Madigan took the manila envelope and opened it. There was ten grand inside. He split the ten grand into three parts, put one third in his pants pocket, one third in each of his jacket pockets. Whatever the hell might be awaiting him when he found Bernie was bound to go easier if he had a stack of cash along as company.

Madigan's first thought was to head back to the Bronx, but that had been Bernie's first thought, that Madigan would be home. Bernie wouldn't come to the precinct—not a prayer—and thus he would check out the haunts where he believed he would find Madigan. They were easy enough to scope out, and it was in the third place he tried that he was almost besieged by a fraught and shaken Bernie Tomczak, and whatever the hell kind of treatment he'd undergone at the hands of Madigan on Monday was just nothing compared to what he had suffered since Wednesday night.

"Jesus fucking Christ, Vincent. I've been looking for you everywhere!" he said. Two of his teeth were missing, the right side of his face was swollen and pitted with burst blood vessels. He had a cut above his left eye that had bled down to the lid, and a thick gob of congealed blood had dried there.

"What the hell happened to you?" Madigan asked, and he actually felt concerned for Bernie. Such a reaction surprised him.

"I got an issue or two," Bernie said. He grabbed Madigan's arm and steered him toward the back of the bar, a quiet place on East

123rd that Madigan sometimes went to when he needed a break from his regular haunts.

"Why the hell didn't you call me?" Madigan asked.

"Ah man, I got another phone and it didn't have your number on it. And I would've called you from a pay phone, but I couldn't remember all of your number . . . Anyway, whatever the fuck, it don't matter. I got you now."

"So what the hell happened to you? You screwed someone's little girl and she—"

"I need some money, Vincent, and I need it fast. I don't know where the hell else to go."

"How much, Bernie?"

"Eight grand. I need eight grand in about three hours, and I—"

"Eight grand? Are you fucking kidding me?"

"Do I look like I'm kidding, Vincent? Do I look like I'm yanking your chain? I need eight grand, and I need it fast."

"And where the hell do you think I'm gonna get eight grand from, Bernie? That's a sizable chunk of cash."

"I don't know, Vincent. I don't know, and right now I don't care. You gotta help me. You gotta—"

"I ain't *gotta* anything, Bernie. You can't just up and ask me for eight grand—"

"I'll pay you back. I'll pay you back for sure, Vincent."

"Just like you paid whoever you now owe this money to, right?"

"Anything, Vincent—"

"I want the phone," Madigan said.

Bernie's eyes widened. "The phone?"

"The phone you recorded the cop on. I want *that* phone."

"But, Vincent—"

"Bernie, don't bullshit me. You need eight grand. I can give you eight grand right here and now in cash."

Bernie smiled weirdly, and then he laughed. "What the fuck you talkin' about?"

Madigan reached into his pants pocket. "That's about three and a half right there," he said, showing Bernie the bundle of notes as discreetly as he could. "I have another bundle like that in each of my jacket pockets, and I'll give you eight grand right now if you give me the phone."

Bernie blinked twice, and then he shook his head. "I can't . . ."

"This money you need . . . Is it for Sandià?"

"No, of course it isn't for Sandià."

"Then you're screwed," Madigan said. "You give me the phone for this eight grand, and then you have nothing to barter for the Sandià debt, right?"

Bernie didn't need to reply. The situation was obvious.

"Okay, Bernie, here's the deal. I need you alive. This is a bullshit thing you've done here. You've been running a tab with some other loan shark bookie asshole, right? Whatever the hell you've done that's got you into this much trouble for the sake of eight grand . . . Jesus Christ, I can't even get my head on with you sometimes . . ."

"Vincent . . . man, seriously, I didn't mean to—"

"Shut the hell up and listen to me, Bernie. I'm gonna give you the eight grand because I can't have you die on me right now. I want the phone, okay? You need to give me the phone. You need to give it to me because I'm gonna look after it a helluva lot better than you, and also because if you screw something else up and get yourself killed then I'm in a hole, okay?"

"But, Vincent—"

"Bernie, what the hell did I say?"

"You said to shut the hell up."

"Good, so shut the hell up a minute and hear me out."

Bernie shut his mouth.

"Okay, so you give me the phone, I give you eight grand, you keep the hell out of trouble and stay alive for a few more days. I'll give you another five hundred and you just go hide in a motel or whatever, and you're on call to me, okay? You do nothing. You go nowhere without my say-so. You understand me so far?"

Bernie nodded.

"Good, so you go hide in a motel someplace, and you call me and let me know where you . . . No, better still, I'm taking you someplace and then I'll know where you are, and when I call you and tell you to do something, you gotta do it, okay?"

"And what about Sandià . . . I gotta pay Sandià too."

"I'm dealing with that," Madigan said. "I'm handling it. I'll keep my end of the deal if you do exactly what I tell you."

"Yes, yes . . . Jesus Christ, Vincent, I don't know what to say."

"Then say nothing, Bernie . . . less likely you'll get into trouble that way."

"Right, right."

"Good, so we're going. Where's this phone?"

"It's in a rented mailbox place about three blocks from here."

"Well, lead the way, my friend. Lead the way."

They went on foot, and en route Madigan stopped at a phone store and bought a disposable cell with fifty dollars' credit on it. He dialed his own number into the directory, called himself, then gave the phone to Bernie.

"You have my number now," Madigan said. "Only number you need. That's the only phone you answer, and this is the only phone you call out from, okay? When I see you I'm gonna check how many times you've called me and how much credit remains. If I find out you've been calling hookers or bookies or dealers or whoever, then so help me God I will drive you to see Sandià myself . . ."

"I promise, Vincent. I promise."

"Okay, so let's get this phone with the recording on it."

The mailbox place was where Bernie said it would be, as was the phone. Madigan checked the recording. It was Walsh all right, no question.

"Okay, so where do you have to get this eight grand to?"

"There's a club up on Marin Boulevard—"

"You're bullshitting me," Madigan said. "Marin Boulevard. There's only one person you could be dealing with if you've got to make a drop there. Jesus, Bernie, what the hell was it this time?"

"It was a ball game, okay? A dumb freakin' ball game. I went double or nothing. It was an outstanding debt from a long way back."

"Jesus, Bernie, sometimes I wonder what the hell is wrong with you."

"It's a sickness, Vincent . . . Gambling is a sickness . . ."

"Yeah, Bernie, sure as hell it is. Just like being a drunk or a junkie or a kiddy fiddler . . . It's all a freakin' illness and no one's actually responsible."

"Vincent, I'm sorry . . ."

"Save it, Bernie. We're going in the car. I'm not walking to Marin Boulevard. And this eight grand . . . This is everything, yeah? This is not, *Get me eight grand today and you'll stay alive, but I want the rest by tomorrow*? It's not that kind of deal, right?"

"No. This is everything, Vincent, absolutely everything."

"It fucking better be, Bernie, or I'm gonna—"

"It is, Vincent, it is. This and the one eighty I owe Sandià, and that's it."

"Just this and the one eighty to Sandià. That's all. Man, you should hear yourself. Don't know anyone in as deep a hole as Bernie freakin' Tomczak."

Madigan heard his own words. There was the lie. The hole Madigan had dug for himself was far, far deeper.

Madigan drove. Neither he nor Tomczak spoke for the duration of the journey. Madigan pulled up outside without even asking where they were supposed to be going.

He counted out the eight grand and gave it to Bernie Tomczak. Bernie looked like he was going to say something, and then he looked like he wasn't.

"Okay, so go pay the man," Madigan said, and Bernie got out of the car.

Madigan waited. Bernie was gone no more than ten minutes. While he waited, Madigan listened to the recording Bernie had made of his conversation with Walsh. It was a good recording—no doubt about the identity of the speaker, and no question what each of them meant. If this ended up in the hands of someone inside the PD, then Walsh's career was done and over. He'd said he'd get rid of the evidence, and—by all appearances—he had.

Bernie Tomczak returned. He seemed relieved.

"They ask where the money came from?" Madigan asked.

"Do they ever?" Bernie replied. "Do they care?"

"No, they don't," Madigan said, and started the car.

He drove Bernie back across the river to Mott Haven, found a motel near St. Francis Hospital. He booked him in for a week, paid up-front, gave Bernie another five hundred in cash.

"That," Madigan said, "is for coffee and cakes, a drink, some smokes, right? Nothing else. I come back and you've gambled that . . ."

"Vincent, enough already. I got it. I really got it, okay?"

"Glad to hear it, Bernie. Now, you take care. Stay inside, watch the porn channel, order food delivered in, a different take-out every time. Stay the hell here until I call you."

Bernie nodded. He stood in the doorway of his new home. "I really appreciate it, Vincent. You know, despite all the shit that's gone down between us, you really are a good—"

"Save it, Bernie. You don't know what the fuck you're talking about."

*

235

Madigan drove back to the precinct, stopping only once at a secondhand cellphone place to buy an identical phone to the one he had taken from Bernie. He recorded the conversation between Walsh and Tomczak on the second phone, and put the first one in the glove box. Back at the precinct he found Walsh, asked him to come to his office. Walsh did so. Madigan sat him down, handed him the phone, and Walsh sat there in quiet disbelief for a good thirty seconds.

"This is the phone?" he said eventually.

"No, Walsh, it's my mother's cellphone. Jesus Christ, of course it's the phone."

Walsh looked set to cry.

"So we're done, okay?" Madigan said. "Now will you go the hell home and get some sleep?"

Walsh got up. "Christ Almighty, I don't know what to say, Vincent."

"Well, like I just told Bernie, why don't you keep your mouth shut for a while and stay out of trouble?"

"Yes," he said. "Yes, of course."

"Good, now get the hell out of here. I have things to do."

Walsh left. Madigan could imagine him exiting the precinct, sitting in his car, playing that conversation over and over and then deleting it, all the while asking himself how much of an idiot he'd been. If such an experience had taught Walsh anything, it would have to be that there was a line. Step over it and you better know what you were doing, and if you didn't . . . well, you'd end up like Bernie Tomczak. Hiding in some two-bit piece-of-shit motel in Mott Haven and scared to go outside.

And maybe, Madigan thought as he left his office once more, that would be his own fate too.

There had been other plays. The game had moved on. Now it was time to bring it all to a close.

46

FIRE SPIRIT

Charlie Harris was at his desk. He seemed agitated before Madigan even started speaking, and when Madigan opened with, "Charlie . . . another question about this Valderas killing, the one with the screwdriver," Charlie looked up at him with this vexed expression on his face. It was then that Madigan knew he was aggravating an open wound. Charlie Harris had something on this case, and he didn't want Madigan pulling threads out of it.

"What?" Harris replied, in his voice an edge of suspicion.

"Just something that's been bothering me."

"Jesus, Vincent, I'm really busy here. I got a reassignment from some dickhead at the 158th because a CI we once used— Ah Christ, you don't even wanna know." He shook his head and leaned back in the chair. "So what is the problem now?"

Madigan took the other chair, hesitated for just a moment, and then said, "The witnesses?"

"Witnesses? What the hell are you talking about? I told you I got nothing, jack squat, nada . . . absolutely nothing on this one."

"Inside the house."

Harris seemed confused. "What about it?"

Madigan then took his turn to frown. "What about what?"

"Jesus, we gonna do this square dance all day? You ask me about the witness in the house, and then you look surprised because I'm asking you what you want to know about the witness in the house. You even mentioned this girl, the one who got sliced and diced. It's all in the file."

Madigan shook his head. "There's nothing in the file about any witness in the house, Charlie."

"Sure there is. I wrote the damned thing up myself. Go take another look."

"I've gone through every page. There's no report about a possible witness in the house."

"What?"

237

"Seriously, Charlie, there's nothing there."

"Well, sure as shit there was someone in the house, and sure as shit I wrote it up. If some doofus in admin has screwed it up and lost a report, then that's their problem."

"What was in the report?"

"Look, Vincent, it's real simple. We get there. There's a DB on the deck with a freakin' screwdriver sticking out of his face like an aerial. Maybe he's trying to catch the WKLM evening show, I don't know. We clear the house, we make sure no one's hiding anyplace with a socket set and a monkey wrench, right? Then I'm in the bathroom, and all of a sudden I'm standing in a pool of piss, right? Someone's peed on the bathroom rug. Then Crime Scene shows up, late as ever, and they're looking at the pooling around the DB's head, and they come back and tell me that there's the edge of a woman's shoe print in the blood, okay? So two plus two makes four. This footprint comes after the blood, not before. So we're straight now. There's someone in the house, some chick, and she's hiding in the bathroom. She's terrified, she knows what's happening. She waits for the perp to leave, she comes out, she's checking out aerial-head, and even as she's standing there the blood pool reaches the edge of her shoes or whatever. Then she takes off—"

Madigan thought of Maribel Arias—decapitated, her torso and body parts divided, bagged, dumped unceremoniously in various locations. A week ago it had seemed insignificant. Now it seemed like a nightmare from the worst of all imaginations.

Madigan wanted to ask Charlie Harris how they had become so cynical. At what point had these people ceased to be people? He caught himself even as he voiced the question in his own mind. Something was happening to him. A week ago he would no more have thought such a question than confess to the Sandià house robbery and the three DBs in the storage unit.

He was losing it. He wasn't drinking as much. He wasn't swallowing pills like they were M&M's. Yes, he was definitely losing it.

"Okay," Madigan said, and started to get up.

"Anyway, you have any other questions about this bullshit you ask someone else, okay? I got too much on my desk to be dealing with history right now."

"I think I'm done, Charlie . . . I was just puzzled about the witness in the house thing."

"Well, we're straight on that now. All done and dusted, right?"

"Right."

Madigan looked back as he left the office. Charlie wasn't watching him, and Charlie had really seemed pretty much the way he always was. And the report from the file? The report that was no longer there? Maybe Charlie wasn't the lead to Sandià. Ron Callow? Hell, it could have been anyone in the precinct. Everyone had access to files, or could get access to them without difficulty. All Sandià had to do was give a nod to whoever he had in the system, get them to keep tabs on an ongoing investigation, keep him informed of what was happening with it, and "lose" the odd document or two to slow down the proceedings. Madigan knew it could happen that way. Why? Because he'd done the very same things himself.

No, intuition told him that this went further than Charlie Harris and a lost piece of paperwork, but he couldn't think who . . .

Back in his own office he put Bernie Tomczak's phone in an evidence bag and locked it in the bottom drawer of his desk. Then he changed his mind, took it out, and hid it way back behind the lowest drawer of the filing cabinet. He counted the few remaining hundreds of Sandià's ten grand, and he wondered what his next step should be. No one else was looking into the Sandià robbery and the three homicides. No one else was looking into the Melissa Arias shooting. The Maribel murder and the killing of David Valderas were on the back burner. With Walsh taken care of, no one was even looking at him. Charlie Harris wasn't filing any more reports, and neither would Madigan. That way, whoever was feeding information to Sandià would run dry very quickly. That would make Sandià dependent upon Madigan. That would also prompt someone—perhaps—to come asking about progress on the cases. Madigan remembered a scene from *The Godfather*. The garden, Michael talking with his father, and Vito told him to look out for whoever came to propose the reconciliation meeting. It was the same here. Whoever asked for progress—nonchalantly, as an aside, a *Hey, Vincent, anything ever happen on that Sandià bust . . . You know, the one where those three guys got whacked in the storage unit or whatever?*—well, that was the man. That's what he had to watch for.

Resolved in his own mind that things were as under control as they could be, Madigan left the office. He took the stairs, headed out of the building, and drove home. It was nearly three, he'd eaten no lunch, had been on-shift since eight that morning. Officially he had a couple of hours left, but no one would miss him. He wanted out for a while. Just a little while. He wanted to be elsewhere—away from this, away from the madness and the lies and the killing.

Something had shifted. Was it the fact that he had Isabella Arias in his house? Was it the fact that he wasn't drugged out of his head half the time? He hadn't even thought about it, but he was taking fewer and fewer pills. He reached his car, got in, and searched through the glove box for the hip flask. It was full. He drank half of it, maybe a little more, and then he leaned back and closed his eyes for a moment. The warmth of the spirit filled his throat, his chest, and he could feel the knot of muscle easing at the base of his neck and across his shoulders. There was that ever-present anxiety in the base of his gut. Always there, always reliable . . . the tension that came with living this life. *At the end of every phone call is another disaster. No victims are created equal. When your day ends, my day begins. Lord God, if nothing else, just grant me one more day . . .*

Madigan set the hip flask aside and started the engine. He pulled out of the underground parking lot and turned right toward home. He was going to stop on the way and get food. He knew a Thai place a half dozen blocks from his house. He would get food for them both, and he would make believe that he was a normal guy with a normal life and that everything that happened today had no bearing on tomorrow or the next day or the next.

For a little while—perhaps—Sandià would not exist, nor Maribel in a Dumpster, nor Valderas with a screwdriver through his face, nor a little girl in a hospital with a bullet hole through her guts. Perhaps.

49

SEXBEAT

"I don't eat oriental food usually," she said, "but that was good."
They sat at the kitchen table, she with a glass of wine, Madigan with a coffee mug half-filled with Jack Daniel's.

"I don't usually eat," he said.

"I know."

He leaned back. "So tell me about Melissa's father." It seemed right to ask her about her daughter. Madigan had called the hospital. The child was doing well, would be there for another few days yet, had asked for her mother, and the attending nurse —the one that Madigan spoke to—had dealt with it well. She'd told Melissa that she was under a *No Visit Order* due to potential infection from outside the ward. The child was fine. The nurse had asked Madigan if the mother's whereabouts had been established. Madigan denied all knowledge.

"She'll have to go with Social Services if the mother doesn't show by the time we release her."

"I understand," Madigan said. "It'll be fine. I'm gonna find the mother. You let me know if anyone from Child Services comes around, okay?"

Madigan relayed the conversation to Isabella, omitting Melissa's request for her. The last thing he needed was for Isabella to be taking off to the hospital to see her daughter while Madigan was at work. Containment was now the key. Containment of Bernie Tomczak, containment of Isabella Arias, and most of all, containment of himself. He had to keep it together. He knew he should not have been drinking, but he couldn't help it. But he was doing better. He really believed he was doing better. What would transpire with the Ariases, he did not know. He had no plan beyond the immediate end of this thing. It was like Alcoholics Anonymous—take everything just one day at a time. Anything beyond that was more than he could deal with right now.

"Melissa's father?" Isabella said. "We were together for some years, but . . ." She shook her head, reached for the wineglass. "But he was not a father. Some men just aren't ready to be fathers."

"Some men are never ready to be fathers."

"You speak of yourself?"

"Myself, and a lot of others."

She shook her head. "Every man is ready to be a father. It's nature. Some men don't want to be fathers because they believe a child will slow them down, stop them living, stop them enjoying things so much, when really it's exactly the opposite."

"In what way?"

"What could be a greater guarantee of your continued happiness and well-being than a child?"

"That's a very basic viewpoint."

"Basic?" she said. "Maybe. But basic can be fundamental, and fundamentals are everything. Without fundamentals there is no structure—"

"What is this? Philosophy and Sociology 101?"

She laughed, but Madigan did not get the impression she was laughing *at* him.

"You pretend to be shallow, but you are not," she said.

"Oh, I'm shallow," Madigan replied. "I have a veneer of awkward misery, and beneath that there is very little else."

"You are too hard on yourself. You are a good man."

"So people keep telling me."

"Maybe it would be good to believe such a thing, then."

"Maybe it would be good if people stopped trying to tell me who I am, especially those who don't know me."

"Like me."

"Like you, yes."

A frown crossed her brow, like the shadow of a cloud across a field. "I have upset you, Vincent?"

"I've got thicker skin than that."

"I didn't mean to upset you."

"You didn't upset me."

"I'm sorry."

"For what?" Madigan asked. "I just said that you didn't upset me." He reached for the coffee mug.

She drank her wine.

There was silence for a moment.

"And your children?" she asked.

"What about them?"

"How many do you have?"

"Four."

"Four? Well, hell, for someone who doesn't want to be a father—"

"I never said I didn't *want* to be a father. I said some people were not *ready* to be fathers."

"But four kids?"

"Yes, four."

"What are their names?"

"Cassie, Adam, Lucy, and Tom. Seventeen, thirteen, six, and three, respectively."

"You see them?"

"Rarely."

"Do you not think it would be good for them to see more of you?"

"Probably not."

"Why, Vincent? Why do you think that a child wouldn't want to know their father?"

"Because that father might not be the best influence on that child."

"You really don't have a high opinion of yourself, do you?"

"Maybe I don't deserve a high opinion."

"You can't have done anything so terrible that you feel this badly about yourself."

"And how badly would that be?" he said. "What the hell is this? What am I getting this third degree for? I'm trying to help you out here, lady—"

"Hey, I'm sorry," Isabella interjected. "I'm not trying to upset you, like I said. We're just talking, okay? Just talking."

"Talking is a discussion, not a barrage of questions."

"Okay, Vincent, no more questions."

"Good. No more questions."

There was silence again, longer this time.

"So what do you want to talk about?" she asked.

"Something other than my children, my ex-wives, my ex-mistresses, or my job."

"Right," she said. "Politics, then? Religion?"

Madigan looked up at her. She looked good. She was angry with him and she looked good.

"I'm sorry," he said.

"For what?"

"Well, I don't know . . . for being an asshole, okay? Just accept the apology and let's move on."

"Accepted," she said.

"So you *do* think I'm an asshole."

"I didn't say that."

"But I said sorry for being an asshole and you accepted the apology, therefore indicating that I was right to apologize, ergo you must think I was being an asshole."

"Fuck off, Vincent."

He laughed.

She laughed too, briefly.

They sat in silence once more.

"I don't know that I've ever felt this awkward," she said.

"Then you ain't lived much," Madigan replied. "This isn't awkward. This isn't even close to awkward."

"I feel like I should like you," she said, "but you seem to make it your business to persuade people that they shouldn't."

"Oh, it's just for you that I behave like this," he said. "With everyone else I'm just the nicest guy in town."

For a moment she wondered if he was being serious. His expression was deadpan, and then he cracked the faintest smile.

"You really are an asshole," she said.

"Why you . . ." he threatened, and he raised his fist.

She was sipping her wine. She coughed, spluttered, couldn't stop laughing. The wine was down her T-shirt.

"Look at this," she said.

"I'll get you some more," he said. "Don't worry about it."

"I'm going to get a clean one," she said.

"Oh, for Christ's sake, it's only a bit of wine . . . Leave it."

"No," she said. "I want to get a clean one."

She got up, walked past him toward the stairwell, and as she passed him she traced a line across his shoulder with the tip of her finger. He did not acknowledge it. It was a split-second thing. He felt her finger, and then she was gone.

Was she hitting on him?

Jesus Christ, was she *really* hitting on him?

Madigan's mouth was dry. He reached for the mug of Jack, decided against it. He went to the kitchen for a drink of water, juice, something else, and then he changed his mind and went back to the Jack Daniel's.

This was not good. Not good at all. This was a complication he could do without. This was not containment. This was something so far from containment . . .

"See?" she said.

Madigan turned. She was at the foot of the stairwell, and then she was walking toward him. She had on a new T-shirt. It was white. In that moment, she looked better than she'd ever looked.

I shot your daughter. Me and my friends shot your daughter. If it wasn't for me . . .

What? he thought. If it hadn't been for Madigan, what would have happened? Maybe the robbery at the house threw Sandià's plans into disarray. Maybe it threw a spanner in the works. Maybe—just *maybe*—had the robbery not taken place, had the nephew not been killed, then Sandià would just have systematically moved ahead with finding Isabella and Melissa, and they would both now be little more than names and files in the unclosed case section of the 167th.

But no, that was not what had happened. Isabella was alive. Melissa was alive too. They were both alive.

Maybe by shooting Melissa he had actually kept them both alive a little longer.

Madigan tried to smile.

"You okay, Vincent?"

"Yes," he said. "Tired maybe."

"You do look tired."

"Yeah, just tired," he said. He went back to the kitchen table and sat down. She followed him, sat where she had before—facing him, smiling now, her clean white T-shirt, her white teeth, her dark hair around her shoulders, her eyes, the smell of her . . . Had she put on perfume?

Oh Jesus, this is not the way to go . . .

"Can I ask you a question, Vincent?"

"Sure."

"You ever get lonely?"

"Sure I do," he replied.

"I mean, so lonely that you just want to be with someone . . . just next to someone, to feel the warmth of another human being right there beside you?"

He looked at her.

Her cheeks were flushed.

If this wasn't an invitation . . .

"No," he said. "We're not going there, Isabella." He tried to sound as definite and emphatic as he could.

"But . . ."

"You're vulnerable. You're lonely. So am I. Jesus Christ, what the hell is this?"

She got up. He *knew* she was going to come around the table.

"Isabella, no," he said, and he raised his hand.

"Vincent . . ." she said, and she sat down once more.

"No," he said. "You can't do this. You do this and you'll regret it."

She got up again. Vincent rose too. He stepped back and the chair fell over, and then he felt himself getting angry.

She was right in front of him, and she had her hand on his arm. He steeled himself and felt tension in every muscle on his body, and then he closed his eyes for a second, preparing himself to do battle with this overwhelming desire to just grab her, but it was too late . . .

He felt her hand on his cheek, and when he opened his eyes her eyes were right there—inches from his.

She leaned forward. She kissed him.

Madigan did not respond.

She kissed him again.

He couldn't help himself.

His arms on her shoulders, pulling her close against him, and the feeling of another body, the heat from her, the smell of her, the sensation of her hair against his skin, and his hands were around her waist, and he couldn't remember when he'd last felt anything as powerful as this . . .

And then he froze.

You nearly killed her daughter.

You are not a good man.

You are an evil son of a bitch, and if she knew what you knew . . .

"I'm sorry," he said. He pushed her away, held her at arm's length, and in her eyes was a flash of hurt and rejection.

"No," he said. "It's not you . . . Seriously, it's not you, Isabella. I promise you . . . Jesus Christ, this is me, this is all me. I can't do this. I have to stay separate from this. I can't get involved . . ."

"Involved?" she asked. "You can't get *involved*? You are already involved, Vincent . . . I am here, right? I am right here in your kitchen. I am living in your house. You are hiding me from the people who killed my sister and shot my daughter—"

That's what you think. You think Sandià was responsible for Melissa's shooting.

"—and if that doesn't make you involved, then I don't know what the hell is going on in your head."

"That's not what I meant," he said. "You know what I meant. It's not that I don't find you—"

"What? You seriously think I give a damn about whether or not you find me attractive? Jesus Christ, you are naive, Vincent Madigan. You really think that this was what it was all about? Hell no, I just thought that maybe we could fuck, okay? You think women just don't want to get fucked sometimes. That's all there is to it, Vincent. Women like to get laid too every once in a while. No strings, no complications, nothing at all but some straightforward sex to ease the tension and take your mind off the pitiful bullshit that your life has become. That's it, Vincent. What . . . you seriously thought I was in love with you or something? That I was all head over heels and you and me were going to get it together, and I was going to be your little Suzy Homemaker . . ."

"Enough," Madigan said. "You're giving me a headache."

"Oh, grow up, for Christ's sake!"

"Shut your damned mouth!" Madigan snapped.

"You shut *your* damned mouth, you asshole!"

She took a minute step backward, and he saw it coming—the roundhouse. She let fly with an almighty swing, but he caught her forearm inches away from the moment of impact. He held her arm in a viselike grip. He was almost amazed at his own reaction time and strength. Her arm came at a hundred miles an hour and he just stopped it dead.

"You were going to slap me," he said.

"You deserved it."

"You're a complete nightmare," he said. "You are worse than both of my ex-wives put together."

"And you were a real hotshot husband, I see . . . That's how come you're still so happily married."

"Jesus Christ, you really have a negative side."

"Yeah, and you're Mr. Happy-Go-Lucky yourself, Vincent."

She backed up, sat down, grabbed her glass, and emptied it.

"Get me some more wine," she said.

Vincent hesitated, and then grabbed the bottle. He poured wine into her glass, overfilled it, saw it spill over the edge and across the table.

He caught her looking at him out of the corner of his eye. She was smiling. He started to smile too.

"You are a hopeless bastard," she said. "Never in my life have I ever seen a man turn down free, no-strings-attached sex."

"Well, sister, if it had been anyone else but you—" He left the statement hanging.

"Oh, you son of a bitch," she said.

Madigan reached for his cup. His heart was going at some phenomenal rate. The adrenaline rushed like . . . like what? He couldn't even describe the feeling.

The taste of the whiskey in his mouth, the feeling in his chest—all of a sudden he didn't want any more, but he knew that if he drank it the urge he had to just pounce on her would pass.

He had to withhold himself. This would not work. This was not the direction to go in.

"Maybe it is best," Isabella said eventually. "I didn't mean to—"

"You don't have to explain or justify anything to me," he said. "Other circumstances, and there would be no question. But we have to keep our minds focused on what we're doing here. For you, for Melissa, for your sister, okay?"

"Now you make me feel cheap."

"I'm sorry," Madigan said. "I don't mean to. I'm not so good at working out this kind of thing. I think what I think and I say it."

"That's a good quality."

"In some instances, yes, but in others that's exactly what you shouldn't do."

"Well, in this instance . . ." She hesitated. "I think maybe you were right, Vincent. I know that in the morning you wouldn't have respected me and I would have hated myself for stooping so low."

Madigan smiled. "Touché."

Isabella leaned forward and put her hand over Madigan's. "You pretend so much to be the tough guy, the unreachable one, but you are just like everyone else," she said. "Underneath all that bullshit and bravado there is a heart."

"I am not who you think I am, Isabella."

"I don't know who you are, Vincent, so it doesn't matter what I think. I've known you for two days, that's all. Seems longer, but it's only two days. You don't get to know anyone in two days."

"If I gave you twenty years you wouldn't know everything about me."

"Oh, I don't think you're so hard to read, Detective Madigan."

Madigan nodded. He smiled. He reached for the bottle. He didn't challenge or deny; he didn't refute or respond. This conversation was going nowhere.

Right now, all he wanted to do was drink himself into unconsciousness, and that—irrespective of what Isabella Arias might say or think—was what he was going to do.

"You gonna drink all of that?" she asked.

"Sure am," he said, "and when I'm done, I may just go get another."

"Well, if you're going to be drunk for the rest of the night, then you can get me a coffee cup and I'll join you."

Later, somewhere in the small hours before daybreak, he woke. He was still dressed, Isabella was too, and they lay beside one another on the sofa.

He stayed silent, motionless, so as not to wake her, to not obscure the sound of her breathing. For that was the only sound he could hear, save for later when a moth wove some invisible web around the kitchen lightbulb in the hope of keeping that light forever.

He wondered about himself, his life, about Isabella and Melissa, about who in the department was working for Sandià . . .

He wondered about a great many things, and yet understood so very few.

It served no purpose to look at himself, and yet he couldn't help it. He looked, he saw; he understood where he had begun and where he had ended up. Had he known that such a life awaited him . . .

And then he closed his eyes, and for a brief while he tried to forget who he was.

50

THE HOUSE ON HIGHLAND AVENUE

Isabella did not wake when Madigan finally got up from the sofa. It was past eight on Saturday morning, and though he was off-shift there were things he needed to do.

Now would have been the moment of desperate regret had they slept together. He was relieved that he had drawn a line.

He sluiced cold water on his face in the upstairs bathroom, got a clean shirt—unpressed—and put it on. He took his jacket, his car keys and cellphone, and—perhaps unnecessarily—he scribbled a note for Isabella.

Out for a couple of hours. Call me on the cell if you need me. Don't go out.

Vincent.

As he drove away from the house, he thought about Charlie Harris. The more he thought about Charlie, the less he believed that Charlie was working for Sandià. Sure, he had said whatever he'd said to Charlie, and a few hours later he'd received the call from Sandià. But Charlie could have spoken to anyone in the interim.

Madigan's working himself foolish over some dead freakin' drug dealer.

Oh yeah, what dealer was that, then?

I don't know, some asshole who got dug in the head with a screwdriver.

And it may not even have been whoever Charlie spoke to. It could have been someone who overheard the conversation. Charlie's manner, his attitude, his seeming lack of concern for what Madigan might have been doing with the case . . . Or maybe Charlie was just a good liar. After all, wasn't he—Madigan—the best liar of all? He was the Patron Saint of Liars. Did he consider that he possessed the monopoly on falsity and deceit?

Madigan looked at himself in the rearview as he pulled to a stop a half block from the precinct house.

He started to question what he was doing.

Don't go there, Vincent.

It's a dark place. You'll get lost.

No, my friend, you really don't want to go there.

It's too late to change things now.

Things have a natural order.

Doesn't do well to go upsetting them . . .

You are who you are. You'll always be this way.

Better to accept it. Fighting the inevitable is futile . . .

Madigan hunted through the glove box for something—anything. A 'lude, a couple of Xanax, some Percocet. There was nothing.

He got out of the car and slammed the door shut. He was frustrated. He was anxious. Anxiety and fear were founded on ignorance, nothing more. And of what was he ignorant? Well, there was an easy answer to that one. Who was working for Sandià? Who—inside the department, inside *this* precinct—was working for Sandià?

Well, as the old saying went, you set a thief to catch a thief. Who could have been better than Madigan to establish who else was an internal line out to Sandià?

No one, that's who.

It was just a question of how to do it.

First and foremost, he had to consider who could be in the frame for this. There was Ron Callow and Charlie Harris in Robbery-Homicide, but that was just one small unit within the precinct. There were the detectives in Vice, Sex Crimes, Fraud and Cyber, and above them their relevant squad sergeants, unit chiefs, the precinct captain, the divisional commander . . . hell, all the way to the top. Anyone with a rank of detective 3rd class or above could access the system from any workstation. Anyone could've taken a look in the Valderas case file and decided to lose some of the paperwork.

It was not feasible to determine the identity from information that Madigan could leak. There were just too many people. To do such a thing would require giving a different piece of information to every single person, and seeing which of those came back to him via Sandià. The precinct guys perhaps, but the divisional commander?

So if he could not go after them, he would have to set it up so they came after him.

That was the only way.

He would have to set some bait and see who came sniffing around.

It was the proverbial "house on Highland Avenue," something that came from his father, and where it came from before that Madigan had no idea. As a child, it was always the answer.

Where are we going, Dad?

The house on Highland Avenue.

Where's that?

You'll see when we get there.

It didn't mean anything. It was just his father's way of never answering the question, of maintaining a mystery. You kept looking for someplace that wasn't there.

Madigan had to get the inside man to go someplace to find something. And it had to be something that Sandià could not ask Madigan to do, someplace Madigan could not or would not go. Somewhere that would compromise their relationship. Then Sandià would have to send his other man, and Madigan would be there to find out who it was. Once that was established, then the second play would have to work, a play that would leave Madigan and Isabella Arias out of the firing line, Melissa too, even Bernie Tomczak. And Madigan had Bernie as a resource, Walsh also, and whoever else he could think of that could be trusted not to talk.

It was chess, that was all, but a game of chess where the opponent was unaware that the game had already started.

And what would raise Sandià's interest sufficiently to prompt immediate action?

The money, of course, but—even more than the money—the possible identity of the fourth man, the one who'd killed his nephew, shot his three accomplices, and then calmly walked away with the proceeds.

Simple, in theory, but in reality? In reality it was something else entirely.

Madigan reached his office and closed the door. He sat down at his desk and closed his eyes. He breathed deeply for a while, tried to focus, tried to center himself, but it was hard. So many thoughts, so much confusion. Isabella, Bernie Tomczak, the motel, the money, the wounded daughter, the dead sister, the fact that he'd nearly compromised everything by sleeping with the damned woman the night before . . .

He needed a drink. He fetched a half bottle of Jack Daniel's from the lower desk drawer, selected the cleanest of two coffee cups from the top of his filing cabinet, and poured a couple of inches.

He downed it in one, felt the familiar and comforting bloom of sensation in his chest.

He thought about Cassie. She was going to be eighteen in twenty-five days. Then he thought of Adam and Lucy and Tom, and he remembered what Sandià had said.

If children grow up without a father there will be things about themselves that they will never understand.

There were two ways to grow up without a father. The father can be absent—physically, tangibly absent. Or he can be mentally and emotionally absent. The former applied to Madigan's own children, perhaps the latter applied to his own father. The "house on Highland Avenue" had perhaps been a metaphor for all things of significance. Had his father ever really been there for him?

In all honesty, there was little that aggravated Madigan more than the whining, victim attitude of those who blamed the past for their current misfortunes. People were not simply a product of their past. They were a product of so many things. There were situational dynamics—elements that came into play from so many different quarters. The whole was greater than the sum of its parts. An only child, a distant father, a timid mother, always in the shadow of her husband, Madigan had had to create his own entertainment. It was always the smarter kids that got into trouble. They bored more easily. They needed greater mental stimuli. Imagination, if not channeled into something creative and constructive, became a tool for manipulation. Some kids were just too dumb and too trusting to tell lies. Madigan, however, had always been a liar. Lying to get what he wanted, lying to get attention, lying to get money, lying to get out of trouble. Lying—in some cases—to get *into* trouble, just as a means by which he could relieve the monotony of being a kid.

Is this what had happened? Is this where it had all started? And had this laid the foundation for the way in which he had failed his own children?

It was a dark place. Such thoughts, such feelings. Was this now where he would live for the rest of his life? Was this all he had to look forward to? On a scale of right to wrong, how far had he traveled, and was there any way back? Perhaps more accurately, was there any way back *alive*?

Madigan had never overly concerned himself with his own memory. What people thought of him after he was gone had never been of any concern. But now? Did it matter now? Was he now anxious for what his children might think of him, what they would be told, what they would find out? That was egotistical in itself. The assumption that they would *want* to know, that they would even care. After all, how significant a part had he played in their lives? What had they already been told? What had Angela told Cassie? *Your father? Jesus, Cassie, don't even bother. He was a loser, a drunk, a liar . . . He was back then, and I'm sure as hell he still is now. People don't change. Actually, no, that's not true. Some people do change. It's people like Vincent Madigan that will always be the same.* And had Cassie's perspective been slanted to such a degree that she would never consider another viewpoint? And if so, wasn't that all he deserved?

But then there was Adam and Lucy and Tom. Why were they any less important than Cassie? Because they were all still young enough to have impressions carry weight and substance. And where would those impressions come from? From the very women he himself had lied to, betrayed, cheated on, deceived, misled, and abandoned. These were the character references for his life. But the kids were also young enough to be influenced the other way, to have their viewpoints reversed. To do that, though, Madigan would have to be there for them. And he was not.

Cassie was the first, had always been the first, *would* always be the first. Cassie was an adult now, she was a young woman, not a child, and every thought he had of her carried the weight of obligation, of responsibility, of duty, of fatherhood, and it seemed now that in all things he had been found wanting.

His life.

Christ, what a fucking mess.

Madigan rose and paced the room. He had to bring it all back together. He had to tie every thread, every loose end, every fragment of this thing together and walk away. Was such a thing possible? Was he delusional, crazy, simply tempting fate and Providence? Had he just done too many bad things to even warrant another chance?

And what about Isabella? How long would it be before she learned the truth of what had happened, that he—Vincent

Madigan, her knight in shining armor—had been the one to put her daughter in Harlem Hospital with a bullet in her guts?

And if she did find out, what would she do? Try and kill him? Go to the department? Forgive him?

Madigan's mind was stretched every which way. The nausea had not passed, not completely. The tension in his chest, his lower gut, now seemed to be spreading like some neural-borne virus throughout his entire body. He had to get out. He had to get some air. He had to *think*.

A block and a half from the precinct Madigan found a diner. He sat in a window-facing booth; he ordered coffee, a Danish. He watched people go by. He looked at their faces, their eyes, their expressions, and he wondered about the truth of their personal worlds. He thought about their lies, their misdemeanors—the infidelities, the broken promises, the deceptions and evasions and family secrets. He thought about the unknown pregnancies, the abortions, the hit-and-runs, the embezzlement, the thefts, the tax evasions. He thought about the truth, how some considered it cheap and expendable, how others considered it a disease that could be cured with just a few more lies. The compassion and humanity of youth and innocence obliterated by degrees. Eventually people were no longer themselves. They were what they believed the world wanted them to be. Because that was what it was all about. That was the real sleight of hand, the real deception. The self-conviction, the self-*convincing* that everything they did, everything they had done, was for the best. *I didn't want to hurt her feelings. I didn't want to make it worse than it already was. Had he known, he would have been devastated . . . I thought it best to keep it to myself. Just for now. Just until I think he can cope.* Bullshit. It was all bullshit. We all spent our lives lying to one another, to ourselves, to the rest of the goddamned world. Why? Because of greed, avarice, lust, racism, hatred, prejudice . . . And what did they say about prejudice? A fixed opinion founded in fear? A *pre*judgment. Madigan had been prejudiced all his life. Prejudiced toward himself, prejudiced against others. It was a lie. Had been then and still was now.

And the truth? The truth was that he would have to lie some more to get out of it.

Madigan drained his coffee cup, left the uneaten Danish behind. He walked from the diner back to his car and turned it around. He headed up First toward Paladino.

Everything was on the line—not only the lives of Melissa and Isabella Arias, but also those of Bernie Tomczak, Duncan Walsh, even the lives of his children. Most of all, perhaps even *least* of all, there was his own life.

Madigan knew he had to talk to Sandià, and he had to talk to him now.

51

THE MASTER PLAN

"Seneca?" Sandià echoed.

Madigan nodded. He tried to smile. He tried to look relaxed. He tried to give nothing away. "Yes," he said. "Seneca."

"And what did he say?"

"He said that luck was nothing more than the meeting of opportunity and preparation."

Sandià considered it for a moment, and then he nodded. "I like that," he said, "but what that has to do with anything, I do not know."

Madigan took a deep breath, but silently.

The strength of the heart had been measured—not in emotional terms, not in terms of love or passion or betrayal, for this was not possible. It had been measured in physical terms, in pounds per square inch, the force with which it could move so many gallons for so many yards at such and such a speed. But the heart, irrespective of its power, was silent until fear presented its face. Until panic or terror or trauma assaulted the senses, the heart went quietly about its powerful secret business. Now Madigan's heart was truly alive for the first time in as long as he could recall. Whatever he might have experienced before was nothing compared to this. Now he was cleaner than he had been in a long time. There was little in the way of drugs and alcohol to quell the anxiety, the alarm, the terror he felt in that moment.

Everything was in the balance now, for Sandià recognized no parameters when it came to exacting revenge for wrongs committed against him.

Madigan lit a cigarette, inhaled, exhaled, closed his eyes for a second and then started talking.

"Just as you said before, we have known each other a long time. Enough for us to share a degree of respect, perhaps a limited degree of trust. I mean, what the hell, eh? In this business you can trust no one completely, but of all the people I deal with, I think it's safe to say that you have always been a man of your word, and I respect you for that."

"That's very good of you to say so, Vincent, but what this has to do with—"

"Bear with me," Madigan interjected. He took another drag of his cigarette. "I have been thinking about this thing that happened, and I have been thinking about trust, and I have also been thinking about Seneca and his viewpoint about luck. Whoever robbed that house did not have luck, good or bad. Whoever robbed that house and killed your nephew had preparation and opportunity . . ."

"Well, that is obvious, Vincent—"

"Maybe so, but this is the thing I don't get." Madigan leaned forward. "People who work for you, right? They get taken care of. I mean, look at you and me for an example. I work on a give-and-take principle. I give you what you want. I take from you what I need. You give me what I ask for. You take from me what you require to make business go smoothly. We've never had any problems. We've never had any disagreements. We've always seen eye to eye, right?"

"Sure, Vincent, sure." Sandià shifted in his chair. He had an expression on his face—implacable, calm, unattached perhaps. This was business. His personal relationship with Madigan— factually—meant nothing. If Madigan was not there, someone else would take his place. He was curious as to where Madigan was taking him with this line of conversation. He was questioning the destination. It had been merely four days since the robbery of the house, the murder of his nephew, and whatever patience he might have possessed was growing thin. He wanted answers. He wanted results. If answers and results were not forthcoming, then people were going to die.

Sandià waved his hand. *Get to the point, Vincent,* that gesture said.

Madigan cleared his throat. "And during all these years we have worked side by side, have I ever given you cause for concern? Have I ever given you any reason not to believe what I have told you?"

"No, Vincent, of course not. As I said before, we have had . . ." Sandià paused. He smiled like he was trying to force himself to be good-humored, to take the edge of seriousness out of the conversation. "We have had what I would call a mutually beneficial relationship."

"So I want you to listen to me now," Madigan said, "and I want you to hear me out, and when I am done we can talk about this thing and see if we can make sense of it."

"Say what you want to say, Vincent. Enough of this bullshit, okay?"

"That's the point right there," Madigan said. "It isn't bullshit. I'm not bullshitting you. I'm gonna tell you something, and this is going to come out of left field, but I want you to consider all options and possibilities before you dismiss this out of hand."

"Okay, okay, okay . . . Jesus, Vincent, you're getting me fucking angry now. Enough with the lectures. Tell me the details here."

"I think . . . Hell, Dario, I think your nephew was going to rip you off."

Sandià looked at Madigan. A frown flitted across his brow. It was there, and then it was gone. He smiled, then he looked intense, confused even, and then he smiled again. The smile became a laugh, and then he was shaking his head and saying, "Jesus, Vincent, you had me fucking going then . . . I thought you were gonna tell me something that made some sense."

"You have someone else on the payroll," Madigan said. "You have someone inside the department on the payroll, someone who gives you information, someone who tells you what you need to know. I have a very strong suspicion that this person may have been working with your nephew and they were going to rip you off for that money, and then your nephew was going to use that money to put some people together, and he was going to come after you. He wanted the territory, Dario. He wanted your territory and he was prepared to do pretty much anything he needed to get it. He had his own relationship with whoever else you have on the payroll, and they figured to take you and me out of the picture and put themselves in our places . . ."

Sandià was silent.

His expression did not change.

That—perhaps—was the most unnerving thing of all. Sandià's initial reaction—one of dismissal—was merely superficial. The truth—harsh though it was—was that Sandià trusted no one. He knew he could trust no one, not even his own family.

That moment, the fact that there was nothing at all in Sandià's eyes scared Madigan more than anything he had ever seen. If Sandià's nephew had in fact tried to rip him off, then the nephew would have been killed. It was business. It had always been business, would always be business.

And then Sandià spoke. His voice was low, a whisper almost, and though the words meant one thing, the feeling behind them was something else entirely. It was as if Sandià was saying things in an effort to convince himself of something he wished to believe, and yet knowing—all too well—that Madigan's words could be just as true.

"This is crazy, Vincent. I know you do some pills and whatever, Vincent . . . but this is crazy—"

"Is it?" Madigan asked. "Is it so crazy?"

"So if that's the case, then how did my nephew end up dead?"

Sandià just asked the question directly. He was not angry, his voice still barely more than a whisper, and his gaze was unerring, riveting, fixed on Madigan.

It took everything that Madigan possessed to meet that gaze and not look away. Not for a moment. Not for a heartbeat.

"Because whoever else you have working for you had no intention of taking you down. He's making too much money. He's onto a good thing. He is approached by this kid, he hears him out, he goes along with it, and he figures he can do the work himself. He can take the money from the house, he can off your nephew and the delivery crew, he can kill his three accomplices. He's away scot-free, he's more than three hundred grand in profit, he keeps his relationship with you, and the only person who knew that he was aware of the money delivery is dead."

"No, Vincent, this is not possible . . . You don't know what you're saying. My own nephew? You think Alex did this thing? That he wanted to overthrow me? My own sister's boy?"

"He wasn't your son, Dario. He was your nephew. He told you what you wanted to hear. He made you believe he was with you all the way, but all the time he had this thing going on, this thing to be the big boss, the master of the house. And he works at this thing behind the scenes; he talks to whoever he can trust. Why does he approach your other police contact? Because a police contact is already compromised. He's a better bet than someone inside the family, right? This guy has to be careful whatever he does. He can't go blabbing around the place. He can't up and say whatever he likes to you. You're dealing with this guy like eggshells already. He knows that. This isn't like someone who can just disappear into Witness Protection if they decide to give you up. This is a cop. This is a brother-in-arms. This is someone who's going to vanish like no one else. Why? Because the department doesn't want this in the papers. They don't want this on the news. There's nothing that hurts the department's image more than a dirty cop. They're going to do whatever they have to keep word of this out of the press. If your contact gives it all up, then they're going to hide him somewhere. He tells them he's been working with you. He says he's on graft, kickbacks, he's doing deals for you, he's passing information, and has been for years. They're scared like you wouldn't believe. This is going to take their reputation back to how it was in the forties. They give him immunity. They listen to everything he has to say. They prepare their case. They get you, your whole family, everyone. They close everything down, and our man is in Boise, Idaho, with a different name, a different life. You're never going to find him. It's all over. End of story. But, then again, it could go the other way. Your nephew plans to take you down, he tells your police contact, the contact tells you. What are you going to do? You're going to get rid of your nephew, but then you're going to have to get rid of the cop as he can tie you to the death of your nephew. Think about it. The smartest thing to do is kill your nephew, take the money, and everything is back to battery."

Sandià was silent. He was hearing what Madigan had to say. He was looking for anything and everything he could recall that would confirm or deny what Madigan was suggesting. What had Alex said? How had he seemed? How had he responded to such and such? That time he said so and so . . . Could that have been a lie? The wheels were going in Sandià's mind. Madigan could hear them. Two things were working for him. One was a small facet of human psychology: Give someone reason to doubt, and they automatically look for reasons to confirm that doubt, not refute it. The second was Sandià's hard-earned suspicion of everyone. A man like Sandià could not maintain such an empire without distrusting everything he heard and everything he saw.

"And if this is true, then why did this other person, this cop, the one in league with my nephew, why did he not go ahead and take me down?"

"Why would he? Why would he need to do that? What possible reason could he have for doing that? You think he wants to be put through the ringer, to have his whole life closed down around him? You think he wants to wind up in Boise, Idaho? He already has it good. He already has you paying him whatever you pay him, and if it's equivalent to what you give me, well, unless he's crazy . . ."

"Or a gambler, Vincent. A gambler and a drunk. Maybe whatever I give him is irrelevant. Maybe he's just like you. Maybe I could give him a million dollars a month and it wouldn't matter a damn because he just spends it on cards and booze and football games . . ."

"I don't think so, Dario."

"And why not, Vincent? Why don't you think so?"

"Because I'm your wild card, my friend. You don't think I know that? You don't think I understand that you're far too smart to have two crazy people working for you? I know you too well, right? I know you have irons in fires all over. I know you have to keep some things straight, and some things can just run wherever the hell they're going to. I know you don't have the attention to worry about two crazy men. You keep me around because I'm the dangerous one. Like a smart investor, you keep some stocks in the old reliables, and you put some money on the wildcat shit that could go bust tomorrow—but maybe not . . . it might just come good and make you a fortune. That's the way you work, my friend. I've known you too long and I've seen too much to doubt you for a second."

Sandià smiled. For a moment he appreciated the compliment, and then his humor vanished as he remembered the point of this conversation.

"You're telling me my own nephew—Alex Calvo—my own nephew was going to betray me?"

"All I'm telling you is that there's too much here that doesn't make sense for anything else *to* make sense. I'm saying there's a chance, a possibility . . . That's all I'm saying."

"And that I need to talk to whoever else I have to talk to . . ."

"I'm not telling you your business. All I'm saying is that there was this rumor that a cop might have had something to do with this robbery, that a cop might have had something to do with the murder of your nephew . . . and a cop might just have had the opportunity to do this. More important, if it was someone on your payroll, then who better to know when that money was being delivered?"

"And if what you say is true, then answer me this. Why would a cop tell me that a cop had been involved? If whoever it was that did this *is* a cop, why would he implicate himself?"

Madigan smiled. "It's the oldest trick in the book. By implying that you could be involved, you exonerate yourself. Offense is the best form of defense."

Sandià leaned back, pressed his hands together as if in prayer, and rested his elbows on the arms of the chair. He closed his eyes.

He stayed motionless for a good four or five minutes.

Madigan could feel his own heart beating. He didn't dare move.

Those minutes stretched away into eternity, and Madigan watched as his own life seemed to be swallowed by that void. If he'd got this wrong . . .

"Vincent."

Madigan opened his eyes. He didn't realize he had closed them.

"Vincent . . . I have to make some calls. I have to deal with some things." Sandià got up from his chair. He came around the desk.

Madigan rose also, and for a moment they stood face-to-face, no more than two or three feet apart, and Sandià looked into Madigan's eyes as if to expose the past, determine the present, predict the future. Madigan did not flinch, he did not glance away; he just looked right back at Sandià as if there was no one else in the world.

Sandià raised his arms and gripped Madigan's shoulders.

"I have killed men," he said quietly. "Even my name . . . it was earned, Vincent, as you know, by something I did that I had to do. I am not a man to find weakness in people. I try to find their strengths. I can use a man's strengths. I can use his honesty and his integrity and his strength. I need a man to be courageous, to tell me the truth, to never lie to me. I need to be able to rely on people. You know that. You know that it is not possible to do what we do with deception and falsehood around us, except where we intend there to be deception and falsehood." He inhaled slowly, exhaled again. He shook his head, but never once looked away from Madigan. "If what you are saying is true . . . If there is even a shred of truth in this, then I will find this out and I will make my decisions. If I find you have lied to me, Vincent . . ." Sandià left the statement hanging.

Madigan did not say a word. He did not breathe.

"Good," Sandià said. "So go, do whatever you have to do, and I

263

will make my calls and speak to people, and we will find the truth together."

Madigan nodded, a barely noticeable dip of the head, but he did not look away.

"And if you are right . . ." Sandià said, and then he released Madigan's shoulders and walked back to the desk. "If you are right, my friend, then it will be a sad day for this family . . ."

"I understand," Madigan said. "But I had to come to you, Dario . . . I had to tell you what I suspected—"

Sandià raised his hand and Madigan fell silent.

"Your loyalty has never before been in question, Vincent, and it is not in question now. Not yet. Let me resolve this for myself, and then we will speak some more."

Madigan walked to the door.

"Thank you, Vincent," Sandià said.

Madigan said nothing. His hand on the door, the door opening, the sense of release, of relief, the letting go of everything, the feeling that he could scream, that he could just run from the building into the street, his heart like a machine, his heart ready to implode, collapse, to just stop in its tracks, his expression blank as he fell to the sidewalk, his life over, everything gone, everything that was anything now meaningless . . .

The weight of his feet as he walked to the elevator. Pushing the button. The sound of the gears and cables. Waiting for Sandià to open the door behind him, to call him back . . .

Vincent . . . just one thing before you go . . .

The elevator arriving. Stepping inside. His finger on the button, looking back toward the door he had just exited.

His mouth and throat like dust.

His eyes wide, almost disbelieving of the scenario that had just played out before him.

Everything was real, but unreal.

The elevator reached the ground. The doors opened. Passing the guys in the corridor, retrieving his gun, and then there was daylight, and the sound of the world beyond the walls of Sandià's empire.

Someone said something, Madigan failed to respond, and then he turned back and tried to smile.

The door, the sidewalk, the hundred yards to his car.

All of it in slow-motion while the rest of the world ran at five, ten, twenty times its normal speed.

Opening the door, climbing in, closing the door, his hands on the wheel, his forehead down against his hands. He was screaming inside, but everything was silent.

It was a long time before he started the engine and pulled away.

52

STRAITS OF LOVE AND HATE

M adigan's heart didn't slow until he was a half dozen blocks from Sandià's place.

He kept thinking about Alex Calvo, Sandià's nephew. Sandià would be turning the thing over in his mind again and again. He would chew on it until he had it all figured out. Until he *believed* he had it figured out. *Why had Alex not colluded with Valderas? Why had he gone to Sandià and reported Valderas's betrayal? Because he was already in collusion with someone else, that's why. And why would Alex want to overthrow Sandià in the first place? Simple . . . The same reasons as everyone else—money, greed, power, control, jealousy.*

Sandià would now no longer be saddened by the death of Alex Calvo in the robbery that Tuesday morning. He would no longer be grieving for his nephew. He would be considering the fact that someone had simply done his dirty work for him. Calvo had become the renegade, the traitor, and now he was no longer a threat. But the other cop? The fourth man? Was he the real traitor? This was the seed of doubt that Madigan hoped to have planted in Sandià's mind, and Sandià—by his nature—would now want nothing more than to challenge this man.

Madigan just hoped he could make it back in time.

He stopped at a car rental place on East 118th, took a non-descript compact, and gave them an extra fifty bucks to look after his own car until he returned. He showed them his ID and they didn't ask questions.

Madigan drove back to Paladino and parked up a half block from the tenement entranceway. If everything moved as he hoped it would, then it wouldn't be long before someone showed up. The only question was who, and whether or not Madigan would recognize them. It could be any cop from any precinct in the city. If he came away empty-handed on the ID, then he was screwed.

*

Ten thirty and Madigan was already on a knife-edge. He needed to take a piss. He couldn't move. Couldn't go anywhere. He wished he had a plastic bottle or some such in the car, something he could piss into and get rid of later.

Self-doubt was the foremost consideration in his mind. He had misjudged everything and everyone. He had talked himself into an inescapable trap of his own devising.

He put the radio on low. He listened to some jazz station out of Long Island.

The music merely served to irritate him further, and he switched it off again.

He thought about Isabella. He thought about Melissa. He wondered what he would do with them if this thing ever ended. Maybe that would be a decision he wouldn't have to make. Maybe they would both be dead. Maybe they would make it through, and he would be dead. He thought about everything that had happened since he and Bernie Tomczak had met in an alleyway only five days earlier. Five days, and everything had changed. The most important five days of his life. No way back, no way over, no way around this. It was straight ahead now, straight ahead and through whatever got in the way. He would either overcome it and see the other side, or it would stop him dead. Literally.

And if he did make it through, what then? Where would he go? Sure as hell he couldn't stay in the department. Or could he? Could he actually pull something like that off? If he dealt with Walsh, with IA, with his own stats, his record, could he just hang in there, make twenty-five, take a pension? He'd be forty-eight, not so old, a good twenty, thirty years ahead of him. The money from the Sandià robbery would be gone. That had to vanish someplace soon. That had to be the incontrovertible evidence to put someone other than himself in that house on Tuesday morning, to put someone else behind the guns that killed Sandià's crew. Could he deal with that? Could he live a life somewhere on a PD pension?

Madigan glanced in the rearview. He recalled that moment when he'd pulled over in front of the chop suey joint. After the meeting with Landry and Williams and Fulton. He'd looked at that same reflection. From how many mirrors in how many restrooms in how many bars had that worn-out face looked back at him? Too many? Or too few? Maybe he'd just lock himself in a motel room and drink himself to death. Maybe that would be simpler. He remembered that thought. He remembered many such thoughts. Seemed the world was full of dark places. He'd seen most of them, lived in a few, and even the ones he'd never visited felt somehow familiar.

Nothing was certain. Nothing was dependable.

Madigan watched the front of the building and he prayed that someone would show up.

By noon he couldn't bear it. His nerves were shredded. His bladder was ready to rupture. He'd chained a half dozen smokes, felt nauseous and light-headed. He could sit there for the rest of the day and no one could show up. What if Sandià's man was way up high in the department? What if he was District, even the Chief's Office? There was no way in the world someone like that would be seen around Paladino. If that was the case, then this was a hide into nowhere. If he did not know the identity of Sandià's other source, then . . .

Madigan shifted in the seat. He glanced back over his shoulder and caught something move in the corner of his eye.

He turned back.

A car drew to a halt a half block up ahead. It was a nondescript sedan, precisely the kind of vehicle provided for duty use from the car pool. Would make sense to use a car pool vehicle. Just as Madigan had said to Sandià about the second source, offense was the best form of defense. Be seen down here in something other than a PD vehicle and it would raise more questions. In a PD vehicle you would be on nothing but PD business, right? Who would be dumb enough to make a personal visit to Sandià's territory in their own car?

Madigan ducked down instinctively, despite the fact that the car had pulled to a stop facing in the opposite direction. He waited. He watched. He wished he had binoculars. He did have his cellphone. He could at least take some snaps of the car and its occupant.

Madigan worked his hand into his inside jacket pocket and retrieved the phone. He got it set up just as the sedan door opened.

A foot on the street, a hand on the roof as the driver pulled himself up and out.

Madigan was unable to take a picture.

He froze. He could not believe his eyes.

He took two or three pictures then—rapid-fire—and then the

phone slipped from his hands and clattered into the footwell. He left it there as he watched the occupant lock the door of the sedan and start across the street toward Sandià's building. Jesus Christ Al-fucking-mighty.

Madigan was breathless, speechless, utterly dismayed. There was no way in the world he would ever have suspected this man of being in Sandià's employ . . . But then there had to be a good few people at the precinct who would have said the same thing about Madigan.

Madigan leaned back. He closed his eyes and breathed deeply. He reached for another cigarette and lit it, almost immediately grinding it out in the ashtray.

Okay. Okay. He had to get his thoughts together. He had to arrange things. He had to work out what he was going to do and how he was going to do it. He needed to speak to Bernie, to Walsh . . . He needed to get Sandià's money out of the house and prepare for what was happening next.

Jesus Christ Almighty.

Madigan struggled with it. He could not refute the evidence of his own eyes. But it made as much sense as anything else. This man had access to every case that was being worked on. Any file, any document, any report. And his viewing of such things would not be questioned in any way. This man was in a perfect position to provide Sandià with anything he needed.

The only question that then troubled him was whether this second insider knew of Madigan's relationship with Sandià. Surely not. Surely Sandià was not so dumb as to compromise his contacts by informing one of the other's existence? Madigan felt sure that Sandià would not have done this. After all, he had known nothing of this man, had he? Above and beyond everything, Sandià was a businessman. The extent of his influence and control was determined solely by what he knew and what others did not.

Madigan started the car. He pulled away and headed back to the rental site. By one he was away again. He had to make some calls, pay some visits, share some words with Walsh about the next stage of his operation.

Bernie Tomczak was about ready to die of loneliness by the time Madigan showed up at the motel.

"Jesus Christ, Vincent, how long are you gonna keep me holed up in this fleabag freakin' joint?"

"Calm down, Bernie. We're going to go out. We're going to get a drink, get something to eat, and we're going to talk. There's something I need you to do for me, and I need you to be straight and clearheaded and calm about this."

"What thing? What do you want me to do?"

"Get your jacket," Madigan said.

Bernie did so, slipped it on, followed Madigan out of the motel to the car.

They drove north, away from Mott Haven toward the Bronx, and then Madigan headed west toward High Bridge. He wanted to be away from home, away from anyone who might recognize either himself or Bernie Tomczak.

Madigan pulled over and they walked a block or two. He chose a nondescript diner near John Mullaly Park. He ordered a turkey and white cheddar sub. Bernie said he'd have the same. Madigan asked for fries as well, a side salad, a couple of beers. He had an appetite. It felt good to have an appetite. He wondered whether it was because he was off the pills.

The food came, the beer also.

Bernie held up the bottle. "What the hell is this?" he asked. "You're drinking barley pop now? What the hell is going on with you?"

"Shut your mouth unless you're putting food in it," Madigan replied. "We eat, then we talk."

"Something's awry with you," Bernie started, and then he shook his head. "What am I saying? Something's *always* awry with you."

"Eat, Bernie," Madigan said.

"Okay, okay. I'm eating already."

Bernie Tomczak ate, every once in a while glancing up at Vincent Madigan and wondering what was going on behind the intense and unsettling expression.

When they were done eating, they talked. They talked for an hour. Bernie asked questions, Madigan answered them to the extent that he was willing, and when he was done Bernie Tomczak just sat there for a while in silence.

Half an hour later Madigan pulled over outside the motel in Mott Haven and let Bernie out.

"Speak later," Madigan told him. "I'll come get you or call you here. Don't try and reach me."

Bernie said nothing, merely nodded and walked back toward the motel entrance.

Madigan turned around once more, headed toward the Bronx. He wanted to see Isabella Arias. He wanted to talk to her as well. He wanted to let her know something of what he was going to do and why.

53

WATERMELON MAN

"You look like you slept good," Madigan said.

"I found some pills in your medicine cabinet and I took one and I feel like crap."

"What tablets?" Madigan asked.

"I don't know . . . sleeping tablets, downers of some sort. They knocked me out. Completely knocked me out, and now I feel like shit."

"You had some coffee?"

"No. I thought to make some, but I couldn't be bothered."

"Jesus," Madigan said. In his voice was a tone of exasperation.

"Hey," she said. "You can fuck off with that attitude. You're not the one stuck in this crappy house on your own worrying about your daughter."

"Your daughter is fine. I told you that," Madigan said.

"I have to get out of here," she said. "This is bullshit. I can't stay locked up in here forever."

"It won't be long now," Madigan said.

She opened her mouth to respond, hesitated, and then shook her head.

"I'm going to make some coffee," Madigan said. He crossed the room and drew the blinds. Why, he didn't know. All of a sudden he felt as if he needed to hide. The room was in semi-darkness. It changed the mood between them suddenly.

"Sit there," he said, indicating the couch.

She did as she was asked, but resentfully. A couple of hours waiting in the car for someone to show up at Sandià's had made Madigan stir-crazy. Isabella had been in the house since Wednesday. He had some small inkling of how she must feel.

But now, now it was all different. Now he had some small appreciation for the extent of this thing. Now he truly understood how much was at stake, and what would happen if it all went to hell. He was screwed both ways if he fucked this up.

Madigan did as he said—made coffee, good and strong. He poured a cup for each of them and took it back into the front room.

Isabella looked worried, more so than previously.

"So what's happening?" she said. "What's going on? How long do I have to stay here?"

"Hopefully not that much longer," Madigan replied. "There's a couple of things I need to do, and if everything goes the way I want it to go then you're going to be off the hook in the next day or two."

"What are you going to do?" she asked, and then she raised her hand. "Don't tell me," she said. "Me off the hook means that you're going to handle Sandià, right?"

"That's the idea."

She closed her eyes then. She just sat there with her hands around the coffee cup, and Madigan heard her exhale. There was something about her body language—a profound overwhelm, a shadow of defeat.

"You think I'm going to get myself killed," Madigan said.

"Yes," Isabella replied. "You go up against Sandià and you're going to get yourself killed, and then where the hell will I be? In this house, completely unaware of what's going on. Sooner or later they'll put two and two together and they'll do to me what they did to Maribel."

"That is not part of the plan."

"You know who you're dealing with, right?"

"I do."

"You do? Really? You know why he's called Sandià?"

"I've heard the stories—"

"Stories? There's only one story here. Only one story that gave him that name. The Watermelon Man, right? You've heard that story?"

"Yes, I have . . . Of course I have. Anyone who works down here, anyone who has anything to do with this man has heard the story."

"But you didn't know her, right?"

"Her?"

"The mother. The boy's mother."

Madigan shook his head. "No, I didn't know her."

"I did," Isabella replied. "Eloisa, that was her name. That was her name from before. She changed it later, of course, but back then she was called Eloisa."

Isabella shifted back. Her face was little more than shadows.

"And you spoke to her about it?"

"I did," Isabella replied. "I knew her. I spoke to her. I was there when she found out what he'd done. And I knew the boy as well . . ."

Madigan's eyes visibly widened.

"Oh yes," Isabella said before Madigan had a chance to speak. "I knew the whole family. I knew what happened, why it happened, and I know what Dario Barrantes did. And when Maribel told me that she was in love with this guy, this David Valderas, I told her to stay away from him. Don't get involved with anyone who works with Sandià. That's the law down here. That's the law if you want to see tomorrow, next week, Christmas. Stay the hell away from Sandià and his people . . ."

"She didn't listen," Madigan said.

"Listen? When did she ever listen to me? No, she didn't listen. Of course she didn't listen. She was *in love*. He was a good man really . . . This is what he told her. And he loved her too, and he had some money coming to him and he was going to take her out of this life and give her the life she deserved. The same story. Always the same story from these people. Well, he gave her that life, didn't he? He gave her exactly the life that she deserved. Short and brutal. Painful. A horror of a life. That's what he gave her."

Isabella's fists clenched. The cup slid between her palms and hot coffee slopped over the rim and scalded her.

"Christ!" She stood up suddenly.

Madigan took the cup from her, set it on the floor. She shook her hand, held it for a moment.

"You okay?"

She didn't acknowledge Madigan's question.

She sat down again.

Madigan lit a cigarette.

Isabella asked for one.

"You don't smoke," he said.

"Did, then I quit, now I'm starting again."

Madigan frowned.

"What, you worried I'm gonna die of cancer before Sandià gets to me?"

Madigan handed her the pack of cigarettes. She took one, lit it, inhaled deeply.

"Like riding a bike, right?" she said, and she smiled awkwardly. She closed her eyes, shook her head slowly. "You really know him?" she asked Madigan. "You really know the kind of man he is?"

"I think I do," Madigan replied.

"I don't think anyone knows what kind of man he is. Not the women he sleeps with, not the people who work for him. I think the only ones who know who Dario Barrantes really is . . . God and the devil. God because He made him, the devil because that's who owns his soul . . ."

Madigan smiled wryly.

"You are not a religious man, are you, Vincent?"

"Can't say that I am."

"Our culture . . . everything is steeped in religion. Everything means something; everything is symbolic. Everything is seen by God, and everything is punishable. They love to hand you the guilt . . . They love to make you terrified for your soul, the souls of your family. Don't do this, don't do that . . . So when someone turns against the church, when they become a criminal, a murderer, they *really* turn against everything that the culture represents. People like Barrantes . . . they are the worst. They have gone to the dark side of their soul completely."

"I've seen some pretty fucked-up people in my time—"

"But to do what he did? To do that to a young boy, a boy who hadn't even started his life . . . and for money?"

Madigan shook his head. "I don't know details. I heard what I heard. I heard a number of different things. Urban legends . . ."

"No, not urban legends." Isabella took another drag of the cigarette. He watched the bright tip of the cigarette, the wreath of smoke, the way her face looked as she exhaled from her nostrils . . .

"It was there," she said. "Right there in East Harlem. Right in that building where he sells his drugs and his guns and his women. He did that thing to that boy, and I knew the boy's mother . . . I saw what he did and how it killed her too."

"So tell me," Madigan said. "Tell me your understanding of what happened."

"You really want to know?"

"Yes," Madigan said. "I really want to know."

"The guy . . . Angel, they used to call him. His name was Angelo Torresola. He was Puerto Rican. He came here . . . when? I don't know, maybe thirty years ago. He was young, no more than eighteen or nineteen, and he was always in some sort of trouble. Never serious, just kid stuff. But then something happened and he ended up inside. It broke him, made him crazy. There was the girl I told you about. Eloisa. He got her pregnant. They were just kids, nothing more. He was in his early twenties by the time he came out, and Eloisa had moved on, had taken the kid with her. Maybe it was jail that broke Torresola, maybe the fact that Eloisa had disappeared with his son, but he was out of it. He was off the radar. He was a great deal more dangerous then than before he went inside. And then there was Barrantes . . . and he'd already started to cut East Harlem into pieces and divide things up like he had some God-given right to do what he wanted with people. And Torresola was home, and he'd heard about this guy Dario Barrantes while he was in jail, and so it started. The territorial disagreements, the little wars, the shootings, the stabbings . . . like a gang culture. People on Torresola's side, people on Barrantes's side, and they would never agree. Once the first stone has been thrown, there is no way to revert to negotiations. After the first casualty it becomes a matter of pride, of principle . . . And they brought the whole neighborhood down with them . . ."

"Torresola I heard about. He was dead by the time I knew Barrantes," Madigan said.

"And when was that? When did you and Barrantes meet?"

"Ninety-five . . . early ninety-five."

"Then Torresola himself was only just dead . . . a handful of months, and the boy, Torresola's son? You should have seen that boy. He was the one who should have been called *Angel*."

"Barrantes killed the boy, right?"

Isabella smiled. It was a mournful expression, as if remembering someone she loved who had passed, perhaps remembering a time before all this, when things were good, when she had her daughter with her and she was not in hiding from the world.

"A watermelon," she said. "It started because of a watermelon."

She reached for another cigarette, lit it, gave it to Madigan, and then lit one for herself.

"What happened?" Madigan asked.

"Torresola was out of prison. It was ninety-three, just after

Christmas. I remember that because I had just turned seventeen. I was thinking about college, stuff like that. I met a boy then . . ." She glanced away for a moment. "Should have held on to him. He was good. He was the right one, you know? He lives outside of New Jersey now, has his own engineering firm. He has a lot of money, a wife, four kids." She looked back at Madigan. "Could've been me. That could have been me out there in New Jersey with a good husband and four kids."

"You can't go backward," Madigan said. "If you'd have stayed with him, you'd never have had Melissa."

Isabella's eyes flashed. The hurt was there. The hurt of truth. She waved the comment aside. "So Torresola . . . Angel, right? He was out. He was in his early thirties. He was the tough guy. He had all his people behind him, and here was this other one, this Dario Barrantes, and he had come muscling in on East Harlem, a territory that belonged to Angel before he went to jail. Eloisa was nowhere to be found. Angel tried to find her, sure, her and the boy, but she had disappeared. It was always the way. He was looking so hard he didn't see her. She was right there under his nose. She changed her name. She called herself Veronica. She had married someone else, had a couple more kids, and he didn't even recognize her. The better part of fifteen years had passed and she had grown up. She knew who he was, but she had another life. She didn't want to be involved with these people. And the boy? Angel's boy? He looked like his mother. He didn't look like Angel Torresola. She'd changed his name as well. His name was now Dominic Campos . . . twelve, maybe thirteen years old. That was the old life, the life with Angel Torresola, and she wanted her son to stay away from it. She had plans to move, to get out of East Harlem, and her husband was a good man, a simple man, and he knew nothing about her former life as Eloisa, and he did not know the identity of Dominic's father. He was an auto mechanic. He had a small place, a little shop, you know? He fixed cars for people. That's what he did. He was about as far from the world of Dario Barrantes and Angel Torresola as you could get."

"So what happened with the watermelon?"

Isabella smiled ruefully. "It all sounds so stupid now. So meaningless. Jesus Christ, these people are animals . . . When it comes down to it, these people are little more than fucking animals."

"What happened?" Madigan prompted.

"The war had gone on. Barrantes killed Angel's people, Angel

killed Barrantes's people. They fought over blocks, streets, alley-
ways. They were both running dealers, hookers, selling guns,
whatever people wanted. It went on for two, three years. I don't
know how many people ended up dead, but it was a lot."

"I heard about it," Madigan said. "I was over in the Twelfth until
July of ninety-four, and then I moved to Manhattan Gangs. I was a
good ways from East Harlem, but I heard about it."

"Nineteen ninety-four," Isabella went on, "and things just
became insane. People were frightened to leave their houses.
Torresola and Barrantes were selling their shit everywhere. Even
the dealers were fighting between themselves, fighting over who
got to supply who with what. The police could do literally nothing. Barrantes had one half of the neighborhood, Torresola the
other. Finally it came to a head. They sent envoys. They arranged a
meeting, a dinner, and Angelo Torresola and Dario Barrantes were
going to resolve their differences, agree on their territories, stop
the war. That was the plan."

"But it didn't work out that way, right?"

"No, and it didn't work out that way because they were as bad as
one another. It was a setup. Barrantes was going to kill Torresola.
Torresola was going to kill Barrantes. It was obvious. Why they
even bothered pretending, who knows? But they came together,
and they talked, and they went back and forth and didn't resolve
anything. They got to the end of the meal, and there they were,
nothing had changed, and Torresola sends for the waiter to
bring watermelon. He wants watermelon to cleanse his palate.
The waiter is paid off, and this request is his signal to call Torresola's people. It means that Barrantes is going to die, that
Torresola's people will come and shoot Barrantes right there in
the restaurant, and then they will begin the operation to clean up
East Harlem. You work for Torresola or you die, it was that simple.
But Barrantes had his own arrangements, and he had his own
people, and they already had the waiter bought off. The call was
never made. No one came. Torresola and Barrantes went their
separate ways. Barrantes could have killed Torresola right there in
the restaurant, but he wanted nothing to do with it directly. He
didn't want to be implicated directly in the death of Angel Torresola, and he knew that if Torresola died right there that evening
then his people would make him a martyr and just keep fighting."

"So he killed the son, right?"

"Barrantes knew about Eloisa. He knew she had changed her

name. He had been there in the territory all the time that Angel had been in jail. He knew that Torresola wanted the boy back, but didn't know where he was. So you know what he did?"

"I heard what he did."

"You heard the truth?"

"That he cut out the boy's heart and put it inside a watermelon."

"And you believe he did that?"

Madigan was silent.

"The boy was thirteen, no more than that. Barrantes had his people take him. They cut his throat. They opened up his chest and they took his heart out. Then they cut a watermelon in half. They took out all the seeds, all the pulp, and there was enough room to put the boy's heart inside it, and then they closed it up and tied it together with a ribbon, and then they sent it over to Angelo Torresola with their love. There was even a message, like with a gift, you know? 'I found your son,' the message said. 'Have a great reunion.'"

Madigan looked at Isabella Arias. Her eyes were wide, full of disbelief, full of horror, and yet she had known of this event for nearly twenty years. The best part of two decades had not assuaged the effect it had created on her.

"Dario Barrantes sent Angel Torresola the boy's heart inside a watermelon. Dominic Campos, thirteen years old . . . dead before his life had even begun, and all because of the sins of a father he didn't even know. This is our people. This is where we come from, you see?"

Madigan reached forward and took her hand. "Not everyone," he said.

Isabella withdrew. "Everyone," she said. "David Valderas is dead. Maribel is dead. My only child is shot and wounded. And now . . . now I am hiding and terrified for my life, terrified that they will find me, that they will take Melissa, that I will be dead or she will be dead and we will never see each other again."

"I told you before," Madigan interjected. "I am not going to let that happen."

"You cannot control this, Vincent. You are just one man. One man cannot make Barrantes disappear. Torresola had an entire army, and Barrantes just crushed him. After Dominic's death Torresola was ruined. Eloisa found him. She knew her son was dead because of him. She killed Angel, and then she killed herself. Left her children behind with the new husband. Lives destroyed.

All of it smashed to pieces because of the vanity and greed and stupidity of two men. And one of them is still alive, and the law cannot touch him. We cannot defend ourselves against him, and he keeps selling drugs and guns and putting teenagers out on the streets to do his dirty work, and no one can do anything . . ."

"I can," Madigan said, and he felt something rushing up in his chest, a feeling like . . . like a burning heat coming up from his stomach. For a moment he strained to breathe, and then the sensation passed and he saw everything with a clear and precise view.

"I can do something about it," he said, and he rose from the chair and walked to the window. He edged the blinds apart and looked out into the street. He did not want to look at Isabella Arias. He did not want her to look into his eyes, to look *behind* his eyes, and see him for what he was. He had been with Barrantes. He was no better than the people of whom she spoke. He may as well have cut out Dominic Campos's heart and delivered it to Angelo Torresola himself. The money, the drugs, the lying, the killing, the deception, the betrayals, forever playing one side against the other, forever saying one thing and meaning something else entirely. The blood was on his hands too. The same blood as Torresola and Barrantes. East Harlem, the Yard, the territories— call it whatever—was controlled by people like this because of people like Madigan.

But he did not feel guilty. He did not feel ashamed. He felt that there was something he needed to do, and if in doing it he was killed, then so be it. That would be his own justice for wrongdoing. And if he survived? If he made it through the other side, then he would have to tell Isabella Arias what really happened in that house near Louis Cuvillier Park, and why her daughter was nearly killed. And he would have to accept her judgment, her retribution, and in doing so he would be at last able to wash his hands of these things and walk away. Or not. Maybe that would be the end of him. Perhaps she would take revenge against him just as Eloisa had taken revenge against Angelo Torresola. If that was the case, then so be it.

This was not vengeance against Dario Barrantes. This was an acceptance of culpability for all he himself had done, and a last-ditch attempt to become a human being again.

"Vincent?"

He turned back toward Isabella Arias.

"I don't want to die," she said, "and I don't want Melissa to die, and I don't want you to die either."

Madigan closed his eyes.

He didn't say a word.

He hardly dared breathe.

54

FROM TEMPTATION TO YOU

Madigan got Walsh's cellphone number from the desk and called him.

"I need to meet you," Madigan told him. "But not in the precinct. I need to meet you outside somewhere."

Immediately Madigan sensed Walsh's anxiety.

"There's a problem, isn't there?" Walsh said.

"Yes, I think so," Madigan replied, "But not what you think."

"To do with me . . . to do with what happened and—"

"No," Madigan interjected. "Not to do with that. But I need your help with something. I just need you to come and meet me."

Walsh hesitated.

"You owe me," Madigan said.

"I know, but—"

"But nothing, Walsh . . . You fucking owe me—"

"Okay . . . where?"

"Corner of 161st and Gerard, right near Yankee Stadium, there's a diner called Subs and Salads. Meet me there in a half hour."

"Okay."

Walsh hung up.

Madigan drove to Yankee Stadium. He waited across the street from the diner until Walsh arrived. Madigan crossed the street and joined him as he went in through the door.

"What's going on, Vincent?" Walsh started.

Madigan shook his head. "Let's sit down."

They took a booth at the rear, ordered coffee. Once the waitress had gone again, Madigan leaned forward and started talking in hushed tones.

"I think I have your man," he said.

"My man?"

"Keep your voice down."

"What do you mean, my man?"

"The fourth man . . . the DBs in the storage unit, the Sandià robbery."

"But this ain't my case," Walsh said. "Bryant took it off me."

Madigan smiled wryly. "Of course he did."

"What's the supposed to mean?"

"If your man was a cop . . . Just say that the fourth man was a cop, then it would be your case again, right?"

"Well, sure . . ."

"So I think we're back to the fact that it's a cop."

Walsh's eyes widened. "You're serious?"

"Serious as it gets."

"And what did you mean when you said that thing about Bryant taking the case off of me?"

"Because I know who the fourth man is." Madigan took a napkin, wrote a name on it, slid it across the table to Walsh.

Walsh smiled, started laughing. It was nothing more than a nervous reaction.

Madigan's expression didn't shift an inch.

"What the hell are you talking about? You cannot be—"

"What? What *can't* I be? Serious? Real? Jesus, Walsh, it makes so much sense. Every step of the way this investigation has been balked. We've got nowhere on the Sandià robbery, nowhere on the three DBs . . . Hell, even this Valderas killing has gotten all screwed up because of paperwork missing out of the file. Charlie Harris put it there, and now it's gone. Just vanished. It makes sense, Walsh. It makes so much fucking sense I'm staggered I didn't see it before."

Walsh leaned back in the seat. His coffee was forgotten. He was in shock, disbelieving, but somehow could see the sense of what Madigan was telling him.

"Jesus Christ," he finally exhaled.

"You have a case now, my friend," Madigan said. "Robbery, seven homicides that we know of, maybe some *compadres* in the department. You got yourself a career-maker, my friend, a freaking career-maker. You understand what I'm telling you here?"

Walsh exhaled. He looked down at the name that Madigan had written on the napkin.

"Soak it up, Walsh. It's gonna get noisy, I tell you. Get yourself ready for some fireworks, my friend. This is a once-in-a-lifetime bust for you, and if you screw it up . . ." Madigan shook his head.

"This is your baby, no one else's. I'm not IA. I've got enough shit to deal with already."

"Jesus," Walsh said under his breath. "Jesus Christ Almighty."

Madigan drained his coffee cup and stood up.

"Wait up," Walsh said.

Madigan paused.

"You said for me to come down here because I owed you, and I get here and you give me a case that could make my career. What the hell is this? I owe you again?"

Madigan shook his head. "No, you don't owe me again. Do this thing and we're even."

"Why? You got something against him?"

"Personally? No, nothing against him personally. This entire fucking thing is a mess, and Sandià is behind all of it. I just want to see him fall, and I want to see him fall hard." Madigan nodded toward the napkin on the table. "And if that means that he has to fall too, then so be it. Things have been too fucked up for too long, and I just wanna get them straight again."

Walsh nodded. "Okay, Vincent, I'll start working on this. I'll let you know what I find."

"Appreciated."

Madigan left the diner. He walked to the car, pulled away from the curb, all the while thinking that the liar inside him would always be there.

Madigan went over to the precinct, put his car in the basement garage and took the elevator. He checked at the desk: Bryant was in his office.

It was close to five. Bryant, if he'd come on at nine was already at the end of his shift. No matter. What Madigan had to tell him wouldn't take long. He knocked on the door.

"Come!"

Madigan opened up and went in.

"Hey, Vincent, what's up?" Bryant asked.

"Need a word, Sarge," Madigan said.

Bryant looked at Madigan.

Madigan did the worried expression well. Perhaps it came easy from all the years of bullshitting people.

"What is it, Vincent? Take a seat."

Madigan sat down. "Don't know how to go around it, so I'm

gonna tell you straight." He paused for effect. Took a deep breath. "I think Walsh is on the take."

Madigan took a secret pleasure in observing Bryant's reaction to what he was telling him. His shift in expression, the smile, the laugh, the abrupt discontinuation of that laugh as he saw that Madigan's expression wasn't changing, was almost the same as Walsh's.

"What the hell are you talking about?"

"I have a CI . . . off the books, you don't know him. Name doesn't matter. He recorded something on his phone. I haven't heard it, but apparently he had a meet with Walsh and Walsh offered to lose some evidence in exchange for some info that Walsh was after on someone here. I didn't get all the details, but I figure that whatever evidence that might have been has already taken a walk from storage."

"What info?" Bryant asked.

"I don't know for sure, but I think it might have had something to do with the fourth man we've been talking about. The robbery last Tuesday, the drug house thing, the three DBs in the storage unit. Apparently this guy, my guy . . . Well, he reckons that the fourth guy *was* a cop, even knows his name, and he was all for buying himself a get-out-of-jail-free card. So he spoke to Walsh . . ."

"Hold up a minute there," Bryant interjected. "You're telling me that your CI has some info on a cop that's in with Sandià, or a cop that robbed Sandià?"

"Looks like they are one and the same guy."

"And your CI offered this info to Walsh?"

"Right."

"What the hell would he offer it to Walsh for? Walsh is IA. How would he even know Walsh?"

Madigan shook his head. "I don't know. I'm just telling you that this guy has a recording on his phone of Walsh agreeing to the deal. In exchange for the name of this cop, Walsh will lose some evidence. It ain't complicated. My CI tells me, I think 'Oh fuck' . . . and here I am telling you so you can do whatever you have to about it."

"Who knows about this?"

"Three people. Me, you, my CI."

"And does Walsh know that your CI taped this conversation?"

"No, I don't think so."

"You don't *think* so?"

"For Christ's sake, Sarge. I'm sitting talking to my guy about some unrelated shit and he lets me have this out of left field. What am I supposed to do? Get all excited? Get a hard-on about the thing like it's some big deal and blow it up? My first instinct was to play it down, make nothing of it, despite the fact that the press would cut their own fucking hands off to get something noisy about the PD in the headlines. I'm trying to act like it's no big deal, that no one would be interested. Meanwhile, I'm wondering what the hell would happen if it got out that Internal Affairs—the very department that's supposed to be dealing with potential police corruption—are as corrupt as the crooks. Jesus, what a goddamned nightmare. That's what I'm thinking. I'm also thinking to get back here as fast as I can and tell you about it so you can take whatever action you need to."

"Good," Bryant said. "Good job."

"It was common sense, Sarge. Jesus, if someone in this precinct is in with Sandià then that cellphone recording is gonna be worth a million to them. Get that phone, and they'll have something on Walsh. They'll have all the get-out-of-jail cards. The shit that Sandià's into, the drugs, the gambling, the hookers . . . IA gets hold of someone who's an insider in the department, then whoever that is, well, he's going away for a long time, right?"

Bryant was elsewhere, as if he hadn't even heard what Madigan was saying.

"Sarge?" Madigan prompted.

"Yes," Bryant said, and snapped to. "Right, yes, of course . . . I'll get onto it."

"Okay, well that was all. Walsh might be a dirty cop and someone needs to do something before it all goes to hell. Aside from that, Walsh might have evidence against an even dirtier cop, and it would be good to know that a storm like that was on its way so we can do as much damage control as possible, right?"

"Yes, for sure. I'll handle it," Bryant said. "You did the right thing, Vincent . . . coming to me. Appreciated."

"Well, what the hell else was I going to do? My CI wanted to go sell it to the press, for Christ's sake. He made a noise about it somewhere and he got word back that someone would be up for giving him a hundred and fifty grand for that phone. Can you believe it? A hundred and fifty grand. But then, if it puts the PD on the front pages of the newspapers for a week it's gotta be worth at least that much, wouldn't you say?"

"More," Bryant said. "More than that. Would be a huge story." He smiled forcibly. He looked overwhelmed. "Thanks for letting me know."

"No problem," Madigan replied, and added, "And if there's anything I can do to help straighten this thing out, then say the word, okay?"

"Sure, Vincent, sure."

55

LOVE CIRCUS

Madigan went down to Evidence and took a half dozen empty bags. Then he headed home. There was one other thing he had to arrange.

Isabella was at the front door even as Madigan opened it.

"You get any word on Melissa for me?"

"I didn't," Madigan said. "I had to handle some things. I can call now if you want?"

"Could you? I've been sick with worry all day. I don't know how much longer I can go without seeing her."

"I told you, she's going to be fine," Madigan said. "Seriously. She's out of ICU. They've got her all fixed up. They've just told her she can't have visitors because of the potential for infection. She's none the wiser."

"But I am," Isabella replied. "Please can you call the hospital?"

"Sure," Madigan said. "I'll do it now."

Isabella looked frayed at the edges, worn-out and stressed.

In that moment he felt nothing but empathy for her. He wanted to sit with her. He wanted to tell what he had done, that he was sorry—more sorry than she could ever imagine, and that he wanted to make it right, make it good, have it all be the way it was before . . .

Madigan ignored his own thoughts. He went in front and made the call. He was back within minutes.

"She's on solids, is eating well, sleeping well, making great progress. They think she'll be out within seventy-two hours. They're just keeping her monitored for any possible complications, infections, usual stuff . . ."

"Infections . . . what infections? What complications could there be?"

"Hey, hey, hey . . . enough of this," Madigan said. He took her hand, sat her down at the kitchen table.

"Your daughter was shot," he said. "She's a little girl and she was shot with a big bullet. There was some internal damage. They've fixed it all up. She has to heal fully, she has to recuperate, and while she's doing that they have to keep watch for anything that might be a problem. Would be the same if she'd broken her leg or had her appendix out—"

"But she didn't," Isabella said. "She was shot."

"She was, yes."

"Kind of person would shoot a little girl?"

"The kind of person who didn't know she was there, Isabella. You know that."

"And that excuses them?"

"No, of course not, but you know how it is around Sandià. You've been aware of what's going on for as long as you've been in this neighborhood. What happened with your sister, what happened with David . . . This is what happens around Sandià. The war was going on long before you got here, and it will go on long afterward. And if it isn't Sandià's war, it'll be someone else's. Melissa just happened to be an unfortunate casualty of that war. And I'll tell you something . . . The robbery of Sandià's house resulted in the death of seven men, and maybe some more are going to wind up dead before this thing has run its course."

"It's all so senseless, so meaningless," she said.

Madigan lit a cigarette for her. For the first time in a day or so he really wanted a drink. He took a couple of glasses from the shelf, a bottle from the cupboard. He fetched ice, poured both glasses, set one in front of her.

She held the glass in her hand, swirled the ice. She took a good sip, closed her eyes as she swallowed.

"It's meaningless to everyone but them," Madigan said. "It's the same wherever you go. People do what they think is best. People do what they believe is the greatest good. Even when people do terrible, terrible things they're doing them because of some misguided belief that they are in the right . . ."

"Not everyone, surely?"

Madigan smiled. "Oh yes, everyone. Even the crazies. Even the psychos, the serial murderers, the sex killers. They have some notion somewhere that what they're doing is solving some important problem somewhere."

"That's just crazy."

"Sure it is, and that's why they're called *crazy*."

She tried to smile.

Madigan took a drink. He felt the liquor fill his chest with warmth. It was good. Too good. Then he reached out and took her hand. It felt cold.

She did not flinch. She did not withdraw. She just looked back at him with such wide-eyed trust and faith that he couldn't help but feel like the very worst liar in the world. It had never bothered him. He had never cared a great deal for what people thought. But now? With this woman? What the hell was going on? Something had changed, and he knew that such a change did not bode well.

Was he falling for her? Was it something like that, or did he feel propitiative toward her because of what had happened to Melissa? Did he now feel that he had to make amends? Had she now become representative of all those he had wronged?

His thoughts were jumbled, his feelings new and unstable, and he did not like it.

Other people could not be trusted, for sure. You never knew what other people were going to say or do, and thus you always anticipated the worst and made appropriate arrangements. But himself? Was he now incapable of determining his own thoughts and feelings?

"What?" Isabella asked. "You are somewhere else all of a sudden."

Madigan gripped her hand a little tighter. "I'm here," he said. "I'm just tired."

"You hungry?"

"Some, yeah," he replied. "I'm going to take a shower," he said. "Get changed."

"Do that, then I'll make us something to eat."

Madigan went upstairs, and before he turned on the shower he went beneath the carpet and the floorboards and removed two hundred and thirty grand. He put a hundred grand in each of two evidence bags, thirty in another, and zipped them up. All three bags went in a duffel in his bedroom. He pushed the duffel beneath the bed.

Madigan took a shower, put on some jeans and a T-shirt. He needed to shave, and he needed a haircut. Right now such things were the least of his priorities.

Downstairs again, he sat on the couch.

"You're not driving anywhere tonight?" she asked, as if a few shots would have made any difference to Madigan.

"No," he said. "I'm not planning on going anywhere."

She turned and half-smiled. "You have a music system in this house?" she asked. "I found some CDs, some blues and jazz and stuff, but I couldn't find anywhere to play them."

"The DVD player plays them through the TV," Madigan said. "It ain't great, but it's better than nothing."

"So put some music on," she said.

"Music?"

"Sure, let's have a glass of wine and listen to some music."

Madigan shrugged. His manner was offhand, distracted, but Isabella seemed to be making an effort to introduce some normality into things. It was a pretense, a charade, but Madigan understood precisely why she was doing it and he humored her.

"Let's try and pretend we're regular people, eh?" she said, as if she could hear Madigan's thoughts. "Just for a little while, let's pretend that we're not hiding out from people who want to see us dead . . ." She laughed awkwardly. She was trying her best to make light of her present circumstances. It didn't work.

Madigan got up. He went to the CDs without thinking, looked through Art Tatum, Gil Evans, Wes Montgomery, chose *Kenny Burrell Live at the Village Vanguard*. He put it on low. It was strange to be doing this—playing music in the house, having a drink with someone. How long since he'd had music here? He couldn't remember. In the car sure, out of his head on something, listening to Tom Waits as he drove out to some crime scene, as he returned to the precinct, as one day blurred seamlessly into the next and he struggled to remember his own name.

But not now. Now things had changed.

"That's nice . . ." she said.

Madigan stood there with the CD case in his hand.

He felt it then, the rush in his chest, the almost overwhelming sense of guilt.

It was me.

Isabella, it was me.

I did this thing.

I robbed that house.

I was there when your daughter was shot. I didn't even know she was there. And then I drove a few miles and I killed three men and took the money, and that money is in a duffel under my bed.

Right here above our heads.

Nearly a quarter of a million dollars in a duffel, another hundred grand under the floor.

It was me.

He closed his eyes. He felt his fingers tighten on the CD case, and he set it down before he broke it.

He took several deep breaths. He wanted another drink, but he knew he shouldn't.

He walked back through to the kitchen. He put a couple of inches of whiskey into a glass, drank it, poured another couple, raised it to his lips, and then he was aware of Isabella right behind him.

"Open a bottle of wine," she said, and then she was beside him, her hand around the glass, lifting it out of his grip, almost as if to say, *Enough of that, Vincent . . . Enough already . . .*

He let her take it.

Madigan fetched the wine bottle from the top of the refrigerator. He took down glasses, poured both half full, gave one to her. His nerves were shredded. His hands shook.

"Thank you," she said, and she was smiling at him through the blurred edges of his whiskey-influenced vision, and once again he felt a sudden rush of emotion toward her, something primal almost, something that made him want to hide her from the world forever.

He drank some wine. The taste was strange and uncomfortable in his mouth.

He swallowed.

She drank too.

"Not bad," she said, "for someone who only ever buys Jack Daniel's."

Madigan drank some more. He sat down at the table, not because he wanted to sit, but because he wanted to be beneath her, wanted to look up at her, wanted to be away from the temptation to just grab her and kiss her.

It was a strong temptation. It was instinctual. It was about sex and lust and remedying the profound sense of loneliness and isolation that had become so much a part of himself. It was about making himself believe that he wasn't as evil as Sandià. Making himself believe that he was still the same person who had fathered Cassie, who had loved his wives, who had been loved by them in return. He hurt—emotionally, mentally, spiritually. Like his heart was crying somewhere in a dark room, and he could only ever hear it, never see it, never reach it, never do anything to make it stop.

Isabella sat down. She put her hand over his again. She had done it before. He didn't want to stop her, but at the same time it simply reinforced what he was now feeling toward her.

"Vincent . . ."

He looked at her.

"You don't know how much . . ."

Madigan smiled awkwardly. "Isabella . . . seriously, I'm just doing my job as best I can . . ."

"No, you're not. I don't believe you. I don't want to hear that. I don't want to think that that's the only reason I'm here. I want to think that I'm here because you actually care for people . . ."

"I don't care for people . . . not in the way you think," he replied.

"How can you care for people any other way—"

"You can pretend to care for people," he said. "You can make people believe you care for them because that way you can control them. You can care for people just because there's something they have that you want from them . . ."

"I don't have anything that you could want—"

He withdrew his hand from beneath hers and picked up his glass. "You have Sandià."

She frowned. "I *have* Sandià? What do you mean, I *have* Sandià?"

"You can put him away. You can put him in a jail cell for the rest of his life. That's what you can do, and that's what I need you for."

"You want me to testify against him?"

"Perhaps," Madigan said. "If he's not dead by the time we're done."

"I can't testify against Sandià. Jesus, Vincent, is that what you thought I'd do? Is that why you've kept me here . . . Vincent Madigan's own little Witness Protection Program?" Her voice carried an angry edge, an edge he had heard before. She was sounding him out. She was determining whether or not the anger she was feeling was justified, whether she should let him have it right now or give him another half chance to explain himself.

"Not the only reason," he said, and he spoke the truth. He had protected her out of guilt, a halfhearted attempt at making amends for some of what he had done. A halfhearted attempt to balance out the fact that her daughter had been damned near killed because of him.

"What's the other reason?"

"Reasons."

"Reasons then . . . Tell me the other reasons I am here."

293

He sighed audibly. He wanted more whiskey. He finished the wine in his glass and reached for the bottle. Her hand stopped his.

"No," she said. "Talk to me first. Get drunk later."

"You are not my wife . . . You are not my mother . . ."

"No, I am not your wife or your mother or anyone else important . . . Oh, except for someone who wants to stay alive, and the idea of being protected by a drunk isn't so appealing right now. You've had enough for now. Talk to me. Explain what you mean. Then you can drink yourself stupid for the rest of the night, for all I care."

It enraged him—not the denial, not the way she stopped him drinking more wine, but the fact that she said those words. *Then you can drink yourself stupid for the rest of the night, for all I care. For all I care . . .*

Is this what it had finally come down to? The only person in the world who actually gave a damn about Vincent Madigan was Isabella Arias? No one else had ever told him, *No, Vincent, no more booze.* No one had ever said that to him.

"We're screwed," Madigan said. "Both of us. You're alone. There's no one there for you. You get your daughter out of the hospital, you're gonna need to leave the city, leave the state preferably. Me? I've got nothing either. No one here for me. That's not me sounding sorry for myself. That's me being real and honest. I'm a drunk. I take downers, uppers, anything I can get my hands on, for Christ's sake. I don't know what freaking day it is most of the time. I'm doing my best to handle this mess, but I don't know that my best is going to be good enough. Truth of the matter is that both of us might wind up dead. In all honesty, I don't think I ever took the idea of you testifying against Sandià seriously. Why? Because I don't think either of us is ever going to get that far . . ."

"You think I don't know this? You think I don't understand the situation I am in? And you think I don't see you for who you are, Vincent? Sure, you're a drunk. Sure, you screwed up your marriages, your kids, your job, everything. Same as me. Same as most of us. It isn't about being perfect. It isn't about always telling the truth and making everything happen the way you want it to. Hell, if that was the way it was, then none of us would ever get into trouble and I sure as hell wouldn't need someone like you to help bail me out." She reached for his hand again, took it, then the other, and she was holding both of them, the sensation of her skin against his almost electric.

"Look at me," she said, and Madigan did so.

"I am who I am. I have no hidden agenda here. I am scared for my own life, for the life of my daughter . . . And you've even gotten me scared for you too. We can't just quit now. I can't just walk away from here. Sandià will kill me. He thinks I'm a witness to what he did to David Valderas, and he will kill you for harboring me from him, and that'll be the end of it. And if he finds it in his heart not to kill Melissa, then she will go to Child Services, and somewhere up the line they'll find someone who'll take her on or she'll be a ward of the state until she's eighteen. And then she'll come back here and turn tricks for crack and die before she's twenty-five. That's what I have, Vincent. Those are the choices . . . All except for one. I can work with you. I can fix this thing with you. Or I can at least give it the best I've got. I just believe one thing, Vincent . . . That you and I could actually work together on this thing. I can help you somehow, surely? There has to be something I can do to help fix this fucking disaster . . ."

"There's nothing you can do," Madigan said. "Everything is in place. In the next twenty-four, forty-eight hours this thing will end well, or it will not. We will walk away from this thing or we won't . . ."

"You think I'm not capable, is that it? You think I'm not tough enough?"

Madigan laughed. "Christ no, Isabella, it's not that—"

"So it's because you don't want to put me in any danger, right? You know Sandià is after me and you want to make sure he doesn't get me?"

"Yes," Madigan said. "That's right."

"And is that because you want me to testify against Sandià, or because you actually give a damn about me?"

"Jesus," Madigan said. "How the hell do you do that? How the hell do women do that? They can take anything you say, anything at all, and somehow turn it around and make it personal."

"Everything's personal, Vincent . . . Everything in life is personal. If it has something to do with people, then it's personal. So answer up. You want me to testify, or do you actually give a damn about what happens to me and my daughter?"

Madigan looked at the fire in her eyes. He couldn't lie to her—not about this.

"I care," he said.

"Sorry?"

"I care, Isabella, I actually *do* care, and though it might not seem like it, it means a great deal to me . . ."

"Then why is it so goddamned hard for you to say what you think, to say what you feel?"

He smiled. "Because I'm a man, and we don't do all that crap about thoughts and feelings. That kinda thing is just for you girls."

"I keep telling you, but you won't believe me. You are a good person, Vincent Madigan—"

"No, sweetheart, you got me all wrong on that one. I am an asshole of the first order. I am a first-class asshole. You have no idea . . ."

"You don't think so?"

"I *know* so."

"You think I don't see what you're capable of? You think I don't recognize the liar, the cheat, the thief, the corrupt cop in you . . ."

Madigan couldn't speak. He wanted to, but he couldn't.

"I'm not so naive, Vincent. I've been around people like you and Sandià all my life. You don't think you're that different from him. Well, you are. It's true what they say. Everyone's a hooker. Everyone is screwing someone for money. You think I don't see the pills in your bathroom cabinet. They're not for anything that's wrong with you. You are not in pain, Vincent Madigan. You're not an insomniac or a depressive. A drunk you might be, but there's nothing wrong with you that would justify taking those pills. And people take drugs and they drink for the same reasons, Vincent . . . Because they're running away from all the bad shit they've done. Not what's been done *to* them, because people get over that. They survive that crap. They can let go of it. But the stuff they've done . . . They can never escape that . . ."

"I am not Sandià—"

"No, you're not, Vincent. And that's exactly what I'm saying. I know you better than you think. You have shadows and ghosts just like everyone else, but you are not evil like Sandià. If you spend your life holding on to those ghosts, well, you wind up a drunk and a pillhead, and that's where you're at right now. It pains me to see someone who can be a decent human being acting like such an asshole."

"Hey, what the fuck is this?" Madigan said, suddenly angered by her accusatory tone.

Isabella held up her hands. "I'm sorry," she said. "It's just I saw the same thing with Melissa's father, a good man gone to waste, and I see it in you and it hurts me. I didn't mean to—"

"Enough," Madigan said. "I'm not playing these games with you. You are here because I give a crap about you, same way I used to give a crap about most people . . . the reason I became a cop and all that. You are also here because I need you as much as you need me, and that's all there is to it. This thing ends one way or the other, and either we'll be alive or we'll be dead or one of us will be dead and one of us won't—and what the hell happens to your daughter I do not know. I hope she makes it out of here. I hope she doesn't wind up orphaned and on the street and turning tricks for crack and dying before she's twenty-five. Well, I really fucking hope that doesn't happen because no one deserves that . . ."

"You want to tell Sandià that no one deserves that? I don't think he has the same viewpoint about it as you and me."

"I think Sandià is going to have a great deal more on his mind than however many girls he happens to be running out of that building on Paladino."

"You're gonna kill him, right?"

"I'm going to do what I can to stop him from killing you."

"And if you have to kill him, then you'll kill him, right?"

"If it's between you and him, or me and him, then yes, I will kill him."

"I want him to die."

"I know you do."

"I would be happy to see him rot in a jail cell for the rest of his life, but preferably I want him to die. Only sad thing is that I will not be there to see it happen."

"I'll make sure you get the full run-down, blow-by-blow."

She smiled. It was brief, almost a fleeting expression, but it was there.

"I am sorry," she said, "for giving you all this crap."

Madigan dismissed her apology. "For a while I thought I was married again."

She laughed at that, not because it was particularly funny, but because both of them were looking for the slightest thing that would ease the tension. Then she rose and said, "I'll get the food." She walked around the other side of the table and put her hands on Madigan's shoulders and just that feeling—the awareness of real honest-to-God physical contact from another human being—made every muscle in his body twitch. Madigan shuddered involuntarily, even let out a small audible gasp, and when she started massaging his shoulders he felt as if he could just sit there and weep until he collapsed from exhaustion.

"Too tense," she said.

"You don't say?"

"How long since someone was there for you, Vincent?"

"Was there for me?"

"Someone who didn't just want something from you, you know? Someone who just gave a damn about how you really felt."

Madigan did not know how to answer her question.

"A long time, right?"

Madigan felt her hands on his shoulders, the tips of her fingers on the nape of his neck. Her touch was gentle, sensitive.

He turned around in the chair, looked up at her. "No," he said. "We went through this before, Isabella. This is not what this is about. We are not getting into this . . ."

Her hands were on his shoulders again. There was no pressure, but the mere fact that she was there made it difficult for Madigan to stand up.

"You don't like me."

"Isabella . . . seriously . . ."

She leaned down. He felt her hair against his ear, his neck, and then the warmth of her breath was on the side of his face. "What's the deal here, Vincent . . . You don't want to?"

He leaned forward. She stepped back instinctively. He took that split second to stand up.

He opened his mouth to say something, anything, but he was speechless.

He just didn't know what to say.

"Nothing to say?" she asked, echoing his absence of thought.

Again, he didn't speak. He wanted to stay. He wanted to leave. He wanted . . . He wanted someone else to make the decision . . .

And she did. Isabella Arias. She took three or four steps, and she held his forearms, and before he understood what was happening she was kissing him and he was kissing her back. And he could see right through himself to the small black stone that was his heart, and around that heart were wrapped all the lies he had ever told, and in the middle of those lies—perhaps the greatest lie of all—was the lie he told himself each and every day.

You did it all for the right reasons, Vincent Madigan.

And a close second—even as he felt her hands around his waist, even as he felt the pressure and warmth of her body against his, even as he passed the point of no return with Isabella Arias—he could see the other lie . . . the thing he'd never said . . . the thing he knew he'd have to one day tell her . . .

I am responsible for what happened to Melissa.

I nearly killed your daughter.

It was me—Vincent Madigan—and no one else.

And then there were thoughts of Sandià, of Larry Fulton and Chuck Williams and Bobby Landry, and blood up and down those stairs, and pieces of people, just fistfuls of human beings scattered back and forth up and down that stairwell. The way in which the bodies had just exploded as they were hit by a wall of gunfire . . . a massacre . . . a turkey shoot . . . No one stood a goddamned chance . . . And Bernie's face in that alleyway and how the blood was on Madigan's hands as he walked away, all because he owed money to Sandià . . . Hunting through the dash for that wrap of speed or coke or whatever the hell it was . . . Meeting with Chico, Harpo, and Zeppo . . . And what in the name of Christ Almighty was he doing?

He tried to step back, but her hands were around him and he was still kissing her. And even as he was fighting it, he was giving in, succumbing to whatever was happening. And he knew it was just as much him as it was her. He felt the tension breaking down, felt the resistance folding, and he was holding her tight, as tight as anything, and he could feel her tongue inside his mouth, and he wanted nothing more in the world than to feel every inch of her, to be beside her, behind her, around her, inside her . . .

He started moving toward the front room, the door to the stairwell.

She went with him. She knew where he was going.

Halfway up the stairs she was taking off her T-shirt, unbuttoning her jeans. She was grabbing at his belt buckle.

"Take it off," she said. "Undo the damned thing, for Christ's sake."

He laughed then, and she started laughing too, and whatever was happening meant everything and nothing. They fell through the door of Madigan's bedroom, and by the time they reached the edge of the mattress most of their clothes were on the floor. And then everything slowed down . . .

There were tears in her eyes.

He saw that much.

Even as he was kissing her, even as she was kicking her jeans off her feet, even as he was aware of her hands all over him, there were tears in her eyes.

"What?" he remembered asking her. "What is it?"

"I don't know," she said, and her voice caught in her throat as if she were having difficulty breathing.

"It's okay," he told her. "It's gonna be okay . . . I promise . . ."

And for the first time in as long as he could recall he believed that he was telling the truth.

Later, after it was over—after they had struggled with this new thing, the closeness, the physicality, the urgency, the passion, the fear, the release—he lay there with her in his arms and thought of the money beneath the bed, and he wondered what kind of human being he was.

He wondered if he could ever want to be near such a person as himself.

He questioned his own reasons, his motives, his rationale . . . and he listened to her breathing, and he tried not to cry.

He had done this terrible thing to her daughter.

He had killed people and lied—oh, so many lies—and he had worked with Sandià for fifteen years. He was as bad as Sandià, or at least on his way. Was there any hope of redemption?

He had to get out of this. He had to escape. He had to save her. He had to get her away from Sandià and all that Sandià represented. Melissa too. She had to survive.

They all did. All except himself and Sandià. They were the ones who deserved to be punished for what they had done.

And he asked himself then, asked himself if it came down to it, if it *really* came down to it, would he give up his own life to see Sandià fall, to see Isabella and Melissa away from this nightmare and Sandià buried in a hole somewhere or some stinking jail cell or anywhere where he could no longer hurt or abuse or maim or kill . . .

Could he give up his own life for this?

And beyond this—more important than any other consideration—could he give up his life to know that his children would never discover the truth of who he was?

Yes, came the answer. *Yes, I could do this.*

And Madigan, terrified at the prospect of such a thing, knew that it was no longer a question of whether or not he could, but simply a question of whether he would.

An eye for an eye.

A life for a life.

Madigan looked down at Isabella Arias, naked there in his arms, and he listened to the sound of her breathing as she drifted into sleep. Amid all he felt, he believed he could hear the echo of that sound in his heart.

He closed his eyes.

He knew that whatever sleep he would find would be awkward and restless.

No more than he deserved.

56

SHE'S LIKE HEROIN TO ME

In the brief hour of twilight before dawn Madigan managed to ease himself out of the bed and escape to his own room. He took the duffel with him, the money within. He was careful not to wake Isabella, careful to make as little sound as possible as he took his jeans and T-shirt from the floor. He made it out to the car and buried the duffel beneath the spare tire in the trunk. Then he went back into the house and took a shower.

By the time Isabella appeared it was after seven. He was dressed, making breakfast in the kitchen, and she was there behind him, her arms around his waist. She felt him tense up, but she said nothing. She merely kissed his neck and said, "You sleep okay?"

"Sure," he said, and he turned and smiled at her as best he could. He did not know what he was feeling, did not know what he was thinking, and he figured the best solution was to get out of there as quickly as possible.

Madigan did not regret what had happened. He could not regret it. He knew from the experiences of too many years and too many mistakes that regret was a futile waste of time and energy. What was done was done. Perhaps he had never really applied what he knew, but in this instance he did. Beyond regret there was only damage control, avoidance, acceptance, and in some cases the ability to make the problem disappear. The situation with Isabella could not just vanish. It had to be faced.

"Isabella—" he started.

She smiled, but there was something hard beneath the expression. "Do not tell me that this was a mistake, Vincent Madigan. Even if you believe it was, do not tell me that this was a mistake. No one likes to be told that they were a mistake, and unless you are now going to throw me out on the street, then we have to go on living beneath the same roof . . ."

Madigan laughed. He appreciated her directness.

"No," he said. "I wasn't going to say that." He reached out and took her hand. He walked to the kitchen table, asked her to sit down. She did so, and Madigan sat facing her, still holding her hand.

"I am not a good man to know," he said.

She opened her mouth to speak.

"Let me finish, Isabella . . . please."

She nodded, didn't say a word.

"I am not a good man. I am a police officer, yes, but that counts for nothing, as you know. I have made a lot of mistakes. I have done a lot of things that I shouldn't have done. It is too late to go back and change many of them, but there are some that can be fixed. I have to fix them now."

"Sandià?" she asked.

"Among others, yes."

She looked away for a moment, and then looked back. "I expect nothing of you," she said. "You owe me nothing. What happened last night was something I wanted to have happen, and it did. I don't know why, Vincent . . . because I am afraid, because I am lonely, because . . ." She shook her head. "I don't know, and I don't think it matters now." She smiled, laughed briefly. "Don't worry," she said. "You don't have to marry me."

Madigan smiled back. "Aw shucks," he said. "And I went and bought the ring an' everything."

Neither of them spoke for a moment, and then Madigan told her he had to go out.

"So eat some breakfast," she said. "I'll finish making it, and then you go."

"Yes," he said. "Breakfast first."

A half hour later he was driving away from the house. He'd told Isabella to stay inside, just as before. Nothing had changed. This was the way it had to be until he said otherwise. She neither protested nor argued. She asked if he could check on Melissa for her.

"If I can," Madigan told her. "I have to do some things. Important things. If I do this right then we're gonna come through the other side of this . . . okay?"

She reached out and touched his face. He closed his eyes, felt the warmth of her hand against his skin. He had missed this. Oh, how he had missed this.

"So go," she said. "Make it right."

And he had gone, all the while asking himself if he could lie to this woman forever, if he could get away with never telling her the truth of what had happened in the Sandià house.

The answer was no. She would have to know. Somehow, sometime, she would have to know. Otherwise he would be starting again with the same old patterns in place.

But then there was another possibility. The good chance that he wouldn't come through this, just as he had considered the night before.

Could he do this?

Yes, he could do this. There was no other way.

Madigan stopped at the motel and gave a couple of bundles of money from the Sandià robbery to Bernie Tomczak. He also returned Bernie's cellphone, the original one that held the recording of his conversation with Duncan Walsh. Bernie knew what to do.

"You made the calls I asked you to?" Madigan asked.

"Sure I did. You think I'm dumb, or what?"

"What time?"

"You know what time, Vincent. Eleven o'clock exactly."

"There's gonna be two of them?"

"Jesus, Vincent, of course there are. You told me what you needed, I arranged it. That was the deal. Just cool your jets, okay? They're gonna be there."

"If this goes wrong . . ."

"Vincent . . . if this screws up . . . Well, it goes without saying that I am screwed too, right?"

"Right," Madigan replied. "We are both in this together. If I get deep-sixed, then you do too."

"Sometimes I ask myself why I like you, Vincent Madigan. I mean, for Christ's sake, a week ago you kicked me down an alleyway and beat the crap out of me. I think I lost my sense of smell."

Madigan smiled wryly. "Well, if that's the case, you ain't never gonna have to take a bath again. I did you a favor."

"Sometimes, in fact most of the damned time, you are such a freakin' asshole."

"Well, my friend, the feeling is mutual."

"You take care, okay? Don't mess it up."

"Same to you."

Madigan left the motel, walked back to the car, headed south-west toward the bridge.

He glanced at his watch. Nine forty. An hour and twenty minutes to go.

Madigan was across the street, a half block from Bernie's place, by ten after ten. He parked near one of the ramps that came down from the FDR Drive. He could hear the traffic thundering across it. He waited until half past and then he called the precinct. He reported a probable cause on the address, said he could do with a couple of uniforms. Dispatch told him he'd have to wait fifteen minutes at least. Madigan said he needed them faster. That didn't help any.

Madigan sat back and smoked a cigarette. He watched as the two guys entered the building, and then he took the duffel and walked over there. They opened up when he knocked, he gave them the duffel with the two hundred grand in it, and said to sit tight until he came back.

"When I come back I'm gonna be with two uniforms, okay? Don't do anything different than what Bernie agreed with you. You fuck this up and someone's gonna get shot, okay? We come in through the front. You go out through the side. You leave the bag behind. End of story."

The taller one—dark-haired, looked like getting angry was a lifestyle choice—just nodded. The other one—lighter hair, an awkward zigzag scar across his right cheek and beneath the ear—said, "It's cool. We know the deal. Bernie told us, okay? Don't shit it. We're professionals."

Professionals? Madigan wanted to ask him. *Professionals at what exactly? Running away?*

Madigan looked at his watch. "Fifteen minutes, give or take," he said. "I'm waiting on backup."

"Go do your thing," Anger Management said, and then he closed the front door.

Madigan walked back to the car. The street was deserted. Hell, even if anyone had seen him they wouldn't be saying anything to the police if they came around. It wasn't that kind of neighborhood.

Backup showed at five to.

"Take your damned time," Madigan told the driver.

"I'm sorry, sir," the uniform said, "but we got a—"

"It's okay," Madigan replied. "It might be nothing, but I know the guy who lives here . . . He's smalltime, but there's word he got into bigger business recently. There's two of them in there now. Associates of this guy. Saw them go in there, and I think they were carrying semiautomatic rifles."

"They got rifles? Hell, you want SWAT, not us," the other uniform said.

Madigan leaned down and looked through the window. "What's your name?"

"Young," he replied.

"And you?" Madigan asked the driver.

"Henderson."

"Well, okay. Here's the way it goes, boys. I know the guy who owns the place. His name is Bernie. He's done some work for me in the past. He's a CI, okay? He does mostly small-time shit, nothing muscular. But he has a cousin—can't remember his name—and he's a player. He's a heavy hitter, part of a crew. Banks, armored vans, this kind of crap, right? So I think that Bernie is away. Christ knows where he is, but he ain't home, as far as I can tell. You got two crackheads in there, part of this crew, maybe the cousin, maybe someone else, but they're in there. I saw them go in an hour ago, and they sure as hell weren't carrying fishing rods. Know what I mean? Now, we can go in there and sort this thing out, or we can cry home to Mommy and send the big boys to do the work. You do this, you'll get commends from me, others from the department; everything's fine an' dandy. You chicken out on me, and I'll write you both up."

"Hey, I'm in," Young said.

"No problem," Henderson added.

"Good," Madigan said. "Now, get your car back over there behind mine; then you make your way down the back of the alleyway and to the rear of the building. You stay on the radio, but keep it down. I'll call you when I'm at the front door, and you come in through the back. It's just a drill, okay? Nothing different from how you learned at the academy. Keep your goddamned heads down, keep looking thirty-five different ways at once, and don't shoot anyone, for Christ's sake. Only time you shoot someone is if you see a bullet actually coming at you. You understand?"

Young and Henderson said they got it.

They seemed bright enough. Last thing Madigan needed was a couple of uniforms killing Bernie's friends. The guys inside would not be armed. That was the deal. Madigan would approach from the front. He would demand entry. Anger Management and Zigzag would do a runner from the side of the property, down the alleyway, out to the street, and Young and Henderson would come in through the back just in time to find them gone. Madigan needed Bernie's people there to create the appearance that someone other than himself been in possession of the marked money from the Sandià house. If he'd just *happened to find it*, then he left himself open to unwanted suspicion. He needed Young and Henderson as unrelated and official witnesses to the duffel with two hundred grand in it.

Simple. Couldn't have been easier.

Madigan watched Young and Henderson as they took their black-and-white around behind his car. They parked, left the vehicle, and then made their way down toward the rear of Bernie's place.

He gave them another three or four minutes and then he called, "You boys all set?"

"Yes, sir," came the reply.

"I'll tap you twice on the handset when I'm at the front door."

"Roger."

Madigan tucked the handset in his jacket pocket. He walked across the street, went up the steps, and stopped at Bernie's front door. He pulled his ID, rapped on the door with the heel of his gun.

"Police!" he shouted. "Open up!"

He heard movement inside. Anger Management and Zigzag were probably just at the side door waiting for the right moment.

Madigan banged on the door again.

More movement. He thought he heard a door open somewhere inside. Then a door slammed.

Voices.

Was that voices?

Someone shouting?

Madigan took one step back and then launched his heel at the front door. It cracked along the jamb but didn't open. He let fly again, and this time the door went through. He rushed into the hallway just as he heard gunfire. One shot? Two?

What the hell was going on?

Madigan—familiar with Bernie's place—ran through the front room, down the corridor, saw the side door open, went through it, and there he found Henderson, his gun raised, Young coming up behind him from the rear.

"What the fuck is going on?" Madigan shouted.

"They came out through the side door," Henderson said. "I was here. I saw the side door and decided to cover it while Young went to the back. They came out through the side door. I shouted for them to stop. I gave them clear warning. They didn't stop. I think I hit one of them. They kept on going, but I think I hit one of them . . ."

"Jesus Christ! What the hell! I told you to go to the back, for Christ's sake. I told you to cover the back exit, not the side!"

"I did the drill!" Henderson said. "I did what you told me to do! I did the fucking drill!"

Madigan lowered his gun. He realized he'd been pointing it at Henderson.

"Jesus Christ Almighty! You shot one of them? You fucking shot one of them?"

"I think so, yes," Henderson said. His expression was one of alarm, confusion, dismay, disbelief. He didn't understand what was wrong. He'd done the right thing. Madigan had told him to do the drill, and he'd done the drill. Cover all exits. Give clear warning.

"Did he have a gun?" Madigan shouted. "Was he carrying a gun? Were either of them carrying fucking guns?"

Henderson shook his head. His eyes were wide. "I don't know. I think so. I . . . Christ, I don't know. I told them to stop, okay? I told them to stop. I gave them warning. I did the routine, all right? I did the routine and they wouldn't fucking stop and I fired."

Madigan lowered his head. "Jesus Mary, Mother of God Almighty." He closed his eyes. He breathed deeply. "Okay, okay, okay . . . Let me think here," he said. He turned, started back inside. "Come in," he said to Young and Henderson. "Get inside, for Christ's sake."

No more than a few minutes inside, Young and Henderson dispatched to search the premises, and Young returned with the duffel.

"You're not gonna believe this," he said to Madigan.

"Oh, I doubt it," Madigan said. "There's very little that's gonna surprise me now."

Young held out the bag, pulled apart the handles. Bundles of money sat there. Dozens of them.

"Okay," Madigan said. "Well, maybe that's a little surprise, yes . . ."

He reached out. Young gave him the bag.

"You wanna split this now or later?" Madigan said. He looked at Young and Henderson in turn, his expression deadpan.

Then he cracked a smile. "Jesus, you guys. You should see your faces. Lighten up."

Young just looked anxious. Henderson tried to smile but was still in the shock of the shooting.

Madigan was panicking inside. This was serious. This had gone seriously wrong. But he had to play it down, had to make light of it. Last thing he needed now was an emotional babysitting case. He had to get back to the precinct, had to turn the money over to Evidence, and then hope to hell that he got the visit he expected.

"Ah, to hell with it," Madigan said. "It was probably just a flesh wound. The guy'll get over it. It'll make him easier to find anyway, right?"

"But what if it wasn't?" Henderson asked. "What if it was a fatal wounding?"

"You ever killed a man?" Madigan asked.

"No, sir, I haven't."

"Well, maybe you have now. Kinda think such possibilities go with the territory. I think it's what they call an occupational hazard."

Henderson looked crushed.

Back at the car he called for Crime Scene. He told Young and Henderson to wait at the property. They were responsible for securing the site until the techs got there.

"And don't shoot anyone else, okay?" he called out to Henderson as he crossed the road to the car.

Henderson raised his hand. He still didn't look any better, poor bastard. Well, hell, there was always a first time. Once you dealt with that, it was no longer a problem. At least that had been the way it'd been for Madigan. Irrespective of how Young felt, there was still the possibility that one of Bernie's associates was wounded. A graze, a flesh wound, a through and through. Madigan had no way of knowing. Maybe the guy had already collapsed and died someplace. This was something he had not predicted. This could throw the entire strategy to shit.

He started the engine, pulled away from the curb, glanced there at the duffel on the passenger seat, and wondered how many more lives were going to be over because of what was inside.

57

YELLOW EYES

It was past noon by the time Madigan arrived at the precinct. He filed his report, put the duffel in Evidence storage, filled out the paperwork, and then went to his office.

He sat patiently until one, and then he went to lunch. He received no word from Young or Henderson, nor from the Crime Scene team at Bernie's house, and there had been no calls from Walsh. He thought to call Walsh, ask him to turn the heat up, but he dropped the idea. Walsh had done what he'd been asked to do, and that would have to be good enough.

It was while he was eating that the call came.

"Vincent?"

"Speaking."

"It's Al. Where are you?"

"In a diner down a block or two. I'm just having lunch. What's up?"

"I need to speak to you."

"Now?"

"Now."

"I'll head on back."

"No, I'll come there. What's the name of the place?"

"You wanna come here?"

"What's the name of the place, Vincent?"

"It's called DiMarco's, up on 115th."

"I know it," Bryant said. "Be there in ten."

"You want I should order you a sandwich or something, Sarge?"

The line had gone dead.

Madigan pocketed his cellphone. He took a deep breath. Maybe this thing would work. Hell. Maybe it just might work.

Bryant was good to his word. He appeared ten minutes later. Madigan was surprised at how calm he felt. He'd even managed to finish his sandwich.

R.J. Ellory

Bryant, however, looked like a wreck.

"Jesus, Sarge, you look like crap. What the hell is going on?"

Bryant nodded to a booth way back in the diner. Madigan didn't question him. He followed Bryant and they took seats. The waitress asked if Bryant wanted anything.

"Coffee, just coffee," he said, and Madigan asked for a refill.

Once the coffee had been delivered Madigan asked what was going on.

"I have Walsh on my case," he said. "This thing you spoke about. This thing about the fourth man at the Sandià house being a cop. Looks like there's some substance to it."

"Oh fuck," Madigan said.

"Oh fuck, exactly. And I can't have this going on, Vincent. Not in my precinct."

"Did Walsh speak to you directly?"

"Sure he did. This morning."

"Did he say who he thought this guy was, the fourth man?"

"No, he didn't, and I don't think he knows. I don't think he's even certain that the fourth guy *is* a cop, but I can't take that risk."

"So even if it is a cop, it could be someone from another precinct entirely, right?"

"Sure it could be," Bryant said. "But am I prepared to take that risk? Hell, no. I can't have my precinct pulled to pieces on this . . ."

Madigan understood. He saw where this was going. Bryant was thinking of the department's reputation. This was not a personal request, but a professional one. Think of the reputation of Bryant and Callow and Harris, even Madigan himself . . . Do the right thing, Vincent. Help us preserve the status quo. We do more good than bad. We get more right than wrong. Let's get this shit sorted out. Let's use what we know to back Walsh off, to get IA off our cases. Let's have everything go back to normal so we can just get the hell on with our jobs. Sometimes you have to do a little bad for the greater good.

Madigan gave the impression of dawning realization. "You want that phone," he said. "You want that phone so you can get Walsh off our case, right?"

Bryant didn't reply.

Jackpot.

"Jesus, Sarge . . ."

"But you understand why, right? You understand why I'm doing this? For the good of the precinct, the department . . ."

"For sure," Madigan said. "I just don't know . . ."

"The money. The guy, your CI . . . He was offered a lot of money . . ."

"A hundred and fifty grand." Madigan stopped dead. He looked at Bryant. His eyes widened.

"For all of us," Bryant said. "I'm thinking of all of us . . ."

"Jesus Christ, Sarge . . ."

"So who the hell knows, Vincent? You, me, Evidence, whichever uniforms you took on the bust?"

"Fucking hell . . . Jesus Christ . . ."

"I saw that memo come in, Vincent, and it all made sense. It was like some kind of divine intervention. You bust two hundred grand from some schmuck's house, and there it is, problem solved. We get the phone off your CI. We back Walsh off. He tells IA to look in some other direction. Everyone goes home happy."

Madigan didn't speak. He looked down at his hands. He didn't know how to describe what he was feeling. He didn't want to *try* and describe it.

"It *is* one hell of a coincidence," Madigan said eventually, and then he looked up at Bryant, and he could see his own face reflected in Bryant's eyes. He could see in Bryant's expression the fact that Bryant believed Madigan was going to go along with this insane idea . . . That there was a way out for everyone, that Vincent Madigan was going to be his ally, his buddy, his *compadre* . . .

He wondered how much Bryant's expression would change if he let slip that the money had come from Bernie Tomczak's place; that Bernie was the one with the phone; that the money that now sat in Evidence was Sandià's own money; that this was the money from the house robbery . . .

Oh shit, would that be a sight to see.

But he said nothing. Bernie's address had not been noted on the paperwork. In fact, had Bryant taken the time to look at anything but the fact that two hundred grand had been admitted under Madigan's signature to the Evidence Room, then he would have noticed that a significant number of pertinent and necessary details had been omitted from the paperwork. Didn't matter a damn, because that paperwork was going in the precinct boiler room furnace anyway. Had never been destined for anywhere else.

"Too much of a coincidence to ignore," Bryant said.

Madigan didn't respond.

"Of course, there'd have to be something in it for you, Vincent," Bryant said.

Madigan waved the comment aside. "We have to think of the good of the precinct," he said. "We have a hard enough time already without getting God knows what bullshit dragged through the papers . . . And sometimes IA can be such a bunch of assholes . . ."

Madigan could feel Bryant relaxing even as he spoke, for Madigan was saying precisely what Bryant wanted to hear and he was heading in precisely the direction Bryant wanted him to go. Then Madigan said, "I will have to talk to the guy, the one with the phone."

"For sure."

"And you need to override the paperwork. You have to pull all the paperwork from that raid, and you have to get that money out of Evidence and hide it, and you have to make all the connections to me go away for good. You understand?"

"Yes."

"And what about Young and Henderson?"

"Who?"

"The two uniforms who did the bust with me this morning."

"I'll take care of that," Bryant said.

"What the hell is that supposed to mean? I'm gonna hear that they were killed in the line of duty tomorrow?"

"Jesus, Vincent, what the fuck? What kind of person do you think I am? Hell no, they're not gonna get killed in the line of duty. Jesus Christ, man, what the hell do you say something like that for?"

Madigan shook his head. "I don't know, Sarge. I'm sorry. This is just some very scary shit going on here."

"I said I'll take care of it. I'll tell them that the money was counterfeit, that it got confiscated by the Treasury Department, that they both get commends for their stellar work, and that the investigation has now been passed over to the feds and the Secret freaking Service, okay? They're just rookies, man. They'll believe whatever the fuck I tell 'em."

"Good. Okay. I just don't want any casualties around this thing. It'll just get complicated—"

"Vincent, seriously, don't worry. I'll take care of it. You just speak to your guy. See if he'll take the hundred and fifty grand for the phone from you, okay?"

"You'll have to make him a better offer. He was promised a hundred and fifty by the press, remember?"

"So see what he'll take. We got two hundred to spend, no more."

"I'll do what I can," Madigan said, knowing full well that in a handful of hours he would come back to Bryant and tell him that after long and tense negotiations Bernie Tomczak wanted exactly a hundred and eighty grand. It was precisely the amount he needed, precisely the amount he owed Sandià, though Al Bryant would never know that detail.

Bryant's shoulders seemed to lower a good four or five inches, like someone'd had his spine in a tourniquet and then released it.

"I don't know how to thank you for this—" Bryant started.

"Hell, don't thank me. Thank the good luck fairy who put two hundred grand in the Evidence Room this morning."

"I'll go handle it," Bryant said.

"And remember, Sarge . . . Nothing, absolutely *nothing* comes back to me, okay?"

"Enough said, Vincent. You have my word."

Madigan watched Bryant go. Bryant thought they were out of it, that he and his precinct were in the clear, that he'd get the phone, tell Walsh to go screw himself, and everyone would walk away unscathed.

Bryant had no idea. Not a single damned clue.

Neither did Walsh. Walsh thought he was off the hook with the duplicate phone Madigan had given him. Now he was going to find out that there was a second phone.

Madigan finished his coffee and left the diner. He drove to Mott Haven to see Bernie. Bernie was intrinsic in this plan. Bernie needed to be kept apprised of every step that was taken.

Ironic, Madigan thought, that only days earlier he had kicked Bernie six ways to Sunday and back to Christmas for the sake of a debt that was about to be paid. The irony did not escape Madigan, didn't escape him at all. Had he known what would transpire in those days as he gave Bernie Tomczak yet another smack, well, he wouldn't have believed it. Even he—Vincent Madigan, he who had seen it all from the top down and the bottom up—would not have believed it.

Life was a joke sometimes, and not always funny.

*

It was two fifteen by the time Madigan reached the motel. He went in through reception and knocked on Bernie's door.

"Who's it?"

"Me. Madigan."

Bernie opened up. The usual barrage of questions did not assault Madigan. Bernie looked sober, a little serious.

"What's up?"

"My guy got shot."

Madigan frowned.

"This morning, Vincent. One of my guys got shot. One of your overenthusiastic rookies took a freakin' shot at my guy and winged him. He's got a through-and-through at the side of his gut, and right now I am trying to find a doctor who will fix him up. This . . . Fuck it, Vincent. *This* was not part of the fucking deal here."

"How the hell do you know what happened, Bernie? Tell me that. How the hell do you know what happened this morning?"

"Because he phoned me, okay? They called me. They told me what happened, and right now he's in a safe place, but he's bleeding, man. He's bleeding bad, and he needs a doctor."

"I told you not to make any calls, and I told you not to take any either, Bernie. You went and gave your number to these guys? Jesus, do you not listen to a word I say?"

"These are my guys, Vincent. My people, okay? They're people that trusted me to give them a good gig here, and you went and screwed it up!"

"Hey, cut that shit out right now, Bernie. You know the deal here. This isn't kindergarten, okay? You take the risks, okay? You take the damned risks, and it comes out the way it comes out. You're playing in the big league here, my friend, and this is how it goes sometimes, right?"

Bernie glared at Madigan. "Vincent . . . Jesus, you just don't get it, do you? It's my brother, right? My fucking brother. He's the one that got shot."

Madigan didn't speak for fifteen seconds. He looked at Bernie's face. He saw what was there. He looked back at the two guys who'd appeared in that house—Anger Management and Zigzag—and he saw the resemblance. The shorter one, the one with the scarred face. Bernie Tomczak's brother. Fuck. Zigzag was Bernie Tomczak's brother. It all came full circle. This was the .22 guy, the gun Madigan had taken from Evidence. Bernie had been trying to protect his brother all along, and now he'd wound up shot.

"Ah, Christ Almighty, Bernie. What did you use your own brother for, eh? What the hell were you thinking? This is not supposed to connect to either of us, man. And you go get your own brother in on this."

"Whatever, Vincent. It don't matter. It's too late to change that now. I made a mistake, sure. You made a bigger mistake. You got the poor bastard shot through the gut, and if we don't get him a doctor he's gonna die. Okay? You understand what I'm saying? He's going to *die*."

"I got it. I got it. Jesus, let me think, okay? Let me think for a minute."

Madigan thought hard. Who could he use? There was an ex-pathologist, retired now, always willing to do some work for a few extra bucks. A gunshot—legally required to be reported immediately—was a tough call. Would he do it? To hell with it. Everyone had a price, and there was still more than a hundred grand under the floorboards in his house. He called from his cellphone. Three rings, four, five, went to voice mail. Madigan left a message. The guy would get back to him, for sure.

"You don't screw this up, Vincent, okay? I need you to handle this."

"I'll handle it. I'll handle it. Don't worry, okay? You think I want your brother bled out somewhere and his buddy all fucked up about it? No, thank you, very much. So where are they right now?"

"They're in a house up on East 123rd. One with a red front door. I don't remember the number, but it's the only one with a red front door."

"You gotta give me your phone, Bernie. And you gotta give me your goddamned word that you won't make any calls from the landline and that you won't go take a walk to some phone booth, okay?"

Bernie hesitated.

"Bernie, don't screw around on this one. This is too big. You got a hundred-and-eighty-grand debt that's about to be paid, and you have a new life waiting for you. You can take your brother with you, wherever the hell you go. I'll even give you some extra money, okay? I'll double up on what I already agreed to pay them. Think about it. You make any more calls and there's gonna be records. Cellphone records, records from the line here, prints all over a phone booth and the number you called at the house where your brother's holed up. Give me the phone, Bernie, seriously, and I'll take care of him."

"You better take care of him, Vincent . . . I'm serious, man, really serious. He dies and . . . Hell, Vincent, I don't even know what I'd do if he didn't make it. You gotta get it sorted out. Get your guy over there and fix this thing up."

"Bernie, I said I'd do it and I will. All right? Now give me your phone."

Bernie—resentfully—took the cellphone from his pocket and handed it over.

"Good," Madigan said. "Now you have your thing to do. You go get a message to Sandià that you're paying off your debt to him tomorrow, okay? Not tonight, but tomorrow. Don't go there, whatever the hell you do. You do not want him asking you where you're getting the money from. You understand? You just make sure that word gets to him. I'm calling Bryant in the next two or three hours. I'm arranging a meet here for the three of us at seven. We come here together, you show him the cellphone with the Walsh conversation on it, and you tell him what we agreed. That means you're gonna have to be in and out of Walsh's house and back here by seven, just as we arranged. Okay?"

"I got it, Vincent. We went over it a thousand times."

"I just need you to make sure you're in this a hundred fucking percent now, Bernie. I get this thing with your brother. I really get it. I'll get my guy down there and he'll be fine. I'll take care of it. You have my word."

Bernie held out his hand. "Shake my hand, Vincent. Shake my hand, look me in the eye, and give me your word."

"I just did, Bernie. I just gave you my word. When the hell have I ever let you down?"

"Do what I ask, Vincent, seriously."

Madigan looked at Bernie Tomczak. He held out his hand, he looked him in the eye, and when Bernie took his hand, Madigan said, "Bernie, you have my word."

"Good," Bernie replied.

"Now I'm gone. You do your thing and be back here by seven, and I'll take care of your brother."

Madigan started for the door.

"His name is Peter."

Madigan turned.

"You didn't ask his name, Vincent. His name is Peter. I just wanted you to know that."

"I said no names, Bernie. I didn't want to know their names. I would have known which one he was, okay? I would have been able to tell the damned difference between the one that got shot and the one that didn't."

"But *I* wanted you to know his name, Vincent. His name is Peter, and he's my younger brother."

"I got it, Bernie. I got it. Now concentrate on what you have to do, and let me worry about everything else."

Madigan left the room, paused for a moment in the corridor. He called the number again—the ex-pathologist—but still there was no reply. He put a half hour reminder on his phone. He couldn't forget. In the panic and confusion of everything, he could not forget about Bernie's brother. Last thing he needed was another casualty of this insane war.

The ex-pathologist, a man by the name of Don Jackson, called back fifteen minutes later.

Madigan explained the scenario.

"So if he's a CI, or connected to your CI, and he was doing some shit that it was okay to do, why can't he get himself to the hospital?" Jackson asked.

Madigan said nothing.

There was silence between them for a good ten seconds.

"He wasn't doing something that was okay to do," Jackson stated matter-of-factly.

Again, Madigan didn't speak.

"East 123rd, you say? Red front door?"

"Right."

"Call-out charge is five grand. Then another five on top for treatment and house calls."

"Deal."

"You ain't gonna haggle with me?"

"I haven't got time, Don. I really haven't. I just need you to fix the guy up."

"I'll be there within the hour. I'll call you back on this number if I can't find the place or he's already dead when I arrive."

"Good man," Madigan said. "Appreciated. We'll work out a time for me to pay you before the end of the day."

"Hey, it's all on trust," Jackson said. "It'll be fine. The guy'll live.

I'll get my money. And you won't find yourself on a murder charge."

"I didn't shoot him, for Christ's sake."

"I don't need to know who shot him, Vincent."

"Go do the thing, Don. Call me if there's a problem."

Madigan ended the call.

Jesus, now he had Don Jackson thinking that he shot Bernie Tomczak's useless damned brother.

Okay, so he was ten grand lighter, fifteen if he cut in Jackson's percentage to get it cleaned. The two hundred from Evidence would now be in Bryant's possession; a hundred and eighty of that would go to Sandià; the remaining twenty would go . . . where? Hell, it didn't matter where it went. It was marked money. The other hundred and twenty or so under the floor in Madigan's house? If Sandià was off the radar for good, then Madigan would give fifty to Bernie and tell him to disappear forever. Bernie would also have to get it cleaned, preferably out of state, and that would cost him fifteen, maybe twenty grand, seeing as how it was federal money. And what was left over? Madigan could put that through a cleaner, get back forty, maybe forty-five. Give ten or fifteen to Isabella and her daughter, something to at least get them started, and he would have thirty left over. Give twenty to the lawyers to keep them quiet, and the rest for Cassie. Maybe she would get a car for her eighteenth, after all. That's if it worked the way he intended. That's if it all went smoothly.

Madigan pulled over before he hit the expressway. He found a bar on 136th. Just one drink. A short drink to quench his thirst and steady his nerves. That was all. It was three thirty, a little after, and he had a couple of hours to kill before he went back to Bryant with the deal.

Madigan took a Jack on the rocks. A double. He sat back in a corner booth and wondered if he should maybe eat something. He had time. He would have to go back to the house. He would have to see Isabella again. He didn't want to, not after last night. He still didn't know what to think about what had happened. He didn't *want* to think about it. He could stay with her, maybe. If she would have had him. But there was no way in the world he could ever live with a woman behind that kind of lie. He would have to tell her about the Sandià house. He would have to tell her that he was the fourth man that morning. And that he could not do. Not a prayer. That stayed with him to the grave. So Isabella was out of the picture. She had to be. The kid was going to be fine. Everything was going to be fine.

Madigan ordered another drink, and just as the girl brought it to his table Don Jackson ran a stop light on Lexington and got his fender clipped by an Audi. He had to pull over. There was no other solution. And before he knew it, the asshole in the Audi, some fat son of a bitch with an attitude, was hauling a cop off the sidewalk into the melee and it was all going to shit.

Jackson did have time to call Madigan, but the music in the bar was loud and Madigan had his attention elsewhere. Jackson left Madigan a message to say that he would not be able to make it to the house with the red front door on East 123rd Street. It wouldn't have mattered anyway, because Peter Tomczak was en route to the hereafter already, bleeding out in a shitty back bedroom, while his friend—Anger Management, his given name Glenn Wilson—tried calling Bernie desperately. But Bernie's cellphone was in Madigan's car, switched off and buried in the glove compartment.

Madigan drank his drink. He listened to the game as best he could over the music, and at eight minutes to four Peter Tomczak's eyes seemed to go yellow, and then they rolled backward into his head.

The guy died in his friend's arms, blood all over the place. Looked like a slaughterhouse. Looked a lot like the room where Melissa Arias had been found just a handful of days before.

58

MOONLIGHT MOTEL

The temptation to take something—just one pill, maybe half of one—was more overwhelming than it had ever been.

Madigan steeled himself, steeled his nerves. This was where it all came together. This was where it could all come apart. If the seams showed, he was dead. Bernie would be dead too. Then they would find Isabella, and Sandià would kill her and her daughter without a second thought. Madigan knew that. He knew it as well as his own name.

Bernie would be out by six, would do what he had to do, and then reach the meet for seven. The negotiation would begin. Bernie knew what was required. Could he do it? Perhaps, perhaps not. Much of it depended on Bernie's ability to bullshit Bryant. The only advantage was Bryant's own fear. Such a fear would make him want to believe that Bernie was telling the truth. Bryant *needed* to believe him.

Madigan went back to the car, called Don Jackson. Once again, there was no answer. He returned to the bar, took one more drink, watched the TV up on the wall. People—beautiful people, people no more than a handful of years out of high school—read truths in crime scenes that could never be found. They used equipment that did not exist. They made their jobs look as good as sex. They did not reveal the depth of filth and rot and shit.

For just a moment Madigan resented the lie they were selling the world, but then he reminded himself that he did not care.

He sipped his drink, and it felt like hard work. The good kind of drunk didn't seem to be there, didn't even want to meet him halfway.

He thought about Isabella, how it felt to be around her. Had he possessed the attention to consider it more subjectively, he would have identified how this was so different from Angela, from Catherine, even Ivonne. In each case, when he withdrew they came at him all the more. They invaded the silences and spaces he presented. Isabella did the opposite. When he withdrew, she withdrew also.

Earlier, when he'd left, her expression had cornered him. He knew she wanted him to be careful.

That expression said all that needed to be said. He believed she'd begun to trust him, at least enough to give a damn about what happened to him. She'd believed what he had told her. She wanted him to come back safe. Of all the lies that he had told, the lie to her was the worst. It was under his skin, inside him, down deep inside, and he could feel it breathing. It was a bad sensation, a sensation he wasn't used to, a feeling with which he didn't wish to become familiar.

He imagined that this was conscience, that this was guilt.

Everything seemed unimportant. What he thought, what other people thought, what had occurred in the past, what would occur beyond tomorrow. If this didn't go right, well, there would be no tomorrow.

Madigan drained his glass, wanted more, didn't dare.

All of this was shit. All of this was meaningless. In the grander scheme of things, what happened to him, to Isabella, to Melissa, to Bernie and Sandià, meant nothing at all. But Madigan, sitting there, his heart driving a fist through his chest, his palms damp with sweat, his scalp itching, a feeling across his back like a thousand insects climbing the length of his spine, simply knew that he did not want to die. Not now. Not because of this. He did not want to wind up in prison. Twenty-five to life, no hope of parole. That was a death sentence. Word would be out within hours that he was a cop. Send him anywhere in the state and there would be people who would recognize him. It would all be over before he reached his first weekend. Worse than that, they'd more than likely blind him, cripple him, let him live without any real life at all. And then he would have to end it himself. Could he do that? Would he have the presence of mind and willpower to end his own life? Would they leave him in a condition where he would still be mentally and physically capable of doing so?

He shuddered. He felt transparent. He believed the whole world could see him for what he truly was, that the world could see right through his chest to the small knotted fist of his dark heart.

He felt ashamed. No, he didn't feel ashamed. He just felt small. Infinitesimally small against the weight of Isabella's conviction, her seeming belief in his ability to make everything right. If she only knew . . .

He tried to stop thinking about her. He didn't want this now. He didn't want anything but a little while to gather himself, to focus on what had to be done, to get his head clear and his thoughts straight.

Madigan closed his eyes. He had to get out. If he stayed with her she would get to him, get underneath him, around him, beside him, and he would not be able to withhold himself from speaking.

He would have to tell her the truth, and deal with the consequences.

Was absolution possible? Was there even such a thing? Would he ever be free of the ghosts?

No, he thought, *I will never be free of the ghosts. Things have gone too far.*

It was unbearable.

Madigan left the bar, and returned to his car.

He did not think to call Don Jackson again. He did not think to double-check that Don had found the house with the red door, that Bernie's brother was getting straightened up.

His mind was elsewhere.

Madigan saw Bryant's car before he came to a stop near the motel. He did not see Bryant clearly, but the car—that generic, dark gray sedan—was unmistakable. There were two dozen of them in the precinct car park.

Bryant got out as Madigan approached. Madigan waved him back inside, walked around to the passenger side and got in.

Bryant had the bag beneath his seat, tugged it out, opened the top a couple of inches and showed Madigan the money within.

"All of it?" Madigan said.

Bryant nodded.

"You need one eighty . . . That's what he'll take; no less."

Bryant whistled through his teeth.

"Hey, it don't fucking matter, Sarge," Madigan said. "He could take the whole two hundred. We can't do anything with it anyway."

"Yes, I know," Bryant replied. "I just never imagined we'd be in a situation like this. A hundred and eighty grand to get IA off our cases."

Neither of them spoke for a moment. The tension was suffocating.

"So the guy's in there?" Bryant asked.

Madigan glanced at the clock in the dash. It was close to quarter to seven.

"Fifteen, twenty minutes," he said. "Maybe sooner."

Bryant closed up the bag of money and tucked it back under the seat.

Madigan could tell that Bryant wanted to speak, but he didn't know what to say. Everything that needed to be said had already been communicated in looks, in gestures, in unspoken words. Madigan knew that Bryant would want to ask questions, to know what Madigan thought, what Madigan believed was *really* going on.

It did not matter. They were here for one reason and one reason only, and no further discussion was required.

Bryant maintained his silence.

Madigan could hear nothing but his own heart.

Bernie didn't look back at the sedan. He had no reason to. He paid the cabdriver, crossed the street, went into the motel.

"We're up," Madigan said, and he reached for the door lever.

Bryant reached out and grabbed Madigan's forearm. "This guy's good, right?"

Madigan frowned. "Good? He's a fucking thief, Sarge. He's a thief and a liar and a scumbag. But of all the thieves and liars and scumbags I know, he's slightly better than most. It don't matter what he's like. He's got something we need. We've got something he wants. And that's the end of the matter. We see him once and once only, and it's all over. Let's just get this thing done. Okay?"

Bryant nodded. He reached for the bag, exited the car, and the pair of them crossed to the motel.

In the motel room, Bernie was pacing. He'd done what was needed, had returned as scheduled. He had the phone with the Walsh conversation on it. But he was nervous. He was worried about his brother, wanted to know that Madigan had handled it, that Peter was going to be fine. Madigan had given his word that he'd take care of it. Bernie had given his word that he would not call Peter or Glenn Wilson. To think of his brother in such a situation made him sick, but he had to keep it together. Screw this up and his debt to Sandià would not be paid. He *had* to make this happen.

There was a knock at the door. He nearly dropped his cigarette. His hands were shaking. He had to act nervous, had to act flustered, but only so much.

He walked to the door.

"Yes?"

"Bernie, it's me, Vincent."

"You got the guy?"

"I got him."

"You got what I need?"

"Bernie, for Christ's sake, open the damned door. Will you?"

Bernie hesitated, and then he slid back the chain, unlocked the door, opened it a half dozen inches.

"Bernie, let us in. It's me and the guy. Okay? That's all. No one else. We didn't bring SWAT."

Bernie opened the door. "That's very funny, Vincent. Make me feel worried, why don't you?"

Vincent was inside. Bryant came in after him. He scanned the room, looked Bernie up and down, took in the whole space.

"You the guy who's after the phone?" Bernie asked.

"No," Madigan interjected. "This is the guy from Subway. He brought you a meatball sandwich 'cause he figured you were hungry."

"You're a fucking asshole, Vincent Madigan," Bernie said.

"No, I'm the guy who's here to save your life."

Bernie shook his head. He walked to the window, started back, nervously smoking the cigarette. "There's been a problem," he said.

Madigan looked at Bryant. Bryant opened his mouth to speak. Madigan shook his head.

"Problem?" Madigan said.

"Well, not so much a problem . . . But I've been thinking, Vincent, thinking a lot."

"And how many times have I warned you about that, Bernie?"

Bernie sneered. "You think you're real funny—"

Bryant stepped up to the plate. "What's going on here?" he asked.

Madigan looked at Bryant's expression. He was agitated. He wanted to know what the problem was. Something had been agreed, and now the something was coming apart.

"Hey, I don't have to deal with this," Bernie said, looking at Bryant.

"It's okay. It's okay," Madigan said, his tone placatory. "I'm dealing with this. Okay? I'm dealing with this. So what's the problem?"

"I can't take that money tonight. I can't take it until tomorrow," Bernie said.

He sensed Bryant's reaction behind him.

"Right. I got to pay Sandià, but I can't pay him tonight."

Bryant stepped forward. "This money is going to Sandià? What the hell—"

Madigan turned. "It doesn't matter where the money's going, Sarge. That's not important here. Bernie's gotten himself into some trouble with Sandià. Bernie has something we need. We pay Bernie. He pays Sandià. And everyone's happy, okay?"

Bryant said nothing.

"So why can't you pay Sandià tonight?" Madigan asked Bernie.

"Because he ain't here. Okay? He's out of town. I got word to his people, and they said to bring it tomorrow morning. Sandià wants to take delivery himself for whatever fucking reason . . ."

"That's the problem?" Bryant asked.

"Sarge, leave it," Madigan said. "I'll handle it."

Madigan looked at Bernie. His expression was intense, focused.

"Tomorrow," Bernie said. "It has to go tomorrow."

"But I need that fucking phone tonight," Bryant said. "I'm not going through this again."

"Give us the phone now, Bernie, and you keep the money—"

Bernie laughed nervously. "You think that's such a good idea? Hell, man, you know me better than anyone. You're gonna leave me here on my own with a hundred and eighty grand?"

"I'll keep the cash safe," Bryant said. "I'll take care of it, and I'll get it back to you in the morning. Whatever the hell happens, I need that phone right now."

Madigan didn't turn too quickly. Bryant had taken the bait, but so much sooner than he'd expected.

Madigan looked at Bernie. Bernie seemed hesitant.

"Vincent?" Bernie asked.

"Safer than with anyone else," Madigan said. "If he says he'll have it ready for you in the morning, then he'll have it ready for you in the morning."

"I give you the phone now, and I got nothing," Bernie said.

"You're gonna have to trust us, Bernie. Or you keep the money here tonight."

Bernie was slow to respond, but he did. "Okay," he said. "Okay, but I need that money back here by eight tomorrow morning."

"It'll be here," Bryant said. "Now, where's the phone?"

Bernie walked back into the bathroom. He returned with a plastic bag, in it the cellphone. Within a moment, Bryant was listening to the conversation with Walsh.

"And there are no copies of this?" Bryant asked Madigan.

Madigan nodded. "Bernie and I have an understanding. Don't we, Bernie? Bernie can lie to whoever the hell he likes, but he never lies to me. Right, Bernie?"

"Hey, man, I want out of this. Once that debt is paid, I am gone. Believe me. I am so gone, you won't even remember my name in a week's time. I don't want anything that connects me to Sandià or you or anyone else here for the rest of my freakin' life." He looked at Bryant. "But I am fucking counting on you to be back here at eight in the morning with that money."

"I will be here," Bryant said. "You rest easy. I'll be here."

Bernie still looked terrified. His face was varnished with sweat.

"You stay low now," Madigan told Bernie. "Stay here tonight. Don't go anywhere. Don't speak to anyone. And when you've paid Sandià, I figure you'd best get as far away as you can."

"I got it all straightened out," Bernie said. "I'm outta here, off to—"

Madigan cut him short. "I don't need to know, Bernie."

Bernie hesitated. "Yeah," he said. "For sure."

"We're gone," Madigan said.

Bryant turned toward the door.

"And that money *has* to be back here . . ." Bernie repeated.

Bryant said nothing. He looked at Madigan. In his expression it was obvious, *What is this? I said I'd do it. Tell the guy to keep talking and I might just keep the damned money. Jesus, what the hell is this?*

"It'll be here," Madigan said. "Seriously."

Bernie Tomczak and Vincent Madigan shook hands. Bryant was already halfway out the door with the duffel.

Bernie watched them go. Then he sat down and tried to start breathing again.

59

RIDE

By the time Madigan drove away from the motel, it was dark. Bryant had said little as they left, clutching the duffel in one hand, the phone in the other, a phone that would never get back to Walsh if Madigan's next call went as planned.

He watched Bryant's taillights vanish. Bryant was headed home. He would stay there until early the following morning, and then return the money to Bernie.

Madigan waited until those taillights had vanished completely, and then he took a cigarette from the pack and lit it. He stood silently for some time, looking down in the same direction, nothing ahead of him but the parallel lines of streetlights, the lights of storefronts across the sidewalk, the sound of distant music playing in a bar someplace out of sight.

There were no cars, no people, nothing.

He dropped the cigarette and ground it out with the sole of his shoe.

He closed his eyes for just a moment, mouthed a few silent words, and then took his cellphone from his pocket.

He dialed the number.

Madigan had found that bar where the music was playing, he had ordered nothing but a Coke, and he'd waited patiently. The call he was expecting came just after nine. As soon as it came, he left the bar immediately.

Beneath his shirt Madigan was sweating profusely. He drove slowly, all the while trying not to think, trying to empty his mind of everything. When he reached for his jacket, he realized his hands were shaking. Just one drink. One Valium. One something.

He exited the car and started walking. He was expected, and he went on up without question or comment.

He was alone in the elevator. He closed his eyes, breathed deeply, again forcing himself to think of nothing.

The door opened.

One of Sandià's people was there, nodded silently, took his gun, walked with him to the door, knocked once, turned, and walked back to the elevator.

"Come!" a voice called.

Madigan opened the door.

He smelled it as soon as he entered. Ammonia. Something else. *Fear?*

Sandià was there. He had no jacket, had the sleeves of his white shirt rolled up, and there was blood on the front of it. Just a tiny spatter, but it was there: unmistakable.

"Vincent . . . so good of you to come . . ." Sandià said. "I have some questions, and maybe you have some answers. You want a drink? The usual?"

"Sure," Madigan said.

"Let us talk about Alvin Bryant."

Madigan took the glass from Sandià.

"He says he knows you *very* well."

"Of course he knows me. We work together. We're in the same precinct. You already know this . . ."

"But how well do you know him?"

Madigan frowned. "What the hell is this, Dario? I called you. I told you where the money was. I told you that Bryant was your fourth man—"

"And he is now in the bathroom," Sandià said.

Madigan frowned. "Here?"

"No, Vincent, in the bathroom at Union fucking Station. Of course here."

"What the hell is he doing here? I figured he'd be dead already . . ."

"He is answering some questions for me."

"Okay, so he's answering some questions. I still get the idea I'm missing something here, Dario."

"Bryant told me that you would know exactly what I was talking about . . ."

Madigan laughed uncomfortably. "No, seriously, whatever the hell is going on here, I need a bit more information. Bryant said I would know *what*?"

Sandià sat down behind his desk. "Bryant said that he had my money because he was dealing with you and Bernie Tomczak. You remember Bernie Tomczak?"

"Sure I remember him."

"I know him as a gambler who owes me a great deal of money, but how do you know him?"

"Same as you. He's just a smalltime crook, a thief, a scam artist. He's little fish."

"Is he also a CI, Vincent?"

Madigan shrugged. "Maybe."

"For Bryant? He's a CI for Bryant?"

"He could be, yes. That's the thing about CIs. Often you don't even know who other officers keep as CIs."

"So Bernie Tomczak could be Bryant's CI, and you might not know about it?"

"Sure."

"So Bryant says he is in possession of two hundred grand of my money because he is paying a debt for Bernie Tomczak."

"And why the hell would he be doing that?"

"The details are unimportant, Vincent. I need to know if there is any truth in this. I need to know if you are aware of this arrangement."

"How the fuck would I know anything about a deal Bryant had made with his CI?"

Sandià just looked at Madigan. Madigan held his gaze.

"I want to know if you know where Bryant got this money from."

"He got it from your nephew, Dario. Bryant is your fourth man. He was the one at the house. He was the one who whacked those three guys in the storage unit. How the hell else would he have your money?"

"And how did you find out he was the fourth man, Vincent?"

"From a guy called Richard Moran, a good friend of Larry Fulton's, and Fulton was one of the guys who did the job with Bryant. Fulton was also one of the three people that Bryant killed in the storage unit."

"Well, Bryant says he had nothing to do with the robbery, and that he didn't kill those three men. He says that you can help him explain everything."

"Me?"

"Sure, you."

"Well, I think maybe he's spinning you a serious line of bullshit, Dario. Seems to me he's saying whatever he can think of to get out of the hole he's dug for himself." Madigan hesitated, and then he smiled. "Hey, hold up a moment here. You're not considering the possibility that I am actually involved in some sort of deal with Al Bryant, are you?"

"I don't know, Vincent . . . Am I?"

"So you're gonna listen to him over me? You're gonna take his word over mine?"

Sandià sighed. "There are too many things that don't make sense, Vincent, and too many questions that don't have answers."

"Well, for what it's worth, I don't have any more answers for you." Madigan didn't know whether he was as convincing as Bernie had been with Bryant back at the motel, but he was trying. Oh Lord, he was trying.

"Like I said, Bryant is telling me that he is not the fourth man, Vincent."

"Well, of course he's gonna say that. Jesus, what else is he going to say? Where the hell is he? Bring him out here. Bring him out and let's find out what the hell is going on."

"He's in the bathroom."

Madigan got up from his chair. "Well, I'll go get him out of the fucking bathroom."

"I don't think he's coming out," Sandià said. "I think we have to go visit him."

Sandià got up, started toward the bathroom door.

"Come," he said. "Let's go find out what is really going on here . . ."

Sandià allowed Madigan to go first.

Madigan prepared himself to be shocked by Bryant's presence, just the mere fact that he was there in Sandià's bathroom. But he need not have worried too much about the credibility of his performance.

Bryant—the way he looked, what had already been done to him—was shock enough.

Bryant was taped to a chair. The chair sat in the bathtub. His wrists were behind him, his ankles bound to the legs. His mouth was also taped, the heavy-duty silver duct tape covering much of the lower half of his face. A thick line of blood had traveled from his left nostril and down the tape to his chin. His right eye was closed. The swelling was almost black, the size of a ping-pong ball, and through his left he squinted at both Madigan and Sandià.

Recognition was immediate and desperate. Bryant was terrified. His hands wrestled against the tape. His left eye darted back and forth—Madigan, Sandià, back to Madigan—and in that desperate and petrified agitation Madigan saw everything that must have been going through Bryant's mind.

Bryant knew that if Madigan didn't step up, then he was dead.

But Madigan had known Bryant was dead in the moment he'd seen that nondescript sedan pull up to the curb the day before. He'd known it when he saw Bryant exit that very same sedan and walk toward Sandià's building. He'd known it as he'd taken pictures of Bryant with his cellphone, as he'd tried to come to terms with the fact that his own squad sergeant—a man he had known and trusted for many years—was the second man in Sandià's employ.

"Bryant is telling me something I find hard to believe," Sandià said.

Madigan noticed that the top of Bryant's left ear was torn, almost separated from his scalp. On the edge of the tub lay a pair of pliers. Sandià had tried to rip the guy's ear off.

Patches of the man's hair was missing, and blood had seeped through the skin beneath.

His right shoe and sock had been removed. His toes were stubs of flesh. The bottom of the tub was smeared with a great deal of blood.

This had been personal for Sandià, just like Valderas.

"I found it so hard to believe that I had to insist he tell me the truth. I applied a little persuasion . . ."

Sandià took a step closer to Bryant and leaned toward him.

"Didn't I, Sergeant Bryant?"

Bryant's left eye closed, opened, widened—that desperate, hunted look.

"So we talked. Didn't we, Mr. Bryant?" Sandià went on. "And you told me that Vincent here would be able to help you explain where this money came from?"

Bryant nodded furiously. He looked unerringly at Madigan with his one good eye, and he tried to speak from behind the thick band of tape that covered his mouth.

"What?" Madigan said. "What is this? What the fuck are you talking about?"

Bryant stopped nodding. His left eye widened. Madigan could sense his terror increase a hundredfold.

Madigan was denying knowledge of the money.

Madigan was signing Bryant's death warrant, and Bryant knew it.

"And so it seems that Vincent here thinks you are full of shit, Al . . . And so, as it happens, do I."

Sandià picked up the pliers from the edge of the tub. He held them tight, and then jabbed at Bryant's temple repeatedly.

Madigan felt sick. He looked at the eye, the blood from the scalp, the smashed toes, the way Bryant just wrestled relentlessly yet hopelessly against the tape that bound him to the chair.

The smell of ammonia grew even stronger as Bryant pissed himself once again.

Sandià stopped jabbing Bryant in the head.

Using the pliers, he gripped the edge of the tape across Bryant's mouth. He tried to tear the tape free in one swift motion, but he lost his grip halfway over.

Bryant screamed from one side of his mouth.

Sandià backhanded him.

"Shut the fuck up!" he said. "Enough of this bullshit!"

He tugged the remaining tape away, and Bryant gasped for air. He coughed, spluttered, started pleading with Sandià.

"Enough!" Bryant screamed. "Enough . . . Vincent, tell him . . . Jesus fucking Christ, tell him where the money came from . . ."

Sandià turned and looked at Madigan.

Madigan shook his head slowly. "I don't know what the hell you think is going on here—"

"Jesus Christ, Vincent, noooo . . ."

Sandià backhanded Bryant once again.

Bryant was silenced. His head dropped suddenly, his chin to his chest, and when he raised it there was blood flowing freely from both nostrils.

"Vincent . . ." he gasped. "Vincent, for Christ's s-sake . . ."

Madigan took a step forward. His face demonstrated nothing but anger and dismay. "What the living fuck are you talking about, Bryant? What are you saying here? You're using me to get out of some deep hole of shit you've dug for yourself? I cannot believe you are trying to implicate me in whatever the hell is going on here . . ."

Bryant's left eye widened once more. "Vincent . . . Jesus fucking Christ . . ."

"Enough," Sandià said. "I believe Vincent, of course. Vincent and I have been working together a lot longer than you and I. This ends here. You tell me where this money came from, or it is finished."

Al Bryant knew it was finished. He'd known it was finished the moment Madigan denied any knowledge of the money.

Bryant opened his mouth to speak.

"You were the fourth man, right?" Madigan interjected before Bryant had a chance to speak.

"You were the fourth man. You took this money from that house last week, and you killed his nephew, and then you killed those three guys in that storage unit . . ."

Bryant shook his head furiously. "I didn't . . . didn't ha-have any-anything . . ."

"You were the fourth fucking man," Madigan repeated. "Jesus Christ, I don't fucking believe it . . ."

Bryant tried to speak again. He coughed, spat up blood, and was breathing too heavily to make himself understood.

"And where is the rest of the fucking money?" Madigan asked.

"I have people searching the rest of his house now," Sandià said. "But I imagine it has gone. Who the hell knows what he owed, and who he's had to pay off."

Bryant's left eye was centered on Madigan. He knew there was no purpose in saying anything. Perhaps he was reconciled to his fate. The end was coming. Maybe all he could now hope for was that it would be swift and final. He could stand no more pain.

Sandià left the bathroom.

Madigan could not look at Bryant. He turned away.

"Vincent . . ." Bryant gasped.

Madigan turned back. "You brought this on yourself, my friend. We make our own justice, right? That's the truth. We all pay for our sins . . . eventually . . ."

"But . . . but, Vin—"

"But nothing, Sarge. It's over. We're done. You were in this as deep as me. We're both going to hell . . . You're just gonna wind up there first . . ."

Sandià came back into the bathroom. He held a .38 in his hand.

"Wh-what the fuck . . ." Bryant started.

Sandià raised the gun and pressed it to Bryant's forehead. "Enough," he said.

Bryant's face creased. He started to heave and sob. He couldn't breathe. He was trying desperately to speak. There was nothing but blood and spittle coming from his lips.

Sandià cocked the hammer, and then he turned and looked at Madigan.

"He has to die," Sandià said. "An eye for an eye, right? He killed my nephew. He took my money, and then he tries to tell me that you were involved . . ."

Madigan said nothing.

"Vincent . . . you see he has to die?"

Madigan looked at Sandià. "No question."

Madigan didn't blink, didn't flinch. His heart had slowed down. His stomach was in his chest. His hands were running with sweat.

Sandià lowered the gun, and then turned toward Madigan. "You do it," he said.

"What?"

"You do it," Sandià repeated. "You shoot this lying son of a bitch murdering bastard in the fucking head. He tried to make you guilty for his crimes. He tried to implicate you. He was ready to trade your life for his own. Now you get to take vengeance . . ."

Madigan looked at Bryant. He looked at the .38 in Sandià's hand. He looked back at Bryant.

Bryant was in shock. He was no longer capable of speaking.

"Do it, Vincent," Sandià said. "I believe you, of course. Now you show me how much I can trust you. Do it. Kill this asshole . . ."

Madigan closed his eyes.

He saw everything behind him. He saw Bernie, he saw the blood and chaos of the house robbery, he saw Larry Fulton and Bobby Landry and Chuck Williams, he saw Melissa Arias lying in a hospital bed, he saw Isabella, the way she closed herself against him and made him feel like the worst human being ever to walk the face of the earth . . .

He reached out and took the gun.

If he killed Bryant then it all ended here.

He was out.

He was free.

He hesitated. He considered the possibility of killing them both, of shooting Bryant, and then Sandià, of undoing the tape, of dealing with Sandià's people, of trying to explain to them that Bryant had managed to get the gun, that he had shot Sandià, that he had then wrestled the gun from Bryant and killed him . . .

It was hopeless.

There were people merely ten or fifteen feet away. With the sound of the first gunshot they would be inside.

Madigan felt the weight of the revolver in his hand.

He *had* to do it. It had come this far, and now there was no choice.

The motion was swift. He did not give himself time to think again. He gripped the gun, steadied himself, turned and aimed and fired.

Click!

There was nothing. No deafening roar. No spray of blood as the back of Bryant's head exploded against the bathroom wall.

Bryant screamed.

Madigan was stunned.

Sandià was laughing. "Now I see who to trust, who is my friend, who is my ally," he said. He took the gun from Madigan. He gripped his shoulder. "You never disappointed me, Vincent, and you never will."

From his pocket he took a single bullet, chambered it, cocked the hammer once more, aimed, and fired.

The noise was so familiar, and yet so *real* and sudden.

Madigan believed his ears had burst.

The carnage against the rear wall above the tub was sickening. As if someone had hosed the tiles with blood and matter.

Bryant just sat there, his mouth agape, his left eye wide open, looking right back at Madigan, the hole above the bridge of his nose dark and depthless and black.

A faint ghost of smoke rose from the barrel of the revolver.

There was a commotion in the room behind them. Two men had come through, just as Madigan had predicted, both of them wielding semiautomatic weapons. They saw Sandià through the open bathroom doorway. The guns were lowered. They backed up and left.

Sandià sighed and shook his head. "The fourth man," he said. "Clever, but not clever enough."

Madigan stood motionless for just a second, and then he turned and left the room.

"You are troubled by this?" Sandià asked, following just a yard behind.

"I knew him for a long time," Madigan replied.

"And now you can remember him for a long time, or you can forget him in an instant."

"I will forget," Madigan said, but he lied, and he knew he was

337

lying. That was what he did and who he was. The Patron Saint of Liars.

"And now . . ." Sandià said. "Now we can resume business as it was. I have lost my nephew. I do not believe I will ever know what happened to the rest of my money. But this is collateral damage. Order has been restored. Things are back how they should be."

"Yes," Madigan said, but he knew things would never be the same again.

He had pulled the trigger. He had not known that the gun was unloaded. He had not known that it was a test. He had been prepared to kill Al Bryant to protect himself.

What kind of person was he? Had he changed at all? Had these past few days done nothing? Was he still the horror of a human being that his wives had finally discovered?

Yes, he was. Nothing had changed. He had just proven that he was incapable of change.

"I must go," Madigan said. "I have things I need to do . . ."

"The earth keeps on spinning," Sandià said.

"Indeed it does."

"I am pleased you did not betray me," Sandià added as Madigan reached the door. "You have confirmed my basic faith in human nature . . ." He smiled, and it was a sincere smile. He was grateful to Madigan for the darkness that he and Madigan shared.

Madigan smiled back. He felt sick. He knew such sickness was visible in his expression, but he hoped that Sandià could not see it.

Madigan opened the door. He went down in the elevator. He made it half a block toward the car, and then he staggered against a streetlight and heaved violently into the gutter.

Looking down, he saw Bryant's blood on his shoes, just as he had seen Fulton's less than a week before.

Madigan heaved again.

60

BLACK TRAIN

Madigan sat in his car for more than an hour. There was nothing in the glove compartment. Nothing at all to help him. His hands shook for twenty minutes, and then they stopped. Then he felt pins and needles in his fingers, his toes, even across his scalp. He was sick twice more, suddenly opening the door and just retching into the street.

He lit a cigarette, but it simply burned—unsmoked—between his fingers, until he felt the heat on his skin and had to put it out.

Every time he closed his eyes, he could see Al Bryant's face. He could see the blood and brain matter on the wall. He could smell the ammonia, the fear, the terror, the sheer desperation of the situation. He could sense that presence in the bathroom, the certainty with which Bryant had confronted the end of his own life, the way he'd looked when he'd realized that Madigan was going to do nothing to help him. The awareness that he'd been set up, that Madigan had seen right through him, that he had been played all along.

When Madigan stopped thinking, he started the engine.

He drove home. He wanted to be nowhere else. He wanted to see what happened when he arrived there. Among the familiar. What would he feel then? Isabella too. He wanted to know whether he would still possess that compelling need to tell her the truth. To confess? To ask for forgiveness? To see if redemption was possible? Madigan did not know what he wanted to feel, but he knew that what he felt in that moment was not it.

Madigan came to a stop outside the house. He killed the engine, sat there for another fifteen minutes and then exited the car.

He went along the side of the house and entered through the rear. The kitchen was empty. He called out. "Isabella?"

Nothing.

She must be upstairs.

"Isabella?" Louder this time, but again no response.

Madigan removed his jacket, fetched a glass from the cupboard, ice from the freezer, a bottle of Jack Daniel's from the shelf to the right of the countertop.

He poured the drink, standing there looking out into the night through the window above the sink, and when he saw the reflection of something behind him he knew.

He did not turn. Not at first. He paused for a moment, his head down, his eyes closed, and then he raised the glass and downed it in one.

He set the glass in the sink.

"Things are never what they appear to be," Sandià said.

Madigan didn't reply.

"You are a smart man, Vincent . . . But you are not as smart as you think."

Madigan turned slowly. He confronted Sandià.

"We untied him," Sandià said. "We untied Al Bryant and we went through his pockets and we found this . . ."

Sandià raised his hand. In it was the cellphone that Bryant had bought from Bernie.

"I found this, and I was interested to know about Bryant's contacts, and whether there was anything here I should know . . . and there was a conversation recorded, a very interesting conversation, Vincent. And this conversation was going on between our friend Bernie and some guy called Walsh from Internal Affairs. Seems that Bernie was setting up Walsh, you know? Seems he taped this conversation for some reason. Seems that Bernie knew something about the robbery, and it got me thinking, Vincent . . . and I had to think long and hard to make sense of it."

Madigan felt everything and nothing. He wondered where Isabella was. He wondered if Sandià had already killed her.

"So I started trying to make two and two add up to four, you know? Bernie has a cellphone with a conversation on it. He intends to sell it to Bryant. Bryant intends to pay for it with my money. Bryant needs to get this Internal Affairs guy off his back for some reason . . . And that reason could be that Bryant was the fourth man in the robbery, or that Walsh suspected Bryant was on my payroll. Either which way, it would be worth it to Bryant to get this cellphone out of circulation. And I started to wonder how Bryant might have ended up with my money, money that you knew was marked, money you knew would serve no purpose for anyone. And then I figured that was too easy an explanation,

Vincent . . . I really did. I didn't want to doubt you, Vincent. I really didn't. And then I started to wonder if you really could be involved in all of this. And so I came over here to talk to you, to really have a heart-to-heart about everything that has happened, to clear the air, you know? I came over here to settle things once and for all, and what did I find?"

Madigan looked up at Sandià. Sandià was smiling. Avuncular, patient, almost compassionate.

"I find the girl, Vincent—the one I've been looking for all this time—and she is right here, Vincent, and she thought I was you. She heard me coming in through the back door and she called out your name, and you can imagine her reaction when she saw me . . ."

Sandià laughed to himself. "You should have seen her face, Vincent. It was a helluva thing to witness."

"So I get her all quieted down and she starts to behave herself, and that gives me a little time to think. Why is Vincent Madigan sheltering this woman? Why is my longtime friend and associate hiding this woman from me, a woman who can implicate me in something that will cause me a great deal of trouble? What is this all about? And then I am wondering if Vincent Madigan feels guilty. Maybe he is doing this out of guilt. And what could he feel guilty for? Why on earth would he feel so guilty that he would have anything to do with this Arias woman? Maybe he has hurt her in some way? Maybe he feels guilty because he has hurt her or harmed her in some way. I am wondering if this could be it, no? And what could that be? How could he know this woman? And then I am thinking that maybe he didn't hurt this woman directly, but perhaps someone she knew. Someone she cared for. Someone like a husband or a sister or a brother . . . or maybe a child, Vincent? Could Vincent Madigan feel guilty because he did something that hurt her child? The one in the hospital? The one that was in my house when my house was robbed and my money was taken and my nephew was killed? Could that be it, perhaps?"

Madigan could not speak. He could not breathe. There was nothing to say.

"Come, Vincent," Sandià said, and he leveled the same .38 that he had used to kill Bryant at Madigan's stomach. "Raise your hands slowly above your head."

Madigan complied.

"And now, with your left hand, take out your gun. Hold it with your fingertips, nothing else, and drop it behind you."

Madigan did as he was asked.

The gun clattered heavily into the sink.

"Walk forward," Sandià said.

Madigan took two steps.

"Raise your pants' leg, each side . . . Show me if you have an ankle holster."

Madigan showed him. There was nothing.

Sandià stepped to the side. He waved the gun, indicated that Madigan should step into the front room.

Madigan did as he was instructed, knowing what he would see when he walked in there, and he could not bear to imagine what she would be feeling.

She was there—Isabella Arias—gagged, bound to a chair, her eyes wide, disbelieving, and Madigan right there in front of her, and she'd heard everything that Sandià had said, and—more important—the lack of denial from Madigan.

Madigan's expression said all that needed to be said.

He could not hide the truth from her.

He had been the one to rob the Sandià house, and irrespective of whether he had been the one to pull the trigger, he had still been there when her daughter was shot.

And if he had been there in the house, then he had been the one to kill the three associates and leave their bodies in the storage unit.

And then Madigan saw the money.

More than a hundred grand, right there on the floor, money that had come from beneath the floorboards upstairs.

"Hard to face sometimes," Sandià said. "Isn't it? The truth, I mean. Sometimes it is just so hard to face."

Isabella Arias just stared at Vincent Madigan.

He looked away. He felt sick, ashamed. He felt like nothing.

"And people are just so unimaginative when it comes to finding places to hide their secrets, Vincent. I am disappointed in you. I thought you were a man of greater vision. Under the floorboards? Come on, seriously." Sandià shook his head. "You are a smart man . . . Or maybe I should say you *were* a smart man, because you just ran out of smarts and you just ran out of future . . ."

Madigan opened his mouth to speak. He wanted to explain himself—not to Sandià, but to Isabella.

"I don't want to hear you lie, Vincent," Sandià said. "I figure you either respect or fear me sufficiently by now to not insult me with any more lies . . ."

Madigan was suddenly without words, once again speechless.

There was nothing he could do, nothing he could say. Just as he had told Bryant, his own actions had brought him here and he had to face responsibility for the consequences. Perhaps his arrival in hell would not be so far behind Bryant's.

He thought of Cassie, of the car she would never get. He thought of Lucy and Tom, of Adam, of Angela and Ivonne and Catherine . . .

He thought of how he had met all of their expectations, satisfied all their doubts, proved them all right . . .

But in that moment it was Isabella Arias that he cared about, her viewpoint, her thoughts and feelings, and he did not know why . . . Perhaps because she had never believed him anything other than trustworthy and honest. Because she had believed him someone other than who he really was. Because she had given him a single, simple chance to get it right, to make it good, and he had failed . . .

Perhaps because of this.

"The question for me," Sandià said, "is who to kill first. You are both going to die, and you are both going to die in the next minute, and I am wondering if you should see her die, Vincent, or if I should let your death be the last thing she sees . . ." Sandià weighed the .38 in his hand. "Oh, and one further thing, Vincent . . . And this is just to recompense you for the death of my nephew. I want you to see this woman's face now as I tell her that I will kill her daughter too. There is no doubt here. I want everyone present to be completely aware of what I am saying . . ."

Isabella Arias—her eyes wide, the sound from behind the gag one of tortured anguish—wrestled against her ties much as Bryant had.

"For the trouble Vincent Madigan has caused me, I am going to kill Melissa Arias. I am going to wait until she is released from the hospital, and then I will take her. I will cut off her pretty little head. I will smash her fragile little body to pieces and I will burn whatever remains until there is nothing. And this I will do because of the betrayal that Vincent Madigan has brought upon me. This I want you to understand and know."

"Dario," Madigan said. "There is no reason to kill the child . . ."

Sandià swept his arm wide, the gun caught the side of Madigan's face, and he fell backward. Blood erupted from his torn lip. He was dazed, sick, and he stayed down for a moment. As he tried to get up again, Sandià let fly with a kick to Madigan's shoulder.

Madigan went down again, stayed down, and lay there silently.

"There is *one* reason to kill the child," Sandià said, "and that reason is you, Vincent. That reason is *you*. This is now personal, believe me. Just like Valderas, just like Bryant. I rely on people and they fuck things up. I relied on you, Vincent, and look where we are now. You can have the best people in the world, but sometimes you just have to make sure it gets done by doing it yourself."

Sandià turned back to Isabella. "I am going to shoot this woman in the face, Vincent. I am going to shoot her in the fucking face, and you are going to watch me do it. Then I am going to shoot you, and then I am going to kill her daughter, and this thing will be done. I will have my money back, the death of my nephew will be revenged, and you and Bryant will be in hell where you belong . . ."

Sandià raised the gun. He cocked the hammer. His finger tightened on the trigger.

Isabella screamed through the gag, and the sound was one of unlimited anguish and terror, not only for her own life, but for the life of her daughter.

Madigan could not bear to see it. He closed his eyes.

The sound was deafening once again, just as it had been in the bathroom, and Madigan lay there for a second more, his eyes closed, his heart a clenched fist, until he dared to open them once more.

The pain and tension in his chest almost unbearable, knowing already what he would see, Madigan opened his eyes one at a time. There it would be—the wide arc of blood on the wall behind Isabella, her head slumped forward, the matted rags of hair, the smell of cordite . . .

Sandià was on his knees. The gun had slipped from his fingers. His head lolled to one side, and then he turned and looked at Madigan, his mouth agape, a single line of blood running from his lower right temple to his jaw line.

The world shifted. Madigan did not understand. Confusion, disorientation, disbelief.

He scrabbled backward until he reached the wall, and then he saw Bernie Tomczak. Bernie stood there in the doorway, in his hand Madigan's gun, his face grim, his eyes closed, his expression one of utter determination.

Isabella was screaming again, her eyes wide and wild, the muffled sounds through the gag like some beaten animal.

It was a minute before anyone moved, and then Madigan was up on his feet, there at Isabella's side, untying the gag, the binding that held her wrists to the chair, and even as she got up from the chair she was coming at him.

Her fists were like hammers, beating against his chest, his face, the side of his head.

Madigan was down on his knees. He could not defend himself. He could not protect himself against the onslaught she delivered.

Bernie Tomczak stood silent. He did nothing to help Madigan, nothing to stop Isabella Arias.

Madigan was curled up, knees to his chest, his hands over his head, doing all he could to protect himself.

And then she had the gun in her hand. Sandià's gun. The .38 with which he had killed Bryant.

"Enough!" Bernie shouted. He raised Madigan's gun and aimed it at Isabella.

"He dies!" she screamed. "He fucking dies for what he did. He shot my daughter. He shot my daughter . . . He nearly killed her. He lied to me. He lied to me about this . . . He was involved in this and he lied to me all along!"

Bernie Tomczak took one step forward and grabbed the .38. Isabella—caught off guard, Tomczak's action utterly unexpected—felt nothing but pain as Tomczak twisted her wrist back. The gun was relinquished, and Tomczak stood there, Madigan's 9mm in one hand, Sandià's .38 in the other. He held them steady, one aimed unerringly at Madigan, now seated on the floor, his back against the wall, the other at Isabella.

"No one else is dying here," Bernie said, and even he was surprised at the level certainty of his own voice. "Enough already. Enough. I came for my money, and I'm taking it. Whatever the hell goes on between you is your business, not mine."

Isabella started crying. She put her face in her hands and her chest was racked with staggered breaths as she sobbed.

Madigan started to move. Bernie shook his head. "You just sit right there, Vincent . . . Seriously. Don't say a goddamned word, okay? It all ends here. This is it. The game is over, all right?"

Madigan didn't respond. He looked at Isabella Arias. Still she sobbed, each gasp of air sounding painful and labored.

Bernie nodded at the money on the floor. "What can you get on this?" he said.

Madigan frowned.

"Don't act freakin' dumb, Vincent. Right now, the next two hours, what can you get me on this?"

Madigan shook his head. "In two hours? Fuck, Bernie, I don't know . . ."

"You know people, Vincent. You know everyone it's worth knowing in this city. What can you get me in two hours?"

"Maybe forty, maybe thirty-five on the dollar . . . In two hours you're not going to get much better than that."

"And how much is there?"

"A hundred and twenty, give or take."

"So what's that? Forty, forty-five grand? That'll do. Put it in the bag."

Madigan hesitated.

"Put it in the damned bag, Vincent. Jesus, what the hell is this? I'm asking you to do something real simple here . . ."

Madigan shuffled forward on his knees. He started scooping wads of money into the duffel.

Bernie Tomczak had to lunge forward and wrest Isabella Arias back. She'd moved to the left and let fly with a kick to Madigan's ribs. Madigan grunted painfully, but he did not stop putting the money in the bag.

"Enough!" Bernie shouted. "Jesus Christ. Enough of this shit, okay?"

Isabella backed up. She sat down again. She glared at Bernie. She glared at Madigan. Her rage was palpable.

Madigan put the last of the money inside and held out the bag.

"You carry it," Bernie said. "Both of you are coming with me."

"Wha—" Isabella started.

"Shut the fuck up!" Bernie said. "Christ Al-fucking-mighty, I'm just about ready to shoot the pair of you. Now shut the hell up and start walking. We're going outside. I'm behind you. Don't you run or anything. I'm just gonna shoot you dead in the damned street, so help me God, if you even take one goddamned step the wrong way."

"Where are we going?" Isabella asked.

"Enough questions," Bernie said. "We're going out to Vincent's car, and he's gonna drive us."

Madigan took his car keys from the kitchen table. He went out of the rear door, along the side of the house and into the street. Isabella walked beside him. He tried to look sideways at her, but the sheer force of hatred that he felt from her dissuaded him from trying to make any gesture.

"You're in the passenger seat," Bernie said to Isabella. "I'm in back."

The three of them got in. Madigan started the engine.

"Where to?"

"Wherever we can get the most for this money," Bernie said.

"You just killed the guy who would have given you the most," Madigan said.

"Shut up, Vincent. Just drive."

Madigan pulled away from the sidewalk. He reached the end of the street and turned right. He did not know how this was going to work, but he had to take Bernie Tomczak someplace where they could get the money cleaned, somewhere where there would be forty grand ready and waiting for them. There was no such place. Nowhere he could think of. Twenty-four hours, maybe less, and he could do it. But now—right now—in the middle of the night? It wasn't happening. He couldn't tell Bernie this. However long he could string this out increased his chances of doing something to extricate himself from this situation. Would Bernie shoot him? Probably not. But he couldn't risk it. Couldn't risk the knee-jerk reaction that might happen if he tried something. The guy had a gun in each hand. He had one trained on the back of Madigan's seat, another at Isabella. Try something fast, something sudden, and he would more than likely just respond by pulling one of the triggers. Enough people had been hurt and killed. Enough damage had been done. It was now a matter of salvaging whatever he could out of this.

"You need to let her go," Madigan said.

"What? What the hell are you saying?"

"Seriously, Bernie . . . She doesn't belong in this. You need to let her go."

"She's insurance. She stays, Vincent, and that's all there is to it."

"I want to stay," Isabella said. She looked at Madigan. Her eyes were red and swollen. Her lips were thin and bloodless. Such an intensity of emotion was communicated in that expression, it was hard for Madigan to even comprehend how much she hated him. "I want to see you die, Vincent Madigan. I want to see this crazy son of a bitch shoot you in the fucking head."

Madigan didn't say a word.

Bernie Tomczak leaned back in the rear seat and shook his head. "Jesus Christ, Vincent . . . You really are not in the making friends business, are you?"

Madigan said nothing. He just drove. He drove in a straight line, turning left or right only when he had to, stopping at lights, moving off again, everything on automatic as he tried to work out any possible escape route.

Maybe this was it. Maybe there wasn't a way out of this. Maybe this was the end of the road.

And then Bernie told him to stop the car. "Pull over," he said. "Just pull over, Vincent . . ."

Madigan did as he was told.

"Out of the car," Bernie said. "Both of you."

Isabella was out first, then Madigan. They stood apart on the sidewalk, ten or twelve feet between them.

"Bernie—" Madigan started.

"Shut the hell up, Vincent," Bernie said matter-of-factly. "Enough. Really, enough from you. Okay?"

Bernie Tomczak seemed uncertain. He looked from Madigan to the woman and back again.

"I shot Sandià," he said. "I freakin' well shot Sandià." For a moment dismay crossed his face. He was elsewhere, his gun hand lowered, and Madigan thought to rush him, to get the gun off of him, to turn the tables on this thing.

Bernie looked up.

"You . . . Jesus, Vincent, the shit you get me into. What the hell is it with you? Everything, just everything you touch turns to shit."

"Bernie . . . we can figure this—"

Bernie Tomczak took a step forward, and he swung his right arm in a sideways arc and connected with Madigan's face. Madigan went down like a felled tree. Blood broke the surface. He felt like his eye had been punched clean from his face. He sat there awkwardly on the sidewalk, one hand against his cheek, the other on the ground.

Bernie kicked him then. A hard, swift kick to the chest. Madigan howled in anguish, fell backward, feeling like every rib in his body had been smashed.

Bernie stood above him, both guns aimed at his head. Madigan dared to open his one good eye. He could see nothing but Bernie's silhouette against the streetlight behind him.

"Not a goddamned word, Vincent! Not a single word. Okay? I've had enough of your shit and lies and crap. Jesus Christ, how the fuck do you get me into this shit? What the fuck is it with you?"

Bernie kicked Madigan again, and then he was leaning down, all set to rail on him again. Madigan's hands were over his head, his face, doing all he could to protect himself against the onslaught that was coming.

A gunshot.

Sudden. Unmistakable. The sound was deafening.

Bernie Tomczak froze.

He looked back, and there she stood—Isabella Arias, in her hand Madigan's secondary gun, the one that had forever sat beneath the driver's seat.

"Enough," she said, her voice calm, measured. She leveled the gun at Bernie Tomczak. "Put the guns down," she said, "or so help me God I will shoot you. Don't think I won't . . ."

"Hey, wait up here," Bernie started. "We're on the same side here . . ."

"I'm on no one's side. I don't know who you are, and I don't care who you are. He got my daughter shot. He did business with Sandià. He cheated and lied to everyone, and he has to take responsibility now . . . He has to take responsibility for what he's done. If you kill him, then he is off the hook . . ."

"I have no intention of killing him . . . I'm just giving him back some of the beatings that he's given me . . ."

"Take the money," Isabella said. "Take the money and go. Disappear. Vanish. This is the end of it for you . . ."

Bernie Tomczak looked down at Madigan. Then he looked back at Isabella Arias. There was something in her expression that told him not to take the risk. He was a gambler, had always been a gambler—but with money, never with his own life.

"I'm taking the car," Bernie said.

"So take it," Isabella replied.

Bernie lowered the guns. He put one in each of his jacket pockets. The keys were still in the ignition. He backed up a step toward the vehicle, and then—almost as a final thought—he kicked Madigan hard, just one more time. Madigan was stunned, winded, and he lay there on his side with nothing to breathe for thirty seconds.

"Fuck you, Vincent Madigan," Bernie said. "I hope you rot in fucking hell."

With that, he turned and got into the car, slammed the door, gunned the engine into life, and pulled away.

Isabella Arias stood there for a moment, listening to nothing but the sound of Madigan's car disappearing toward the city, the sound of Madigan himself gagging and retching for breath on the sidewalk, the sound of her own heart as it thundered in her chest.

"You nearly killed my daughter," she said.

"I—I . . ."

"I don't want to hear it," she interjected. "You did whatever you did. You made a mess of your life, and you made a mess of so many other peoples' as well. You are a piece of shit. You are nothing. You are supposed to be a cop. To protect and serve. Protect your own interests, serve your own ends. That's what you do. That's who you are. You say you care for people. You say you want to do the right thing. Fuck you, you selfish, lying piece of shit motherfucker . . ."

Isabella Arias took one step forward and aimed the gun at Madigan's head.

He tried to look back at her. He tried to hold her gaze. He tried to steel himself for the blaze of fire that would come from the muzzle, the sound, the impact, the silence that would follow.

This was it. This was where it ended. Killed by the very person to whom he had wished to confess.

This was justice. This was his redemption. This was the end of all of it.

"Where did you shoot my daughter?"

Vincent opened his eyes.

"Where, Vincent?"

"I didn't shoot your daughter—"

"How do you know, Vincent? How do you know who shot her?"

"I—I d-don't . . ."

"So where did you shoot her?"

"In her stomach," he said. "She was shot through the side of her stomach . . ."

Isabella Arias leaned forward. She held the gun against Madigan's gut, right there to the left of his solar plexus.

"Here?" she said. "Was it here that you shot her?"

"Isabella . . . please . . ."

"Yes or no, Vincent. Yes or no."

He nodded, his eyes wide, his hands up in some sort of defense, the look in her eyes unrelenting, unforgiving, implacable.

"Y-yes," he said, and he closed his eyes once more.

"Good enough," she said matter-of-factly, and she pulled the trigger.

61

THE FIRE OF LOVE

Vincent Madigan did not bleed out.
    Nearly, but not quite.
He was found by a passerby about an hour after the shooting. He was unconscious, and had he remained undiscovered for perhaps another thirty or forty minutes he would have been dead.

As it was, the ambulance got to him in time, and they shipped him on out to St. Francis Hospital, very close to the motel where he had hidden Bernie Tomczak for those few days.

It was the early hours of Monday morning, January 18th, just one week since Madigan had taken Bernie Tomczak down an alleyway off of Third and kicked him good for the money he owed Sandià. Now Sandià was dead, lying there on the floor of Madigan's front room with a hole in his head.

Bernie Tomczak was somewhere with a hundred and twenty grand of dirty money. He had the opportunity to retrieve his phone from the glove compartment of Vincent Madigan's car, and when he switched it on he found a message that broke his heart.

The thing came full circle, and it arrives back with Madigan.

It wasn't until Tuesday that Madigan was capable of answering questions. Who had killed Sandià? Who had shot him and left him to die in the street? Where was his car? What had happened to Bryant? Had Sandià killed Bryant?

Officer-Involved Shooting were assigned. A Board of Review. Walsh was on it like white on rice. He came back time and again, and each time Madigan said nothing that made any sense. He did not give Bernie Tomczak's name. He did not tell Walsh that Isabella Arias had been hiding out in his house.

After three days, Madigan was released. The bullet had missed vital organs, had passed through the side of his torso cleanly, and though a month of recuperation was advised, he could still walk;

352

he could still do the things he needed to do. Walsh told him to stay away from the precinct, that this investigation would more than likely result in his suspension, perhaps his dismissal.

"I know you are not cooperating," Walsh told him. "I know things happened and you know details, names, and if you don't tell me . . ."

Madigan didn't even respond to it. Walsh was still gun-shy, still walking on eggshells. He would never know if there was further evidence of his own complicity.

That same day, the 23rd, merely hours after being released from St. Francis, Madigan went into the 167th, ostensibly to see Callow and Harris. Apparently a social visit, nothing more, but while he was there he went in to the Evidence Room, located the box that held all of Sandià's possessions, and from it he took the cellphone. He left the precinct a little after two in the afternoon, and he hailed a cab to take him home. He paid no mind to the gray sedan that followed him to the bridge and then turned to the right and disappeared.

On the morning of the 24th, Walsh again came to Madigan's home. Madigan did not answer the questions, and when Walsh became agitated, implying with every statement that the situation Madigan had created was becoming all the more untenable and unrealistic, Madigan produced the cellphone he had taken from the precinct. It was this cellphone that Madigan then discussed with Walsh, and Madigan watched as Walsh visibly paled. Madigan gained Walsh's agreement to look no further, to close the internal inquiry, to make it all disappear.

It would disappear, Walsh assured him. It would vanish, just like Bernie Tomczak.

"There is something else I need from you," Madigan told Walsh. "There was another officer-involved shooting you looked into a little while ago. You know the one I mean, right? It is scheduled for tomorrow. You get tomorrow's review indefinitely postponed. How you do it is of no concern to me, but I need your word that you will do it. Then, after an appropriate time, the investigation just folds quietly and is never heard of again, okay?"

Walsh said nothing.

"We understand each other, Duncan?" Madigan asked.

"Yes, Vincent, we understand each other."

Madigan showed Walsh to the door, and he let him out and watched him cross the street to his car.

Again, Madigan was paying little attention to anything but Walsh, and thus did not notice the gray sedan at the end of the street.

Later that same day, Melissa Arias was released from East Harlem Hospital into the care of her mother, Isabella. Duncan Walsh was assigned to follow up on Isabella Arias, to gain her agreement for Melissa to be questioned about what she might have seen when the Sandià house was robbed. No such discussion took place, and no such agreement was made. Later, Madigan would check up on her. She had gone, left the apartment, taken Melissa out of school, vanished into some uncertain future. He thought to find her. It would have been easy—credit reports, forwarding addresses, the police database—but he did not. What was done was done. He let her go, and he wished her well. He knew that she would never consider him anything but an evil man—not now, not after what she had learned. But this he accepted. She had survived, her daughter too, and this was all that mattered.

On the morning of Thursday, February 11th, Vincent Madigan stood in the shower and let the hot water run over his face and down his back. The pain in his side had diminished markedly. He had taken nothing stronger than Vicodin for the last eight days. No Quaaludes, no Xanax, no Percocet, nothing. He had to do something, and he needed his thoughts clear, his nerves steady.

He thought often of Isabella Arias, of Bernie Tomczak, of Dario Barrantes. He thought of the morning of Tuesday, January 12th, of the robbery, the subsequent deaths of Larry Fulton, Chuck Williams and Bobby Landry. He thought of Duncan Walsh, of the cellphone that he possessed, of the hundred or so grand that Bernie had walked away with. He thought of many such things, and all of it paled into insignificance against what he now needed to do. This was something he *had* to do, regardless of what else might happen.

He left his house a little before nine. The previous day he had rented a car—a dark blue compact—and he drove southwest toward the bridge. The gray sedan followed him. It stayed a good half block behind, but it didn't lose him. Whoever was inside seemed to want Madigan alone, to make sure that no one else was tailing him, that the PD, Internal Affairs, maybe even Sandià's people, were no longer marking Vincent Madigan's every move. It had been this way for days, ever since Madigan had been released from the hospital. But Madigan—involved in little but his own internal world—had remained unaware.

Madigan drove downtown, on past the precinct, down Second Avenue, turning right only when he reached East 96th. Here he joined Third, drove a half dozen blocks and crossed to Lexington. He pulled up on the corner, waited for a good fifteen minutes, and then made his way back across the street to a brownstone walk-up a half block back.

Madigan knocked on the door, waited patiently, and then knocked again. When he heard movement inside, he stepped back, his hands in his overcoat pockets.

Karl Benedict did not conceal his surprise.

"We need to talk," Madigan said.

"About?"

"About the fact that your OIS review was postponed. But I am not talking to you about it in the street, Karl. Open the door, let me in, and I'll tell you what I need from you."

Benedict stepped back, held the door wide, and Madigan went in.

The gray sedan sat across the street a hundred and fifty yards back, and whoever was inside seemed to possess all the time in the world.

Inside Benedict's apartment, Madigan stood in the center of the kitchen. Benedict walked to the sink and stood with his back to the window.

"I got your review postponed," Madigan said.

Benedict didn't reply.

"I got it postponed indefinitely, and I can get it canceled."

Benedict frowned. "Wha—"

"Seven thousand dollars," Madigan said.

"You what?"

"Give me seven thousand dollars, Karl, and the whole thing goes away."

"Seven thousand dollars."

"Yeah, seven thousand dollars. Not a dollar more or less. Give me that now and I walk away, your review never happens, and whatever you're so scared about them finding out isn't a problem anymore."

"And how do I know . . ."

"What? That I can do it? Well, you don't know how I got last week's review postponed, but I did. It's that simple. Your review never happened, and *will* never happen if you give me seven thousand dollars."

"Now?"

"Right now."

"I have your word?"

"You have my word."

"I'll get a jacket," Benedict said. "We'll go to the bank now."

Madigan waited while Benedict got his jacket. He felt calm, levelheaded. This was it. This was what he'd needed to do all along. This was maybe the most important thing he had ever done.

Benedict was with him inside two minutes, had his car keys, said simply that Madigan should follow him; it was no more than a half dozen blocks.

They left the house together. Benedict led the way, Madigan followed. Twice he had to ask Benedict not to walk so fast. Painkillers aside, his body hurt a great deal. They drove off, Benedict ahead, and then pulled up at the corner of East 95th and Third. Benedict got out, walked back to meet Madigan. Madigan lowered the window.

"Five minutes," Benedict said.

Madigan nodded, raised the window once more.

He put on the radio. Tom Waits. "Lord I've Been Changed."

Madigan smiled at the irony, but did not believe it for a moment.

He smoked a cigarette, lit a second from the stub of the first, and then Benedict was leaving the bank and crossing the sidewalk to meet him.

Benedict walked around and got in the passenger side. He produced a brown envelope from inside his jacket. It was a good inch thick.

"Seven grand," he said.

Madigan took the envelope.

"We're all done, right?"

"All done," Madigan replied.

"I never hear another word about this."

"Not a single word," Madigan replied.

"Okay, then."

Benedict reached for the door lever, lifted it, got out. He walked back to his own car, reversed a couple of yards, and then turned into the flow of traffic and disappeared.

Madigan finished his cigarette, started the engine, drove away.

The gray sedan followed.

All the way back to the Bronx, and then—on the corner of 169th and Findlay—Madigan pulled over again and got out of the car. He crossed the street to a plain-looking house three or four down from the end of the street.

He knocked on the door, waited, and when a middle-aged woman opened the door they shared a few words. The woman smiled, seemed pleased to see him and let him in.

Madigan was in the house no more than ten minutes. When he reappeared he held a bundle of papers and a set of keys. He walked around the side of the house, and a moment later he pulled out of the lot in a metallic blue 4x4. A Hyundai perhaps, the driver of the gray sedan thought. It was small for a 4x4, like a mom's car, something for dropping the kids off to school, picking them up again, fetching the groceries.

Madigan's rental stayed on the street, the sedan followed the 4x4 back downtown, back over the bridge, and then on toward the Village. The driver of the sedan did not know where Madigan was going, and did not care. All he wished to know was that there was no one following him—no cops, no IA, no one but himself.

This was the end of it all. The end of the lies, the bullshit, the end of everything.

They drove for a good half hour, and then Madigan was slowing, drawing to a stop on the sidewalk.

He got out of the 4x4, walked back across the street, and came around the corner to an apartment building.

Why he hadn't stopped directly ahead of the building was unknown.

Madigan knocked on the door. Within seconds a woman answered. They shared a few words. The woman seemed surprised. She disappeared back into the house and returned again, this time with a teenager—dark-haired, pretty.

Bernie Tomczak got out of the sedan as Madigan and the teenager started walking back toward the 4x4. He came around the corner just as Cassie Madigan started screaming at the top of her voice. Bernie stepped back out of sight, watched them together.

*

"I don't believe it!" Cassie shouted. "Oh my God! Oh my God! No way! Jesus Christ . . . Dad! Oh my God, a car!"

Madigan held out his arms. He closed Cassie inside.

"Happy birthday, sweetheart," he said.

Madigan closed his eyes. He was tired. So damned tired.

There were other people to see—Ivonne and Adam, Catherine, Lucy, and Tom too. There were things that needed to be said. Things that needed to be worked out.

But for now there was just his daughter, the feeling of her right up close against him, and the words she said that navigated the circuitous path to his dark and broken heart.

"I love you, Dad . . . You know that, right?"

"I know, sweetheart. I know."

"Don't ever forget that, okay?" She looked up at him—wide-eyed, her mascara smeared awkwardly like bruises. "You promise me now."

"Yes," Vincent Madigan said. "I promise."

And this time—perhaps for the first time in as long as he could remember—there was no word of a lie.

"I have to get Mom," she said excitedly. "I have to show Mom . . ."

Madigan released her, watched as she ran back to the house, calling after her mom, telling her mom to come see what her dad had bought her for her birthday.

Madigan believed he had never felt anything so real in his life.

He looked back toward the car, and then he turned.

Bernie had a gun in one hand, his cellphone in the other. The gun was aimed directly at Madigan.

"You wanna hear his voice, Vincent? You wanna hear what my brother sounded like while he died in that fucking house?"

It all came back. All the shit he had done came back, and now here he was.

"I am sorry," Madigan said.

"Sometimes that's just too fucking late," Bernie replied.

Cassie Madigan heard the gunshot from the kitchen.